THE

HUNGARIAN

THE

HUNGARIAN

VICTORIA
DOUGHERTY

THE HUNGARIAN

Published by Wilderness Press

ISBN (paperback)   978-0-9974657-5-4
        (ebook)   978-0-9974657-6-1

Visit the author at www.victoriadoughertybooks.com

JOIN MY COLD READERS CLUB
AND GET A FREE BOOK

WWW.VICTORIADOUGHERTYBOOKS.COM

BUT ONLY IF YOU LOVE BLACK AND WHITE PHOTOS, BAD WOMEN AND GREAT WHISKEY...

For Jack.

"I trust no one. Not even myself."

—*Joesph Stalin*

SPRING, 1956

CHAPTER 1

THE SOUTH BOHEMIAN COUNTRYSIDE, CZECHOSLOVAKIA

The ticketing agent's heels squeaked across the linoleum, adding a tinny accompaniment to his poor whistling.

"Lístky, tickets, Fahrkarte!" the man droned—a welcome interruption to his little symphony.

Pasha Tarkhan slipped out of his first class compartment, intercepting the weary-eyed fellow.

"*Lístky*," Pasha said, producing two stiff cards from his breast pocket.

The agent appeared a bit ruffled at first, shifting his feet and tugging on his shaggy walrus mustache. Pasha loomed over him—more than a head taller, dark and imposing, not the kind of man you'd want to meet alone. But the agent took the tickets, stamping and returning them to the Russian's hand. Avoiding eye contact, he whistled a scarcely recognizable refrain to "Virgin and Whore," an old Czech folk tune, then continued his stroll down the aisle. Pasha took up the song as well, concluding the last, weeping note as the ticketing agent disappeared into the next car.

Pasha looked down at the tickets.

They were neatly stamped with a round ČSSR insignia, and a delicate gray cigarette paper was implanted between them. Pasha ran his thumb along its seam. Peering out the aisle window, he caught a glimpse of an old, mustard-yellow farmhouse surrounded by fruit trees before it all went dark. The train had entered a tunnel, and the Russian closed his eyes, relishing the grinding rhythms beneath his feet.

Pasha Tarkhan had loved trains since he took his first

one from Tbilisi to Moscow when he was sixteen years old. It was a three-day trip that took him through Stalingrad, Tambov and Tula in the coveted window seat of a crowded compartment smelling of days-old perspiration and live roosters. As a boy who'd never been out of Josefov (population 222), he found every hour of his journey a delight— even sleeping with his cheek sucked against the window like a piece of calf's liver. His sore neck and back were a small price to pay for the opportunity to go to school in Moscow and fulfill his socialist destiny.

He took airplanes and luxury automobiles to most places now, but whenever circumstances permitted, he booked a seat on the rail. Pasha's car and driver couldn't provide him with the shuffling and hard-stepping of the locomotive wheels, the smells of spilled cognac and fine cigarettes that always permeated the first class cabins and, best of all, unspoiled views of the countryside that even the back roads couldn't offer. Traveling through Czechoslovakia was a particular treat.

The southern part of the country reminded him of his native Georgia, which he hadn't seen in the almost twenty years since he'd left for Moscow. Not the people or the style of housing as much as the rolling hills speckled with wildflowers and curling rows of trees meandering in and out of the valleys like rivers. The climate was similar, too. The sun felt hotter in the southern Bohemian countryside than it did in Austria, only a few kilometers behind him. Hotter and brighter, like a Georgian summer. He remembered how dark his mother would get when she worked outside in the fields, tending to the sprouting grains.

Poor Mama, he thought. She'd begged him to come home once more before she died, but he was living in Rome at the time and couldn't get permission to return.

To be honest, he hadn't tried. His life had taken him so far away from his farmboy roots that he had no idea how to come home and explain to his parents and siblings what he'd become. He could've pretended, the way he did every day at work and at embassy functions with his comrades, but his family would've seen through him. His mother, especially, would have known that he was changed, and that realization would've put his life in danger. She would've rather seen her son in a gulag in Siberia than have hidden a Judas from Stalin's ever-watchful eyes. Josef Stalin had been her hero, and socialism her religion. In the end, it had been better to let her die with the knowledge that her boy, Pasha, was a high-ranking and trusted member of her government, and that she and her family in Josefov would always get their flour, sugar and butter for free.

Pasha opened his eyes as the train exited the tunnel and the countryside he'd been delighting in came to view once more. He turned his attention back to his tickets. Reaching into his trouser pocket, he retrieved a packet of fine tobacco—floral and earthen in its scent. He unfolded the little paper between his fingertips and sprinkled the tobacco onto it. As he began the delicate process of rolling his cigarette, he read the neat, black script printed on the gray paper's edge: BICK 3:00 PM TOMORROW.

Pasha ran his tongue over the black ink and finished rolling his smoke. He lit it, taking a deep drag and smiling at his memory of the comely Miss Bick and the safe house she would be offering him the next afternoon. She had tendered her bed in the past as well, but he wouldn't be taking her up on that particular pleasure this visit. The information he would be passing was far too critical for him to don the casual air of an affair, and Pasha didn't want to risk making her feel too at ease with the service she was providing. He would never want a helper to be jumpy and chance attracting attention, but then again, a woman in love could get sloppy, and Miss Bick had murmured that endearment into Pasha's ear during their previous liaison. It was a fine line to walk and one he didn't particularly revel in, despite Miss Bick's generosity in tending to his more immediate needs.

Miss Bick. He didn't even know her first name, but she was the kind of woman who would've made a fine wife to a more conventional man. A doctor perhaps. Or a shopkeeper. If only she hadn't decided to involve herself in matters of espionage.

Pasha often wondered if he'd be a happier man if he'd taken a job on the farm where his father repaired tractors. If he'd gone to trade school and chosen the life of a mechanic—a problem solver—his dreams would've remained as simple as his youthful perceptions of Soviet life. He would've married a local girl, had local children and loved nothing better than the smell of manure baking in the summer sun. The farthest he would travel would be to the Black Sea, where he could rent a cottage for a few rubles and put his feet up. That, instead of going from city to city, meeting to meeting, party to party, drinking vodka and wine and eating rich food to excess, while everyone talked of politics.

It was a shame Miss Bick couldn't accompany him on some of his engagements. An architect—and a good one at that—she had fine tastes and refined interests. He'd found their post-coital conversations unexpectedly rich. Miss Bick, however, had a difficult time containing the iron streak of nationalism she'd inherited from her father, and that wouldn't do. For a man in Pasha's position, it was important to have a mistress who was either an overt Soviet sympathizer or simply too stupid to have any of her own opinions.

"Oh, Pasha, are those poppies? I love fields of poppies."

Brandy France peeked her head into the aisle, summoning Pasha back to their compartment. Once there, she guided him down onto the bench and sat next to him, smoothing a crease in her yellow Chanel suit. She wore a matching hat with veil.

To Pasha, Brandy looked like a canary bird, but a very pretty one. Thousands of the tiny, red flowers she was admiring were reflected in her eyes, swarming over the grassland, looking all the more vivid against the backdrop of her blue irises. They were a deeper red than even Brandy's painted lips.

"You've seen poppies before—they grow anywhere."

"But they're better here, aren't they? Poppies of the worker's paradise," she chirped, putting her head against Pasha's massive, rounded shoulder.

"Yes, the worker's paradise," he repeated.

Pasha had met Brandy in Rome, where her husband was producing a romantic comedy starring a well-known American actor and an unknown Italian hopeful. For months she offered her crude espionage services to him—talking up politicians at political fundraisers—coming to Pasha with mostly useless bits of jargon that at first he let her blabber to any of his colleagues who would listen. It made him look good that he was able to enlist the enemy, regardless of the caliber of information.

Only weeks after he was transferred to Vienna, Brandy and her husband, Buster, moved there for yet another film. At the time, he thought it was a coincidence.

He was already growing tired of her and planning a graceful exit when she mentioned quite accidentally that her husband had taken to carrying a funny little metal card with the letter "t" engraved on it. A "good luck symbol," he called it, a prop left over from one of his films. Brandy had followed him to a tiny church near Schedenplatz, where he'd visited a number of times—speaking in hushed tones with a Jesuit there and even donating money. A lot of it.

She'd feared her Jewish husband wanted to convert, but Pasha knew better. In the lining of his suitcase he carried a similar card, only his was engraved with the Russian word for soul. Its meaning, however, was the same: subversive, spiritualist and, in Pasha's case, traitor.

From that moment on, Pasha couldn't let Brandy go as he'd planned. Furthermore, he had to figure out a way to keep her mouth shut and her visibility low, until he could extract himself from the relationship without injuring her pride. Or injuring her, if it came to it.

For that, he'd appealed to her overly developed sense of drama.

"The Austrian Premier's wife may have been using the word 'stockings,' but my dear, 'stockings' is the word Western spies commonly employ to mean weapons."

"Pasha!" Brandy had gasped. "I've heard so many of the ministers' wives use the word 'stockings' in the ladies room."

Before long, she forgot all about her husband's "conversion" and spent more and more time going to parties at the homes of government officials. It was to Pasha's great relief when Buster France went back to Los Angeles, taking his wife with him. Brandy visited as often as she could, but for the most part she was out of his hair. He even missed her now and then, and her company on the Czechoslovakian leg of his trip would be just enough time spent with her.

"Is it anything like Russia here?" Brandy leaned her head back against the cushion and sighed, humming one long note. "*Russia*. Even the word is beautiful. When will you take me there?"

Pasha smiled and moved a platinum blonde curl away from Brandy's eye with his finger.

"I think Prague will be better attuned to your interests."

"Oh, my interests are political!" she insisted. "World events. Buster thinks it's an obsession, really, but I'm worried that the whole planet's coming apart. It's all gotten quite out of hand, don't you agree?"

Pasha nodded.

"I've been a lucky woman all of my life. I know I have, and I intend to pass on some of that luck to the less fortunate. We can all make a difference, Pasha. Here I am. Here you are. We're making a difference just by talking about it. Not that I'm all talk. I'm action, too. But action begins with talk and talk begins with thought, thought begins with . . . well, I'm not sure what thought begins with, but it's important."

Brandy lifted her hand to her lips and laughed at herself. She had a throaty, sophisticated laugh—practiced and summoned effortlessly.

"In that case, I'll have to take you to Moscow as soon as possible. Perhaps when my ex-wife brings our daughters to Leningrad."

Brandy hooked her arm through his elbow and held his hand, intertwining her fingers with his. Her husband, Buster, never listened to her the way Pasha did.

"How much longer until we get to Praha?" Brandy stretched her arms above her head and pointed her toes, yawning. She hated trains.

"Darling, I told you: at least four more hours, and that's

without delays. We can be grateful we have no more borders to cross."

"It took so long at the border. Why did it take so long?"

Brandy stood up and cracked the window, looking out onto a row of tiny steeples in the distance. The country air didn't cool the compartment enough or ease her claustrophobia. Unbuttoning her jacket, she fanned her breasts with her lapels, finally getting some relief.

"The Soviet Union takes security very seriously."

Pasha Tarkhan's last word dropped off as he watched Brandy's mother-of-pearl silk camisole ripple like water against her skin while she fanned. It was when she moved like this—unconscious and graceful—that he remembered why she'd attracted him.

Pasha reached up and tiptoed his fingers over her collarbone, running them down the middle of her torso and onto her leg until reaching her knee. He slid his hand under the fabric of her skirt and up her slender thigh, pulling her down to him and kissing the curve of her ear.

"Pasha, what if one of those men comes again? They just barge in whenever they want to—I've seen them."

He suckled her entire ear, slipping his fingers into her panties.

"They know who I am and have no reason to bother us."

Brandy arched her back and 'mmm'd' like she did after taking her first spoonful of a chocolate mousse—her favorite dessert.

"Are you sure?"

Pasha helped her pull off her camisole and bent his enormous head down toward her breasts, kissing each one like he would the tops of his young daughters' heads.

"Positive."

She stood up and undid the back of her skirt, shimmying

out of it and kicking it onto the seat opposite them, doing the same with her panties. That left her in only her garter belt, stockings and yellow, patent leather pumps—just how Pasha liked it. He kissed her breasts and belly, then lifted her effortlessly, as if she were merely a glass of champagne, and set her shapely derriere on the window ledge. Brandy loved the strength of his arms, his thrilling combination of brute force and gentility. Pasha slid down until his face was between her thighs, then knelt and let her wrap her legs around his neck.

"Tell me more about what life is going to be like after you conquer the world."

"Oh, darling," he said, trailing kisses up her inner thigh. "It'll be beautiful."

CHAPTER 2

MONEMVASIA, GREECE

The rosy sun skimmed the water, as if dipping its toe to test the temperature. The simple beauty of the sky made Lily smile. It was one of the few uncomplicated things in her life right now. The sun, the water, and Etor, the hotel gigolo, who sat beside her imparting his particular brand of wisdom.

"A woman should never travel alone," Etor chided. "Especially one of childbearing age."

Lily chuckled at how he could sound like a prim schoolmaster, all the while sporting a most fashionable pair of chartreuse swimming trunks that left little to the imagination. She tossed her head back, enjoying the tickle of a lone droplet of sweat that rushed down from her neck and into her cleavage.

"I'm not alone," she teased. "I have you."

Etor had taken to joining Lily around sunset, sitting cross-legged on the rocks, as they watched jellyfish bob on the swelling surface of the Pélagos Sea. His lined face was still handsome, but Lily figured he was only a couple of years shy of retirement, as men half his age courted the attention of the same vacationing countesses who used to buy Etor's supper and handmade Italian shoes. The ladies were only a decade or so older than the bronzed Cretan now and stared with growing resentment at the silvery roots of his auburn hair.

"You need a man," Etor asserted. "A Greek man. The Americans can't handle you."

Lily had had a man. Richard. Of the Philadelphia Putnams, not the Boston Putnams, as he'd been quick to point out.

Aquamarine eyes, a thick, ungovernable mane of honey and rust hair, and a mother who hummed "Tangerine" as she sneered at Lily through her gin and tonics. Pooh was her name, of all things. Pooh, short for Abigail. Pooh, as in *Oh, Pooh. No, Pooh!* And *Pooh, you didn't!* Pooh, who'd talked of Richard's old girlfriends—girls who hadn't seemed quite right to her in their time—with a breathy nostalgia usually reserved for the one that got away. And Pooh, who had bullied her son into law school and dangled that victory in Lily's face like a diamond watch. Never mind that Richard would make a terrible lawyer, at least as Lily saw it. Even if he did continue to breeze through his studies with the same ease that he claimed to absorb Byron.

Poor Richard. He has the soul of an artist, his friends would say. *Although not the talent,* Lily had wanted to add on more than one occasion after their relationship had begun its slow flush down the pink porcelain toilet of his mother's new powder room.

Poor Richard, he's too much of a gentleman to give that Greek girl the heave-ho now that it's come this far. No one actually said it—that Lily knew of—but the sentiment was there. It was the uninvited guest at every party she and Richard attended together, every family dinner, unrelenting in every look, polite question and feigned interest in what Lily was reading. Even that was subject to censure in the most well-bred possible way, naturally. It was, to the people in Richard's circle, unseemly for a woman to enjoy Bellow, Hemmingway, O'Connor or, God forbid, Nabokov.

But it wasn't Richard's friends who really got to Lily in the end. It was the barely concealed look of relief on

Richard's face the night she "released him from their engagement" that Lily found so damned infuriating. His crafty, humiliating way of manipulating her into doing his mother's will.

Spineless bastard.

"Lilia, Lilia, Lilia," Etor yawned, splashing his suntorched chest with palmfuls of chilly salt water.

Lily patted Etor's shoulder and ran her fingers through her waist-length hair. The thick, black threads tangled around her knuckles, as day upon day of sunbathing was making her ends brittle.

"Would you mind?" she asked, removing a tall vial of olive oil from her beach bag. Etor sprinkled the oil over her hair, massaging it into her dry ends.

"Of course Kástro is no place to find a husband," Etor reminded her. "Only adulterers and seducers come here."

Kástro, or Old Town Monemvasia, as it was known to tourists, was notorious for offering what the flashier getaways never could—secrecy. Lily had nothing to hide on this—her *last*, she swore to herself—trip to the tiny peninsula, but she had plenty to hide from. And it wasn't just a broken engagement; one that came with the added embarrassment of having to admit once again that she was a screw-up when it came to matters of the heart. No, Lily realized, the heart was too specific a category. Most people back home just thought she was a screw-up. Period.

It was why she'd grown to hate Boston. And the whole Eastern Seaboard, except for New York. Because despite how hard she'd tried to fit in—at Dana Hall, at the goddamned Junior League—Lily just couldn't stand the stuck-up, intellectual pomposity of the men or the prim, icy-cool affectations of girls who moved in cliques so armored you needed barbed wire cutters just to say hello.

The same girls who feigned propriety with the right kind
of boy from seven to nine p.m., then slipped a cute waiter
a little note about where to meet for some real fun. Lily
knew all too well that she wasn't the only girl at Dana
Hall who'd had more than the prescribed three lovers
you could take and still remain vaguely respectable. The
snooty pricks who'd wooed her onto their plaid couches
knew that, too, but it didn't matter. All that mattered was
that she wasn't one of *them*.

She'd thought Richard was different.

And he was, at first. Late night coffees, introducing
her to poets she pretended not to know, finding her family funny and eccentric instead of brash. Richard was the
only non-Greek guy who'd ever had the guts to take Lily
home; she had to give him that. But putting up with the
long silences, the droll weekends at his parents' "beach"
house—a place set on the frigid, un-swimmable waters of
Northeast Harbor, Maine—had proved to be too much.
For both of them.

Her father told her not to think much about Richard
of the Philadelphia Putnams. He was destined to spend his
life in old money oblivion, breathing rarified air and eating
bland food.

Not like her, Daddy said. Lily was the daughter of a
Hellene. One who came to America at fifteen—alone—
and made his own way. Theron Tassos had worked the
docks, then the avenues and the markets, among other
things, while the fathers of boys like Richard sipped their
brandies and talked of the world's stage as if they were on it
as anything more than a ceremonial ribbon.

Malakas, her father called them. *Jerk-offs.*

They may have been just that, but it didn't change the
fact that Lily's father thought too highly of her. If Lily

was the mighty Hellene in Theron Tassos's fantasies, she would've never tried to gain entry into Richard's world in the first place—pining for their stamp of approval like a hungry beagle. She would have never put up with the not-so-subtle inquiries, *Are you going to wear that to mother's?* The dry, fervent kisses followed by the panted pleas to *go down.* That was something the Betsys and Lindys of Richard's world didn't do. Not well, anyway.

"Go to Greece," her father had urged. "A few weeks on the Peloponnese will remind you of who you are."

Only it hadn't. It didn't. It wouldn't.

Greece, while a virtual banquet of indulgences, had never been a place of clarity and motivation for Lily. Come to think of it, no place had. Not even New York, with its busy inhabitants who reveled in variety—enjoying life like they would an assortment of frutti di mare on a big silver plate.

Furthermore, what Lily hadn't counted on was how well Kástro in particular kept its confidences. The rocky cape trapped them like ghosts in a long-abandoned cemetery, and as Lily walked the winding trails and footbridges, nearly every blooming bush and Medieval ruin murmured a story of some time or another when Lily had ended up flat on her back with her dress hiked above her hips.

"What place could be more pleasing to the senses?" Etor beamed, uncorking a bottle of Malvasia wine as he beheld his adopted home.

"Please," Lily yielded, and Etor poured a liberal serving into her pewter goblet. She swished it around, watching the wine twirl.

"You don't have time to sit on Monemvasia for weeks like a Danish tourista," Etor insisted. "By age twenty-five you won't be marketable anymore."

Lily looked at her watch and nodded.

"I don't know that I was meant for marriage," she said aloud, but not specifically to Etor. Lily had never been in love. And the only man who'd ever really cared for her was her father—a man whose tender bearing at home and zeal for his family felt at times like Lily's only true tether to her heart. Of course, his dealings with the outside world were less benevolent, she'd learned.

"Miss Lilia!" Stavros, the concierge, called. "A note for you."

Stavros waved the sealed envelope in his hand as he teetered over the melon-shaped rocks. He nearly tumbled into the water twice, as if he didn't make the journey from the Hotel Malvasia's lobby to the seaside at least a dozen times a day.

"It just appeared on my desk," he marveled. "I didn't see who could've left it."

It was a plain, white envelope—the size of an invitation—and *Miss Lilia Tassos* was scribbled on the back, looking more like *Miso Lihila Tssas* to the untrained eye.

"Thank you, Stavros." She tucked the envelope into her beach bag and looked back at the jellyfish, which were now floating out to sea.

"Open it," Etor demanded. "It could be from an admirer."

Lily smiled at the Cretan gigolo, retrieving the envelope and tearing it at the seam. She pulled out a short note scribbled in the same slapdash handwriting. Tucked inside its crease was a simple, metal card with a plus sign embossed on one side and a six-pointed star on the other. It was the size of a calling card and engraved with eight tiny Cyrillic letters.

"Well?" Etor pressed. Lily patted his hand.

"No admirer, I'm afraid. Just a man."

Tony Geiger sat on a partial fortress wall that looked down over the sea and a rocky perch that Lily Tassos had fled around dinnertime—a tawdry Greek Romeo on her tail. He'd hiked up from the waterfront an hour early to sit amongst the ruins at the top of the peninsula and smoke Chesterfields in the cool evening air. The night required a jacket, but Tony had underdressed on purpose. It kept him sharp when he'd had a lousy night's sleep—taking the red-eye from Berlin to Athens and then driving another five hours to Monemvasia.

"*Fuck*," he said, flicking his last good cigarette into a bush of wildflowers. He watched the butt glow like a lightening bug then fade under the frizzy bloom of the white buds. He wished he could buy a decent pack of smokes in Greece.

"Well, it's about time," he murmured as he watched Lily scramble up a corkscrew rock path from behind a collapsed church wall. She was twenty minutes late and dressed in what looked like a white linen bathrobe that flew behind her like a spinnaker. Though he knew and understood fashion and finery, he'd never learned to appreciate it.

"Tony," she called.

Lily had the kind of looks Tony could appreciate, complete with a big nose and a full set of lips that saved her from cuteness. As far as he was concerned, she wrecked everything she had going for her with flashy clothes and too much perfume. Despite her Boston upbringing, she looked and behaved like a new-money Greek.

"You might as well go ahead and blow my vacation," Lily muttered, stumbling over the broken castle steps.

Geiger rubbed the thick stubble on his cheeks and shook his head.

"Come on, Lily. What's a girl like you got to take a vacation from—shopping?" He smiled and folded his arms. "Besides, something vaguely resembling a job might actually be good for you. Get you away from the Lotharios that hang around in places like this."

Lily put her palms to her temples then shook her hands as if she were chasing away an odor. She caught herself smiling at him and changed her look to a smirk. "It's amazing what a girl will do for a guy who keeps threating to put her daddy in jail."

Geiger pushed away from the fortress wall and pointed a finger in her face. The force of the gesture caused Lily to stagger backward and trip on her white linen train. He grabbed hold of her arm before she could fall and drew her close.

"Your father's an arms dealer, lady!"

He let go of her and glanced around. Geiger leaned back onto the stone wall, spitting over his shoulder and watching his foaming saliva disappear over the cliffside into the black air.

"You should thank me for letting you keep living this life of yours. You understand treason? How about seizure?" Geiger hoped the Greek baron would eat a bullet one day and figured that sooner or later, he would. "What's it gonna be, Lily?" he said.

Lily tucked her hair behind her ear. She hated it when Geiger popped up out of the blue like this. The funny little errands he'd sent her on—going to the Russian Tea Room at exactly 5:15 pm wearing a red skirt or leaving her purse at the Seven Sisters tube stop in London—weren't much more than an inconvenience, but his brown eyes told a much longer story than his thirty years, and the way he sucked in his cheeks whenever she started talking made her feel like the kind of woman she feared she was—bored and rich, with the wrong kind of money. Lily had seen enough to know that wasn't the way she wanted to spend her life, but she wasn't sure what options there were for a girl like her. She looked at Geiger—into his eyes, which she often avoided—and nodded.

"What have you got for me this time?"

Tony Geiger reached down and moved a fallen stone about the size of a gold brick. He produced another envelope with Lily's name on it, this one long and thick with folded papers. Lily grabbed the envelope and opened the flap, pulling out an airline ticket, itinerary, visa and various receipts in her name.

"This is going to Moscow."

"You're going to Moscow," Geiger corrected.

"Why would I go to Moscow?"

Geiger scratched his head and shrugged.

"All the good parties are happening in Moscow these days—the rich Pinkos love it."

"I'm not a Pinko."

Geiger smiled, for once looking sweet, lighthearted and his age. "Lily, you're not an anything."

Something inside her wanted to smile back at him despite the insult, but instead she rubbed her lips together as if she were redistributing her lipstick.

"Moscow, huh?"

"A little sightseeing—Lenin's Mausoleum and all that. You know you can view his actual body in Red Square. The Bolshevik Fuehrer."

"That's disgusting."

"No, I've seen it. He doesn't look that different than he does in photos." Geiger lit another smoke and inhaled deeply. "You still got that little present I sent you?"

Lily tucked her index finger into the bust of her dress and slid the odd metal card he'd conveyed through the hotel concierge over her collarbone. The gesture was meant as a joke—a play on something you might see in a French movie—but Tony Geiger didn't even smile.

"Don't lose that," he warned. "It's more important than your passport."

Lily took the card and flipped it over a couple of times, running her index finger over the Cyrillic lettering. She'd thought of taking Russian at Wellesley, hoping to rule the cocktail party circuit with unfiltered phrases from *Anna Karenina,* but ended up learning Arabic instead. Languages were the only thing she'd ever been really good at, and she collected them the way some people collected amusing dinner guests.

"It looks like a belt buckle," she remarked.

Geiger shook his head. "For your purposes, it'll get you a suite at the best hotel in Moscow, provided you show it to my good friend Fedot at the front desk. It'll also help you know who your friends are."

Lily mouthed "Fedot" and shrugged. "And?"

"And, on a separate note, you're now a member of the American Communist Party. Back-dated three years, of course. Like you joined in college."

This time Lily laughed out loud. "What if the Ruskies find out I'm not?"

"Oh, but you are. I've made sure of it. It makes getting you into Russia all the easier. And getting you out a little more interesting."

Lily stopped laughing and squeezed the card in her palm until one of its pointy edges dug into her skin. She held it up between two fingers and flicked it at him. Geiger caught it.

"Are you out of your mind?" she said.

"Lily, keep it down."

Lily paced in front of Geiger and then stopped, pointing her finger in his face the way he had to her. The wind was turning wild and cold, blowing her dress every which way. She wished she hadn't worn it. "Is this about my father? Or is it about something else?"

If only, Geiger thought.

"Your father's in Boston and he's not going anywhere that I know of—you can call him if you want. And as for something else?" Tony folded his hands together as if he were praying. "Look . . . it's not even on my radar."

Lily hardly ever thought about that night in New York anymore, either. Until she thought about it, that is—the night she'd first met Tony and assumed, wrongly, that it was by chance. He'd approached her outside of her hotel as the bellman hailed her a cab. He said he was late and asked if he could share the ride.

They talked about the weather—it had been lousy—and about Faulkner—whom they both loved. Then he asked her out for a drink. It occurred to her, as she found herself making love with him standing up behind a beer truck outside of Chumley's, that he'd lied about being late for an appointment. She could never, for the life of her, understand how it was that men knew they could have her without even the polite formality of a hotel room.

Then Tony just stopped in the middle of everything.

"You want to go somewhere else?" he asked.

In the cab back to the St. Regis she found he spoke Greek and Italian in addition to German and Hebrew. She didn't speak Hebrew, but they took turns impressing each other with the languages they had in common. They also shared a love of black comedy, and Tony told her he'd never actually met a woman with a real sense of humor. He said women he'd known liked laughing at jokes, but rarely made any.

Somehow, though, despite all of the laughing and the teasing and the fact that she was pretty sure she was the best-looking girl Tony had ever gotten into bed, they "couldn't close the deal" as he mumbled right before passing out. He blamed the two bottles of wine they'd shared when they got back to his suite, but he hadn't seemed all that drunk to her.

Now, as she looked at him—a year and some later—he seemed a hell of a lot older than he did then. She watched as Tony Geiger bent down and picked up the metal card she'd flicked to the ground. He dusted it off and held it flat in his hand as if it were some kind of peace offering, the lines on his palm looking like deep scars.

"Lily, I don't like your father very much, but I've got nothing against you. This is just something you can do pretty easily for me, that's all."

Lily rolled her eyes, but instead of Tony giving her some smart-ass comment, he looked down and swallowed hard.

"Look," he said, meeting her eyes again. "I need you to do this for me."

Geiger stepped closer to her and held his hands up as if he were going to put them on her shoulders. For a second, she thought he was going to kiss her. And for a second, he wanted to.

"You'll walk around for a couple of days, go to a party or two, and on the third day you're there—three minutes before noon—a man with a doctor's bag is going to ring the bell at your suite. When he arrives, you'll show him the card, go to the safe in your chest of drawers and give him the contents. The combination will be your birth date. Easy to remember."

"I don't need it to be easy—I remember everything."

"Yeah, you do, don't you?" Tony said. It was funny to him how she remembered every line from every book she'd ever read. It was not funny how he remembered the soft curve of her hips and the way her toes tasted in his mouth. "Anyway, you can go home any time after that. Or stay and see Mr. Lenin's mummy if you want."

Lily backed up and eyed Geiger from close-cropped hair to tightly laced shoe. This was definitely different from the other times, and Lily didn't like it. Tony was edgy and distant—but as if he was acting that way on purpose. It wasn't like he was a soft, warm blanket the other times they'd met, but he wasn't stiff either and could laugh here and there, even if it was at her expense. She wondered if everything else up until now had been a warm-up—a series of little tests meant to help him discern whether or not she could cross a line. And whether Tony ever acted real at all.

God, she was sick of men.

"I'm going back to my hotel."

"Lily!" Geiger called as she turned on her heel and stomped toward the slim path leading back to the castle. A thornflower bush caught the painted silk scarf Lily had tied around her waist, and the wind blew it off the tiny dagger of a petal, catching it around Tony Geiger's ankle.

"Lily! Are you going to leave a legacy or a residue?"

Lily stopped and spun around.

Geiger opened his palms and smiled like he meant it.

"This," he said, holding up her airline tickets, "is a legacy." Tony Geiger bent down and retrieved her scarf, letting it flail in the air. "What do you think a thing like this is? Bet it cost a pretty penny, but what's it worth?"

Lily rolled her eyes and turned back toward the path.

It was one of her favorite scarves—and it had cost a pretty penny—but he could keep it.

"Who'd you tell, Lily?"

Lily stopped and cocked her head.

"What?"

"Who'd you tell I was here?"

"Nobody."

Tony Geiger took a step forward and wobbled a little. He closed and opened his eyes like he was shaking off a hangover, then fell over onto his face.

"Jesus. Tony!"

Lily sprinted over and knelt beside him, running her hand down the length of his back. Something small and shaped like a pen cap was stuck between his shoulder blades. She pulled it out and saw that the thing had a thick needle that protruded from the top. Lily gasped and threw it to the side.

"Can you talk?" she asked him.

Tony's eyes were open and his lips were still moving— not as if he was trying to tell her something, but rather in a struggle to keep breathing. She took his hand on impulse, holding it and squeezing his fingers until Tony Geiger was gone and she was alone.

"I didn't," she whispered. "I didn't tell. I swear."

Lily wanted to cry, but her head wouldn't let her. She stood and rubbed her eyes, inching cautiously back from Tony's corpse as she watched the sky and the sea. They mingled together into one black mass that could only be distinguished by sound—a whistle of the wind and whoosh of the waves.

"Oh, God," she murmured.

She looked down into Tony's face and swallowed a sickening pool of saliva that had collected under her tongue. It almost made her vomit. "Dear God," she said, fully aloud this time. Tony's eyelids were half-closed, like he was falling asleep to the sound of a radio show. Lily thought about what it was Tony might like to listen to when he was alone. Maybe one of those detective stories her mother was so fond of.

"God damn," she shouted. She'd drunk with Tony and made him laugh. She'd fed him pieces of smoked trout from room service china. He'd been inside her, for Christ's sake!

And he'd been one of the good guys. Maybe Lily didn't know all that much about the dead man at her feet, and maybe she hadn't loved him, but part of her wished she had. Because if there was one thing that she was one hundred percent sure of, it was that in the big picture Tony was okay. More than okay.

"Bastard—where are you?" she gasped. She squatted down, waiting, watching.

Nothing changed—at least not out there. Inside, though, she could feel the shift, the adjustment from her old life—the one with Etor and Malvasia wine and without a thing to do—to her new one.

The new one she knew nothing about, except that a CIA agent was dead on top of the ruins of Monemvasia and she was hunched there on a cliff with a billowing, white dress on—an easy target for another poison pen cap. Lily took in a sharp breath and started untying her belt and fumbling with her buttons. Her fingers were shaking and wouldn't cooperate, so she grabbed the top of her dress at the neck and yanked as hard as she could, until half the buttons popped off and it fell to her ankles. Her tanned skin blended well with the night air, and she figured at the very least Tony's killer would have a hard time distinguishing her from a Greek fir. Lily ducked behind the eroded fortress wall and pulled her airline tickets and the metal card from under Tony's fingers.

Running naked back to her hotel room, Lily did not go unnoticed in the Hotel Malvasia's lobby. But this was Kástro, after all, and there was little that could have surprised the hedonistic clientele or jaded hotel clerks.

Once inside her room, she locked the door and drank three shots of Ouzo—compliments of the house. Out her window, the one she'd left open for fresh air, Lily saw the same panorama she had admired earlier in the evening after she and Etor had returned from the seaside. The little lane, two floors down, had been bustling, a stream of worshipers filing out of the only church on Monemvasia—a small Greek Orthodox temple with a domed roof shaped like a breast. Now, the lane was gloomy and still, with only the click-clack of a pair of high-heeled sandals sounding off its cobblestones. The footsteps seemed ominous, like they could have, conceivably, belonged to Tony's killer, and Lily shuddered.

After closing the window and locking the latch, Lily crouched down and slithered beneath her bedframe, pulling with her the copper spine of her bedside lamp and the coverlet from her mattress. She balled the soft, cotton spread into her arms like a loved one and hid under her bed in the dark—naked, but with her wits about her—until the sun rose out of the sea and filled her room with its butter and lemon glow. It was there, under her bed, and in a fetal position, that Lily got hold of herself and made some decisions about her life.

CHAPTER 3

BRASOV, ROMANIA

The static fizzed at Beryx Gulyas's ear, an unwelcome background noise to an already troubling conversation.

"You're certain?" Gulyas demanded into the telephone receiver. He rubbed turquoise and pyrite between the fingers of his left hand to soothe himself. The minerals, according to his fortuneteller, aided digestion—and Beryx was suffering from terrible heartburn after eating smoked lard, washed down with a glass of *palinca* brandy for lunch.

"Yes, of course," Etor insisted. Even through the poor reception on the line, Etor's voice cooed like that of a crooner.

Beryx hated that about Etor. And he hated to delegate any of his work. He'd spent too long and worked too hard to allow blunders to sully his reputation. He'd only delegated one other time, and it had kept him up for two nights in a row, drinking a near overdose of morphine as he awaited word that the job had gone off fine. It wasn't without a hitch: the idiot Spaniard had left the woman alive, bludgeoning her with a silver-bound new edition of *The Conquistadors,* of all things, rather than using a pistol or a knife. An amateur should never get creative, Beryx Gulyas believed, and to him everyone was an amateur. Everyone but himself.

The woman was still in a sanitarium somewhere, cleverer than the leeches the doctors used on her bedsores, but not quite as sharp as the pigeons that perched on her windowsill. Gulyas would've done the job perfectly, but in fairness, the Spaniard's work had been adequate enough. The injured woman's husband left politics altogether, and Gulyas's boss, Nicolai Ceausescu, was elected to the Politburo less than a year later.

It was lucky for Beryx Gulyas—and it was *luck* and not the Spaniard's skill—that the black hole of a vegetative state had an even more menacing effect on Ceausescu's nemesis than a clean kill.

"You'd better be right," he told Etor.

Beryx slammed the phone down, chipping the cradle in the process. Etor was a lousy assassin, but the only assassin available in Greece—let alone Monemvasia—on such short notice. His effete tastes irked the Transylvanian native, especially since he knew Etor had spent most of his adolescence and early manhood as a rough for a Cretan gangster known as Baru. Now he sashayed around like he was better than everyone else and took assignments from Baru only when he was broke. Beryx would've made an example out of him if he were the big Greek, but there went Etor, eating his fancy food with his fancy girlfriends. Beryx Gulyas hated the Greeks almost as much as he hated the Romanians.

"Burn that little turd . . ." he said aloud before catching himself. He looked back into the living room and was relieved to see his Aunt Zuzanna was still asleep on the couch and hadn't heard his crass slip of the tongue.

Whenever Gulyas came to Brasov, he stayed with his Aunt Zuzanna, his uncle's second wife. She lived on the edge of the valley, where the gondola left hourly for the tops of the Southern Carpathian Mountains. The views were stunning, even if her cottage was marred by peeling paint and fungal growths.

Zuzanna thought he was some big shot party official, and

Gulyas proved her right by sending her twenty American dollars every month. It was a fortune for her, and he was sure that she'd saved every dollar he'd sent and kept it buried in her yard somewhere. This simple pay-off allowed him the freedom to come and go as he pleased and discouraged his aunt from gossiping for fear of losing her meal ticket. These were the practical reasons he sent her money. The personal reasons were more complicated.

His aunt had taught him how to make love some two and a half decades earlier. She was slender then and a youthful thirty. She had shapely calves, and full hips, and almost no bosom. At the time, she was perfection to him, and he would favor her physical type all his life.

They had eight encounters total, but it was the first that was most exciting and played over and over again in his mind when he needed to summon the proper enthusiasm with his wife. He'd seen Zuzanna sunbathing in her yard, lying face down, with her bathing suit pulled slightly past her hips so that just a wee bit of her cleavage showed at the top of her buttocks. He lost himself staring at her and was startled when she called his name and summoned him to her side.

"There's some oil in the kitchen, would you bring it out here for me?" He nodded and ran back into the house, retrieving the oil.

"Now, rub it on my back, will you?"

Gulyas bent over to cover his lap as he massaged the oil into her skin. Without any warning, she turned over and poured the oil over her tiny breasts and stomach. Zuzanna took young Beryx's hands and dipped them into the oil, guiding them along her curves until he took over the motion himself.

"Such fine-looking eyes," she purred. "I could pluck one out and wear it on my finger like an emerald."

The tension in his loins became unbearable, and to Beryx's horror, suddenly released. Zuzanna giggled, and he wanted to slap her. Instead, Beryx ran into the house and closed himself off in the cellar. It was quiet for several minutes there—he could hear no small, bare feet making their way into the house, and no voice giving gentle words of apology. Only the squeak of a fruit bat that had entered the house in a basket of freshly picked crab apples.

After little less than an hour, Beryx grew tired of the dark, damp cellar and made his way back to his room again. The house was quiet and still, and Zuzanna was nowhere in sight—neither in the kitchen, her usual place, nor outside on the lawn, where she'd been sunning.

It was to Beryx's great surprise when he opened his bedroom door and found Zuzanna, naked and asleep, on his bed. She pointed her toes, stretching a bit at the sound of the door, and slowly opened her eyes. He'd sworn she said 'come here,' and he walked over to her, shaking and fiddling with his trousers. Zuzanna helped him get undressed and then took over for the rest.

How different it was seeing her now. She'd become pear shaped and grown weary, having been shunned by her neighbors. Marrying a Hungarian was almost as bad as being one in those hapless years.

Zuzanna had tried to rekindle their affair once, but Beryx could no longer look on her with desire the way he had when he was seventeen and she was beautiful. He used his wife as an excuse, but Zuzanna knew the real reason behind his faithfulness. It was then that he started sending her money, and she started treating him like a nephew.

She dithered over whether he'd eaten enough and spent entire days washing his laundry, trying to erase age-old stains from fine shirts that were too good to throw away.

This was all done without affection, and Beryx now felt like a young boy with a distant mother when he was in her company. The hungry lover in his fantasies bore no resemblance to the busy, ashen woman who kept his underwear clean and smelling like cedar mulch.

"Have you eaten?" she asked without looking at him. She got up from the couch and pushed her feet into her slippers.

"I'm not hungry," he told her.

Regardless of their past, Zuzanna had never fully liked him, as she had never fully liked her late husband, Beryx's uncle by blood. They were, after all, ethnic Hungarians, and she was no Hungarian, as she'd liked to remind them— even during their most intimate moments.

"*Az apád faszát,*" he snarled to himself in Hungarian— do it to your father's cock. Beryx Gulyas fingered his ring—a bequest from his grandfather's time in the Royal Hungarian Army.

Though Beryx was born and raised in Transylvania and carried a Romanian passport, he'd never felt like one of them, and the Romanians would never let him forget that he was by origin a Hungarian. Despite the overt snubs he'd endured throughout the years, his birth country had not left him uninfected by its history and culture, either. He loved the brittle air of the Southern Carpathian Mountains and the wide, sensual faces of the women who called them home. Their broad shoulders, made strong by carrying milk jugs, piles of pelts, and heavy buckets to and from the water pump, were rippled from behind and particularly alluring when covered with perspiration. Romanian women sweat like their men and smelled like animals.

And there was a palpable sorrow present in even the freshest newborn—a thirst for the agonies of life that courted lucklessness for the sheer thrill of surviving it. A Hungarian, though also drawn to the melancholy and macabre, might kill himself to end his grief, while a Romanian—particularly a Transylvanian—would hang on to the bitter end. Beryx Gulyas had a Hungarian heart, unable to truly love anyone except one of his own, but he possessed the soul of a Transylvanian.

"I'm going out," he said as he retrieved the keys to his new Berlina from a wooden bowl by the door. He told her he wouldn't be coming back for at least a week and would appreciate the holes in his trouser pockets being mended by then. It was a terrible inconvenience not being able to wear them, and they were his favorite pair—forgiving in their cut and capable of retaining their shape and crispness for hours longer than the other pants he owned. They also made him look at least five kilos slimmer.

Strangely, the pants meant more to him than the Berlina, which had been a recent gift from his boss. He'd "oo'd" and "aah'd" the way he was expected to, but a car was little more to him than a vehicle that got him from one place to another. Certainly, it spared him the inconvenience of having to take a bus or a train, but even at that moment, with his foot pressing the pedal to the floor and nothing but an empty, winding road ahead of him, Beryx did not feel the rush of adrenaline that consumed so many ardent drivers. There was only one thing that gave him that kind of rush.

A muffled groan pierced his reverie.

"Quiet!" he bellowed, and finally there was some peace in the car. Beryx had grown used to the incessant whining of the doomed over the years, but Leon Kunz, his regular pilot, had begged the whole ride on the way to Zuzanna's that afternoon and was now starting up again, repeating "Please, no," over and over again in various intonations like an actor rehearsing his one big line. Although the moans were hushed by the trunk walls, they were beginning to wear on Beryx's already raw nerves, and he'd almost pulled over and shot the man like he had his co-pilot back at the airfield before lunch.

"What have you done to yourself?" he'd demanded, as the co-pilot had begun slurring and sputtering that they weren't expecting him—no one had called.

"You're too drunk to hear a phone, you mongoloid."

Beryx had broken their bottle of Boza on the concrete floor and carved the word *idiot* into the man's forehead before shooting him in the groin, stomach, and finally mouth. That was when Leon Kunz started whimpering, and "Please, no," became the only words in his vocabulary. It was a common enough phenomenon amongst the very frightened—getting stuck, like a needle on a defective record album—but Beryx was in no mood for it tonight and was relieved that the German had been able to reign himself in. Now, he could sit at the wheel for a few moments after pulling over into the dead stillness of the mountain overlook and think through what he wanted to do in the next twenty-four hours.

Anyone who had ever heard of Beryx in a professional capacity would know better than to lie about a botched job, but Greeks were unpredictable, and men like Etor had a far less exacting definition of success than a man in Beryx's position. He couldn't look Nicolai Ceausescu in the eye until he knew without a doubt that Tony Geiger was dead and there were no loose ends to be tied up. That realization changed his plans for the night. He tucked his gun into his holster, slipped on the thick, tobacco wool turtleneck Zuzanna had knitted for him, and stepped out of the warm car and into a freezing drizzle.

"Get up, Leon," Beryx ordered as he unlocked the trunk. Leon Kunz was rolled up into a ball with his face buried in his knees.

"Please, no," he started, and once he said it he couldn't stop.

"Leon."

"Please, no."

"Leon!"

"Please, no."

"Shut up!"

"Please, no. Please, no. Please, no."

"Leon," Beryx whispered, taking a long, deep breath. "I'm not going to kill you tonight, Leon. I'm not even going to beat you."

"Please, no,"

"I'm an honest man, Leon. If you were going to die, I'd tell you. And if I was going to torture you, I would torture you. We wouldn't have to talk about it."

Leon Kunz stopped begging but continued to cry, keeping his eyes closed tight and his kneecaps pressed against his brow.

"Let tonight be a lesson to you, Leon."

Leon Kunz nodded feverishly and vomited.

"Now take your stinking clothes off before coming into the car. It's almost dawn, and you're flying me to Greece in an hour."

CHAPTER 4
PRAGUE

"Couldn't we get a better hotel?"

Brandy France stood outside the Hotel Yalta and squinted up at the glimmering, concrete monolith. It looked like a vertical ice cube tray and was positioned in stark contrast to the centuries-old buildings that also lined Wenceslas Square.

"My dear, this is the best hotel in Prague."

Pasha led her inside.

Bulo, a young bellboy of about sixteen, neither greeted them nor offered to take their bags until Pasha made him get a luggage cart. Miffed at having to exert himself, he sucked in his pimply cheeks and pouted all the way to their room.

"I'm glad you didn't tip him," Brandy sniffed as the boy stomped away, but Pasha wasn't listening. He opened the large metal door of their suite and held it for Brandy as she peeked inside.

The room was as big as a regular suite—in fact bigger, like everything else in the Hotel Yalta—but with hardly any furniture and none of the usual amenities. No bar, no welcome basket or pretty chocolates, and no robes or slippers to get cozy in. Ironically, what little furniture the place had was downright miniature compared to the antique bedroom set in Brandy's Vienna suite. If it weren't for the uniformed bellboys in the lobby—dressed like performing monkeys—the place could have doubled for a sanitarium.

"Don't just stand there, my dear," Pasha said, as he pulled their luggage cart from the entryway. "Come in."

The suite was a patchwork of beige and white, except for the institutional yellow linoleum in the bathroom. Their two low, single beds had been pushed together and were even harder than the ones in Austria. Brandy sat down and bounced a little on the corner of one of the mattresses. They were as stiff as dry sea sponges. The covers had been pulled tight, like they were in a military barracks, and the pillows were no bigger or softer than the decorative ones adorning the sofas of countless American living rooms. Those might read King and Queen, respectively, and be stuffed with wool. These were plain white and looked to be stuffed with crumpled tissue paper.

"I don't think I'll even be able to fit all my things into these little drawers," Brandy lamented of the bureau. "That man at the desk bragged that this hotel is state of the art. Better than anything in America. He said it's only been open for a month and pointed to that big banner that read, 'WELCOME TO THE HOTEL YALTA' as if it was some sort of proof. Clearly," Brandy huffed, "the man is a liar."

"And what is it exactly you want me to do? Shall I ask for another suite?"

Pasha opened his suitcase and began placing his folded clothes into the top drawer of their bureau, leaving the three drawers beneath it for her. Years of travel had taught him to make himself at home immediately and not live out of his baggage.

"I don't know. Some of the older hotels we passed looked nice." Brandy squinted out of their white nylon curtains onto Wenceslas Square several stories below. "I rather like the look of the Hotel Europa. It seems comfy and pretty."

"The Hotel Europa is falling apart. At least we'll get

working faucets here." Pasha eased up behind Brandy and massaged her delicate shoulders. He wanted to say "welcome to the worker's paradise," but he knew the irony would be lost on her.

"Hotel Yalta, my dear, is where men of my position stay. It's a monument to socialist productivity and skill." Pasha opened his palms in a grand, presentational style. "How would it look if I stayed in one of the older, bourgeois-built hotels?"

Brandy hung her dresses—a robin's egg Oleg Cassini, jade Givenchy and watermelon Dior—in a wardrobe not much wider than their bureau.

"I just don't see why anyone would care who built a hotel and when they built it. And it's not as if this place is cheap. It's just . . . big."

Pasha had forgotten how much Brandy liked to complain. Normally their liaisons supported only a few minutes of talk—thirty at most—as they were short on time and wanted to get down to business.

"Will you excuse me, darling? I'll need to shave before the party tonight. Zablov should be here any minute. You remember Kosmo Zablov, don't you? He was in Paris before getting assigned here, and used to come to Rome."

Pasha took his razor and shaving soap out of his toilette case and entered the bath, closing the door behind him. Brandy heard the faucet turn on and the unmistakable click of the door lock.

"Pasha . . ." she started, and then thought better of it. A practiced wife and mistress, she knew a man needed his privacy sometimes. Brandy didn't really feel like company right then anyway. She had a splitting headache and was upset that her clothes were all squashed together in an ugly wardrobe.

Brandy marched over to her luggage and searched her

Louis Vuitton chest until she found the matching makeup case at the bottom, under her brassieres. She opened it, rummaging through her hair combs, toothpaste, mascara, eye shadow, Rouge Classique nail polish, Chanel #5, Crème la Perle hand cream, night oil, eye balm, sedatives, her toothbrush, breath mints, countless tubes of lipstick and a small vial of "pick me up's." She laid every item on the bed like they were evidence, but among all of her beauty supplies, powders and pills, there was not one single aspirin to help relieve the rhythmic pounding at her temples.

"Pasha!" she called, but he couldn't hear her with the water running. "Pasha, do you have any aspirin?"

Brandy sat down and put his toilette case in her lap. She unzipped it and pulled out several medicine bottles, leaving his hair balm, a comb and pillbox inside. Amidst the antacids, laxatives and boric acid lay a small, brown bottle of Myer aspirin.

"Pasha, I'm going to have one of your aspirin, okay? My head's about to split."

She opened the bottle and tipped it over into her hand, but nothing came out. She shook it, hearing a swooshing inside, and stuck her pinky into the bottle.

"Pasha, I think I'm taking your last one? Is that all right?"

Her pinky dug further until her nail hooked onto something that was sliding against the wall of the bottle. Slowly, she pulled her finger out, dragging with it a long, curly stretch of what looked like camera film, only smaller. She held the film up to the light and looked closely at some tiny Cyrillic letters printed on what looked to be an architect's drawing. She'd seen one of those when she and her husband, Buster, built their beach house.

"S-P-U-T-N-I-K," she sounded out. Pasha had taught her his alphabet.

"What are you doing?"

Brandy hadn't heard Pasha open the bathroom door and jumped up, dropping the film and the bottle onto the bed with all of her other beauty products. He was standing before her in his royal blue bathrobe with only his trousers on underneath. He didn't look angry exactly, but all of his usual warmth was gone, replaced by nothing but a stare.

"I just wanted an aspirin, that's all. Didn't you hear me asking you?"

"No."

"I'm sorry." Brandy swallowed and looked down at the coiled roll of film. "Do you have any?"

"What?"

"Aspirin?"

Pasha took a deep breath, relaxing his shoulders and letting his features soften. He knew that unless he was smiling, he could look terribly mean.

"Of course," he said. "They're in my suit jacket."

Pasha went back into the bathroom and came out a moment later with his suit jacket draped over his forearm. He handed her a plain, clear bottle of pills and a cup of water and watched as she took two pills out and swallowed them.

"Thank you," she said.

He nodded.

When she finished drinking her water, he took the cup out of her hands and placed it on the bedside table. He walked to the end of the room and hung his suit jacket on his valet, turned back to her and grabbed her wrist, abruptly twisting it behind her. He slit her throat with his shaving blade, splattering their white curtains and a bad painting of a grain-processing factory with an arched spray of her blood.

She would die in less than a minute, and he was glad.

Pasha hadn't wanted her to suffer and made sure that the cut was deep and completely severed her artery. Though she would be unconscious, at least, if not dead, by the time she fell to the beige carpet, he guided her body down slowly and into a position that would be comfortable. When she seemed at rest, he went back into the bathroom and washed her blood off his hands and wrists. The arms of his bathrobe were finished, so he peeled it off, rolled it into a ball, and threw it into the bathtub. He rinsed his arms one more time before putting his white undershirt back on.

Pasha cursed himself for having put the microfilm in an aspirin bottle. He should've put it into his stomach medication, but the Myer aspirin bottle was the same brown color of the film and a safer bet. It had been since before his last regular mistress, Aprilia, that he'd traveled with a woman, and he'd forgotten the way they got into everything.

It didn't appear as if she'd gotten a look at the film, and she wouldn't understand how to read a blueprint if she had—especially one of a spaceship. But the fact that Brandy had seen it at all sealed her fate. He could've made up a story that she would've believed the way she believed everything else he told her, but that would've been one more lie on top of the many he'd already woven, and he had to draw a line somewhere.

And she was eminently capable of making a slip in front of one of his colleagues or pestering him for a deeper involvement in his so-called patriotic missions for Mother Russia. When the time came to break things off with her completely, she might've even put some of the puzzle pieces together and blackmailed him. It never ceased to amaze him how a woman of limited intellect could become uncharacteristically sharp when her ego had been bruised and her heart broken by a lover. His mistresses had always been fair-minded, but he'd seen it happen before. A more rational man might have killed Brandy after she'd mentioned knowledge of the metal card, but Pasha was an emotional creature, whose heart was made up of poetry. He had a soft spot for his mistresses.

Pasha rolled up the microfilm and put it back in the aspirin bottle, tucking it into his pants pocket. He would be delivering it to the safe house late that evening. Plucking Brandy's beauty products off the bed, he placed them in her makeup case according to size, returning it and her clothes to her luggage. Pasha then removed some bogus classified documents—Russian—from the lining of his suitcase and laid them out on the bed, throwing a mini-camera—the type used in American espionage—on top of them as if it had been dropped there. He dug a small pistol out of the same lining where he'd stored the bogus documents and opened Brandy's hand, placing the pistol in her palm and squeezing her fingers around the handle. He always carried props with him in case of an emergency. Remembering the bathroom, he went to the tub, removed his bloody robe from its cradle and filled it a quarter of the way with cold water. He was finishing hanging his suit jacket and dress shirt on a rack in the bath when Kosmo Zablov came knocking—late, as usual.

"Why aren't you dressed, you ox?" Kosmo feigned outrage when he saw Pasha in his undershirt. He, on the other hand, was dressed in his usual close-fitting, second-rate clothes, trying to affect the look of a Venetian gangster.

"What the . . . ?" It was hard to miss Brandy's body and the copious amounts of blood she'd spilled. Kosmo glimpsed her nearly severed head from the doorway and entered the suite to get a better look at her.

"You could've at least saved the artwork, my friend. What did it do to you?"

"She's an American spy."

Kosmo looked down at the surprised look on Brandy's face, and at the gun in her hand.

"This little idiot?"

"No idiot, I'm afraid." Pasha picked the documents up off the bed and held up the camera. "I've been trying to trap her for months."

Kosmo whistled his approval of his comrade's cool air. He assumed the same kind of detachment as he eyeballed the contents of the documents in Pasha's hand.

"You just leave those around for anyone to find?"

"These?" Pasha held up the documents. He'd enjoyed taunting the agent with them, but it was time to wrap up this whole ugly scene. "These are useless. Go ahead—look at them. I made them up."

Kosmo grabbed them, devouring the first page.

"This is great stuff," he chuckled. "How did you come up with it?"

Pasha shrugged. "I wanted to arrest her, not kill her, but she tried to shoot me."

Pasha went into the bathroom and returned with his suit jacket and dress shirt. He dressed slowly as Kosmo sat on the edge of the bed and continued to amuse himself with the false documents. He had one foot on the bloodied carpet and one resting on Brandy's shoulder. When Pasha finished tying his tie, he tore the top blanket off the bed and covered Brandy's body with it, making Kosmo put his feet up elsewhere.

"Have this cleaned up, will you? I need to go downstairs and request another suite—one with a clean carpet."

"You are a cold bastard, aren't you?" Kosmo stood up, slapping Pasha's back before going over to the telephone. "I'll get right on it. You know this is going to get some attention. She's a Hollywood type—the denials will be fervent and angry."

"We have the evidence right here—they can deny it all they want."

Kosmo smiled, revealing his crossed front teeth.

"What the hell?" he said, picking up the receiver. "I've always loved to annoy the Americans."

He dialed the three-digit number, but the front desk was busy.

"Of course, you'll be sent back to Moscow for this," Zablov continued. He dialed again and this time the line rang. "And you'll miss your dinner with the French President next week. Bastard—you always get the greatest of the great boondoggles. President Coty has the most exquisite chef—or so I've been told."

Pasha Tarkhan nodded and tried his best at a smile. "We can fly back together."

"I'm afraid you'll be flying back alone, my friend," Kosmo Zablov lamented, placing his fingers over the mouthpiece. "You know General Pushkin and how he likes to keep our satellite countries in line. I have to go to Romania now—they've been very naughty you know, those Romanians."

The phone stopped ringing and a bored voice came on the line. "Yes, hello, front desk?" Zablov inquired. "We have a dead mouse up here."

CHAPTER 5

BUCHAREST, ROMANIA

Kosmo Zablov's neck was killing him. The damned cots in the overnight compartment on the train from Prague to Bucharest reminded him of the war. Not that he'd seen much action. Ironically, a neck injury he'd been able to exaggerate had kept him busy and mostly out of harm's way. But he'd still had to brave those cots. Too short and too thin, they actually did give him something of an injury. His neck had never been the same.

He was sure Pasha Tarkhan wouldn't be complaining of a sore neck. Or a sore anything. He'd flown back to Moscow in first class like he always did, while Zablov had to make his way to Romania on his considerably smaller travel budget.

Kosmo Zablov loathed Romania, but it was the only way he could meet with Nicolai Ceausescu and his ever-present wife, Elena, without arousing suspicion. And he detested coming to their home. For reasons beyond his understanding, the Ceausescus eschewed fresh air and kept the doors and windows of their villa closed tight, trapping the stenches of their pantry, the daily "accidents" carried out by their coiffed pack of lap dogs, and Elena's dreadful perfume of waxy lipstick, talcum powder and mustard-laced breath. Of course, he went a long way back with the Ceausescus, and aesthetic grounds were no reason to discontinue his relationship with them.

Zablov, it could be argued, had helped insure Nicolai Ceausescu's election to the Romanian Politburo by alerting him to his greatest competitor and inspiring him to act upon that information, much like he planned to inspire him about Pasha Tarkhan today. Ceausescu's old rival had been ten times the intellect of Nicolai Ceausescu, and twice the intellect of Kosmo Zablov. The man had a promising career indeed before his wife's tragic injuries.

Unfortunately, the rival's intellect and promise had uncovered Zablov's weakness as well: that he had no idea how to do his job and had risen in the ranks of the KGB by inventing espionage escapades that allowed him to save the day and passing off the blame for the very real exploits he'd overlooked. Politics were where Zablov's core abilities lay, and it was imperative that he rise out of the KGB and into areas of diplomacy. There, his inadequacies could take years to surface, giving him much more time to invent a trail that could transfer the blame.

For the time being, however, he still had to deliver real results, and his terror of getting caught "improvising," as he liked to call it, was starting to wear on him. The nightmares, the tremble in his pinky finger, the days of insomnia before any meeting with a superior, and the crushing lower back pain that seemed to start at his arches and shoot up to his buttocks before lodging itself at the base of his spine had all intensified as expectations of him increased and he was finally being considered for the very positions he'd been striving for, but had never got offered.

Finally, not two weeks before, Comrade General Pushkin—Kosmo Zablov's superior—had revealed to him that a diplomatic post was indeed in his future, but not for another two to three years. By then, Pasha Tarkhan would be taking his seat at the big table in Moscow, and Zablov could replace him on the lobster and Lafite circuit, as it was called.

Two to three years was an eternity under his present circumstances. Not only could a colleague stumble upon his shortfalls, but a foreign agent could exploit them as well—the way Tony Geiger had done on numerous occasions.

Of course, what Zablov lacked in aptitude, he made up for in malevolence. He had learned a lot from his time under Stalin. When Geiger had made inquiries about him at Zablov's favorite brothel in Berlin, the Russian agent knew it was the last straw. Kosmo Zablov was but one slip-up away from his whole house of cards collapsing, and this meant but one slip-up away from a bullet in his skull, or worse, a gulag, where he would die slowly. This was no time for him to be conservative.

So, once again Zablov created a trail of stolen documents and double agents, laying them at General Pushkin's feet and prompting the order for the elimination of Tony Geiger. It was true that a couple of honest agents would be trampled in the crossfire, but Kosmo Zablov couldn't make that his problem. Besides, confirming Tony Geiger's death for the general gave Zablov the perfect cover for his trip to Romania, where he could finally do something to further his own career instead of merely protecting his hide.

"You're early," Nicolai Ceausescu said, devoid of his usual deadpan tone. "What a delight."

Kosmo Zablov took a languid step over the threshold of the Romanian politician's villa. A guard ushered him into Ceausescu's library, while Elena, Nicolai's wife, ran to the kitchen and pulled a bottle of private reserve Russian vodka out of her icebox. She put the vodka on a serving platter with some slices of Brânză de burduf cheese and two exquisite crystal glasses the President of Czechoslovakia had sent her, nearly dropping one as she fumbled to get it firmly in her grasp.

"Comrade!" Elena wailed, as she entered the library where her husband and the Russian were waiting. She put the serving platter on a French Renaissance coffee table and forced an open-mouthed smile that put nearly all of her irregular teeth and receding gums on display.

"I have ached every day since your last visit, and now my heart can sing once again," Elena lathered in Russian as she kissed Zablov on both cheeks. The men sat, and she knelt between the two of them.

For the Ceausescus, a visit from a high-ranking member of the KGB was an event on par with a call from a head of state, a public appointment with the Secretary General. Especially now, when Romania was vulnerable to a Soviet crackdown.

"You're too kind, Madam," the Russian responded. Even putting their grotesquerie aside, Kosmo Zablov had never liked the Ceausescus very much. They were gruff, common and grossly sycophantic—like a lot of power couples these days. Still, they had their uses. "Nicolai, my comrade, I want to thank you personally for ridding me of my annoyance in Greece yesterday. My man in Athens tells me there has been a positive identification. Tony Geiger is out of our hair for good."

Nicolai Ceausescu nodded.

"I always know I can count on you—the way you always know you can count on me to favor you in my reports—even if you've always been a little too independent at heart for Soviet tastes."

"We are here to serve the great Union of Soviet Socialist

Republics," Elena interrupted. "We are happy to be slaves for you and would dig our own graves with our very own hands if we ever thought we had displeased you."

Zablov crossed and uncrossed his legs.

"That won't be necessary, Madam. Really, I'm only here to extend my thanks." Zablov drank half of his vodka and picked up a slice of cheese, smelling it before putting it back down on the serving platter. "Of course, there has been a minor snafu in my regular report."

Nicolai Ceausescu tilted his head, and his usually neutral mouth curved downward at its corners.

"Not on my end. Never that. I'm afraid a man in our diplomatic corps—a bit higher up on the food chain than I am—has had a few unfavorable things to say about you particularly, as well as some mildly derisive observations about your esteemed Secretary General."

"But this is an outrage!" Nicolai Ceausescu blurted. "I mean, we have done nothing but served in our most humble and loving way."

Zablov sighed.

"Of course you have. I know this. You know this. But I'm afraid Comrade Tarkhan—oop." Zablov covered his mouth and shook his head with a slight tremor. "I'm afraid my Comrade, who I cannot name, believes your government has retained its Stalinist leanings despite the Politburo's private condemnation of our late leader's policies. You know these young up-and-comers. They're not nearly as tolerant as someone of my experience."

Nicolai Ceausescu slammed his open palm on the coffee table, causing the cheese platter to tremor. "I despise the cult of the individual as much as Comrade Khruschev! And I can say with supreme confidence that our esteemed Secretary General, whom I will serve till my death and have known since we rotted together in a concentration camp, deplores the actions of Comrade Stalin in the years after his great contribution to the Revolution."

Nicolai Ceausescu rose and leaned his squat body against his bookshelves, fingering several volumes entitled *The Glory of 1917*.

"Did you know I owned every book ever written on Comrade Stalin?" Nicolai Ceausescu barked, putting his fist to his chest in an awkward, dramatic gesture. "But when I learned of his treachery and realized that I, too, had succumbed to believing he was a god—even if it was against everything my Marxist-Leninist beliefs were whispering— no, *roaring* from my heart—I burned every volume myself, putting out the fire with my bare hands."

Nicolai Ceausescu opened his hands and shoved them in Zablov's face so that the Soviet agent could see the scarred, wrinkled skin of his palms. In reality, the scars had been from a childhood incident concerning a dare and one hot piece of coal. His mother had whipped his burned palms when she found out, further mauling his skin.

"You've never needed to convince me of your loyalty, Comrade," Zablov assured him, leaning back and brushing aside the Romanian's hands. "But this is all nonsense that I'm sure can be cleaned up during your questioning after I'm forced to turn in the report next month. I wouldn't worry about it at all." Zablov stood and walked to the coat stand, taking his hat and raincoat as Elena Ceausescu struggled to help him dress.

"Please stay, Comrade," she begged. "Our maid is a wonderful cook and we can make for you anything you love."

"My dear Madam Ceausescu." He smiled, touching her nose with his fingertip. "I've taken up too much of your time already."

Kosmo Zablov thrilled to the feel of the cool, spring rain as he left the Ceausescu's stuffy residence. He removed a small flask of Becherovka from his breast pocket and inhaled a deep sniff of the herbal liquor—a gift from Tarkhan for helping clean up the mess with his dead American mistress. He took a copious gulp. It was good.

Yes, Pasha Tarkhan had to go, and Nicolai Ceausescu was the perfect man to get rid of him.

CHAPTER 6

MOSCOW, RUSSIA

Moscow was chilly and sullen, not at all the city of contradictions and enchantments from some of Lily's favorite novels. She took an instant dislike to it, one cushioned only by the fact that the Hotel Rude—her new home, at least for the time being—felt as warm as the hearthbed of a ski chalet. It was a pleasant contrast to the crisp "spring" air that Tony Geiger's friend Fedot was extolling the virtues of as he led her away from the registration desk. With her suitcase in his little hand—he was at least a half-head shorter than Lily—he pressed the elevator call, then ushered her inside with a bow. Fedot stood next to her in the car, staring and smiling into her face without a trace of self-consciousness. Somehow, despite his odd demeanor, she felt a certain affection for him. But maybe it was just because he was a link to Tony, and Tony's ugly death was still plaguing every moment of her waking life.

"And this is the Soviet Women's Liberation from Tyranny Suite," Fedot instructed, as he carried Lily's suitcase through the sizeable double doors. Lily only smiled and nodded as she followed him, feeling acutely aware that the most casual observers—a grimacing woman dressed as a maid, but who carried herself with the authority of a police sergeant, and a toadying man from the concierge desk—were watching her every move.

Lily's attention wandered to an unframed portrait of a woman. It hung above the camelback of a Biedermier sofa in desperate need of re-stuffing, and its artlessness clashed with the sofa's scrolled arms and Sabre legs. The woman was depicted wearing a plain, pale blue babushka that matched her eyes and stared impassively at the suite before her. Lily thought she looked a bit like her mother without makeup.

"And if you need anything at all," Fedot pledged, "Our front desk will be happy to assist you. Merely pick up your telephone and you will be connected to the lobby. The lobby is the only number your phone is suited to dial, but it's also the only number you will need." Fedot pointed to the plain, black phone as he took Lily's suitcase into the bedroom and laid it on the bed. He grinned before opening it for her.

"So, you will like your stay at Hotel Rude," he said.

"Yes, I'm sure I will."

"I wrote some places down for you," Fedot informed her, holding out a folded, brown paper. "Places of interest to enjoy with or without my assistance."

Lily had no idea what it was that Fedot was trying to tell her, but she knew he believed he was being helpful. Every sentence he spoke seemed coded, and she realized that she and Tony had only begun to talk about her trip to Moscow when he was killed.

If she had a brain in her head, Lily thought, she would fly back to Boston and tell her father everything that had happened, including her short and mildly sordid—certainly strange—relationship with Tony Geiger. But for reasons that seemed to have nothing to do with self-preservation, she couldn't bring herself to go that route.

The words "legacy" and "residue" wouldn't stop resonating through her head in Tony's offhand tough-talk, and Boston was nothing but residue for her. Broken promises, juvenile love affairs, frivolous friendships and, above all, a complete lack of inspiration awaited her there. That in itself was a kind of death.

"Tony," she whispered. Lily couldn't get the sardonic New Yorker out of her head. She wondered if he had a mother and siblings, or if he'd left behind a wife and kids. Somehow she doubted all that. She imagined that the only person he'd really left behind was her, and the more she thought about Tony, the more he mattered. He'd had a job—a job important enough to die for—and he'd really never been anything but fair to her, even if she didn't matter much to him. She realized she was envious of him, and that envy was what had drawn her to his friend, Fedot, and Soviet Russia with a peculiar metal card and a membership in the American Communist Party. Tony Geiger had given her a taste of what it was like to be a part of real events, and once she'd tasted that, she wanted more and more of his world. Truth be told, she wanted Tony's life, and as Fedot blabbered on about the wonders of communism and the liberated woman glowered at her like a strict nanny, she knew now that she was going to take it.

"With or without your assistance," she repeated. "Of course."

Fedot bowed before he left, leaving Lily with a sloppy pile of her warmest summer clothes heaped on her bed.

"Fedot," she called, but he'd already closed the doors behind him. She'd forgotten to ask him where she could buy a jacket and a warmer sweater. Moscow was a good thirty degrees colder than Greece, and except for the brief respite of the too-warm Hotel Rude lobby, Lily had been freezing since she stepped off the plane. Freezing and hungry.

"Hello, room service please?" she inquired in English, then French, then German, but the line turned to static and went dead. Lily grunted and slammed the phone down, sitting at the edge of her mattress and taking in her suite for the first time.

She was perched on a French antique bed, flanked by incompatible modern lamps from a German designer. Three ornate Russian writing tables littered the living area and were, according to Fedot, built by a carpenter who had made a name for himself by building libraries in the late Czar's family residences. Before his death, he'd become an ardent communist, Fedot had assured her.

All of the furniture had flaws that might have been fine had they been part of a collection in a home but made the hotel appear sloppy even when the floors and appliances shined. The bed was a bit lopsided, the tables were scratched with jagged, awkward strokes as if they'd spent time in a child's room, and the lamps were plain and ugly.

It was as if Hotel Rude had been decorated by a burglar. One who had no taste of his own, but had assembled mismatched yet expensive furniture that he'd pilfered from variously styled mansions. Even the telephone, which was old but a standard enough model, didn't quite look like it belonged. Lily stared at it for a moment, and it started to ring—as if she'd willed it.

"Hello. Yes, hello, is this room service?" Lily yelled into the phone. "I'm sorry, speak up—I can hardly hear you. I'd like some breakfast, please. *Breakfast.* Borscht? From last night? Look, don't you have . . . hello? Are you still there? Hello? Yes, good. No, borscht will be fine. Can you bring it up to room 1036? Oh!"

The line went dead again. Lily set the receiver into the cradle and folded her arms in a huff. She looked down at the royal blue hand-woven carpet that spilled out from under her bed like a large puddle. It had once been stunning and must have cost its original owner a small fortune. Her eyes followed its tattered edge to the base of a short and stout dresser that Lily had at first mistaken for a writing table.

"Happy birthday," Lily said, remembering Tony's directives. She treaded one careful step at a time to the dresser and crouched down, pulling open the bottom drawer. Inside was a safe the size of a modest hat box. Plain, but sturdy. Lily reached down and turned the dial, entering her birth date and drawing the door up slowly.

The contents of the safe were anti-climactic. An olive-green folder lay at the bottom topped with a small, brown bottle of Myer aspirin—like a cherry on a sundae. Lily picked up the aspirin bottle and held it to the light. It looked empty. She uncorked it and, on instinct, sniffed the contents. The interior smelled bitter and chemical, not at all like aspirin. Lily dipped her index finger into the bottle and explored the inside. As she ran her fingertip along its inner wall, she felt something a little slippery and pulled it up and out of the brown glass. It was a tiny roll of film, so small it seemed made for a doll. Lily backed up from the dresser and sat back down on the bed, clicking on the reading lamp at her bedside table. She positioned the film under the light, beholding the strangest blue print patterns she had ever seen.

"What on earth?" Lily whispered.

The doorbell buzzed, and she nearly leapt off the bed.

"Just a minute," she called, tucking the film into the top of her stocking and dropping the empty bottle back into the safe. Lily kicked the drawer closed.

"Who is it?"

She tried to sound casual as she walked to the door. There was no peephole, so Lily put her ear to the lacquered wood, as if the visitor's movements could tell her something.

"Room service," the Russian replied in a voice that was like thick paper rubbed between a thumb and index finger.

"That was awfully fast. What do you have for me?"

"Borscht," he answered.

Lily cracked the door first, and then opened it wide. An impressive man in a dark, tailored suit stood before her. His black hair was slicked back and shiny, looking like the grooves on a record album, and his shoulders and chest overshadowed the rest of him.

The dark man's eyes swept the suite before focusing on Lily. She could smell his breath, anise and cigarettes, and his cologne, citrus.

"Where's my borscht?" she asked.

The dark man raised his eyebrow and smirked, entering the suite without her invitation and closing the door.

"Where's my dossier?" he countered.

Lily shook her head.

"The dossier in the small safe at the bottom of your wardrobe over there." The dark man pointed to the squat, three-drawer dresser.

"I haven't even unpacked yet," Lily said.

"But you know the combination, so why don't you open it for me?"

Lily wasn't afraid of him, but she knew she should be. "No," she told him.

The dark man took a lugubrious breath and walked to the wardrobe himself. He opened the bottom drawer, lifted the safe and entered Lily's birth date. The door popped open, and he placed the contents of the safe—the folder and the tiny bottle of Myer aspirin—into his breast pocket without ceremony.

"I'm sorry," Lily began. "But you're two days early and I didn't want to take any chances."

The man rubbed a medicinal balm over his lips and shook his head. "I wasn't supposed to come at all. I received a message to come here shortly after I got off my plane."

"From who?"

The man put his fingers to his cheek and ran the tips of them over his chin.

"I would think you'd know that."

Lily stepped closer to him—not because she was compelled to, but because she wanted him to know that she wasn't afraid. "I knew enough to get here, didn't I?"

The man laughed in a tender way that was at odds with the cruel character of his fused eyebrows.

"Tony Geiger was supposed to take the contents of the safe from you," he enlightened her. "But apparently he couldn't make it." The man clutched the bottle of Myer aspirin in his palm and shook his head. "I was hoping to never see this again."

Lily squeezed her thighs together and felt the microfilm chafing between them.

"So, Tony was the one who was supposed to come here?" she asked. "Jesus Christ. Are you sure?"

"I'm positive. I received a message from him before I left my previous destination a couple of days ago. It changed my plans considerably."

Lily shrugged and looked at the ground.

"Tony's always full of surprises," she mumbled.

The dark man smoothed his hair and adjusted his suit jacket in an oval mirror above the telephone table. The contents of the safe were well-disguised under the wool of his jacket and in the soft pillow of his breast.

"Madam," he said, before turning to leave.

"Wait a minute," Lily called, and the dark man turned his head. She could feel the film slither under the lace trim of her stocking. "Are you staying here? In the Hotel Rude, which is an appropriate enough name?"

The man shook his head.

"Rude, in most Slavic languages, means red, not un-mannerly," he informed her without condescension. "It can also mean beautiful."

"I know that," she said, her cheeks burning. "I was trying to make a joke. What's your name, is what I'm really asking. I mean, shouldn't I know your name just in case?"

His voice was tender again when he answered her. "You shouldn't."

The door clicked shut, and Lily waited until his foot-steps faded down the corridor before pulling the film out of her stocking. She wound it into a tight coil that fit easily inside her lipstick tube. Lily didn't know what she was going to do with the film and could've kicked herself for having pocketed it in the first place. Damn Tony for sending his contact so soon. She supposed she could have come clean, but that Russian hadn't exactly seemed like the kind of guy who would understand why the film was under her skirt instead of where it belonged. She needed to think hard about how she was going to get the contents of the Myer aspirin bottle back into the hands of Tony's Russian before he figured out what she'd done.

Lily couldn't stay in her suite right then. Apart from the fact that the place was not growing on her and that she felt like there was always a fly on the wall, Lily was one of those people who needed to move in order to do her best thinking. The sounds of the city—the cars, pounding the pavement, and the ever-present cool wind—would give her a sense of security that her quiet suite of pilfered treasures could not. She grabbed her purse and a wrap and headed to the lobby.

"Greetings!"

The concierge smiled a big, disingenuous smile at her as she stepped out of the elevator, and Lily averted her eyes, only to catch Fedot trotting after her.

"Miss Tassos, I would so like to join you for your day. I promise to make my company of you exquisite."

"Thanks, Fedot, but I'd like some time alone today."

Fedot bowed his head, still smiling, and held up the newspaper that had been folded under his arm.

"I'll go for my jacket. You'll see good times with me."

Lily was about to get emphatic with him when she caught a glimpse of the front page of the Moscow city paper.

"Fedot, who is that?"

Fedot looked down at the grainy photograph and then back to Lily.

"Miss Tassos . . ."

"His name. I just need to hear his name."

Fedot bit his bottom lip and adjusted his collar.

"Pasha Tarkhan, of course."

Lily repeated the name to herself. It wasn't at all familiar to her. The man, however, was very familiar. She'd met him not fifteen minutes earlier in her suite when he came for Tony's dossier.

"Can you translate the article for me, please?"

Fedot gave her a Cheshire cat grin and laughed.

"Fedot . . ."

"Forgive me, but the article is awkward, I'm afraid."

Lily swallowed, wondering if Fedot had been eaves-dropping on her and Tony's big, dark Russian. Perhaps he understood a great deal more about their simple exchange than she did.

"Just translate it, Fedot."

The slight Russian shrugged and took out a round pair of reading glasses, balancing them on his nose.

"Pasha Tarkhan, who is . . . uh . . . how you say? Perhaps Under Secretary? He has honored his country when he was made forced to kill the American spy Brenda France of Los Angeles California United States. The American woman breaked into his hotel room in Prague, was trying to steal from him and took gun on him to killed him, but he was able to fight her and forced to unfortunately killed her. The United States Americans have aggressively deny she was spy, but we all know that they are biggest liars in world. Because USSR is greater than they are, the United States Americans are jealous of us and want to know the secrets of our Utopian society. The United States, as we know, is filled with nothing but Capitalist poverty and its people are dying and would wish to come to USSR, so the American government wants to kill us . . ."

"That's quite enough, Fedot. Thank you."

The article was funny in its own way, but Lily had a difficult time finding humor in anything at that particular moment—especially as she recalled the sheer size of Pasha Tarkhan, his inscrutable eyes, and his tender laugh. She had no doubt that he was, in fact, capable of murder. She'd heard the same ring of truth when Tony Geiger had first acquainted her with the knowledge that her father was not exactly what he appeared to be. And when her mother told her that she was just like her father.

"I'll get my coat," Fedot reiterated. "We'll have nice day."

"Of course," Lily told him, but as soon as he reached the front desk, she slipped out the door. She knew he would follow her, as would a half dozen other "employees" of Hotel Rude, but she wanted at least a head start with some time alone. If Pasha Tarkhan was a monster, then he might've been the one who killed Tony, which meant Lily had just given him at least some of what Tony was trying to protect. But a monster would've had no incentive to leave Lily alive, she deduced, and she could've been so easily disposed of in a hotel room—just like Brenda France. Whatever the case, Lily and Pasha Tarkhan had some unfinished business.

"Miss Tassos!" Fedot cried, as Lily quickened her step. "You have forgotten me, but I catch you!"

CHAPTER 7

ATHENS, GREECE

Beryx Gulyas champed his stuffed grape leaves until they were the consistency of over-boiled tripe. He was a fast eater—too fast—and was trying to slow himself down in an effort to control his portions. It was a joyless way to consume his favorite Greek dish.

He looked across the table at his lunch companion and cocked his head, scrutinizing the easy, languorous way in which Etor chewed his food. The Cretan gigolo sat idly in his chair, relishing the hustle and bustle of the Plaka as if the bounty of seafood before him was incidental. It was no wonder he was so trim. He took his time, and treated his lunch like a casual mistress. One whose company he took pleasure in throughout the night, but didn't need to enjoy his coffee with in the morning.

Etor. He was not as stupid as Beryx had originally thought him to be. He was careless. He was trivial. But he wasn't an idiot, like Leon Kuntz's co-pilot had been, as testified by the crude carvings on his forehead.

"I shouldn't use so much salt," Etor reproved, helping himself to a liberal pinch for his baked eel. He had finished explaining to Beryx why he'd chosen to kill Tony Geiger with poison instead of the sniper's rifle the Hungarian had championed and was now looking forward to digging in to a costly lunch that wouldn't cost him a thing.

"What if you hadn't used enough of the toxin?" Beryx queried.

Etor shrugged and shook his head in the same manner he had used to dismiss their waiter when the young boy offered them another bottle of Retsina. The noonday sun was beaming into his eyes, but the gigolo wouldn't squint. It put his wrinkles on display.

"Then he would have died in three hours instead of three minutes. You only need enough to cover the head of a pin. And there's no antidote."

"Good," Beryx murmured.

Throughout the ages, poison had been referred to as "the coward's weapon," but the Hungarian assassin disagreed. Poison took knowledge and a strong stomach. It could disfigure, distort and liquefy, forcing the perpetrator to watch an often gruesome process. It wasn't a coward's weapon, no, but it was certainly a feminine one.

"An Arab's kiss, you called it."

"Arab's kiss, yes. Very potent. Fast acting. It's cultivated from a type of passionflower that grows in the Middle East. They call it a . . . a . . . I can't remember, but it's a nice word. Beautiful. Like a woman's name—Alehlah."

Although Etor relayed all of this with his mouth full, he managed to avoid looking uncouth. He spoke equally with his hands, which moved in sensual, dancing motions and drew attention away from his lips.

"Alehlah. A very clever poison," Beryx acknowledged, and Etor smiled.

"Of course, if I'd used a gun, I would've been better prepared for circumstances created out of my control. If something or someone else emerged, I could've fired another bullet. The darts are more complicated. They're difficult to handle, because you don't want the poison to come in contact with your skin."

Etor stuck his fork into a heavily salted yellow potato

the size of a walnut and held it up while his tongue fished a piece of eel skin out of his back molar.

"But," he continued. "The fact is I've never liked blood. It's ugly and it stains the clothes."

Beryx knew how to get a man like Etor going. Initially reticent, the gigolo was growing more forthcoming with every glass of wine. All he needed to be assured of was a sympathetic ear, which would give him permission to bask in the sound of his own voice and boast an expertise in something other than luxury clothing and women's genitalia.

"Who could get in the way?" Beryx probed.

"I don't know. A lover, perhaps. Someone who wasn't supposed to be there."

Beryx moved closer to Etor, putting his hand on the gigolo's thigh.

"A lover?"

Etor nodded and leaned in to the Hungarian, his lips brushing the curve of his ear. He didn't desire men sexually—in fact, he preferred the company of women on almost all occasions—but his days of picking and choosing were over, and men like Beryx Gulyas had deep pockets.

"A very good lover," he whispered.

Beryx smiled, showing his teeth, which he didn't often do. Not out of vanity, although the state of his teeth was nothing to be proud of, but because it felt entirely unnatural to him. Smiling on command was difficult enough, but grinning was so contrary to his character that he looked more like an animal baring its teeth than a happy, amused human being.

"Then let's go to your place."

Etor pushed his plate away and leaned his elbows on the table.

"My place is small. I'm not here very often. A couple of months here and there—mostly in the early summer."

"I don't like hotels," Beryx insisted. "They don't have kitchens. I must have a kitchen."

Etor shrugged, thinking, *Suit yourself.* His Athens apartment was a depressing concrete matchbox of a place, and unlike Beryx Gulyas, he loved hotels. They were always so clean—the good ones anyway—and everyone did everything for him.

"We should ask for a carafe of wine to take with us."

"Oh, yes," Beryx agreed. "In a glass carafe. Only a glass carafe will do. Because they're so *pretty.*"

The Hungarian hadn't struck Etor as the type who cared much about pretty things, but then people often got very particular when it came to sex. And the Cretan didn't care if the man wanted a glass carafe or a glass giraffe, as long he got paid in American dollars.

"I'll make sure to get the prettiest one."

Beryx smiled again and waved a hundred drachma note at the waiter. He got up to use the toilet, telling Etor he'd meet him outside. Having not had anything to drink, he didn't need to go, but he did need to purge himself of the heavy lunch he'd shared with the gigolo. Beryx was planning on having a nice dinner with a girl that night and wanted to save his appetite for his real date. He also wanted to look trim and was depressed that he'd lost only two kilos. This, despite nearly starving himself on a diet of raw vegetables and vomiting every time temptation grew too great and he cheated with a sweet pastry or a sausage. He was sure to build up a good sweat with Etor, though. Maybe once he was finished with the Cretan, his pants would fit just a little bit better around the waist.

"Are you ready?" Etor cooed, pushing his shoulders back and sucking in his stomach.

Beryx Gulyas nodded.

"Tell me," he said. "Do you have any salt at home, or will we need to stop at a market?"

"Ah, salt—it's good for the skin." Etor nodded, rubbing his palms over his chest.

"It's good for so many things," the Hungarian told him.

CHAPTER 8

ATHENS, GREECE

Adonia was clearly an invented name, and Beryx imagined that the youngish woman the madam had offered him was born an Agatha or Acacia in some remote Greek fishing village. These thoughts about her were ruining his fantasy, and he swept them away as surely as he'd swept away the salt and broken glass on the floor of Etor's cramped city apartment. When he hired a woman for the night, he liked to pretend that they had met somewhere other than a brothel—in this case a bus stop—and would instruct the woman to bump into him and look up—or in this case down—into his eyes. She would feel an immediate and uncontrollable passion for him and agree to dinner, knowing full well that he intended to take her afterward. She would love it and be anticipating it all night—frightened, ashamed, titillated.

"What's this place called again?" Adonia asked, gazing up at the lighted Acropolis, which sat high above the tiny, outdoor restaurant her customer had chosen. Forgetting to act in his thrall, she recovered quickly by licking her lips and pushing her bust together, while she stroked his calf with her open-toed sandal.

"Socrates's Prison. The chicken is good."

"I like chicken," she cooed. "Do you like chicken?"

"Yes, I like chicken," Beryx breathed. From his pocket, he removed five stones with properties for bolstering willpower—rose quartz, black onyx, rock crystal, chrysoprase, and tiger's eye—and lined them up on the table in front of him.

Adonia was just his type: Black hair, a small bust and soft, rounded hips. She would pucker her lips and whisper when she talked of sex—the way all of them did, the girls for hire. The way Etor had.

Etor. He'd been an idiot after all.

Not only had he admitted to leaving his gloves in his hotel room—discouraging him from loading another lethal dart if the need had presented itself—but he acknowledged leaving a witness behind.

"She's a harmless girl," he'd begged. "A tourist. I liked her."

He was adamant that she hadn't seen him and positive that she had nothing to do with Tony Geiger professionally.

"They probably m-m-m-met somewh-where and ag-ag-agreed to m-meet for a p-p-private rendezvous," Etor had insisted. He was stuttering by then, so it took him a considerably long time to say what he needed to say.

"Then why wouldn't they meet in a hotel room?" Beryx had snarled. He'd left Etor's handsome face intact, but carved a Hungarian insult into him whenever the gigolo said anything stupid. *Geci* (asshole) joined *kurva* (whore), and *puhapócs* (impotent), which were engraved on his buttocks, chest and thigh as Etor hung—arms above his head—from a water pipe in his kitchenette.

Beryx despised sloppiness in his line of work and took enormous pride in leaving no loose ends. He was particularly contemptuous of assassins like Etor, who took occasional jobs and wanted to get them over with as soon as possible—leaving behind bystanders because they *liked* them.

"Where," he had demanded, "is there room for favoritism in what we do?"

Etor hadn't been able to answer, as his throat was filled

with nearly a pound of finely milled sea salt. The Hungarian had broken the Cretan's jaw, prying his fingers behind the man's teeth and pulling hard until he heard a crackling noise—like splintering wood—that made Etor shriek. It was a sickly sound that Beryx didn't like, but the gigolo was unable to close his mouth afterward, and it made pouring the salt down his throat a much easier task. Beryx was unclear as to whether the gigolo had died of cerebral edema—the most common outcome of salt poisoning—or asphyxiation, and wrote a note to himself to remember to contact the medical examiner and find out.

Whatever the case, Etor was gone and Beryx was glad. He was yet another black mark erased from Beryx's profession.

"I like the little lights around those poles," Adonia mused. "They're like twinkling stars." She never got to go to restaurants, let alone nice ones where a husband might take his wife.

"Those aren't poles," Beryx explained. "They're prison bars. For Socrates's Prison."

"Oh."

The waiter sauntered by, depositing two plates of chicken, broiled in an oily tomato sauce and accompanied by the small, yellow potatoes that Etor had liked so much. Adonia smiled and bit her lip, digging into the food with her knife and fork, and dripping grease from her lips into the hollow of what would have been her cleavage, if she had any breasts to speak of.

"So what did he do, the man who owns this place?" Adonia not only chewed with her mouth wide open, but spoke with it full. "You know, why'd he go to prison?"

"He didn't," Beryx enlightened her. "Socrates was a teacher who was poisoned in his prison cell a long, long time ago."

Adonia grimaced. "They name a restaurant after a guy who was poisoned? That doesn't seem very smart." It was only once Beryx heard her say a full sentence—without food in her mouth—that he realized she was no girl from a village. Adonia spoke a lower class Greek dialect direct from the Athens tenement slums.

"Ew, poison," she shuddered, looking down at her oily chicken.

Beryx smirked and ran his crooked index finger from her elbow to her wrist, tracing it all the way down to the tip of her thumb.

"Are you saying you have no craving for dessert?"

Adonia knocked back her glass of Retsina and slammed the empty pewter goblet onto the table with gusto.

"Hell, yes, I want dessert. I want baklava and strong coffee."

She laughed and tipped her ear to her shoulder, kicking off her sandal before wedging her foot between his legs and tickling his groin with her big toe.

"Oh, and I want that kind of dessert, too. I've just got to go take a piss first."

Eying her ample bottom as she wiggled away from the table, Beryx believed in that moment that if he and Adonia had become acquainted under different circumstances— perhaps at a grocery store or in a doctor's waiting room— without her madam as a middleman, that she would've been with him tonight regardless of whether he was paying her. He could tell by the easy flow of their conversation, and by the way she looked to him for explanations about the simplest things. She wanted him, he was convinced, more than she'd ever wanted any man and would do to him things she'd never done—even to her best customers.

"Excuse me, sir." The waiter bowed respectfully and

presented Beryx with the key to an airport locker. "The young woman asked me to give this to you. She said not to worry, that a man with a mustache had taken care of her, and that you would know what she meant."

Beryx sighed, his fantasies shattered like the carafe of red wine he'd smashed against Etor's bedroom wall. It was time to go back to work, and Nicolai Ceausescu didn't pay him to have romantic encounters in foreign cities. He knew exactly what he would find in the airport locker: A photograph of his next mark, a schedule of his usual comings and goings, and a deadline.

The Hungarian paid the check, leaving a little extra for the waiter, and hailed a cab to the airport. Perhaps on his next visit he could ask for Adonia again, and they could finally consummate their passion.

CHAPTER 9
MOSCOW

The chilly, miserable rain that had descended on Moscow in the previous weeks had finally lifted, paving the way for Kosmo Zablov's favorite time of year in his birth city. It was a shame he couldn't enjoy it. Not when so much hung in the balance and Pasha Tarkhan was still walking around free to attend lavish functions and accept glorious promotions. Ones that rightfully belonged to Zablov, at least in terms of seniority, and were now looking blurry and distant, like the fine print he could no longer read without a magnifier. What was worse, there seemed to have been a shift in temperament that had occurred at work while he was visiting with the Ceausescus in Romania and plotting the next phase of his career.

For starters, upon Zablov's return to Moscow from Bucharest, he knew immediately that his office at KGB headquarters had been searched. He'd sprayed his files ever so lightly with fig leaf oil, so that finger smudges would appear on the manhandled pages within a few hours of contact. An ingenious solution for when he was away on short trips, the sensitive oil would evaporate automatically within a few days if it had never been interfered with.

The search in and of itself was troubling, although it didn't necessarily have to mean anything, Zablov reminded himself. Searches were fairly routine, meant to keep people on their toes as much as actually uncover anything. Unless, of course, they wanted to uncover something, but that was another issue entirely. KGB bosses were notorious for "discovering" so-called treachery when they wanted to be rid of someone for one reason or another.

At that thought, Zablov's stomach dropped. He began cataloging all of his more recent encounters at headquarters, desperately trying to figure out if he'd tripped over any mines that could've been laid for him by a jealous colleague, or a superior with a grudge. Nothing. His only real interactions had been with Pasha Tarkhan in Prague and the Ceausescus in Bucharest. Naturally, he'd made his share of enemies, but Zablov had always been sure to destroy any possible detractors fully.

"When there's a snake in your bed," he murmured. "You cut off its head to kill it, not its tail to teach it a lesson."

Zablov's schedule over the past year had been erratic and international, too, hardly giving him time to cultivate the kinds of resentments needed for a real ambush. But then again, Kosmo Zablov understood that no one ever needed a reason other than self-interest in Russia. What, besides being younger, smarter and more talented, had Pasha Tarkhan ever done to him?

Zablov's fear turned to outright terror when Anya, his secretary, informed him that General Pushkin wanted to see him at once.

"Damn Anya," he cursed after she closed his door—always so noiselessly—and returned to her desk. She seemed the slightest bit happy whenever there was any possibility of bad news for her boss. And the redhead had appeared especially pleased when she spoke the words "at once" to him. Her top lip had curled, and her sleepy eyelids quivered so that she almost looked like she was batting her eyelashes.

"Good morning, General. How was your holiday? I hear the Urals are lovely this time of year," Zablov practiced, before opening his door and marching by Anya's desk and toward the narrow corridor that lead to his commander's corner office.

The general was always angry when coming back from a holiday with his family. He much preferred the company of his mistresses to the whining of the three-year-old son and one-year-old daughter he'd had with his new wife.

Zablov hated seeing him on the day after his vacation.

When he caught eyes with the general's secretaries, his right pinky started to tremble. They both stood, rushing to usher him in without exchanging a single pleasantry. Zablov's bladder contracted, and he came within a hair of wetting his pants—an involuntary act that would have communicated only one message to his superior: GUILTY.

"Good Morning, General. How was your—?"

"Sit down," General Pushkin ordered, and Zablov obeyed. The general's cheeks were flushed and his gray eyes had dark, blue rings underneath. He folded his hands in front of him and began to pace, as if he were dictating a letter.

"Several days ago, a woman named Bick, an architect by trade, was captured trying to enter Germany by crossing the Czech border." The general paused briefly, taking note of the look on Zablov's face. He was a master at detecting that tiny glimmer of recognition that registered in the eyes of even the best spy when confronted with a familiar name.

"After a couple of hours of questioning, this architect revealed that she allowed the house she occupied in Prague to be used as a safe house—mostly for the Americans. Over the next few days, she continued to be generous with her knowledge. Much of it meant little, or was a moot point by now, but she was able to offer one bit of tantalizing information."

Zablov did his best not to move a muscle. He knew

nothing of this architect woman, nor of the safe house in question, but the very coincidence that he'd been in Prague recently was enough to make him suspect.

"This architect was able to describe a man we all know quite well. Handsome, in an imperious sort of way. Dark, cultured, well-dressed. These are her words. And quite a lover, she admitted."

Bick, Zablov said to himself, or had the general said *Buck*? Several women he'd had came to mind, but no. No architect, certainly not in a house in Prague! *Bick, Beck, Buck, Bock.* Nothing. Of course any woman could lie about her name. *But good God, whoever she was, she was describing him to a T.*

"A man who she claimed had visited her safe house at least twice very recently," the general hissed. "A man thought in most of our circles to be beyond reproach."

Pretending to adjust his zipper, Zablov squeezed the tip of his penis to block any potential urine flow. He knew he should remain silent, but despite his experience and his training, everything inside him wanted to stand up and scream, "It's not me! For God's sake, it's not me. I've been framed!"

"Architects have sharp memories attuned to detail, wouldn't you say?" the general asked him. "And our lovely little friend was exceptionally detailed in her description. Unmistakably so."

"Could she be a plant?" Zablov inquired, maintaining his regular tone, though softer than usual.

"No," the general whispered.

"Perhaps if my man Jarko could question her? There's no one better at what he does."

General Pushkin shook his head with a measure of genuine sadness. For once, he didn't seem to be enjoying his work.

"The architect is dead. Furthermore, her legitimacy has been established."

Zablov swallowed and nodded.

"What I need from you is something else. I need what you allege to be best at—gathering information."

The word "allege" was not lost on Zablov. He'd felt the general's scrutiny before—during one of his most recent "improvisations" when he'd engineered the assassination of a Canadian operative. An annoying, but nonetheless perceptive would-be intellectual had taken the fall for Zablov's failure to detect an American attempt—no, success—at infiltrating their Canadian operation. The young man had warned Zablov that there was something amiss, but the Russian agent had been too busy fucking the undercover American to pay attention.

"Anything," Zablov sighed. "You know I'd do anything for you."

What the general said next nearly caused Kosmo Zablov to void both his bowels and his bladder.

"Then find Pasha Tarkhan and bring him to me."

CHAPTER 10
MOSCOW

Lily and Fedot had started the afternoon by walking around Red Square admiring buildings that looked like elaborate marzipan cakes, but it was so cold that she had to duck into a store called "Textiles" and buy the first coat she could find. It was, quite possibly, the ugliest thing she'd ever seen. Besides keeping her warm, the coat did serve a purpose, though. It made her fit in better. Lily didn't know if that was good or bad for sure, but Fedot seemed impressed.

Near the Bolshoi Theater, a tiny woman with a faint mustache was standing, hands stiffly at her sides, singing an operetta. Her eyes followed Lily as her voice swelled, and Lily wondered, for a moment, if the singer was yet another finger of the Soviet police state, or if she was simply intrigued by a foreign-looking woman in a communist-issue coat.

"Dunayevsky," Fedot said, smiling.

"Who?"

"The song," he continued. "It's by Dunayevsky. He died last year. A great Soviet."

And so the day went.

By dinnertime Lily was dying to get away from the little Russian's constant stream of idioms and helpful observations, but Fedot goaded her into the hotel bar for "just one da-rink."

He ordered four vodkas right off the bat.

"In case our bartender is too busy," he said, although they were his only patrons.

The bar itself was a study in assorted reds: blood-red,

royal-red, fire-engine-red, claret, ruby, scarlet, crimson, burgundy, cherry. Much like Lily's suite, it was a mishmash of old and new, cheap and luxurious. The chairs lining the bar counter were antique and wooden—their cushions covered in an ancient velvet that had worn into the shape of the average buttocks that had graced them. The bar counter, clearly a replacement, was fashioned out of dented metal and what looked like press-in-place tiles. A sickly shade of cement-gray, it was the only thing in the whole room that was conspicuously not red.

"Fedot," Lily said, sipping from her shot glass. "What do you know about this Tarkhan fellow? I mean, apart from what you translated for me from the newspaper article."

Fedot rubbed his shot glass between his palms and sprouted a closed-lip smile. Right then, he looked no older than twelve.

"Oh, he's a fine communist," he said.

"Yes, I'm sure he is," Lily sighed. "But do you know him? Have you seen him around the hotel or around town? Hotel Rude seems to be host to plenty of visiting dignitaries—would a man like Tarkhan come to meet them here?"

Fedot bobbed his head.

"A comrade like Tarkhan has many friends, certainly."

"Certainly, yes," Lily concurred. "I, for instance, would like to have a friendly meeting with him here. Is that something you could arrange?"

A man in a thin, woolen sweater the color of winter grass and crisp, navy trousers sat down next to Lily at the bar. Except for a flash of his vivid green eyes, Lily didn't get a good look at his face. But his comportment favored a man well into his forties who ate a few too many pastries. The man spread his elbows apart and pushed into Lily, grunting at her.

"Pardon me," she said. "I said *Pardon me!*"

The man had his back to her and barked out his order for brandy.

Fedot leaned in to Lily. "A Hungarian, I think," he said, pointing to the man's ring. It bore the insignia of the Royal Hungarian Army.

"You know what they say about Hungarians, don't you?"

Lily shook her head.

"If you see a Hungarian on the street," Fedot explained, "go to him and slap him. He will know why."

Lily laughed. It sounded like something Tony Geiger would say, and she wasn't sure if Fedot had gotten it from him or the other way around. Tony had always had a way of crystallizing things—observations about situations and people that stung a bit but were largely true. Lily leaned away from the Hungarian fellow and lowered her voice.

"Fedot," she whispered. "Why do you think Tony was killed?"

"Miss Lily," Fedot replied, his small, wet lips parting just enough to let a word escape. "I am hungry. Are you not?" He flagged down the bartender and ordered a plate of bear meat cutlets.

Lily tipped back into her bar chair and sighed. No easy answers in Russia. No easy answers about Tony anywhere, but at least she was sure now that Fedot knew Tony was dead. She had a feeling he had known from the moment she walked into the Hotel Rude—even if Pasha Tarkhan had seemed ignorant of the fact.

"Fedot, do you ever get the feeling that something really big is going to happen?"

Fedot poured a shot of vodka down his throat and swallowed.

"I didn't feel it the night I met with Tony on Monemvasia,

but I feel it now. Like I'm at the top of a roller coaster, getting ready to scream."

Lily reached for her purse and dug inside, producing her room key and dangling it before Fedot. The keychain was oval and brass, displaying her room number—1036—on both sides. "But not before I get a good night's rest," she said.

Fatigue had come upon her like the flu. Lily felt she couldn't possibly say one more word, have one more idea, receive one more piece of information, no matter how trivial. Russia had done that to her—its otherness, its complete inversion of the rules she was used to. It was no wonder Tony Geiger seemed to age five years for every one. He was always playing against the rules in places where cheating was like breathing.

"Good rest is imperative," Fedot agreed. "But so is good food."

The bartender slid the bear meat cutlets in front of them and deposited their silverware in a noisy pile, absent dinner napkins or salt and pepper.

"Eat, eat," Fedot encouraged.

Lily took a halfhearted bite of a lukewarm cutlet and put her fork down.

"Was it not the prophet Elijah who was told by the Lord to eat as he awaited word as to whether he would be put to death or saved?" Fedot inquired.

Lily looked at Fedot—open-mouthed and utterly depleted. "I have no idea," she said. "I hated Sunday school."

"Well," Fedot continued. "I would say Elijah was waiting for something very big to happen, and he needed food for that very big thing."

Lily reached back into her purse, but instead of her room key, this time she removed the metal card Tony had given her. She didn't know what made her want to take it out and show it to Fedot again, the way she had when she first came to the Hotel Rude. The way Tony had instructed her to do. It was as if a bell rang in her head, signaling that it was time.

"Miss Lily," Fedot murmured softly. "I am first and foremost your servant. You must understand this."

Lily cupped her hand over the card.

"It is per my training at Moscow's finest hotelier school," Fedot crowed. "Your wishes compel me."

Fedot sprang up from his seat and bowed. Without another word, he left the red-hued bar and took his place at the night desk—as if he'd never left it. He made no attempt to catch Lily's gaze as she walked to the elevator next to his desk and pressed the call button.

From the bar, the Hungarian watched Lily Tassos step onto the elevator and greet the operator with a weary smile. As the elevator doors closed, he slid the plate of bear cutlets beneath his chin and dug in with Lily's knife and fork. In less than two minutes, he had consumed everything on the plate—even the garnish of grated carrots soaked in white vinegar.

The Hungarian then lifted his empty brandy glass and shook it at the bartender, who obliged.

"Charge it to room 1-0-3-6," he said, exhibiting the key he'd lifted from Lily's purse and laying it on the gray-tiled counter. Pasha Tarkhan had left her suite that morning, and her long hair and pretty face were the last images Tony Geiger had seen before it all went black for him. A tourist, Etor had said. *Dunce!*

He got up from the bar and walked to a corner of the room, where he was sheltered from the bartender's view by a potted rubber tree. Swallowing a massive breath of air, the Hungarian bent over and vomited into the urn-shaped pot that held the rubber tree's roots. He had become expert at gagging and heaving, able to do so with nary a sound that might alert a bystander or member of the staff.

Once back at the bar, he stood as he drank the brandy and petted a piece of amber the size of a quail's egg. It was the Hungarian's favorite gemstone, his most powerful, imbuing the body with vitality and absorbing negative energy. He had paid a whopping five American dollars for it, but it had been worth every penny, as it contained a spider, possibly as old as twenty-five million years, that had been trapped in the fossilized resin just as it was about to feed on a dance fly.

CHAPTER 11

ATHENS, GREECE

The blood and broken glass on the vinyl floor of Etor's kitchen had been cleaned up, more or less—the largest pieces from the smashed carafe swept to the side and the sticky mess of body fluids swabbed with wet towels by a gang of grizzled and beefy Greeks. The men had performed their task in complete silence, not daring a glance at their master as he walked around Etor's mangled body.

"This is unspeakable," the Cretan gangster lamented, running his thick hand—made for chopping wood, spear fishing and gripping a man at the throat—over his bald head. "What kind of animal would do this?"

Baru o Crete, as he was known, stood eye to eye with Etor, studying the death grimace on the gigolo's face as his gruesomely abused body still dangled from the water pipe in his kitchenette. The congealed blood had been wiped off Etor's smooth, tanned skin, but the gangster's men had yet to cut him down. He'd asked all of them but his man, Christo, to leave him alone with his boy. The men had filed out, one by one, as if in a funeral procession.

Until that day, Christo had been the only one who had known Etor was Baru's son. The two Cretans had grown up together, and Christo had been there when Baru became a father at thirteen. It was Christo's parents and not Baru's mother—a notorious drunk and whore—who had raised Etor as if he were their own.

"He'll die a worse death, this Gulyas," Christo assured him, but both men knew Baru's fingers didn't extend very far beyond Greece. The Cretan didn't understand the Soviet Union and cursed himself for having taken a subcontract from one of their assassins. He thought he was doing his boy a favor by throwing him work and hoped the prospect of more plum assignments would lure Etor away from the folly of resorts and rich women and back into the folds of the family business. Baru o Crete could have finally introduced Etor as his son, instead of protecting him like he had and letting him have his fun. The Cretan gangster had thought he was being a good father, allowing his only son to indulge his fantasies, but what he'd feared had finally come to pass. Etor's frivolous pursuits were interpreted as weakness, and a more hardened predator had trapped and killed him.

"There's Zeki in Istanbul," Christo continued. "His men are appropriately vicious."

"But not very smart," Baru countered. There were at least a half dozen other gangsters with whom he was on friendly terms who either owed him a favor or would've been happy to have a debt they could collect upon in the future. None of them were a match for a man like Beryx Gulyas, whose reputation had grown so fearsome in such a short period of time.

"He's not unbreakable," Christo said. "He just knows how to make a statement."

Baru took out his handkerchief and spit on it, using the cotton cloth to wipe the white dribble caked around Etor's mouth. On impulse, he tasted the sediment—salt.

"I know how to make a statement, too," the Cretan snarled.

Christo put his hand on Baru's shoulder, and the gangster shuddered.

"You know what you have to do. He owes you a thousand debts and should be honored to get justice for Etor."

As any father would desire, as any Cretan would demand, Baru o Crete wanted the pleasure of at least watching Beryx Gulyas die, if not crushing his skull with his bare hands. But Baru's men were parochial Greeks, who spoke no other languages and had no heads for strategy. Hunting down a prized assassin required an international operation with ties deep inside the Soviet Union.

"Get my boy down," Baru ordered, stepping away from his bloodied son. "I want to bury him myself."

CHAPTER 12
MOSCOW

What had begun for Kosmo Zablov as a mere simmer of jealousy had raged into a full boil of hatred.

Hatred for Pasha Tarkhan.

Zablov hated his intellect, despised his panache and found his rise in Moscow deplorable, his beautiful mistresses loathsome and his facility with language utterly contemptible. The funny thing was, despite the fact that Zablov had arranged to have Nicolai Ceausescu put out a kill for Tarkhan, he hadn't actually hated the man until the moment Pushkin had identified him—"dark, cultured, dapper," and let's not forget "quite a lover"—as a traitor. *A man like Tarkhan couldn't be satisfied with ascending to the top of the Soviet hierarchy, could he?* Zablov vexed. *He had to become a philosopher on top of it all and start working for the other side!*

All of this would have been fine if Zablov didn't have the niggling feeling that General Pushkin had commanded him to do the honors of bringing in Comrade Dark and Cultured for a purpose. But what purpose? And why not use a lower-ranking brute—one who had the muscle to fight Tarkhan if need be? Tarkhan was, after all, nearly twice Zablov's size. It was a nightmare-inducing quandary.

"On the pavement of my trampled soul, the steps of madmen weave the prints of rude, crude words." *The steps of madmen, yes,* thought Zablov. *And on my soul!*

These were the poet Vladimir Mayakovsky's words. Mayakovsky, who was perhaps the only thing Kosmo

Zablov and Pasha Tarkhan truly had in common. Both his and Tarkhan's favorite poet. They had even mused about Mayakovsky on that most damning trip to Prague only a few days ago.

"He's Georgian—like you," Zablov had told him.

"Yes, but that's not why I like him," Tarkhan said. "His energy was demonic, and his words a disjointed lullaby."

Of course, everyone had a favorite poet in Russia. Several, as a matter of fact. But for Zablov, his affinity for Mayakovsky went so much deeper than an appreciation of the poet's way with words or feverish rhythms.

Vladimir Mayakovsky committed suicide at the age of thirty-six by playing Russian roulette until he lost. Both poet laureate and shameless Bolshevik flack, he'd always fascinated Kosmo Zablov, and the KGB spy found disturbing parallels between his own life and that of the young, brooding poet's.

First and foremost, what Mayakovsky was and what he wanted to be were two very different things, and Zablov knew this pain well. Although he wasn't a poet and had never cared about being a revolutionary like his imagined counterpart, Zablov was a remarkable manipulator who had always wanted to be a brilliant tactician.

And Mayakovsky had no interest in nature or things spiritual. He'd embraced the beauty of industry and the simple logic of atheism as suddenly and completely as Constantine had embraced Christ, yet his poetry, quite unintentionally, exemplified the very things the poet disdained.

Tender souls! You play your love on a fiddle, and the crude club their love on a drum. But you cannot turn yourselves inside out, like me, and be just bare lips!

Similarly, Zablov had no grasp of situations in their whole, yet was somehow able to flawlessly execute any plan that revolved around his own self-interest. He'd never questioned his instincts in this regard and certainly never considered any moral implications.

What wouldn't he have given, he wondered, for the mental agility that could've freed him to apply his gifts of self-preservation to his actual job? It seemed like such a small leap, and yet somehow he'd never mastered it.

If Zablov could've been more like Pasha Tarkhan in this regard, he'd be a much less troubled man. Then it would be he who hobnobbed with world leaders instead of having to associate with the likes of Nicolai Ceausescu and his rat-faced wife.

The problem was made worse by the fact that Zablov had no insight into his one and only talent, either. He didn't know how he had come to the decisions he'd made or why things had always worked out for him. He only knew that his judgment had so far remained intact. It was important that Zablov reminded himself of this, as he tried desperately to shake the curly-headed man with the dented face General Pushkin had sent to follow him. The Neanderthal had made no effort to hide his intentions and strolled around the metro station—hands in his pockets—admiring the Cathedral ceilings and giant Deco chandeliers until he hopped onto the same coach Zablov was taking.

"Try this, you box-eyed bastard," the spy grumbled as he muscled his way out of the train's sliding doors before they closed and jumped onto another train going in the opposite direction. Pushkin's thug was left wedged behind them—stuck on a coach to Oktyabrskaya.

Zablov needed all the time he could steal in order to get in and out of the secret apartment he kept in Leningradsky Prospect. It had been a stroke of genius on his part to secure the place for his own use—genius and blind luck. The one-bedroom flat had been formerly used to spy on a biologist who ended up dying in a drunken skiing accident. Instead of having the flat reassigned, Zablov had burned all files on the unfortunate scientist and transferred the place to a man he'd invented.

While the flat was certainly nothing to write home about, it did possess one critical perk, apart from its non-existence. It had a working telephone.

"Immediately, please. I want to place a call to Bucharest, Romania." Zablov used his best Belarus accent to disguise his voice. All outgoing and incoming calls were recorded and deliberated ad nauseum by young intelligence officers eager to make a name for themselves.

Zablov hung up the phone and waited for the operator to call back, hoping against hope that for once the Moscow switchboard would operate with a modicum of efficiency. There was no food in the cupboards, only a few satchels of tea, so Zablov made himself a cup and sat a few feet away from the window.

"Mother of God!" he yelped, nearly falling off the old piano stool that served as the only chair in the flat. Pushkin's thug—with his smashed-in face and walk like a rhinoceros—was lumbering down Tverskaya Street, his shape unmistakable under the lamplight. He nodded at an old woman carrying a beehive satchel and crossed the street, looking up at Zablov's apartment.

"Bastard!" Zablov cried, crouching to the floor. It would've been impossible for the thug to see him, but he was taking no chances. The agent reached up and dialed the phone again, peeking just enough over the window to see the top of the thug's head as he entered the building.

"International operator," he begged. It took a little under four minutes for a normal man to walk up to the ninth floor. This allowed time for a half minute rest on the sixth floor and the eighteen paces it took from the top of the staircase to Zablov's apartment door.

"Operator, I called a few minutes ago regarding a line to Bucharest. Yes, yes, I know. Very busy, I'm sure." Zablov held his palm over the receiver and took two deep breaths before continuing. "This is an extreme emergency, you see. My mother is very ill. It could be any moment now."

He nodded as the operator explained procedure and ground his knuckle into a groove on the telephone table.

"Yes, I'll hold."

It occurred to him suddenly that he hadn't put together what he was going to say to Nicolai Ceausescu. He couldn't tell him the truth for obvious reasons—that killing Tarkhan now would make it look like Zablov was trying to rid himself of a co-conspirator. One who could implicate him—wrongly—as a double agent. The Romanian couldn't care less about the mess Zablov had stumbled into.

Great news, my friend. The report will be glowing after all! Zablov tried it on, but it was wrong. Nicolai Ceausescu would never buy it.

Call it off, unless you want to lose your only advocate in Moscow.

"No," Zablov murmured. Far too much information, and no guarantee that he was the Romanian's only advocate.

You're in danger. Call it off.

"Perfect."

The message was simple and mysterious—just the right combination for a man as paranoid as Nicolai Ceausescu.

"Yes, I'm still holding," he stuttered. Zablov put the telephone receiver down and crept to the foyer. He held his breath as he put his ear to the door, as if any noise he made could be yet another piece of evidence against him.

He could hear, on the seventh floor, the unmistakable thud of a pair of police boots climbing the stairs at a steady pace.

"Too soon," he whispered.

The thug was making excellent time, having foregone the need for a rest stop. Zablov's shoulders dropped, surrendering into a slouch as he pondered his predicament. The catalog of his alleged crimes, he realized, was impressive: treason, conspiracy, murder. He could even hear himself listing the evidence against him, as Jarko, his enforcer, stood behind him with a billy club.

Isn't it true you met with Pasha Tarkhan in Prague?

Isn't it true you were his accomplice in treason against the Soviet Union?

Isn't it true that you had Pasha Tarkhan murdered before he could corroborate any evidence against you?

"Horrific coincidence," Zablov wailed.

It was, to Zablov, profoundly unfair that a mere scheme for a promotion had entangled him in much larger events that he had so little control over. He reached into his wallet and took out a small, twenty-six-year-old newspaper clipping detailing Mayakovsky's unfortunate end. It showed a picture of the poet—taken when he was twenty-two, but looking forty. Even then, when he was in the thrall of his revolutionary dreams, Mayakovsky's eyes looked doomed, and Zablov wondered if his own eyes, at twenty-two, had told a similar tale.

It was a mere fifty-seven seconds later when the thug, or Rodki Semyonov, as he was known to General Pushkin, called his chief to let him know what had happened.

"I wouldn't have seen it, but once the blood started to

drip down the wall, the words became visible. He wrote, 'I've set my heel upon the throat of my own song.'" Semyonov squatted under Kosmo Zablov's body and listened as the General vented his frustrations about the dead agent, calling Zablov a moron and a traitor, then demanding to know the meaning of his last written words.

"He liked poetry, I guess—but then, who doesn't?" Semyonov remarked. "There was one more thing, though." Semyonov reached over to the window and took Zablov's tea cup off the sill, drinking it down in three, large gulps. It was hot and stung the back of his throat.

"The operator was on the line. He was trying to reach Romania." Semyonov looked up at Kosmo Zablov— slumped on the piano stool, but still leaning against the wall, as if he were bent over, trying to light a cigarette in the wind. The spy's gun was cradled in his hands, and his lips were wrapped tightly around the barrel. Semyonov, who possessed all of the acumen Kosmo Zablov had coveted while he lived, was able to listen to the general's detailed instructions and simultaneously observe the dead man's body as it slid down the wall—slowly and deliberately, as if the spy was still controlling his motions. He appreciated the beauty in such a moment. It was, he realized, a rare event to witness a man's body so soon after his death, and Semyonov felt a deep respect both for life and life's end— even if he was unsentimental about the person who had actually died.

"He'd just returned from Bucharest a couple of days ago," Semyonov explained. "If I had ordered an assassin there, I wouldn't be too eager to keep making contact." He nodded and hmm'd. "Yes, a moron, as you said."

He took a tin case out of his pocket and retrieved a thickly rolled cigarette from it. He peeled off the paper and deposited the tobacco into his palm before scooping up the dried leaves with his lips and lodging them between his lower gums and his cheek.

"I'll go back to the Hotel Rude," he told the general. "I can be there within the hour."

CHAPTER 13

MOSCOW

"*Kon da ti go natrese!*" a formally dressed Bulgarian shouted as he bolted out the door to the toilet in the *Revolution Room* at Hotel Rude. He shoved by Pasha, pursued by the man he'd told to go "get fucked by a horse."

Pasha Tarkhan waited until the ruckus had passed before entering the men's room—now quiet and empty. Toilets at most crowded gatherings like this were used primarily for homosexual encounters, so the majority of guests piddled outside. The dark Russian, however, wanted to avoid mingling with the other partygoers and thought it better to brave the odors of semen and concentrated urine.

"Don't allow anyone to enter," he'd told the toilet minder, slipping her five American dollars that she promptly hid under the reserves of weak, gravelly toilet paper she meted out for a coin. His donation would allow him at least a couple of minutes' peace while he relieved his bladder and thought about how he was going to convince Tony Geiger's Lily to leave Russia with him.

"The urinals are clogged," the old woman reported as Pasha closed the door. Men's room urinals were foul as a rule, and Pasha never used them. He entered the second of only two stalls, having glimpsed a full bowl of excrement in the first, and unzipped his trousers.

Pasha's instincts had always been sharp, and the tiny needles of truth that pricked at him like acupuncture had told him his cover had been blown. There had been no searches of his villa or out of the blue discussions about fantastical promotions, but there had been a change in the air that Pasha could smell as surely as a peasant farmer could smell an oncoming drought. Having stolen the information about *Sputnik*—though his greatest and most recent transgression—was hardly his only one.

The moment he'd caught a whiff of the danger, he'd left his offices at the Kremlin—casually—and disappeared into the Moscow maze. At least until now, when he'd shown his face in the Hotel Rude's *Revolution Room,* at a party for a South American official. He could hide in the shadows by day, but in the night, it was better to take cover in a crowd—especially a drunken one. Part of him had hoped that he might run into Lily Tassos there. If General Pushkin was on to Pasha, then it couldn't be long before he found his way to Tony's Lily, and the sooner he, the girl and the *Sputnik* information got out of Russia the better.

But Lily had been out all day and Pasha was feeling worried about her. She was clearly an amateur wanting to play in the high stakes game of espionage—and worse, she was an amateur with a good measure of pluck. Her association with the likes of Tony Geiger and her reckless deed of taking the microfilm from the contents of the safe were evidence of that. Pasha had tried to send a message to Geiger—it was possible Tony had learned of his compromise at the Kremlin and had asked his Lily to take the film as a safeguard—but to no avail. Tony had gone "AWOL," as he would say.

It occurred quite suddenly to Pasha that he had taken a liking to the American girl, and this made him the slightest bit uneasy. Although their encounter in her hotel room that morning had been brief, he'd found himself thinking about it throughout the day, when his mind should have been on other things. Instead of presuming duplicity on

her part for taking the film, he had assumed h
And now, he found himself concerned for her
er than bothering first about his own. Chivalry
paid off for Pasha. He'd seen first-hand what a ....ty a
kind heart was in Russia, and had worked diligently over
the years to harden his.

> *Mortals! Hear the sacred cry:*
>
> *"Freedom, freedom, freedom!"*
> *Hear the noise of broken chains,*
> *see the noble Equality enthroned.*
> *The United Provinces of the South*
> *have now opened their very honorable throne.*

The Argentine National Anthem was being warbled by
a drunken chorus of diplomats and bureaucrats. Pasha remembered that it had always played at midnight in Buenos
Aires on official holidays. It was performed any old time
by Argentine tourists after they knocked back a few drinks.
The music swelled as the door to the men's toilet opened
behind him.

> *And the free people of the world reply:*
> *"To the great Argentine people, Cheers!"*

Pasha couldn't know if it was chance or instinct that made
him raise his arm to his neck after closing his zipper. He
howled as a needle dug into his forearm while a substance
that felt at once hot and cold bubbled under his skin.

"The more you struggle, the faster you'll die," the assassin hissed as he wrapped his arms around Pasha's neck.
But the Russian moved too quickly to let the man grip his
elbows in a stranglehold. He backed up and slammed the
assassin against the wall, then used all of his weight to push

evenly against the man's chest to keep him from being able to take a breath. It was a difficult way to kill someone—requiring a lot of strength—but Pasha had done it before. The problem was, his arm felt as though it was being liquefied, and the poison the man had injected into it was giving him fever and draining his stamina.

Pasha could hold on only long enough to render the man unconscious and then collapsed to the floor. The burn had spread to his shoulder and into his chest cavity, and taking a simple breath was agonizing.

Pasha turned to look at his assassin: the man was dressed well, but pudgy and pale with maroon circles under his eyes. He wore a distinctive ring bearing the insignia of the Royal Hungarian Army. The Russian had never seen him before and had no interest in meeting him when he awoke. He pulled the syringe out of his blistering forearm and aimed to inject his would-be killer with whatever poison was left. His vision failing, he missed the man's femoral artery and ended up plunging the needle close to his groin.

Pasha crawled to the door and managed to turn the handle after several tries. He struggled past the disinterested toilet minder—now ten American dollars richer—and exited through the service elevator just as the assassin began to stir.

CHAPTER 14

"Hi, Mom," Lily said to the painting of the Soviet woman liberated from tyranny as she strode into her suite at last. She felt oddly at home there after a day of Moscow peculiarities, including the loss of her room key somewhere between the bar and her suite on the tenth floor. The bartender shrugged with indifference when she quizzed him about it, and Fedot was forced to produce another key for her. He seemed disturbed about having to accommodate her in this way—even reluctant—but it wasn't Fedot's mood that alarmed Lily when she re-entered the lobby. It was a man—thick and muscular, with a face like a Picasso—who had made himself at home in one of the lobby chairs. He looked at her in a nakedly curious way that made it unclear as to whether he was really dumb and couldn't figure things out or wickedly smart and questioning everything. Whatever the case, his brazen attention prompted Lily to hurry back to the elevator, get off on the seventh floor, and take the stairs the rest of the way.

On impulse, she went to the bureau where the safe was housed. Nothing. The safe had disappeared as surely as her room key. It would be just like Tony to pull a trick on her like that—taking her key and the safe to put her off balance. He'd always liked to razz her, and for a moment there, she missed him.

It was an odd thing, missing someone you didn't know all that well, but Lily was more than aware that what she really missed was the fact that Tony had existed at all. After watching the guy get murdered and spending only one full day in Moscow, Lily was, for the first time in her life, aware of what it felt like to be in danger. Not just the kind of danger that could get under your skin when you walked through a dicey part of town, but the kind of danger you didn't have any control over. The kind you couldn't be rescued from by a good Samaritan, like when a guy snatched her purse on 7th Avenue and a hot dog stand owner chased him down for her.

By the end of the day, Lily had found herself wearing the same disillusioned expression that all the Russians she'd seen in this city wore. It was a hell of a difference from New York, she marveled, where people wore their personalities on their shirtsleeves, and Boston, where they wore their smug self-satisfaction.

Only Fedot, who had the energy of a small child, and Pasha Tarkhan had seemed different. The big Russian had a level of confidence that Lily had observed in none of his fellow countrymen, and an élan that was conspicuously absent in almost all aspects of Moscow life, except for the pre-Revolutionary architecture and the mismatched furniture in her hotel. Pasha Tarkhan could've belonged to the Czar's Russia, and Lily Tassos wondered what the hell he was doing in Moscow at all. She stepped out of her shoes and into her bathroom, taking the bobby pins out of her twist and letting hair fall down her back.

"Holy Mother of God!" Lily cried. Now she had to wonder what the hell he was doing in her bathroom.

"Don't scream," he whispered, but it was too late.

Lily made the kind of noise she'd only been able to imagine herself making in the middle of having a baby or maybe making one—assuming it could ever be that good. Pasha Tarkhan was lying in her bathtub stripped to the waist. His suit jacket and shirt were crumpled behind his back, and his legs were hanging over the side. Cold water dribbled from the faucet onto his arm, which looked as if his skin had been ripped off, and he was shaking. She touched her hand to his forehead and found he was having cold sweats—not a fever.

"What happened to you?"

Pasha didn't respond except to breathe in quick, outward breaths like a human time bomb. It was Tony all over again, she thought as she was seized by a sudden desperation to keep Pasha Tarkhan alive.

"Fedot, get up here!" she shouted into the telephone receiver after dialing the only number that worked and reaching the only line it allowed. Whoever had answered the phone hung up and left her with nothing but an annoying buzz cranking in her ear.

"I can help you," she said, but more to herself than to Pasha.

Lily pulled out two small towels the maid had left in her vanity and soaked them in hot water before placing one on Pasha's head and the other on his chest. She then rifled through her makeup bag until she found her last remaining bottle of aloe vera gel. Lily turned off the water and dried his arm delicately, spreading the burn-soother all over it, being careful not to irritate any of his blisters. They were monstrous—filled with bright yellow pus. Finally, she thought to strip the covers off her bed and tucked them around the Russian. It didn't make him stop shivering, but he at least looked more comfortable.

"Miss Lilia?" Fedot inquired, and Lily nearly fell into the bathtub with the half-dead Russian.

"Jesus Christ, Fedot, can't you announce yourself?"

Fedot ignored her, bumping her aside as he knelt by

Pasha and took his arm in his hands, examining it like a scientist would a jar containing a diseased liver. He said something in Russian and left the room without another word. Lily heard the door to her suite close and thought for a minute that she should get out of there, too. It was only a thought, though. She couldn't leave the big Russian like she had Tony's body on Monemvasia. At the very least she could concoct some story when Fedot brought the Moscow police back with him.

But he didn't bring the police. He brought an acne-scarred guy in a red sweater who helped him pick up the Russian and carry him into the suite next to hers. They didn't do it the regular way—out the door and through the hallway—but moved the Biedermier sofa and the liberated Soviet woman to reveal a door that connected the two suites.

"Get your coat," Fedot instructed her, having lost most of the nasal tone he employed when he was "at your service for you." His English had gotten better, too.

She grabbed her ugly new coat, shoved the lipstick tube containing the microfilm into its pocket and followed them into the neighboring suite. There, slumped over an antique British office desk not nearly as nice as the desks in her suite, was her neighbor. She'd only seen him once before, wearing the same eggplant suit that made his skin and hair look even whiter than it was. Quite dead, he was staring dreamily into oblivion.

"Do you know him?" Lily asked. Fedot, surely, had killed him.

"A Swede, I think," Fedot grunted as he and the man in the red sweater heaved Pasha onto the bed. "And a malicious hotel spy." Fedot injected the big Russian with something, and Pasha's body relaxed as his breathing slowed. He opened his eyes, and Lily smiled.

"He looks better," she said.

"He's not," Fedot countered. "He's just not in pain anymore."

Fedot signaled the other man, who wheeled a gurney out from the bathroom. Lily watched as the two men went to work strapping the hulking Russian to the underside of the gurney before laying the Swede on top of it and covering him with a sheet.

"I'm coming with you," Lily said.

Fedot seemed at first as if he were going to protest. "Button your coat," he told her. "And when we reach the lobby, slip out the back, then follow around to join us at the entrance. There will be a medical wagon waiting."

But when they stepped off the elevator and into the lobby, Lily began to wail. "Oh, my God," she cried. "He was fine before dinner!"

Fedot's eyes widened, his lips parting.

"And he was so cute," Lily spluttered. "I thought, you know, that maybe he could be the one."

Lily buried her head in her palms, moaning and sniffling a cry that sounded pretty real to her if not anyone else. She then threw herself over the gurney and heaved a sob, gripping its sides and making sure neither Fedot nor his cohort could leave her behind the way she bet they'd planned to.

Nobody addressed her in the quiet lobby, because no one was there. Hardly anyone, at least. Just the concierge and a bell boy who snorted awake when he heard the commotion. It was only right before Lily crawled into the medical wagon behind Fedot that she spotted the brute with the messed up face who'd eyed her earlier. He stood between the double front doors of the Hotel Rude and stared at her like he knew exactly what she was doing—even if she didn't have the faintest idea. Right then, his eyes looked more sad than mean, but she guessed you could say that about almost any Russian. He turned and walked back inside the hotel as the man in the red sweater closed the wagon doors, pounding twice on the back before slipping into the driver's seat and revving the engine.

Inside the wagon, Lily sat beside the gurney on a small stool bolted to the floor. Tin buckets filled with ice water lined the back and sides of the vehicle like votive candles surrounding an open casket at a wake.

"Miss Lily, your performance was unwise," Fedot said.

"Oh, you thought I was going to stay back there alone?"

"Not alone," Fedot said. "I would have made accommodations for you."

"I don't need accommodations," she told him. "Now, where are we going?"

Fedot pushed the Swede's corpse off the gurney and released Pasha from its underside. Reaching behind him, Fedot grabbed a bucket and dumped its contents over the diplomat's unconscious body. Ice cubes scattered over the floor and Lily screamed, jerking her feet up to keep her shoes from getting soaked.

"To see about a sorcerer," he answered.

CHAPTER 15

Rodki Semyonov turned his back on the medical wagon, untroubled about letting the American girl get a few steps ahead of him. Russia, for all of its big cities and vast terrain, was as small a place as any other police state. Especially for a first-time visitor whose passport had been in the hands of a front desk clerk and now resided in Semyonov's coat pocket.

General Pushkin would've preferred he have an encounter with the girl right away, but Semyonov opted for a more subtle approach. He hated to beat women. It was at times a part of his job, but he went to great lengths to avoid such confrontations. That was work for the secret police and KGB.

"The key sticks," the woman dressed as a maid told him as she accompanied him to the tenth floor. She jiggled the lock before it released, letting him into Lily Tassos's suite.

"She bought a green coat at a textile store near the Kremlin," the woman testified, "a bowl of sausage and pickle soup in the Red Square cafeteria, a coffee, two creams and no sugar, Kulich bread—though she didn't eat it—four vodkas, bear cutlets—of which she had only one bite—and stole a pencil from the front desk." One of ten assistants to the deputy head of hotel security, the woman was intent on distinguishing herself to the Great Detective. "I was told she's a communist."

The Great Detective nodded. "So was she."

The woman didn't understand exactly what he meant

but pretended to, raising her eyebrow as if they were in on a very important clue together. But the Great Detective never returned the gesture and remained in the middle of the living room, his eyes fixed on the Soviet woman liberated from tyranny.

"Comrade Detective," the woman entreated, "I hope it is not imprudent of me to tell you what an honor it is to meet you. If I can be of any help to you at all, I could go to my death a satisfied woman."

She hadn't intended on propositioning him, but his quiet demeanor and general ugliness had emboldened her. Had he appeared conceited, she would've never thought that a woman with her pleasant but ordinary features could interest him. Especially since men had often accused her of having a stern manner that lacked sensuality.

The Great Detective, for his part, gave no witty remark or double entendre. He simply buried his face into her hair and took her against a scratched-up writing table. Its delicate, fawn-like legs clashed with the assistant's upturned thighs and ankles, and the Great Detective thought briefly that the writing table reminded him of his late wife. That thought alone made the encounter worthwhile.

When they finished, Semyonov helped the woman restore her appearance, and with a sufficient amount of respect, he asked her to leave while he performed his investigation. She saluted him before departing—even clicking the heels of her walking shoes.

Semyonov liked being in a room so recently after its inhabitant had left it. It allowed him to touch upon what his subject might have been thinking as well as doing. Had Lily Tassos really gone back to her suite to freshen up before joining her new lover next door—and discovering his body—she might've washed or at least put on lipstick.

But it was clear she'd done none of those things. Her toiletries remained largely untouched, and her bath, though wet, contained a couple of straight, black hairs—the kind from a man's head. The floor in the bathroom had been wiped down, as had the path from the bathroom door to the sofa, and a white bottle containing a clear gel appeared to be the only grooming product she'd used. The detective didn't have to touch her bedding to see that it was wet.

At the bottom of her makeup case, underneath a disk of powdered rouge, he found a small mirror—the kind that could fit in a pocket book and be used to touch up lipstick. The Great Detective slid the mirror out of its embroidered linen sleeve and noticed that something remained inside the silk lining. Casually, he slipped his finger behind the lining and pulled out a metal card embossed with a plus sign, a star and the Russian word for tree, *derevo*.

"Unless you have an urgent message for me, I would prefer to continue my investigation alone," Semyonov announced. The smell in the air had changed. It was infused with the scent of a man who bathed every day—an uncommon practice in Russia and Europe.

Beryx Gulyas put his gun away quietly.

"Pardon me, Comrade," Beryx said in Russian. "I met a girl at a party downstairs and she gave me her key. I hope something terrible hasn't happened."

"Are you from Bucharest?" Semyonov asked in Russian, and then repeated the phrase in Romanian, pocketing the metal card before turning to face the intruder.

"I'm Hungarian," Beryx answered. "Here on holiday."

The Hungarian spoke in a distinctive Transylvanian accent. Semyonov had never been particularly good at speaking foreign languages, but he had an ear for detecting dialects. It was a skill he'd sharpened on the police force, when he'd been required to shadow visiting aliens.

"I've never been out of Moscow, but I encountered a student from Budapest once," Semyonov continued. "He sent me a recipe for stuffed cabbage that he wrote on cigarette paper and smuggled to me through one of the prison guards. He was crazy. I still haven't made the cabbage."

"Are you the house detective?" Beryx asked.

"Yes, I'm a detective." Semyonov yawned and cracked his neck, feeling an attack of bursitis coming on in his shoulder. "Most of my job is boring, but being sent after a nice-looking girl isn't so bad."

Beryx forced a smile. His crotch burned from the Aqua Regia injected into it, and he was in no mood for small talk. Though most of the acid had gone into the Russian's arm, it didn't take much of it to cause an inexorable amount of damage. Aqua Regia was, after all, primarily used to melt gold and platinum, as the inflamed blisters poking out of his pubic hair could attest.

"Can you tell me anything about her?" the detective inquired.

Beryx shrugged.

"Not really. Pretty piece of ass. Throws her money around."

Semyonov continued to rifle through Lily's toiletries, picking through them one by one and lining them up on the bathroom counter. "Do you know where she gets her money?"

Beryx curled his lip and folded his arms across his chest. "Maybe her daddy," he replied.

Semyonov took out a small pad of poor-quality paper and made notes for himself in his own shorthand. There was an unmistakable clarity to finding the spigot of any investigation—the person from whom all of the answers would flow sooner or later, in one way or another. It was the same when he'd been investigating murders and black market rings and was especially true now, when his detecting revolved solely around espionage.

"Must be her daddy," he agreed. "Say, you wouldn't want to have a drink with me, would you? Since your plans with the American girl have fallen through?" Semyonov's nose pointed left as he smiled, and the Hungarian was transfixed by the man's features. His interest turned to annoyance when the Russian detective put his arm around him and squeezed his shoulder.

Beryx Gulyas shrugged him off and walked out of the suite. He knew it was imprudent to be rude—even to mid-level hotel employees—but he didn't plan on sticking around Moscow long enough to need any favors or fear petty repercussions.

The Great Detective, for his part, had expected the slight.

CHAPTER 16

ATHENS, GREECE

"It was taken just this Christmas," Theron Tassos expounded as he removed a photograph from his ostrich leather attaché case.

Baru o Crete adjusted the pocket square he'd hastily tucked into his jacket, its indigo dye leaving a faint stain on his fingertips. He dipped them in his tea and wiped them on a linen napkin before taking the Polaroid from his younger brother and holding it at a distance to get a proper look. Baru hadn't seen his niece in nearly a decade and was struck by what a beauty she'd become. The sight of the color photograph—a rarity in his world—was equally impressive. He could even make out the eggplant tint of Lily's eyeshadow.

"She favors you," Baru commented, scrutinizing the picture further.

"You think so?" Theron Tassos dismissed him. The man Lily called Daddy looked hardly at all like his daughter. It seemed to him she had absorbed all of her mother's lovely features as she developed in the womb. Her high cheek-bones and plump lips. Her wide-set eyes.

"She doesn't resemble you, but she does favor you," Baru insisted. "It's here," he said, pointing to the girl's nose. "And here," he continued, indicating her eyes. "It's not their shape, no, but what's behind them."

The two brothers nodded.

"Gulyas is his name, you say. That's Hungarian," Theron concluded as he slid Lily's picture back into its home in a

plastic sleeve and restored it to his case. They'd been drinking tea for over an hour, having indulged in the kind of
over-the-fence chatter that would've been impolite to forgo
entirely. Even under these grave circumstances.

"No, he's Romanian. Perhaps a Hungarian by family
origin."

Theron knelt down on two of several Turkish pillows
that were strewn about Baru's living room, and the Cretan
gangster followed him.

"And it's important to you that he suffers."

"More than Christ," Baru hissed.

Theron put his hand on Baru's bald head. His hands
weren't as lethal as his brother's—made for holding weapons, not being them—but possessed the even touch of a
man long accustomed to power. "No one can suffer more
than Christ."

It would've been sacrilegious for him to contend otherwise, but Theron Tassos had indeed made men suffer much
more than Christ. Christ, it could be argued, had the added burden of humanity, which made his suffering infinitely
greater from a spiritual perspective, but pain is pain when
you're made of flesh and blood, he believed.

Etor himself had once narrowly escaped one of Theron
Tassos's punishments after he'd been late with a one-time
delivery to an Oriental. It was a small order from a bit
player in an even smaller country, so it was just as easy for
Tassos to tell Etor to get lost and stay lost than it was to
teach him a lesson.

But he'd never forgiven Baru for his poor judgment.
The two, who had once been as close as soldiers in a death
battle, had become distant in the seven-odd years since the
Etor incident. While they'd never officially fallen out with
one another, they hadn't spoken in all of this time, either.

"Do you wish to be present?"

Baru exhaled and closed his eyes for a moment.

"Oh, yes," he whispered.

Whatever their conflicts over family and business, a Greek would never deny a brother his revenge. Especially over the death of a child—no matter how disappointing that child might have been.

"Do I know the man you'll use?" Baru asked. The Cretan's eyes were leaden and glassy, bearing the look of an old man's eyes in the long year before his death.

"I'd never use a Greek," Theron insisted. "He must be a Russian. I never trust anyone but a Russian to inflict pain."

Baru straightened his shoulders and swallowed hard, as if confronting his first glimpse of Etor's mutilated body.

"This Gulyas. He's no Russian, yet he's built a savage name for himself."

Theron Tassos lit a cigarette and shrugged. He knew that men like Beryx Gulyas came and went all the time—burning bright for a few short years before descending back to earth—or rather, beneath it. Sadists rarely lasted very long. Egoists let their vanity override their intellect. Gulyas had both marks against him.

In the arms dealer's experience, it took an impersonal character—someone imminently flexible, who took neither pleasure nor pain from his work—to last for any meaningful length of time.

"Don't worry," he said. "I have the perfect man in mind."

CHAPTER 17

SERGEI POSAD, RUSSIA

Lily was drenched from her waist down and freezing. Fedot, despite her vigorous objections, had flung bucket after bucket of ice water on Pasha Tarkhan at ten minute intervals. He did so with the precision of a physician, as though performing life-saving surgery on the ailing Russian and not merely making the ride in the back of the medical wagon unbearable.

"Can't you just soak his arm?" Lily implored. "It's the only part that's blistered." Fedot's clothes were as wet as Lily's, but he seemed unbothered by the fact. "Hey, hey! Are you talking to me?"

It became increasingly clear to her that he was not. Fedot was standing over Pasha Tarkhan, half singing and half chanting a Russian verse. For the third time in their two-hour journey, Pasha—as Lily had taken to calling him in her mind– opened his eyes wide and took in his surroundings. Fedot ignored his awakening and continued chanting until the wagon came to an abrupt halt.

"Quickly," he ordered.

Fedot opened the doors and hopped down, helping Lily into the darkness before wheeling Pasha out. He pounded twice on the back, and the wagon pulled away.

They were standing outside a tall, white wall that looked like it belonged to a fortress. In the night, with no streetlights to provide guidance, it appeared as if the wall went on forever. A village surrounded the wall, nestled into the countryside. Even in the darkness, it looked old, though not as old as the stone fortress wall that sat in its midst. The village was, Lily thought, post-medieval, but not by much. Clearly, the wall and whatever lay behind it had come first.

"Miss Lilia," Fedot whispered.

Lily spun around, but Fedot and Pasha were gone.

"Down here."

Lily followed the voice and spotted Fedot's head popping out of a trapdoor hidden in the grass.

"How did you get down there?" she asked him.

"There's a ramp," he said. And yes, of course, she saw it now. It folded out of the trapdoor.

Fedot held out his hand, and Lily accepted it, locking eyes with him as she descended into a stone tunnel lit every few meters by two crisscrossed torches. The tunnel was narrow and the sandy color of the desert pyramids that she'd seen as a child on a family trip to Egypt.

Pasha stirred, letting out a groan as Fedot pushed him along. The little Russian placed his palm on the big Russian's forehead and seemed to put him at peace. It occurred to Lily that Fedot, like the pyramids, was perhaps one of the Seven Wonders of the World.

"Where are we?" she whispered.

"Sergei Posad. About seventy kilometers north from Moscow," Fedot answered.

"That's very exact of you, Fedot, but I was referring more to this tunnel, these walls, this place."

Fedot stopped and looked at her. He took off his glasses and placed them on top of Pasha's chest. Lily's eyes tracked the movement, and she found herself focused on the numbers of Pasha's wristwatch, positioned behind the lenses. Even in the torchlight, Lily could see that Fedot's lenses did nothing to magnify the numbers of the watch. They were plain glass.

"Miss Lilia," Fedot said, prompting Lily to look into his perfect, tiger-brown eyes. "You're standing beneath the Lavra—the seat of the Russian Orthodox Church."

Fedot turned away from her and grabbed the last torch at the end of the tunnel. He walked another ten meters to a metal door and rang a hollow-sounding bell—like a cowbell—which hung from the ceiling. Within seconds, they could hear the rattle of a series of locks being opened on the other side, until finally the door wheezed open.

"Ivanov," Fedot breathed.

In the doorway stood an uncommonly tall, athletic man with flowing, white hair and a thick salt-and-pepper beard. He was dressed only in white undershorts and held his arms out wide, repeating the same chant Fedot had sung inside the medical wagon. When he had said the verse three times, he put his arms down and smiled, extolling a greeting in Russian.

"What did he say?" Lily inquired.

"He said, 'Good morning, my babies,'" Fedot told her. "And I will answer, 'Swathe us in your holiness, sainted one.'" This he apparently said before bowing at the white-haired man's feet and kissing them both.

CHAPTER 18

Porphyri Ivanov bounced up the stairs on the balls of his bare feet. He hummed as he helped Fedot carry Pasha to the surface and stopped once—not to rest, but to tighten the straps that held the Russian to the gurney and to kiss the man's damp forehead. When they reached the top of the staircase, Ivanov kicked open the door and strode into the pale, blue light of early dawn.

"Soak me in your liquid brilliance, oh, too good to be true to have lived another day," he praised in English as they entered into the great courtyard of the Lavra.

Lily felt that she'd penetrated a world that had become all but extinct in Russia. Although only forty years had passed since 1917, the force of the revolution had erased religion from daily life, replacing it with an apathy that loomed every bit as pervasively as God had before Mr. Lenin and his cronies had come along. The Byzantine structures before her looked like pieces of chipped pottery, but there was an aura of purpose in the air, embodied in two cloistered monks who were now scampering to first Mass at the Holy Trinity Cathedral—the centerpiece of the Lavra.

"This is a monastery," Fedot explained as he draped a scarf over Lily's head and pointed out the various religious structures. "Do try to look pious."

Though she was not pious, the decaying majesty of the Lavra was comforting to Lily. The Trinity Cathedral still held services, as did the Assumption Cathedral, the Church of the Virgin of Smolensk and the half a dozen other churches and chapels that had been erected on the grounds since the start of the fourteenth century. The rooftops—shaped like Hershey's kisses—were pointing to the sky for a reason.

"It's beautiful," Lily uttered.

"Oh, yes, beautiful!" Ivanov pronounced. "The shrubs are beautiful, the air is beautiful, my fingers are beautiful, your lips are beautiful—it's all beautiful and beauty is beautiful."

Most of the holy buildings Lily had seen in Moscow had been turned into monuments to bureaucracy. Churches had been converted to museums or libraries if they were lucky and factories if they were not. Many weren't converted at all, but destroyed, along with their priceless treasures. Ivanov pointed to the empty bell towers and described the horror of the faithful as the bells—including the sixty-five-ton Czar's bell—were removed from their places and smashed to smithereens.

Why is this still here? Lily wondered to herself, and Fedot answered her as if she'd said it aloud.

"After a brief interlude as a civic institution," he said, "Stalin returned the Lavra to the Russian Orthodox Church."

From a practical standpoint, it seemed to Lily that even Josef Stalin had to admit that the Lavra was one of Russia's most important cultural heritages. As a result, it became an island left largely alone, with visitors kept out and the inhabitants of the monastery kept in. Ivanov described it simply as "God's will," but Fedot had another explanation.

"The Holy One prayed for its return, and it was returned. How else could a man like Stalin change his heart and go against his own dogma?"

Lily looked to Ivanov, but the Holy One had moved on from their conversation.

"My Lord, my Jesus," the Russian mystic chanted as he spun and danced, pausing to hug a tree in the central courtyard. He fluffed its leaves and kissed its branches, calling it Tatiana, and explaining that she was the love of his life, apart from his dear wife in Orekhovka, and God, of course.

"Of course," Lily repeated.

The man Fedot referred to as a living saint led them around the blue and white baroque bell tower to a minor, wooden chapel in ruins. Inside, Ivanov had made a bed of hay, pulled cotton, wool and leaves that lay where the altar once presided, surrounded by half-destroyed Byzantine frescos dating back to the fifteenth century.

"Lay my new baby here," he said, pointing to his nature bed.

Lily took Pasha's feet as she and Fedot lifted him off the gurney and placed him beneath a fresco of St. Sergius of Radonezh, the founder and patron saint of the Lavra. Lily knelt next to Pasha, stroking his hair and checking the status of his burns, while Fedot left the chapel.

Ivanov's mood hadn't changed. He sang to himself as he picked at his toes, largely ignoring Lily and Pasha, until Fedot returned with a monk named Matvei, who flashed a smile of tea-stained teeth resembling tombstones. Like Fedot, he made kissing Ivanov's feet his first priority.

With that out of the way, Fedot and Matvei stripped away Pasha's remaining clothes and carried the naked Russian to a tiny rectory adjacent to the chapel. The walls were thin and bare, and the windows had long ago been robbed of most of their stained glass, leaving the room open to the elements. In the center of the rectory sat a substantial tin tub filled nearly to the rim with ice and water.

"You're not going to put him in that!" Lily cried.

Fedot and the monk not only immersed the unconscious Pasha Tarkhan in the ice bath, but poured several ladles of the frigid water over his head, as if they were basting him.

"Only for a few minutes at first," Fedot explained.

Lily felt the urge to protest again, but did nothing. She was inside a chapel within an Orthodox fortress, in a Godless country surrounded by religious zealots. She looked down at Pasha, who seemed serene, though he was turning blue, and watched as Fedot and the monk lifted him out of the tub, continuing to ladle him with ice water until he opened his eyes and panted like a man who'd been holding his breath for too long. After blotting him dry with an oil cloth, they lifted Pasha off the floor and carried him back to the nature bed, where Ivanov was waiting.

"This is happiness," the Russian saint declared before sitting at Pasha's feet and pulling his muscular body into a tight knot. He closed his eyes and expelled a breath, not seeming to take one again for nearly a quarter hour. When he did, it was a soft inhale, like the ripple of a wave, instead of a sharp intake of air.

"The lake of your soul must be absolutely serene. Only then can God be reflected in it," Fedot enlightened her.

"Is he praying for Pasha?"

"No," Fedot smiled. "He's not praying at all. Only Pasha can save himself. We merely give his body the tools."

"Ice water?"

Fedot nodded.

Fedot sat behind Ivanov and knotted himself like his master. Unwilling and unable to follow in their example, Lily moved anxiously around the chapel and examined the frescoes that were wasting away on its walls. She assumed they were replicas of the great icons from the Holy Trinity

Cathedral, as the showpiece was Rublev's *The Trinity*. A copy had hung in her Greek Orthodox Church in Boston and over her parents' dining room table.

"Lilia," Ivanov breathed behind her.

"You scared me," she said, turning to Ivanov's collarbone and tipping her head up to connect with his eyes. They were compelling, his eyes, she had to admit, but she didn't see in him what Fedot saw. She saw only a kind, puckish man who cut a hell of a figure and was willing to risk his life to help total strangers. Perhaps that was enough to make him a saint.

CHAPTER 19

MOSCOW

Beryx Gulyas shifted the telephone receiver from his left ear to his right. He fingered three stones in his trouser pocket, though he couldn't remember which ones and what they could be for. He hoped persuasion, assurance.

"I'm sure he's dying as we speak," the Hungarian editorialized.

Nicolai Ceausescu said nothing, letting the drama of his breath do the talking.

Gulyas didn't often provide his master with predictions, preferring to stick to the facts and not make any promises he couldn't keep or verify. It occurred to him for one unpleasant second that he was sounding like Etor.

"Of course, I don't make my plans based on assumptions," he added.

"Yes," Ceausescu grumbled. Gulyas could hear the unmistakable Elena, her voice like a muffled buzz saw, demanding to know what had been said. The line went dead before her husband could answer her. Gulyas hesitated about calling back, but then dialed the operator. It had been a spring storm and not a poor connection that had ended the conversation, and Gulyas was grateful. He would call back when he had good news to report and hurried out of his hotel room—grabbing his own towel and loufa sponge—before the lines were restored and the phone could ring again.

Finding the hospital or clinic that was tending to Pasha Tarkhan's injuries was but a small impediment to his scheme compared to getting his hands on another firearm in Moscow. Guns were not a readily available commodity in Russia, and apart from mugging a KGB agent, Gulyas didn't have a lot of choices. Comrade Ceausescu could no doubt have helped him secure one, but Gulyas had no intention of letting on that he'd lost his gun.

The Beretta had vanished at some point between his leaving the Hotel Rude and arriving at the less glamorous Park Pobedy hotel, where he was staying. He'd taken a brief nap on the subway and was sure that was when the theft had taken place. A greasy-haired youth for whom he'd taken an instant dislike sat behind him at Arbatskaya, but had gotten off by the time Gulyas jerked awake to the sound of his stop being announced.

"Good morning," the pretty receptionist bid him as she checked her appointment book. Gulyas nodded instead of returning the greeting. He hated speaking Russian.

As soon as he slipped the unmarked, bulging envelope into the mail slot, the girl found his name, saying, "Yes, here it is," and reached behind her for a towel, which Gulyas rejected.

"I brought one," he explained, and the girl told him to suit himself but insisted he take her towel anyway. Rules were rules.

Gulyas seized the graying rag and threw it to the floor as soon as he entered the bathhouse.

"Fabi," Gulyas called to the preparatory masseuse. Fabi was dripping in perspiration—a pool of it having formed in a palm-sized ledge perched at the top of his domed belly. When he tipped forward to crack his knuckles, the pool dribbled over Fabi's middle and tinkled off the tip of his penis as if he were taking an unconscious piss. The masseuse then smacked his hands together three times, letting the echo bounce off the sopping tile walls of the steam chamber and signaling to Gulyas and a meaty woman who had come in behind him that it was time for them to strip naked.

Fabi took Gulyas first, slapping and pounding his back and legs, before grabbing the Hungarian's head in his hands and cracking his neck in two quick spins to the right and left. It was a sudden and unlikable way to be handled, but left Gulyas feeling strangely titillated—much like he felt after completing a job.

With a slight bow, Fabi took Gulyas's hand, shaking it hard, before moving on to the woman. She raised her arms over her head—as if she were being arrested—and Gulyas watched the masseuse slap her breasts with a towel.

The key Fabi had given him was cupped tightly in his palm as he entered the next chamber. Gulyas would've loved to bypass the rest of the gauntlet and head straight to the locker room for a rendezvous with his new gun, but once he entered the bath house, he knew there was no turning back or skipping any of its prescriptions. With his usual resolve, the Hungarian looked out onto the four marble beds and chose the one closest to the single gas lantern that illuminated the chamber. He placed the key inside his cheek, laid down on his stomach and waited for one of the baton girls to come. To his chagrin, he got a fatty with yellow skin tone and sodden pubic hair.

"Take it easy around my bladder," Gulyas ordered. He'd forgotten to use the toilet. The girl ignored him, and he watched her belly-folds waggle as she beat him with a club wrapped in a hot, wet towel until his muscles felt like noodles.

His luck in treatment providers got no better until he entered the fifth chamber, where he was oiled by a fair brunette. Fit and graceful, her only shortcoming was an engorged upper lip. She was also kind enough to use the loufa he provided instead of the ones dubiously sanitized by the house. He thanked her by patting her bare buttocks.

"Atta girl," he grumbled.

Gulyas felt good and was especially glad that he'd chosen not to eat that morning. The gauntlet was a vigorous cleansing ritual that partnered well with a liquid diet, and the Hungarian decided it was high time for a forty-eight hour reprieve from solid food. He entered the last chamber—the sauna—confident that his reflexes would be sharper and infinitely more precise due to his fast and looked forward to handing Fabi's son the key in exchange for a rolled bath mat that contained his new weapon.

"Hello there," a reclining man rasped, clearing his throat and trying again. "Hello, I said. Fancy meeting you here." The ugly hotel detective sat up, resting his elbows on his knees.

"I'm sorry, have we met?" Gulyas lied.

"Quite late last night. At the Hotel Rude."

Gulyas leaned forward and squinted as if he was struggling to place him.

"Yes, yes of course. I'm not wearing my eyeglasses, so I didn't recognize you."

"Nor were you last night. You must be ashamed of them, like I am. I've yet to touch mine and they were imposed on me over a year ago."

The detective sat up and leaned against the wall, his bent-up face at odds with his body. Back at Hotel Rude, he'd looked rather lumpy in his overcoat, but here, naked and in unforgiving light, his physique revealed itself as lean and muscular.

"You lift weights?" he asked.

Gulyas shook his head.

"You should try it," the detective counseled. "It helps keep the weight off. Look at me—I'm over fifty, although I won't tell you by how much—and I don't look much different than I did twenty years ago."

He patted his taut abdomen, and Gulyas's face flushed.

"No, really," the detective continued. "I know it works. I fight—or at least I used to. What's more, I use a punching bag in the mornings."

Gulyas sat down on the wooden bench facing the detective and stood up again. He looked out the small porthole of a window into the locker room, but Fabi's son was nowhere in sight. The masseuse had asked him explicitly to wait in the sauna until his son was ready for him.

"You should try it."

"What?"

"A punching bag," the detective clarified.

Gulyas sat down again, crossing his arms over his chest. "I travel a lot," he mumbled.

"All the better," the detective prodded. "Pillows and blankets make decent punching bags, and it's much easier than finding weights—unless you don't mind lifting furniture. But I don't recommend that. You can strain your back."

Gulyas nodded, looking out the porthole window again. "I'll take a crack at it," he grunted.

"Wonderful," the detective exclaimed. "Say, I could show you some moves. I've got time. Besides, lunch is coming up, and what better way to work up an appetite?"

Gulyas didn't answer.

"Don't you think?"

"Hmm?" Gulyas scowled.

"Punching works up an appetite, I said."

The detective put his fists up again and mimed a few

fighting moves. Gulyas stared numbly at his dodges and thrusts until Semyonov punched him with a right cross that propelled the Hungarian backward onto the wooden bench and left him slumped nose to bellybutton. A few drips of water plunged from an IV onto the hot rocks, and a billow of steam obscured the assassin's head until evaporating into the parched air.

"Bombah!"

Fabi's son, a frizzy-headed youth with a faint, black mustache and candy-red lips imitated the Great Detective's knock-out punch before pulling open the sauna doors. He took Beryx Gulyas by the feet, dragging his sweaty body off the bench and letting his head thump to the floor and down the single step into the unisex locker room. The meaty woman from Fabi's chamber followed, still naked, but bone dry as if the heat had no effect on her. She carried a coil of steel wire and pulled up a chair—not for herself, but for Gulyas, whom she proceeded to tie to it.

"Mr. Gulyas," the Great Detective urged, slapping the Hungarian's cheeks and dousing his face with a cup of coffee with cream that had been sitting on top of locker thirty-two since the early morning. "Are you ready for that drink now?"

CHAPTER 20

Long before he became known as The Great Detective, Rodki Semyonov had harbored different ambitions. They were grand in neither scope nor mission, but they were ambitions nonetheless. He wanted his own apartment, where he could live with his wife, Polina, and not have to share space with a gaggle of relatives. He wanted a decent factory job in the burgeoning industrial town where he was born, and he wanted to have one child of either sex that he hoped would inherit Polina's earth-brown eyes.

The job had been provided for him, as he knew it would be. A man of his size and strength was a welcome addition to most factory crews. Rodki was confident the child would come once he and Polina were settled. But obtaining an apartment for him and his family alone was another story altogether, and Rodki Semyonov knew he would have to use his brain more than his back if he were to pull off such a coup.

"Az isten bassza meg a bu'do'sru' csko's kurva anya'dat!" Gulyas spat, spraying blood and a chipped tooth into Rodki's face.

Rodki broke Gulyas's nose with the back of his hand for the insult. He didn't appreciate the visual of God "fucking his stinking, wrinkled whore mother," especially considering the way she'd died—in a gulag, he was told, buried alive next to his Polina.

It was his mother who had told him not to enter into the Shchelkovo underworld, but Rodki Semyonov had seen an opportunity for himself. The bare-knuckle tournaments that went on after the factories closed for the day promised big bucks and, more importantly, could win him some influence with the Housing Authority.

"It's illegal," his mother had warned. "Maybe they look the other way today, but tomorrow is always another story."

She was right, of course, but not about the fights. Those were protected by a man named Belnikov, who was at that time a favorite pet of Stalin's. Belnikov loved the tournaments and grew fond of the eleven-time tournament champion, whom he had personally nick-named *The Iron Knuckle*.

"Mr. Gulyas, I know who you are and what you do."

The Great Detective held Gulyas's Beretta above his bloody nose, letting him get a good look at it.

"It has an abnormal land and groove pattern, did you know that? It's a manufacturer's defect that makes it easy to track from a ballistic standpoint."

Gulyas eyed the gun, reacquainting himself with its blunt nose and quarter moon trigger. It had been cleaned.

"Antosha Sidorov, Lev Kretchnif, Teo Anghelescu, Anna and Magnus Karlsson, Charles Monks . . . I have thirteen other confirmations in addition to five other assassinations I suspect can be attributed to you, although no gun was used. It would appear you've branched out into other methods lately."

Rodki Semyonov had always found interrogations distasteful, but they were a fact of life. There was nothing that made a man reveal his secrets or his character better than discomfort. Beryx Gulyas, of course, had no intention of disclosing any information, no matter how badly he was beaten. Rodki had encountered his type before, but their exchange wouldn't be for nothing.

"I'm confused, Mr. Gulyas, why you would be dispatched here to kill an American tourist when your prey is normally so distinguished?" Rodki lit a cigarette and put it in the assassin's mouth. "You can't have fallen on hard times when there's so much work out there."

Gulyas spit the cigarette out, and Fabi's son picked it up and began to smoke. It was a fine Turkish brand.

"Unless there's someone else you're after and the girl is incidental. I'd be careful about these incidental players, though, if I were you. You never know who they are."

Rodki Semyonov produced the metal card he'd found in Lilia Tassos's suite. He held it up close enough for Gulyas to see and then put it back into his breast pocket.

"Funny little thing—wouldn't you say? Your friend— the American girl—had it amongst her belongings. You wouldn't happen to know what it is, would you?"

Rodki punched Gulyas in the kidney before he could answer. He bore down on the assassin's shoulder—not enough to break it, but enough to make Gulyas wonder if it was broken.

"My biggest question to you, Mr. Gulyas, is—what now?"

It had become a stock phrase for Rodki Semyonov. He'd first used it on a British naval officer who was trying to pass himself off as a Kim Philby ex-patriot, insisting that he was eager to betray his country and move to Moscow. Rodki knew he was a spy the moment he saw him in his civilian clothes. Dressed to appear like a disillusioned member of the British upper classes, he wore a gold-tinted watch that he'd recently scrubbed free of tarnish and attached to a new leather band.

It was one of his first cases after being recruited into the Moscow police force. Belnikov felt they needed more good fighters on the force and thought *The Iron Knuckle* would be a boon at interrogations. He'd never suspected that Rodki Semyonov could be useful as anything other than a strong man, and Rodki Semyonov never suspected that his natural gift for puzzles and mysteries would draw him into Stalin's inner circle.

"Junior?"

The Great Detective stepped back and let Fabi's son box Gulyas's ears and kick his groin. The Hungarian bore the abuse well, so Rodki took a couple of gentle cracks at him to make the eager youth feel like less of a lightweight.

Long before joining the ranks of the Moscow police, where socialist protocol made mediocrity essential, Rodki Semyonov had learned not to flaunt his talents. It could be dangerous to distinguish oneself on the force, even if it was more results-focused than the postal service or the universities. Rodki had always been a likeable fellow and figured out how to handle threatened superiors by using just enough working class humility and appearing genuinely surprised when he solved a case—as if it were by accident.

Belnikov wasn't fooled.

"Aren't you a revelation?" he'd always remark when he visited Rodki at his office. "Stalin has his eye on you."

It would appear Stalin had his eye on Belnikov, too: The trusted advisor's intestines were gored at his whore's apartment on New Year's Day in 1938—the same day they came for Polina and the rest of Rodki Semyonov's family.

Comrade Stalin felt he needed a personal detective without any conflicting loyalties, and in one stroke, Rodki's personal life had ceased to exist.

"Mr. Gulyas, I'm sure you understand that whoever sent you—perhaps your Secretary General or one of his henchmen—is himself a servant of Moscow."

Rodki clutched Gulyas by the hair and yanked his head

backward. The Hungarian, choked by his own blood, coughed and gurgled, taking deep gasps of air as the fluids from his nose drained to the back of his throat.

Gulyas took a good look at his tormentor and noticed for the first time that there was a piercing intellect behind his plum-black eyes. It wasn't the kind a bookworm would value, but it was the most effectual kind—the kind paired with instinct and experiential knowledge. Had his lips not been so swollen, he might've smiled.

"All we want to know is why you're here," Rodki said. Like the Hungarian, he was bored. Both men knew a thing or two about applying and surviving pressure, so their encounter was becoming an endless game of tic-tac-toe.

Gulyas rolled his eyes into the back of his head as if he were about to have a seizure, but Rodki would brook none of his dramatics. He beat the Hungarian with his knees and elbows until the man really was on the brink of unconsciousness and, perhaps, just the slightest bit sorry that he'd tempted fate with such a wise-assed move.

"You're looking tired, Mr. Gulyas," Rodki teased. "I think you need rest."

Fabi's son was keen to continue the interrogation, but Rodki Semyonov took him aside and explained how things were done. He wanted to give the Hungarian a bit of time to get his confidence back before he destroyed it again.

CHAPTER 21

SERGEI POSAD

A day and night of tossing and sweats had been followed by a regimen of ice water, dumped bucket by bucket, over Pasha's head and body—as if those were separate entities. Fedot assured Lily that they were and talked with scientific specificity about the various "elements" the cold water addressed. He was able to deliver his medieval logic—based one part in faith and the other in alchemy—with a tone so utterly reasonable that Lily found herself chanting with him at times, urging Pasha to find it within himself to heal.

There was a selfish motive behind her sudden leap of faith. Lily didn't want to be left alone in this place, with these people, without Pasha. Though in truth she understood him least, he seemed like the closest thing to home.

"Sit with him and take his hand," Fedot prescribed as he covered Pasha with a thin, dry blanket. "He'll be coming around soon."

Lily did as she was told, noting that Pasha's hands resembled T-bone steaks. *God, I'm hungry,* she thought. The monk, Matvei, had been providing them with a single noon-day feeding of thick, borscht-like stew with bread. Although it had only been three days, Lily had come to rely on her only daily meal with the focus of a laboratory rat and was well aware that the monk was over an hour late with their food.

She couldn't help obsessing over the stew's contents and the various reasons why Matvei had been detained. It was a disturbing combination of appetite and paranoia that lead her from analyzing the taste profile of marjoram to worrying if their whereabouts had been discovered. She imagined a hard-stepping mob of KGB agents were on their way to the broken-down chapel.

"Lily?" Pasha whispered.

Lily jerked at the sound of his voice. His eyes were glassy and soft, the most gentle she'd ever seen them, or any pair of men's eyes for that matter. Lily hadn't appreciated until that moment how handsome he was.

"Lily," once again.

It was lovely to hear the sound of her name on his tongue.

Pasha slurred a request for drink and it occurred to Lily that she was gazing at him like a school girl, so she turned her attention to his comfort. She saw her mother in herself as she began offering him water and stuffing her green coat under his head. He was fully awake now and not merely opening his eyes for a brief second and mumbling the way he had been. She asked him his name, his age, and the town where he was born, but he was more interested in recounting what had happened in the men's toilet of the *Revolution Room* at Hotel Rude.

"Why did you come to my room?" she asked him. "How did you know I'd help you—or that I even could?"

Pasha reached across his belly and touched the arm savagely burned by the assassin's chemical.

"It wasn't a master plan, my dear. I had nowhere else to go."

The dark Russian accepted another sip of water but declined her stew, feeling sickened by the smell of food. Lily spooned a few hot morsels into her mouth and put the bowl down.

"I should thank you, Lily, for saving my life. I should also tell you that I think under the circumstances I probably wouldn't have done the same for you."

Lily grinned at him and realized it was the same lopsided grin she used to give Tony Geiger after he'd insulted her.

"I'm not sure I believe that," she told him.

"You don't know me," Pasha explained. "My altruism is largely dependent upon my situation."

"You're a pretty lucky guy, then," she quipped. Like Tony, he could never let a moment be, and always had to impose upon her the realities of the situation—as if she was prone to forget.

Pasha smiled at their cultural impasse.

"If I were truly lucky, I would've never been born a Russian," he lamented.

Lily could hear Ivanov outside the chapel, his mellifluous voice as distinctive as his playful step. Fedot was with him.

"Welcome back to the natural world," Ivanov greeted Pasha. "Did you happen to speak to our Lord while you were away?"

Coming from anyone else, such a comment could've been interpreted as a tease, but Ivanov was never anything but sincere.

"I'm afraid not," Pasha answered. "But it is an honor and a pleasure to see you, Holy One."

Ivanov reached on top of a crumbling pedestal and retrieved a small crucifix he'd fashioned out of a dead birch tree branch, laying it on Pasha's chest. The Russian fingered the crucifix and thanked the mystic, who bent down and kissed it. Fedot looked at the cross as if it had come alive. Lily could see how badly he wanted to touch it.

"When and how can we get out of here?" Lily asked.

Fedot tore his eyes away from the crucifix and folded his hands in front of him. "You're in the only good place in Russia."

Unspoken was what Lily knew he should have said— *You're the one who wanted to come.*

"Yes, but we can't stay here forever," she insisted. "I'm an American. I came here to do . . . something for someone, but I have to get back to America."

Fedot's expression didn't change, and Ivanov smiled at Pasha. Lily felt as if she were the only one of them not in on a tantalizing piece of gossip. It occurred to her that maybe Tony knew it would be this way—that she could get stuck here and never be able to return home—and in that moment, she hated him for it.

"I want to go home," she whined, and then she hated herself. It was, after all, she and not Tony who decided to come here after he was killed. And it was she who had decided that she wanted his life. Now she had it, and like some two-bit Welsher, she was trying to give it back.

"What I mean is: I've finished the job I came here to do."

Pasha reached back with his unburned arm and adjusted Lily's coat, propping himself up and straining to lean forward.

"Fedot," he said. "Would you be so kind as to bring me the extraneous contents of my clothes?"

Fedot stood and removed an old collection box from underneath a pile of cushion stuffing that had been heaped inside the remains of the sacristy. Within it was the dossier Pasha had taken from Lily's suite and the brown bottle of Myer aspirin. Pasha moved his injured arm for the first time, and Lily watched him grimace. He shook off the pain and stretched his fingers, using them to peel away several pages from the dossier and handing them to Lily.

"I know you can't read Russian," Pasha explained. "But I've read them and can tell you roughly what they say. In no less than two years, the Soviet Union plans on launching a vessel into space, intending to beat our greatest rival—your country—into the universe by a comfortable margin. The blueprints for this vessel—called *Sputnik*—are located on a piece of microfilm that used to be inside the little bottle Fedot is holding in his hand."

Lily bent over Pasha and drew her lipstick tube from her ugly coat's pocket. She opened the container and plucked out the microfilm as if it were a long, wavy hair.

"Is this what you mean?" she asked.

Pasha Tarkhan chuckled and shook his head. "I think a better question is: do you understand what it means?"

Lily looked down at the film she was holding and the papers Pasha had furnished.

"That America will be embarrassed, I suppose?"

Pasha took Lily's hand and pulled her closer. A few of his scabs cracked and tiny beads of blood sprang to the surface of his ravaged skin.

"In my village, when I was a boy, there was a man who gave out candy to the local children. His name was Andrei, and we loved him. Our parents loved him, because he gave us joy and offered us things they could not afford."

He took the film from her fingers and watched as Lily tightened her grip on the papers, crunching them in her impatient fist. Pasha squeezed her forearm.

"When the revolution came to our doorstep, it was Andrei—so beloved—who made the call for us to rise up. How were we to know that Andrei was no better than a pimp and that he—and many like him—had come to the far reaches of the countryside, not to give happiness to some poor farmers, but to incite a peasant revolution?"

Lily let go of the papers and intertwined her fingers with the Russian's. Her brow wove into a tight braid across her forehead, and her eyes welled up. She watched three of her tears drip in succession onto one of Pasha's broken scabs. She'd always hated the weak, and right then, more than any other time in her life, she felt like one of them.

"I don't understand," she said.

"I think you do." Pasha looked up into the chapel ceiling and traced the remnants of a hand that had once been attached to yet another devastated artwork. It was probably the hand of Christ, given its location above the missing altar.

"Man's entry into the universe is not about *Flash Gordon*. The military implications are great—as arsenals will undoubtedly make their way above the Earth. But there is a more immediate threat than that. We are battling for people's imaginations. In my tiny village, it wasn't candy alone that led us down a false path, but I can tell you, my dear, that I remember the way that candy tasted to this day."

Pasha took a deep breath and moistened his lips. "And the launch of a vessel into space is a very big piece of candy, wouldn't you say?"

Lily wiped her eyes and cheeks, pushing the hair off her face and using a tattered oil cloth to blow her nose.

"I don't know what you want from me," she said. "I've never done anything like this before—I go to parties and I go places where I can get a tan. That's what I do. I didn't even finish college when I had one class to go. I can speak a few languages—I've always been good at that—and I've got a memory like a Kodak camera, but I don't know that I'm any good at this."

Ivanov had been standing next to the pedestal with his arms folded across his breast plate like a sarcophagus. He went to Lily without any of his usual effervescence, stepping soundlessly across the rotting floor. There wasn't a hint of either a smile or frown on his face. He touched her forehead, nose and chin with a finger that felt more like a cool breath of air than a pillow of flesh and blood.

"Every morning when I wake up, I have no idea how to talk to God," he told her. "It is as if I've forgotten our common language during the simple course of a night's sleep. Yet I find that no matter what I say—no matter how poorly I phrase it—God understands me."

Lily took a shallow breath and nodded, trying to seem appreciative of his comforting words. She felt she owed him that.

"I don't believe in God, Mr. Ivanov," she whispered. She'd never admitted that to anyone, but it had been true for as long as she could remember.

"And I don't believe in evil, Miss Lily. But that doesn't mean it doesn't exist."

CHAPTER 22

MOSCOW

Fabi's son had a look of both surprise and determination frozen upon his face. His lips—no longer the color of cherry candy—had faded into a grayish-white, and blood ran in one smooth line from the pellet-sized hole above his right eyebrow into his hairline, where it disappeared. He was lying on the floor, just outside of the sauna, clutching a baby blue towel with his left hand. His right hand—the one that had held Beryx Gulyas's Beretta—was empty, but his fingers looked like they were still coiled around the thing.

Fabi himself had been moved to one of the marble tables in the second chamber, where his big, round belly pointed to the vent in the ceiling. His brains remained in the first chamber, where they had already dripped down the wet tile walls and slid toward the drain in the center of the floor. A blob of them jiggled over the drain, causing it to slurp.

"I'm leaving my key on the front desk," the receptionist said. The noise of the drain made her queasy. She'd been in the toilet when Beryx Gulyas showed himself out and had stayed there until Rodki Semyonov, The Great Detective, returned from his lunch.

"I'm impressed with his accuracy," Rodki told General Pushkin's assistant.

While Fabi's son had been shot at close range, Fabi had been a moving target who was blasted at a distance of several meters. That was no easy feat for a man who had been worked over as thoroughly as the Hungarian—a man whose eyes were nearly swollen shut, his body bruised to the bone, and his nose completely shattered. Rodki held the assistant's gun and followed what he imagined the Hungarian's movements would have been.

"Right there," Rodki said, as he moved into the first chamber and found the angle at which Gulyas had shot the gun-trading masseuse. Coming in from the second chamber, the assassin would've been totally exposed and Fabi would've had all of the advantages. There would have been no time to position for a shot—only a moment's grace to allow Gulyas to aim by instinct and fire a single round.

"Perfect," Rodki whispered.

Gulyas, he recognized, was the highest caliber of professional. Despite his skill, Rodki could see why General Pushkin hadn't snagged him for his office and let him continue working for one of the lesser states. Sadists had never bothered Pushkin, but instability did—and Beryx Gulyas's penchant for creative murder was a sign of both deep insecurity and staggering hubris.

If he could manage to stick to one method and do what he did best—as he had with poor Fabi and his son—he could have a long career ahead of him.

"The general will be most unhappy about this development," the assistant carped. "If they weren't already dead, he would have purged this operation of these two hacks and replaced them with more talented operatives."

Rodki nodded. His special status left him largely immune from blame for problems like this. Fabi and his son may have been hacks, but they were KGB hacks and it was their responsibility to keep the Hungarian in line. If their superior had any common sense, he would've immediately noticed that this father-son team was a losing proposition. Rodki had noticed. In fact, he had counted on it.

"What should I tell the general?" the assistant implored.

He tried not to seem worried about being the bearer of bad news.

"That I'll follow Mr. Gulyas and let the comrade general know as soon as I discover anything."

The general held his cards close and hated to surrender any control. Rodki knew, on the other hand, that surrendering a bit of control was precisely what broke a case wide open. The Hungarian would've rather died than talk, and all they would've gained by detaining him indefinitely was another prisoner. With Beryx Gulyas loose, Rodki Semyonov could wait for his movements as if he were monitoring a radar screen for a cloaked submarine. Eventually, it would have to surface.

"What if he disappears for good?" the assistant whined.

"It's possible, I guess. But trust me, my friend; I did quite a number on him. And he'll be far more likely to make stupid errors after the trauma of one of my interrogations—they take a lot out of man. You can tell that to the general."

The assistant seemed pleased.

"In the meantime, I'm afraid I may need permission to leave Moscow in the near future. It's just a hunch, but I'd rather the general give me authorization now instead of waiting until our friend reappears and risk losing him again."

It had been eighteen years since Rodki had been allowed to leave the Moscow city limits. Stalin had guarded him so jealously that he hadn't even been allowed a visit to the provinces and conducted all of his investigations—no matter how far-reaching—from the city proper. When Stalin died and he acquired a new master, the restraints upon his movements didn't change. But then, he'd never questioned them either.

Rodki Semyonov didn't know exactly what made him question them today. He didn't want to leave Moscow. It had become a comfortable cell for him after all these years. But something inside him, something perhaps all too human that had nothing to do with his desire or ability to solve this case, made him want to get a look beyond his city prison.

"One more thing," Rodki added, as the assistant looked up from his notepad. "If I'm to follow this man myself, I'll need a gun."

CHAPTER 23
SERGEI POSAD

Lily entered the Holy Trinity Library and sat at a little corner table behind a soaring row of free-standing bookshelves that housed dozens of gold-leafed volumes. They depicted the lives of Russian saints, church officials, noteworthy nobles, politicians, builders of cathedrals, fighters of crusades and others who—in short—had lain the foundation for much of Russia's spiritual existence prior to the demise of the House of Romanov. The library was quaint by Byzantine standards—a perfect square with high, high ceilings—and favored density over expanse. It felt strangely informal to Lily as well, despite its cool climate and sumptuous woodwork—like a great room belonging to a man of science rather than industry.

Lily held in her hands Fedot's translation of the *Sputnik* papers Pasha had squirreled away from his office in Moscow. In the spiritualist's direct language, he distilled highlights of the emerging Soviet space program along with factoids of his own meant to help clarify the situation for Lily.

1955—In announcements made four days apart, the United States of America and the Soviet Union publicly state they will launch artificial Earth satellites by the end of the 1950s decade. This was the starting shot, as Tony Geiger might say, and was preceded by the pillage of the Nazi German V2 ballistic missile program after the war. Liquid-fueled rockets capable of flying long distances at high altitudes, they are the very foundation of astral voyaging.

Von Braun, a German, heads the design team for United States, while a man whose identity is a state secret heads the Soviet design team. His name is Sergei Korolev and he was recently brought out of retirement after spending many years imprisoned in Siberia; a victim of Stalin's Great Purge in 1938.

Eisenhower will not allow Von Braun to use any military launchers for United States satellites because he fears looking like a warmonger. As a result, Von Braun must develop his own, non-military launchers for his satellites. Soviet Union places no such restrictions on their designer, giving them a timeline advantage.

It is known by Pasha Tarkhan that propaganda is not the only victory Soviet Union hopes to gain. If the Sputnik launch is successful, Soviet Union hopes by end of decade to launch the first of a secret nuclear arsenal into space.

Lily put the papers down and folded her hands. She couldn't bear sitting for another moment. Tucking Fedot's *Sputnik* translation into her coat pocket, Lily ran outside. There, in the front yard of the library, she found shelter under the very stars and moon the Soviets and Americans were hoping to claim. She located Venus immediately, and the planet stared back at her while the surrounding stars twinkled. The moon, nearly full, was bone white. It was an unspeakably clear and beautiful night. Serene. Deceptive. Lily had never wanted the dawn more. She went over to the one great Manchurian Maple in the Lavra and sat at its foot, leaning against its trunk and hugging her knees.

Peering through the maple's paper-thin leaves, Lily made a wish on the moon, as her father had taught her when she was a little girl. "The moon is the closest thing to God's face," he'd told her.

She wished to go home, but the wish felt hollow. Lily, herself, felt like a shell. She struggled to find the things within herself that had always given her comfort—humor, the love of her parents—but those were lost to her.

"Tony," she said. "You can take your damned life."

The words had barely left her lips when Lily became aware of a faint chorus of chants approaching her from behind. The chorus began to swell and Lily turned to see a procession of monks filing one by one into the Holy Trinity Cathedral. Each of them was holding a candle and staring ahead with stanch concentration as if hypnotized, their voices blending together like a fine meal.

Tears came to Lily's eyes. Her heart beat hard and felt as hot and dense as a basalt stone. The voices of the monks seemed to want to gain entry to her. She breathed them in through her mouth, their resonances pulsing through her lungs. She felt them pierce her skin and inhabit her internal organs.

Lily dug the bases of her palms into her eyes and wiped her tears away with the backs of her hands. She looked up at the moon again and made another wish—but this time, she meant it. She wished she'd never shared a cab with Tony Geiger, had never gone on his errands, had left his tickets and his metal card with his dead body on top of Monemvasia, had never met Fedot, or Ivanov, or Pasha Tar . . . her mind's voice stopped its litany of regrets as Pasha came into her thoughts. Somehow, she didn't wish she'd never met Pasha Tarkhan. Lily closed her eyes at this unexpected realization, but before she could debate its merits with herself, Ivanov knelt at her side and placed his long fingers on the back of her neck. In his other hand was a small book of poetry, which he held out to her.

"*The Death of the Orange Blossom* by Mansoor Nassa?" She shook her head and accepted the volume, laying it onto her lap. These people and their poets, she thought. It was like an obsession for them. Lily had heard of Nassa, of course, but had never felt any inclination to read him. "Inscrutible" was how he'd been described to her.

"I think Nassa will be very helpful for you," Ivanov told her. He removed his hand from her neck and placed it on the front cover, stroking his thumb over the poet's name. He closed his eyes and began breathing deeply, as if he were praying.

"Who are you people?" Lily asked. "And what do you want from me?"

"You're mistaken, Miss Lilia," Ivanov said. "It is you who wants something."

Lily opened her eyes but wouldn't look at the Russian holy man.

"That's what I thought, but then why do I feel like a fly that's been caught in a web?"

Ivanov smiled and petted Lily's neck. "Yes, yes—you are in a web," he said. "But I think that web has been waiting for you all your life. And maybe you are the one who spun it, and we are the ones caught."

Lily stood and turned her back to Ivanov, leaving *The Death of the Orange Blossom* in the grass. She wanted nothing to do with him right then. Not his flowing hair and philosopher's beard; certainly not his truth-seeking phrases and rhetorical questions. And not his damned poetry. What began as merely a march away from Ivanov became a trot, and then an all-out run back to the dilapidated rectory. She ran past a sleeping Pasha and to the ice bath, where she picked up the ladle and began spooning the freezing water over her head. When she was finished, Lily felt lightheaded and undone, but better somehow.

Reluctant, or perhaps unable, to get to her feet, Lily crawled into the next room, where Pasha lay. She watched him for a moment—his wide shoulders rolling with each breath. Lily inched toward the door, her eyes fixed to his sleeping form. At the doorway, she pulled herself up and started to leave, to go anywhere—back to the library, or maybe into the tunnel and out of the Lavra.

"Are you alright?" Pasha asked. His voice was tender and uncomplicated; a real question asked with genuine sentiment.

"You lied," she said. "Nuclear arsenals are a bigger piece of candy than imaginations."

"Perhaps." Pasha turned on his side and took a long, deep breath. "Please don't go," he said.

Despite her wish on the moon, Lily supposed she'd always known she wasn't leaving. Not the chapel, not the Lavra, not the life she'd taken from Tony Geiger. Most of all not Pasha Tarkhan. She was scared. Scared of her own thoughts and desires, scared of dying, scared of living like this. Lily was scared of becoming like her father and scared that if she left right now she'd just go back to being what she had been until the night she'd watched Tony Geiger take his last breath on Earth. And she was scared of what she was feeling for Pasha and even more scared that he could never feel the same way about her. *Could anyone?* she wondered. The worst thing was that it felt like being scared was just a part of her life now, as being bored had been. And the scariest thing of all, perhaps, was that part of Lily liked it.

"Fear of the Lord is the beginning of wisdom," she said.
"Hmm?"

"It's the hundred and eleventh psalm and repeated in
the first chapter of Proverbs. And something my dad always used to say when I was growing up." Lily sighed. "I'm
sure he still says it—I just haven't heard it in a while. Funny
how these things come back to you out of nowhere."

She sat beside Pasha and stroked his hair.

"Pasha?" she whispered, but he was asleep again.

Lily snuggled down next to him, spooning him the way
her mother did when Lily had a fever. His body was hard
and felt immoveable—like the wall of a citadel; its essence
seemed to know right from wrong and truth from fiction.

"I knew you would stay," he murmured.

"No, I can't leave," she said. "There's a difference."

"And what difference is that?"

Lily rolled onto her back and looked up at the free-float-
ing hand painted on the ceiling—graceful and delicate, except for two intertwining rivers of thick, blue veins.

"The difference that destiny makes, I suppose." Lily
closed her eyes, letting sleep overcome her. It didn't take
long.

Pasha Tarkhan turned over and propped himself up on
his elbow. He leaned over and smelled her hair—hints of
lavender and rosemary. Lovely. Pasha watched her for a
long time.

SUMMER, 1956

CHAPTER 24
THE OUTSKIRTS OF MOSCOW

Beryx Gulyas stole a freshly plucked chicken from a local farm and nailed it to a piece of plywood with its wings and thighs spread pornographically and its limp head dangling in the middle, across its chest. He turned and walked forty paces before pivoting again to face the dead bird. Shooting its limbs off was simple—he almost hadn't bothered. The more difficult shots were the head and heart—especially since his shoulder was still sore from the beatings he'd taken at the bath house. The pain made it difficult to hold his gun steady once fatigue began to set in.

He took another ten paces and got the heart in two shots, but only because he burped suddenly as he fired the gun the first time, splintering the wood that lay just where its head would've been. The chicken's head had slumped to the side, so he didn't have to adjust his position in order to shoot it clear off, which he did in one steady shot.

Satisfied with his performance, Gulyas left the torn, raw chicken behind for the animals. He tucked his gun into his pants and walked out of the eye-shaped clearing and back through a short distance of forest until he reached Grigori's car—an eighteen year old Mercedes Sedan that had been cared for with all the love Grigori would have reserved for his family, had he ever married.

Although Gulyas would never consider Grigori a friend, his wife's cousin had fulfilled his obligation well. He'd cared for Gulyas's injuries with enormous diligence after the Hungarian's escape from the bathhouse—even if Grigori was a liver specialist who hadn't endeavored to treat broken facial bones since medical school. Gulyas's wife had been surprised by his call, since he hadn't contacted her in over a year, but she, too, had delivered, calling Gregori immediately. She must have put a real fire under the man, as Gregori had not only tended to Gulyas but fed him a diet of meat and noodles almost every night. It must have cost him a fortune. The food was uncommonly good for Russian fare but had cost Gulyas dearly as well. His weight was up three kilos from the four he'd managed to lose. He reached into the front pocket of his trousers and fingered two marbles of rutilated quartz and tiger's eye—for will power.

In the past, Gulyas had always been able to rely on his strength and reflexes, but his new bulk made him feel vulnerable and slow. Turning forty had been a physical milestone for him, and he could almost remember the day that he realized he could no longer eat what he liked. Now, only three years later, he was out of breath when he ran and had a difficult time rising from a crouching position. Bending down was fast becoming a nuisance. The only skill he had that remained fully intact was his aim. Nobody could shoot like him. Just ask the chicken, he sniggered to himself.

But the chicken, instead of crumbling in defeat, teased him mercilessly—striking delectable poses on the roasting pans of his imagination. He'd originally taken the bird for dinner and as a way to thank Grigori, but thought better of it when he caught a glimpse of his belly in the reflection of a shop window. He only liked chicken when it was baked with butter, garlic and bacon, or fried in sour cream and breadcrumbs, so there was no point in trying to make it a light meal. He would eat roughage tonight: crisp vegetables and lettuce with lemon juice and fresh dill. A sad way to spend an evening, indeed. As for Grigori, he'd leave him twenty American dollars and two of the pens he'd taken from the bathhouse reception desk. But not until the man did him one more favor.

"I want you to do a little bit of investigating for me," Gulyas ordered, as he took out a pen and paper and began to draw.

Grigori gave an eager nod, scrutinizing the work he'd done on Gulyas's nose. Grigori was proud that the nose looked as good as it did, considering the extent of the Hungarian's injury. His nose would never be straight or thin again, but it would function properly.

"Take a look at this," Gulyas instructed. He showed Grigori his drawing of a rectangle with an X and the word *tree* written beneath it in Cyrillic.

"It was made of metal and double sided," Gulyas continued.

Grigori shook his head. "I've never seen anything like it."

"You work in a hospital, Grigori. You see all types of people. I'm sure someone, somewhere has seen something like this. Would you be so kind as to inquire amongst your colleagues?"

Grigori readily agreed.

"I want this information fast," Gulyas forewarned. "I'll be leaving the day after tomorrow and I'll need to know where the hell I'm going."

CHAPTER 25

SERGEI POSAD

Hot days didn't come often during June in this part of the country. And rarely did the sun ever get strong enough to encourage a Russian to do what Pasha was doing—soak in a tub full of ice water, while Lily sat on the ground, occasionally dipping an oil cloth into the frigid bath and patting the back of her neck to cool off.

She'd been dressing Pasha's burns and helping him get in and out of the tub since they'd arrived, so sitting with him as he alternated bobbing naked in the water and drying out on a cotton blanket should've seemed normal to Lily, but it didn't. The Russian was well enough to care for himself now, and Lily no longer felt like his nurse. And the way that his eyes would roam her body made her feel unexpectedly shy, too. While the way her own eyes would linger too long over his chest and abdominal muscles made her feel downright ridiculous.

"Could you bring me my robe?" Pasha asked.

Fedot had supplied Pasha with a monk's robe, and the Russian had worn it every day since he was able to leave his bed. It flowed loosely over the tender parts of his skin, and he always appeared comfortable in it, although Lily thought he looked no more like a priest than he would a cowboy had he donned a ten-gallon hat.

"Feel better?" she asked.

"Immeasurably."

Evening was at hand, and Pasha wanted to take a walk in the gardens. He said he hadn't been able to truly enjoy the outdoors since he'd left Vienna and wanted to breathe in the perfume of the Asessippi lilacs that the monk, Matvei, was cultivating.

"When do you think we'll be able to leave here?" Lily tried not to sound too eager.

Pasha put his arm around her and steered her toward a row of powder pink rosebushes that looked as if they were made of crepe paper.

"Fedot is working on getting us out of the province, while His Holiness is arranging for us to leave the country."

"*His Holiness,*" Lily repeated. "How?"

Pasha plucked a rose from the bushes and tucked it behind Lily's ear, arranging her hair so it parted at the side and fell away from her face. His smile right then was almost boyish.

"Ivanov is a man of many resources—if he can be called a man at all," Pasha told her. "When he asks for help, he receives it."

Lily touched the flower at her temple. Though she'd begun to take for granted the way the monks in the Lavra kissed Ivanov's feet and hung on his every syllable, his effect on people didn't seem natural when she contemplated him in any other environment.

"What do you mean—*if he can be called a man at all?*"

Pasha took Lily's hands and led her to a stone bench that sat amidst a crescent of tall fire bushes, their yellow buds having only just bloomed. It felt like their own private room within this sprawling garden.

"Porphyri Ivanov is not an ordinary man. He was born quite ordinary—in a peasant town with working parents—and he was an ordinary boy. But as a young man, his true nature emerged."

Lily blinked and looked down at the grass before engaging

Pasha's eyes again. It was a gesture Pasha would come to recognize in her—a polite indication of her hostility to anything she deemed irrational.

"A man like Ivanov is as much a disturbance to the world around him as he is a comfort to those who follow him," Pasha continued. "He certainly disturbed my life."

Lily leaned closer to him. Pasha's eyes, which had been puffy and fatigued even before he was attacked, now looked as lively as Fedot's. His expression was fixed, as if he was recounting an extraordinary dream.

"Are you one of these people?" Lily asked.

The Russian reached down to his shoe and pulled a small metal card from a seam in his leather upper. Like the one Tony had given her, it had a cross on one side, a star on the other, and a series of Cyrillic letters embossed under each symbol. He ran his fingertips over the grooves of the letters and briefly shut his eyes before meeting hers again.

"Some years ago, when the Nazis occupied Ivanov's village, they decided to test the holiness of the so-called Russian saint," Pasha began. "His followers tried to protect him, but Ivanov urged them to allow his fate. That fate, as it turns out, was to spend four hours submerged naked in a frozen lake during the middle of winter and another two being ridden around—wet—on a motorcycle in the frigid air. His

hair broke off at the shoulders like glass thread, but otherwise Ivanov remained as healthy as he had before his torture. Any man I've known would've died."

Lily looked down at her lap and saw that she had taken Pasha's hand and interlocked her fingers with his. He didn't seem to mind.

"Were you there, at the village?"

Pasha shook his head.

"The story could've been exaggerated by his followers," she reasoned.

Pasha nodded. With his free hand, he adjusted his monk's robe and fanned his healing skin.

"Ivanov's popularity grew as a result of this—possible myth, as you say—and his name became known throughout Russia. Needless to say, our esteemed leader was none too pleased. Stalin had barely tolerated Ivanov before the war. By the end of it, he would've liked nothing better than to have eliminated him, the way he eliminated anyone who bothered him. But, instead of killing Ivanov—which might have created a martyr and greater competitor—he had him committed to a psychiatric hospital. Spiritual seekers are the most difficult subjects for brainwashing under any circumstances, but Ivanov was a case unlike any other."

Lily looked down at the grass again, but Pasha placed his finger under her chin and tipped her head up, making her look into his face. Earnest. Grave. Resigned.

"This I saw with my own eyes," he said. "Not only was I present when he was injected with the neuroleptic drugs, but I was his principal interrogator and brainwasher. I beat him and I tortured him and I drugged him. It was, you could say, part of my Foreign Service exam. And the beginning of my political disillusionment."

Lily let go of Pasha's fingers and laid her face in her hands. The Ivanov of Pasha's tale was one she couldn't reconcile with the happy, robust man who spoke to the trees in the Lavra compound as if they were close friends. The Pasha of newspaper articles that detailed his gruesome acts and of torture chambers inside psychiatric hospitals was one she could hardly comprehend. Especially as he traced his finger around her ear and stroked her hair while he spoke these things to her.

"Like you, Lily, I don't believe in God," he told her. "But I do believe in Porphyri Ivanov. And I believe in this." Pasha held up the metal card. "This is the symbol of *Derevo*, the Russian Spiritual Underground, of which I am a member. We have no leader and we have no directive other than to do what is right—or at least what is least wrong."

The Russian put his arms around her, cradling her shoulders and expelling a deep breath into her ear. "I believe in the human spirit, Lily. And if I'm wrong and my rational mind is as limited in its understanding of the universe as I fear it is, then I hope the God I have denied will forgive me."

Pasha squeezed her closer, and Lily could hardly move.

"You've done so much for me, Lily," he whispered.

Lily nodded, wrapping her arms around his neck. Pasha no longer smelled of healing flesh, and his breath was tinged with the wedges of apple that Matvei had given him that morning. His faint smile wore a soft jumble of raw emotions—the kind she had always hoped to see on a lover's face.

"I want to do one more thing," she told him, her eyes tracing the thick line of his jugular vein. "I want to be your lover."

She had not imagined herself making love with him. Despite Pasha's lusting eyes and delicate touches. Despite her own emerging desires for him—this killer, spy, diplomat, spiritualist. But it was exactly what she wanted. In fact, Lily had never wanted anyone or anything like she wanted Pasha Tarkhan.

She moved her hands to his face and trickled her fingers over his cheeks and neck, gliding them down over his chest. Lily untied his robe and let it drop to the ground, at last allowing her eyes to drift over his naked body without feeling the least bit ridiculous.

"Right here," she said, and laid down beneath the fire bushes. They were ferocious in their color, pungent, with hundreds of tiny barbs growing along their stems like hairs. And they were beautiful.

CHAPTER 26

They had been communicating the way secret sweethearts might have during the Dark Ages. Beryx threw the first rock over the fortress wall, having wrapped it in a piece of crisp stationary he'd taken from Grigori's desk. He'd used crayon to write the message so that, in the event of rain, the words wouldn't run together.

The following night he came across the same rock—this time wrapped in cheap school paper—sitting on the outer lawn, waiting to be found. The message had been written in pencil. It had been a remarkably easy and straightforward exchange.

For this, he had to give Grigori credit. In the span of a half-day, his wife's cousin managed to locate a doctor who had performed an unsuccessful operation on a young man who'd taken a nasty fall some months before. The youth had been attempting to repair the roof tiles of a dilapidated church at the St. Sergius Lavra. He'd fallen nearly four stories before landing in the holly bushes that wrapped like a wreath along the base of the outer wall. It had been the young man's misfortune that nobody within the compound had seen him tumble. He was discovered only when a local widow took her Schnauzer for a walk and heard him whimpering for help. The young man had kept repeating just one word in his agony: "*Derevo.*"

Grigori hadn't wanted to risk breaking into the coroner's files, but he did it anyway, and the Hungarian rewarded him with ten additional American dollars before he left the man's home for good. The file had been worth at least fifty, but Grigori had no way of knowing that. To him, all it had revealed was the young man's name and the contact information for his brother. His personal belongings had seemed more promising and contained a metal card like the one Gulyas had seen during his interrogation.

It was that same card that Beryx revealed to the young monk who crawled out of a hole hidden in the grass around the outer ring of the St. Sergius Lavra. The night was cloudy, with little natural light, but the monk's teeth—a clumsy row of tablets too large for his mouth—gleamed.

"Murdered," he murmured. "But how can that be?"

Gulyas shrugged and tried to appear concerned.

"I believe your brother had stumbled onto something and that this was an inside job."

The monk shook his head violently and stepped back from the Hungarian.

"How else can you explain that no one saw him fall—or found him for hours?" Gulyas pressed. "There's a rat in your midst. You mark my words."

The young monk folded his hands and exhaled. His bit down hard on his fleshy bottom lip and thrust his chin forward. Gulyas hadn't won him over.

"I hope I'm wrong," Gulyas continued. "But this has been eating at me for months now, and I had to at least do my part—as a God-fearing man and a doctor—and share my suspicions."

Gulyas turned toward the fortress wall surrounding the Lavra.

"If I'm right, of course, all of you could be in danger."

It was too dark for the monk to look into the doctor's eyes, but it didn't matter. He didn't like his voice and now regretted meeting with him at all.

It had been decided by the Lavra elders, after the rock and the note had been found on the path to the bell tower, that the message was a lure or a hoax. Fedot, in particular, had been adamant about not initiating any contact with outsiders—especially while the diplomat and the American woman were still there. But Maxim had been the monk's twin brother. They had formed from a single egg and been nurtured side by side in one womb. They had come to the Lavra together, and the monk figured they would die together. How could he ignore a message that read: MAXIM FEODOROV WAS MURDERED. DO YOU KNOW WHO KILLED HIM?

"I have to go back," the monk said.

"I want to come with you."

The monk put up his palm and backed toward the trapdoor.

"That's not possible. You have to go, please. Don't come back here."

"But, what about the woman?" Gulyas blurted.

The young monk flinched but recovered quickly, straightening his shoulders and shaking his head.

"You know, the American woman. Long, dark hair and a pretty face. Surely you've noticed her."

The monk heard the man's clothes rustle in the moment before he was knocked to ground. His left side stung, but it was his hand that made him shriek. The bullet had torn off both his index and middle finger before burrowing beneath his rib cage.

"Why?" the young monk begged.

"Why not?" Gulyas answered as he placed the mouth of the silencer between the monk's eyebrows and fired.

CHAPTER 27

"Was Tony your lover?" Pasha asked. They were sitting naked in the tattered rectory as Pasha scraped the new shaving blade Fedot had acquired for him up the curve of Lily's calf. He rinsed the blade in the tin tub—still full from their bath.

"No. Sort of. We got drunk and did it once, but I don't even think he finished." Lily leaned over and kissed Pasha's lips as he ran the blade up her thigh. "I know I didn't. He told me he was a salesman." She laughed as Pasha finished erasing the last line of soap and stubble from Lily's leg.

"Tony was a salesman," Pasha reminded her.

"Then he told me my father was an arms dealer and that I was working for him now if I didn't want Daddy to go to prison."

Pasha appraised the work he'd done on her legs.

"Ah, yes, your father. Was this before or after you got drunk with him?"

Lily dried her calves and thighs, scooting closer to Pasha. She wrapped herself around him and put her lips to his ear.

"It was when I tried to sneak out of his hotel room without saying good-bye. Maybe he took offense."

"Tony took offense to nothing," Pasha said, kissing her earlobe. "And Tony couldn't have had your father arrested even if he wanted to. I'm not sure anyone could."

Pasha chuckled in a baritone hum that had grown on Lily. It was the laugh of an old soldier and reminded her of an uncle she hadn't seen since adolescence. Pasha was too young to laugh like an old soldier, but then, he'd seen a lot in his thirty-six years. By the time he was sixteen, the full weight of manhood rested on his shoulders, and by his mid-twenties, it was the full-on burden of the world. Lily had been remarkably free of burden until she'd met Tony. Since then, it had been like she was cramming for finals every day, trying to figure out how to get a passing mark in what Tony called simply "the real world."

"Matvei's late again," she whispered as her stomach growled.

The monk had taken to leaving their stew just outside the door, as he knew what had been going on in there over the past few days. He would put the tray down, knock twice and scamper away without uttering a word. Lily could swear it had been two hours since his usual time, but Pasha didn't seem concerned, so she wasn't about to get worked up again.

"Did you hear that?" Lily sat up straight. Pasha hunched closer to the ground, becoming very quiet.

The cries came first. They were shouts of disbelief, then panic. Almost as quickly came cracks from a firearm. Lily could hear the heels of the simple loafers worn by the monks of the St. Sergius Lavra as they dug into the stone pathways— and the occasional thud of a body hitting the ground.

"Throw me my trousers," Pasha ordered. He'd eschewed his comfortable monk's robe for his original clothes—laundered by Matvei only two days before. Lily had barely managed three buttons on her blouse before Fedot darted into the rectory.

"Intruder!" he barked.

Fedot corralled Lily and Pasha into the chapel, brushing aside Ivanov's bed. He stood on his tiptoes and removed a crowbar from a tiny ledge that ran above three bullet-shaped windows studded with broken stained glass. He used the crowbar to dislodge a flat chunk of stone that, in part, made up the chapel floor. Beneath the stone was a passageway, lit by the same crisscrossed torches Lily had seen in the tunnel that led into the compound.

"The microfilm!" Lily demanded.

"I'll retrieve it and meet you at Alyona's." Fedot had moved the microfilm into the tabernacle in the Holy Trinity Cathedral. The chapel had been too exposed to the weather, and the Russians feared that all it would take was a good summer storm to corrode the film and render it useless. The printed documents had been left in the collection box, but buried beneath an assembly of rubble that formed a loosely contrived pyramid near the entrance to the rectory. Fedot ran to the pile of refuse and began digging through it.

"Forget the papers," Pasha said, urging Lily down the ladder and into the tunnel. "It's the film we want."

Fedot threw an eroded brick aside and went to the tunnel entrance. With Pasha's help, he guided the stone back over the descending stairway and remade Ivanov's bed—patting and arranging it until it looked lived-in again. A heavy heel thudded on the stone sidewalk outside the chapel and then sprinted into a run. Fedot knew the hard step couldn't belong to one of the monks at the St. Sergius Lavra and listened as the intruder headed toward the Holy Trinity Cathedral.

Fedot walked to the fresco of Rublev's Trinity, kissed it, and removed an old Cossack's Shashka sword from a hidden panel behind the Angel of the Holy Spirit. He pulled it from its black sheath and ran his finger along the edge of the curved blade before dashing out of the chapel in pursuit of the stranger.

CHAPTER 28

Fedot trampled into the field of white tulips swaying across the front lawn of the Trinity Monastery. The intruder had disappeared, his hard step no longer heard on the pathways that snaked in and out of the various chapels. He could've entered any one of the surrounding buildings, yet there were no screams coming from their interiors. The wails of the wounded still echoed from the Pilgrim Tower, as did the tapping feet of the monks who were trying desperately to care for their fallen brothers, but the intruder's rampage had seemed to end as suddenly as it had begun.

Fedot lowered the Shashka sword to his side and strode into the Eastern entrance of the Holy Trinity Cathedral. Mass was in session, the cantor reading from the Epistle—a letter to St. Paul. Fedot locked eyes with one of the altar boys and beckoned him. The boy turned from the altar, gliding over the oriental runner that led to the sacristy. There wasn't so much as a stir amongst the congregation— a small gathering of monks who peopled the first ten rows and a few lone stragglers that dotted the other pews. Hitching his sword to his trousers, Fedot donned the boy's robe and took his place at the altar as the Gospel reading came to a close.

From the altar, Fedot could get a good look at the monks who had come to hear Mass. Immersed in prayer, they hadn't heard the cries that would've just barely pierced through the thick walls during the early stages of the massacre. Fedot, himself, could hear nothing of the outside world, and for a moment he envied the monks their ignorance—even if their peace of mind was to be shattered the moment they filed out of the cathedral doors.

But one of these men wasn't ignorant. Fedot had always had a fine nose for the presence of evil, and that nose had drawn him to the Holy Trinity. He studied each of the kneeling monks, evaluating their posture and the rhythm of their collective breath. It was a phenomenon he'd first noticed in the Lavra several years ago, when he was still living here. As the holy men prayed in any communal venue, they began to breathe as one—their intake of air as well as their exhale coming together in a single motion as if they had only a pair of lungs between them.

Two of the monks rose, retrieving the wine and Eucharist and carrying them to the altar. Fedot stepped down as if he were going to intercept them. Instead, he strode past the cloaked men, gripping the Shashka sword hidden beneath his robes. He walked beyond the pew where a lone monk sat—his hands folded in his lap and his head bowed. He was the one monk whose breath was not in synchronicity with the other praying men. Fedot turned suddenly, and as he leaped over the pew, drew his sword.

"Pōcs!"

Beryx Gulyas screamed a Hungarian expletive and threw himself over the next pew, as Fedot's sword ripped through his robe, carving a slice of flesh out of his left arm. Gulyas ignored the gush of blood that streamed over his elbow and grabbed a small monk by the hair, dragging him into the aisle for cover. He drew his gun.

Shouts and bawls from the sparse congregation echoed throughout the cathedral, but only a couple of the monks scrambled out of the church. The rest of them—confused

and frightened—stayed behind with their endangered
brother, who Gulyas held close to his chest. A hush fell over
the church again as the Hungarian stared down the monks,
pressing the mouth of his gun behind his hostage's ear. The
monk with the Shashka sword had disappeared, and the
Hungarian could only guess that he was either hiding behind one of the pews or had taken a place amongst the
other monks, who from his point of view seemed nearly
indistinguishable from one another.

The Hungarian pointed his gun and shot off his hostage's toe. He muffled the man's scream with the late Matvei
Feodorov's robe sleeve and watched the other monks gasp
and beg for their friend's life. All of them except one—a
small man with thin lips and round glasses. The Hungarian
raised his gun again, but Fedot was too fast for him. He'd
seen through the attempt to smoke him out and dove behind a marble holy water fount, calling for the rest of the
monks to take cover.

"Monk . . . monk . . . dead monk!" The Hungarian
sneered, picking off three of the scurrying holy men with
an even hand. Fedot watched his childhood friend, Artur,
fall dead to the stone floor.

"You can't escape from here," Fedot called to the
Hungarian intruder.

"Is the hand of God going to stop me?" he hissed.
"Because it's not going to be you with your Shashka against
my gun, is it?"

The Hungarian backed up, pulling his whimpering hostage with him until he could lean against a statue of St.
Anna of Kashin. His arm stung, and a gush of tepid blood
soaked down to his wrist and dripped to the floor, mixing
with the blood of his hostage's foot.

"I don't have a quarrel with you or with your brothers,"

he continued. "I only want Tarkhan and the American girl. I can shoot them quickly and easily—ending all of this bloodshed. Or I can shoot my way to them and you can bury a dozen or more of your friends. It makes little difference to me."

Fedot held the Shashka sword up to the light. Its beams filtered through the panes of stained glass, and its rainbow colors reflected off the Shashka's steel blade, striping the Russian's face with green, indigo and violet.

"You ran right by them," he said. "They were last in the old rectory."

"You better be sure of that," the Hungarian warned. "Or you'll all go down."

Both Fedot and the Hungarian were men of their word.

"Oh, I'm sure."

Fedot never carried a gun, but at times like this he acknowledged that a gun would've been a far more expedient way to handle the Hungarian assassin than a Shashka sword. Still, he believed creativity to be a far more powerful weapon than firepower and was confident at being an immensely creative individual. He waited for the side door to thunder closed before standing up and addressing the monks.

"Whatever you do, don't leave here," he said. The men were crowded around their wounded friend, whom Beryx Gulyas had tossed to the floor as he made his exit. "Not even to get a doctor."

Fedot marched to the tabernacle, removed the microfilm, and left from the same door as the Hungarian.

CHAPTER 29

Beryx Gulyas tore into the old rectory with his gun squeezed into his hand. He wasn't surprised to see it empty, but had a gut feeling that the answer to where the girl and the Russian had gone lay somewhere within its decaying walls and broken windows. A crude bed had been assembled in the middle of the floor and looked well-used, while off to the side, in an adjacent room, stood a tin tub filled with ice water. He could smell a faint perfume of sex in the air.

He had expected to hear a soft-shoed scuttle of monks by now, circling the rectory, but the Lavra had returned to its previous state of pensiveness—the same state he'd found it in before he'd stirred things up. It was odd and he didn't like it.

"Little man—you're not a monk, are you?" he called out.

He sensed the man with the Shashka sword was close by, even if there was no sound of him. There was simply a prevailing aura of danger. The man was no gangster or Soviet agent, but neither was he an Etor. It was refreshing, Gulyas thought, to have found a type of man he'd never encountered before.

Swiftly, he pulled Matvei Feodorov's robe over his head and threw it down. It was a cumbersome thing to wear with street clothes on underneath, and Gulyas needed to be able to move. Especially with the added burden of his blubbery middle. Damn his wife's cousin and his scrumptious meals.

The Hungarian heard a crackle outside the rectory door, like a match being struck. Seconds later, the smell of gunpowder and burning wood hit his nostrils. Gulyas leapt away from the door. He darted over the nature bed Ivanov had made for Pasha Tarkhan, rushed past the alcove where Matvei Feodorov used to leave two bowls of hot borscht with brown bread and dove into the icy tub before the entryway of the rectory exploded.

He held his breath for what felt like eternity, and when his head finally broke the surface of the water, Gulyas found himself staring into the point of a Shashka sword. He wanted to raise his gun and shoot the Russian square between the eyes, but knew better than to move until the man instructed him to do so. Only his heaving chest defied Fedot as he endeavored to get his panting under control.

Fedot ran the blade over the Hungarian's nose and chin, then down his neck, stopping at his jugular.

With a slow, deliberate movement, Gulyas inhaled a lungful of smoky air. Not only was the atmosphere gray and thick, but it was getting hot. "This place is going to blow," he said.

Fedot didn't even stir, but Gulyas hadn't expected him to. He was just trying to buy time.

"You're going to crawl out of that tub feet first," Fedot told him. "With your hands and your gun flat against the bottom and your head under the water."

Gulyas nodded. "Whatever you say."

Fedot's sword followed the Hungarian's head beneath the surface, and he waited as the man snaked his legs over the side of the tub. He then straddled the Hungarian and plunged his hand into the ice water, gripping Gulyas by the hair and pulling him out. The gun was still in the Hungarian's hand when he thunked to the floor, but Fedot took advantage of his disorientation and kicked the weapon out of his palm.

"God weeps at your existence," Fedot told him. "You do not please him."

He said this as if it was the worst possible insult—as if he were calling the Hungarian a child-fucker, a defiled sphincter, a carcass.

The Russian began to chant—a monk's chant, Gulyas surmised—a sort of prelude to what the Hungarian imagined would be his gruesome end. He had read somewhere that Shashka swords were particularly good for goring when handled by an adept master.

"I want to die standing up," the Hungarian said. But Fedot Titov wasn't taking requests. He continued to chant, swaying his upper body as his voice rose in decibel, filling the chapel.

Gulyas looked to the ground as the monk's rapture intensified. He couldn't bear to watch a grown man sing— especially one who meant to slice him from head to foot. It was embarrassing. His eyes settled upon a wooden square stamped with gold cursive that read *Grand Hotel Wien*. His mark, Pasha Tarkhan, must have stayed there recently. Or maybe it was the American woman. Travelers like Tarkhan, the woman, himself; they were always picking up boxes of matches wherever they went. Gulyas had a coil pot filled with them in the studio apartment he kept in Bucharest. And a waterlogged book from the Hotel Rude lay in his hip pocket.

"The Hotel Rude," Gulyas said. "That's where I've seen you before."

It was an observation of little consequence, but to a man who is accustomed to hiding his identity, such a comment could put him off balance, make him engage, concoct a lie—*I've never been to the Hotel Rude. You don't know what you're talking about.*

"You were the man at the front desk," Gulyas continued. "I asked for coffee, and you said there was none today. Only tea."

The Russian would not be distracted. He finished his prayer and held the Shashka sword askew, an arm's length away from the Hungarian's neck. He didn't have time to inflict on the assassin the death he deserved. Gulyas would die quickly, his head plunging to the bottom of a cold bathtub.

"And I don't like tea," the Hungarian said. "And it was you in the bar, too, wasn't it? You're a lot different here, I have to say."

The hay from Pasha Tarkhan's bed began to hiss as a plume of black smoke floated to the pointed ceiling. The chapel, a tinder box, had not fared well from the makeshift stick of dynamite Fedot had employed against Gulyas. A spray of sparks from the blast had ignited a series of incidental fires, and the woolen bedding on top of the hay began to fry and curl, like human hair. In a single *poof* that resembled a trick in an illusionist's show, the fire doubled in size, engulfing the fresco of St. Sergius, blackening his tranquil face.

Fedot cared about none of it, not even the chapel and its remaining treasures: ancient, battered, yet still amenable to restoration. What drew his eyes to the pyre was the simple crucifix fashioned by Ivanov from his favorite birch. The holy man's creation lay engulfed in the flames, and Fedot could feel its agony as if he were the one burning. The pain tore through his spine—a lit fuse that then consumed the Russian's brain stem. His eyes began to bulge and tear.

Fedot could withstand all manner of physical torment,

but spiritual anguish was more demanding. Right then, he didn't know if he had the ability to kill the Hungarian successfully—to thrust the sword deep into his abdominal cavity or slice his head clean off. Ivanov's handmade crucifix was all that mattered to him—a holy relic made by a holy man. A thing of purity. It was as if Ivanov himself was speaking to him through his birch branch crucifix, saying, "Don't be hasty, his time will come."

Fedot, with a single, fluid motion, swept the Shashka through the fire, depositing the crucifix onto a pile of bricks. Instantly, his pain abated and he was able to stand and breathe with his usual grace. He wiped his eyes and nose on the sleeve of his cassock.

Gulyas took his opportunity. He dove for his gun, aimed it squarely at Fedot's head and fired, but the Russian was uncommonly fast. He had anticipated the Hungarian and dropped to his knees, rolling behind the metal tub.

"Like a jackrabbit," the Hungarian chuckled.

He was out of cartridges. Gulyas hadn't planned on firing his gun so generously. Monks, in his imagination, were creatures of fear and docility. He certainly hadn't anticipated an adversary that could match his own skills. Russia, it was proving, was filled with all manner of professionals. It was no wonder that the men who called on Nicolai Ceausescu from Moscow had never demanded that the Romanian turn over his most prized assassin to them, the way they insisted upon a national tithe of rye, sugar beets and wine grapes.

The Hungarian went to the brick pile and picked up the wood branch crucifix. It wasn't charred too badly, considering, and was the sort of thing his Aunt Zuzanna would have lying around the house. Not as a symbol of piety, but as a charm meant to deter werewolves.

He tucked his gun into the back of his trousers and held the crucifix high over his head.

"If you drop your Shashka into the basin, this may not have to find its way back to the fire."

The fire in and of itself was fast becoming a concern. It had spread from the nature bed to a wooden beam and was licking its way up to the rafters. The flames were blocking a gap the explosion had created at the entry, and the best way out was past the Russian. Gulyas, although his clothes were still soaking wet, was beginning to perspire.

"I'm going to drop it," he repeated. "Unless you get rid of the sword and let me by."

The Russian said nothing. Did nothing. He remained behind the metal bath—as still as a reptile.

Gulyas could feel the air around him changing. It was dense, blistering, but it was also hollow, like the tip of a bullet. It wouldn't take long for the entire chapel to combust. And the Hungarian had always hated fire. To be burned at the stake, the way heretics used to be, had to be the worst manner of death.

"Get up!" he shouted. But still, there was nothing. He could see the little Russian man's foot peeking out from behind the metal basin. It was tilted to the side, and appeared relaxed, as if he had all the time in the world.

Gulyas looked past the metal washtub to the only free path out of the chapel. He contemplated jumping over the tub and making his way out, but he knew the little man could cut him off at the knees in one stroke. His eyes were beginning to water uncontrollably, and each breath made his lungs feel as if they were being massaged with sandpaper. Through the wall of fire where Pasha Tarkhan's bed had lain was a broken stained glass window with only a few jagged teeth left in its frame. It was a large window. A grown man could easily fit through by tucking his head.

The Hungarian threw the crucifix into the fire and took a running start. He ran through the wall of fire and lunged headfirst into the broken window, slicing a perfect straight line over the skin that covered his spine. Upon landing in the grass, he rolled to put out whatever fire might have caught his clothes. There was none. His shirt and trousers, which had been sopping wet before he ran through the flames, were now nearly dry. His hair and eyebrows were singed, but otherwise, he had escaped with only the cut.

Something white flew past him, and then another, and another. For a moment Gulyas thought they were doves or pigeons that had taken his cue and escaped the chapel. But as his eyes adjusted to the light, he saw they were not birds, but papers flying out of the chapel window. As he ran to the fortress wall, the Hungarian picked up as many of the papers as he could along the way. There, he rolled them, stuffed them into his pants and climbed to the top. He stopped briefly to look at the chapel before he jumped and saw the Russian. He was still inside, still unhurried, and was holding the wooden crucifix up above his head, aiming it at Beryx Gulyas as if to say, "You belong to me."

CHAPTER 30

When Rodki Semyonov stepped off the train in Sergei Posad, his stomach fluttered. The soles of his shoes seemed to sink into the concrete platform, and for a moment he merely stood there, bathing in the sensation of *other*: the smell of tulips, spring grass, chicken feathers, scalded coffee; the feel of sunshine, unhindered by pollution and dense architecture.

He had not left the perimeter of Moscow in nearly two decades, and now here he was only a few dozen miles away, and it felt like another continent. All of this for just a traitor.

In the first years of his urban confinement, he had chaffed at his master's paranoia and felt limited in his ability to solve the very cases the Soviet State had mandated. Stalin in particular took great pleasure in asking the impossible, all the while waving an executioner's mask as the consequence of failure.

For years Rodki spent his nights tossing this way and that, dreaming of his mother and his wife Polina in their shallow grave. A grave he believed he would one day share. In his dreams, he would be digging for them until he found Polina's fine hand—its skin gray and nail beds a shadowy blue. Still, it was a beautiful hand, and Rodki would take it in his and bend down to kiss it. As his lips brushed each of her knuckles, Polina's hand would start to come alive and grip his, pulling him down into the soil to be with her.

Part of him wanted to go, but only a part.

And as Rodki Semyonov continued to unravel puzzle after puzzle, as if playing a game of chess without the privilege of looking at the board, Stalin became downright enchanted. He treated Rodki as a pet, though not necessarily a pampered one. The Great Leader never wanted his Great Detective to lose his edge, as so many of his ministers had done. Even the most ruthless of those had begun to grow soft the moment they indulged themselves in the very luxuries that used to be reserved for aristocrats but were now the exclusive domain of the politicians and their enforcers.

Over time, Rodki had convinced himself that there was no better place for him than Moscow. That if he ever left the Russian capital—even for the provinces—his late wife Polina would be gone from him forever, as would his mother and the last remnants of his former self. It was only when he let the Hungarian go—when he had ever so slightly loosened the reins and the assassin, with his badly broken face and pain in every joint of his body, used whatever strength he had to run—that it occurred to Rodki that perhaps this instinct was at the very heart of humanity. And that he, too, was still human. Polina, he felt, would understand. He was not leaving her memory, her slender silhouette of a ghost that sat most mornings at his kitchen table, sharing his coffee. He was doing what was natural for someone who was still alive.

"Taxi?" a bored young man offered, but Rodki waved him away.

He could have requested a driver in Moscow but refused, as the monastery was only a kilometer or so from the station. Rodki wanted to see the village and its people—the babushkas with their baskets of fresh eggs, local workers riding decades old bicycles. Things he used to see daily before moving to the big city for opportunity.

"Zdravstvuyte," he said to the monk who greeted him at the entrance to the Lavra. The monk was frightened of him and held his head down, averting his eyes as he led Rodki through the courtyard. Rodki wanted to tell him he had nothing to fear, but then he didn't know for certain that was true. He never knew what Moscow had in mind, after all. He was merely a detective.

A tall row of fire bushes bowed as the wind blew over them; the same gust of warm air rode through Rodki's hair like fingers. It felt so good that Rodki forgot himself. He reached out to a birch tree, caressing its smooth, white bark, and shuffled along a pathway of small, pink rocks that looked like tourmaline.

"By His mercies, we have been kept from complete destruction," the monk murmured.

With a trembling finger, the monk pointed out where the intruder had entered, explained his murderous route, its seemingly random pattern, and his eventual escape after blowing up a small chapel with gunpowder. At the place where the chapel had stood was a section of blackened ground framed by parts of the structure's foundation.

"Perhaps he was a fanatic," the monk offered. "And, you know, hated the church."

"You mean a Satanist?" Rodki asked.

The monk nodded.

"Interesting theory."

The monk guided him into a small office behind the Baroque bell tower. Three other monks sat in attendance, hands folded, heads down.

"You see, that is all we know," his monk informed him. "I wish I could tell you more of this diabolical deed."

Rodki nodded. "May I go to the chapel? The one ruined in the fire?"

The monk looked to his brothers then back to the Great Detective.

"But it's destroyed," he said. "You saw it on our walk here."

Rodki looked behind the monk to an old map of the Lavra that hung against the wall behind him. "Surely there's something left," he said.

The monk swallowed and shook his head. "We were busy, you see. Tending to our wounded and our dead. We couldn't save it."

The Great Detective cast a side glance at the three monks seated in a row to his left. They were there as witnesses, ready to be questioned and ready to answer exactly as his monk had.

"Brother . . . ?"

"Albert."

"Brother Albert, there's not even a brick, a splinter, a candle holder, nothing, nothing left of this ancient chapel?"

The monk shook his head again.

"I see. May I speak to Mr. Ivanov then, please?"

The monk looked up from his hands, his eyes wide, mouth open.

"Mr. Ivanov is not here anymore," he mumbled.

"He was given permission by Moscow to leave?"

One of the seated monks stood, removing the hood of his cassock and revealing a thick head of well-groomed salt-and-pepper hair.

"Ivanov left this morning for his village. To be with his wife."

This monk looked the Great Detective straight in the eye. His hands were at his sides, and his voice was measured and definitive.

"Naturally, as a Soviet citizen he's free to do whatever he

wishes, but I'm curious as to how he would return to his village without securing the proper papers?"

"The Holy One needs no papers," the monk said.

The Great Detective removed a bag of tobacco from his pocket and rolled a cigarette. He offered it to the gray-headed monk first, then lit it after his decline.

"How about the American girl? Doesn't she need papers to travel Russia?"

The gray monk looked him up and down, but not in order to assess his character, it seemed. No, to the Great Detective it looked as if this monk was deciding whether or not he should kill him right there.

"I don't know what you're talking about," he said.

The Great Detective smiled.

"It's nothing. Believe me. Just a person of interest. Worth a try, though. Everything's worth a try."

With that, the Great Detective uttered the usual pleasantries and started to let himself out. He turned back at the doorway and pointed his finger at the gray-haired monk.

"I was wondering, Brother, when will you be returning to your home country?"

The monk cocked his head and stood back, as if offended by the question.

"You are from Greece, are you not? At least judging by your accent. I would say you haven't lived there in some time, however. Nor have you been living in Russia."

The Great Detective took a deep drag off his cigarette and exhaled.

"Your Russian is excellent, though. You truly have a gift for languages."

The Great Detective left the Lavra alone. There was nothing else he needed there.

CHAPTER 31

BUCHAREST, ROMANIA

Nicolai Ceausescu thumbed through the crinkled white pages—nineteen of them—that Beryx Gulyas had discovered in the Lavra. There were many pages missing, and they were out of order, but their meaning was unmistakable.

"A spaceship. Do you think it's true, or merely Russian bravado?" the Hungarian asked.

His question was perfunctory and designed to flatter his master's strategic thinking rather than raise an important point. Beryx knew very well that it didn't matter if it was true. What mattered was the possession of the assertion of truth. What mattered was leverage against Moscow. What mattered was power. Without any real commerce going on, power was the only product being traded day to day in the phantom socialist stock market. And everyone had a piece of the action, no matter how small. Even a housewife could acquire some for herself if she paid attention—to the comings and goings of her friends and neighbors, to late-night conversations whispered behind closed doors, to the way her butcher grimaced while mouthing the words of a socialist anthem at the mandatory May Day Parade.

The Hungarian watched Ceausescu as he leaned back into his chair, holding the documents close to his chest. His piece of the action had just gotten much, much bigger.

"You're a lucky Hungarian," he told the assassin.

Beryx Gulyas sniffed and stiffened his back. "I earn my luck. I'm worthy of it." It was a bold statement, Beryx knew, especially since he was very well aware that luck, like beauty, made no distinction between the worthy and the unworthy. Still, he had to say something after his debacle at the Lavra. The papers in Nicolai Ceausescu's hand were the only thing standing between him and a dank, one-room basement apartment shared with three other discarded failures. Already his Berlina had been taken from him. He had returned to Bucharest to find his spot in the airport parking lot empty.

"*Sputnik,*" Ceausescu said. "I want it."

Beryx Gulyas nodded.

"I want it!" Ceausescu sprang to his feet and kicked a painted plaster statue of Lenin that stood next to his desk. Lenin's head hit the edge of a long, wooden file cabinet, decapitating the Soviet hero. "I want the plans! I want to build it. Not the idiots in Moscow! Me! Me! Me!" Ceausescu swept the perspiration from his forehead and smelled the tips of his fingers. He sat down at his desk again and proceeded to perform the remainder of his odd collection of compulsions: smelling his pants, knees, crotch, then his armpits. He scratched his scalp and sniffed his fingers, then relaxed—finally satisfied. "In the service of our esteemed Secretary General, of course, whom I will gladly serve to my death."

"Yes," Gulyas said.

"Our esteemed Secretary General will be pleased that we've found a pathway to the heavens, don't you think?"

I found it, Gulyas wanted to say. "Very pleased," he answered.

"And you'll be leaving tonight?" Ceausescu told him.

Gulyas nodded. "The plans this time. The plans."

He didn't know if Tarkhan or the other Russian had the plans, but even if they didn't, they had to know something.

He could make them tell him. Or make the American girl tell him. Women were much easier to break.

"You won't fail again?"

Beryx Gulyas sucked in his belly. He was ashamed of the weight he'd gained from his wife's cousin's cooking and was sure Ceausescu had noticed his expanded girth.

"Never again."

CHAPTER 32

NEAR THE BORDER OF RUSSIA AND AZERBAIJAN

"I had that dream again," Lily whispered. Ivanov, his eyes black like deep water under the light of a full moon. "He was hungry this time."

Alyona, pale as an eggshell and nearly blind, sat in the middle of her kitchen, boiling water for Lily's tea over a glowing cow patty.

She sang almost constantly—her voice like a Ney—mixing Russian and Arabic melodies the way a talented hostess might mix a cocktail. But she stopped singing when Lily started talking about Ivanov again.

"I touched him," Lily continued. "And he felt so real. My God, it's like he was there. He was warm and I could smell his breath." Lily took her tea from Alyona's crooked fingers and blew on it, watching her breath make ripples on its glossy surface. "Then I woke up, but it seemed like he was still there, you know what I mean?"

Alyona glanced sideways at her, pressing her thin lips together. Her russet hair, unmarred by gray and clipped into a Dutch boy, hung heavy at her ruddy cheeks.

"Pasha says Ivanov has that effect on people. At least he doesn't think I'm crazy."

Alyona placed her palm on Lily's forehead as if feeling for a fever. She ran a long, white fingernail down the slope of Lily's nose and tickled the tip, almost playfully.

Lily smiled.

Ivanov had told Lily about Alyona—the woman who would help smuggle them out of Russia. Those who knew

Alyona believed she was a witch, but Ivanov said he knew better. He said she was more a mole than a human being and that witchery of any kind was nonsense. His description had the flavor of one of his many eccentric observations. Much like the way Ivanov believed Pasha Tarkhan was a banyan tree with deep roots and an unending capacity for expansion—at least where his mind was concerned. But the holy man's characterization of Alyona Artemieva as a mole was more literal.

To begin with, she lived underground beneath a flat, grassless wasteland of dense, unfertile soil the color of milk chocolate—its only inviting feature. Her home, a series of subterranean rooms near the border of Russia and Azerbaijan, was laid out like an apartment. What had begun as merely a kidney-shaped hole no bigger than a coffin was now a living room, kitchen with seating area, bedroom, bath and guest quarters. Over a period of years—two, Alyona claimed—she had dug out her five rather spacious rooms with only a garden shovel, spackling the walls with clay and decorating her new home with bright, oriental pillows and surrealist drawings by her younger self. It was no wonder people thought she was a witch.

Lily took Alyona's hand into her lap. "I wrote down the name of the poet he mentioned back at the Lavra. The Persian. He said it again in my dream last night."

Alyona wore a sizeable opal ring on the middle finger of her left hand, and Lily began to twist it the way she would the diamond ring on her mother's hand as she suffered through church Masses as a young girl.

"Mansoor Nassa," Alyona said.

"Yes, yes, that's it."

Lily wondered if perhaps Alyona had talked to Ivanov after all.

"Fedot?" Lily heard Pasha say. She leapt from Alyona's side and scampered into the living room, where Fedot had just lowered himself from the surface. Pasha embraced him like a bear, then took his face in his hands and kissed him wet-lipped on the brow.

"We all made it," Pasha said, removing the cork from a bottle of Alyona's vodka. He passed it first to Lily.

"Of course," Fedot nodded. "The Holy One foresaw as much."

It had been nearly a month since they'd seen Fedot on that day in the Lavra—the day of the massacre. That time had been spent mostly underground, as Lily and Pasha traveled by day hidden within a circus caravan and by night lived with various *zemljanky*—subterranean dwellers like Alyona, who had deserted their city apartments and dug homes for themselves in the countryside. It was, as Alyona described, the only way to escape Russia without leaving it.

"You came just in time, my friend," Pasha said. "The caravan is returning from Derbent the day after tomorrow. From there, they've obtained permission to travel to Baku, then down the coast to Astara."

Fedot took another swig of the vodka, then sat cross-legged on a large pillow quilted from a prayer rug. Alyona peeked in from the kitchen, and Fedot greeted her in Russian. It was an informal greeting—one reserved for friends and family members.

"Perhaps the caravan can get us close to the Armenian border. If we get into Armenia, it's not hard to make the cross from there into Turkey."

Lily scratched her finger along the brushed dirt wall and tried to catch Pasha's eye. "We're inclined to make our way to Tehran," she said, before Pasha could weigh in.

He looked at her with a sharp turn of his head but said nothing.

Fedot leaned against the wall, accepting a bowl of *kufta* with *sangak* bread that had been passed from Alyona to Lily to him. He dipped the bread into the broth and scooped up one of the meatballs.

"Iran is friendly with the Americans," he said. "But that's precisely why it might be harder to enter."

Lily nodded. "Isn't it the Americans we have to see—and the sooner the better?"

"I don't like having the microfilm so long," Pasha said. "It needs to find a home—and fast—before it's dropped into the wrong burrow and we, ourselves, tumble into an unmarked grave."

Fedot removed the brown bottle of Myer aspirin from his pant pocket, holding it up to one of Alyona's oil lamps. "*Spaceships.* Do you honestly believe this is real?" he asked. "And not some sort of propaganda?"

Pasha held out his palm, and Fedot laid the bottle gently in its ample center. "It's real," Pasha said.

Fedot accepted this confirmation. Cradling their steaming bowls in their laps, the three of them ate, for the most part, in silence.

"Loy Henderson is still in Iran, is he not?" Fedot inquired.

Pasha shook his head. "It's a man named Chandler now. A new type of American agent—cynical, factual to a fault. But I've seen him be brilliant as well."

"Agent, you said?" Lily asked. "I thought he was a diplomat."

Pasha put his hand over hers. "My dear—I am a diplomat, too."

"I see," Lily said.

Pasha was a professional liar, as he'd said on more than one occasion. Even if his lies were morally justifiable in a way. He was unequivocal and unapologetic when it came to this fact about himself, and it was in moments like these when Lily wondered how freely Pasha's lies of necessity could flow from his professional to his personal life. It was quite reasonable under the circumstances that he could be making love to her in order to manage her better. What disturbed Lily most of all was that this possibility was even more unwelcome to her than the mortal danger in which she'd found herself.

"It's not that we couldn't work something out with him," Pasha continued. "I just wouldn't be too quick to trust a man like Chandler. Especially without an intermediary of some sort."

"What about Mansoor Nassa in Tehran?" Lily proposed. Pasha squeezed her fingers.

"The poet?" Fedot asked.

"I think so."

Fedot chewed his last meatball, blotting his lips with Alyona's hand-embroidered napkins. "There's only one Mansoor Nassa."

"So, you know him?" Pasha asked.

Fedot shook his head. "I've read him. Why would I know him?"

"Because Ivanov does," Lily said.

Alyona entered the living room again, talking animatedly—her ring-clad fingers whizzing about her head and shoulders like dragonflies. Fedot sat, unmoving, and listened to whatever she was saying. Lily caught none of it—not even a word. Although Russian had begun to ring familiar in her ear, Alyona's dialect was alien—filled with elongated vowels punctuated by a terse staccato of consonants. Not at all the mellifluous parlance spoken by Pasha and Fedot.

"What else did the Holy One say of this man?" Fedot pressed, turning his attention to Lily.

"Where is he?" Lily asked. "Ivanov, I mean."

Fedot shrugged. "He left the Lavra weeks ago and has been staying in his village with his wife."

Lily put her face into her hands, inhaling the sickly sweet smell of tarragon and dried cherries on her fingertips. A mixture Alyona had said was Porphyri Ivanov's favorite, Lily's fingers had smelled of it from the moment she woke up. She'd told no one about that—not even Alyona.

"Ivanov spoke of the poet at the Lavra, and in my dream last night," she said. "Do you think I'm losing my mind?"

"Miss Lily," he said. "You assume what you call your mind was yours to lose in the first place."

Pasha chuckled, cupping his hand over her shoulder.

"It's not funny," she said. "Are we making our plans based on the visits of a ghost of some sort in one of my dreams?"

"He's not a ghost," Fedot said. "A ghost is the spiritual remains of a dead person. Porphyri Ivanov is very much alive."

"And apparently able to infiltrate my subconsious—unless I've gone insane."

Fedot put his bowl of *kufta* down and folded his hands in his lap. "Miss Lily," he said. "What if I were to look you in the eye as I do now and say, yes, foolish woman, I think you're crazy?"

Lily closed her eyes and remembered the way Ivanov had first appeared in her dream, humming "Rum and Coca-Cola." She was sitting with members of the caravan—not the performers or the side-show freaks, but laborers, a group of hard-living Mongols who on most evenings roasted over a large bonfire whatever rodents had wandered across their path—two chinchillas and a squirrel turned over the flames. The Mongols were drinking and whispering amongst themselves, and Pasha was dozing off, his head cushioned by Lily's thigh when the humming trailed off and she heard Ivanov start to giggle. He appeared—characteristically—from behind a tree, beckoning her into a stretch of woods but a few yards from the caravan. She was wearing the long, white dress she'd had on when Tony died on Monemvasia, and it was stained in blood. When she jerked awake, she thought she was still wearing it, but no. Lily had been naked and wrapped around Pasha like ivy.

"If you were to say I was crazy?" she said. "Fedot, I would be relieved."

Pasha laughed, stroking her hair, and Fedot drank the remaining broth in his bowl. Lily put her bowl aside and pulled her knees close to her chest, resting her chin upon them.

"I guess it's settled then," she said. "We go to Tehran, where we will meet with the Holy One's poet, as he prescribed."

"In the absence of any other concrete ideas," Pasha said. "To have God pointing us in the right direction seems as good a plan as any."

Lily sat up straight, tucking her toes beneath Pasha's seat cushion. "Ivanov isn't God, exactly."

"No," Pasha granted. He took her feet onto his lap and tugged off the colorful, knitted slippers the Mongols had given them. Lily's toes were cool, and he began to massage them. "But he is the only one of us who seems to be in regular contact with Him. And you, my dear, seem to be

the only one of us Ivanov will speak to directly—dream or
no dream."

Fedot slept as soundlessly as Alyona, his arms at his sides
and his head cradled in a soft, loosely knit sweater. He and
Alyona were sharing her bed of foam rubber and Red Army
blankets—utterly motionless, the both of them.

"It's the sleep of the dead," Pasha chuckled.

Pasha and Lily had made their bed on the floor—under
one of Alyona's drawings. It was ostensibly of a human skel-
eton, but only parts of the skull were recognizable as such.
The rest of the image appeared both cubed and melted at
various points. Lily reached up and traced her finger along
a sinuous ribbon that may have been a spine.

"I wonder what she calls this one?" she asked.

"The lovers."

"Nice." Lily's face broke into a smile. "If this is what she
thought of her love life, it's no wonder she dug a hole in the
ground and stayed there."

Pasha ran his fingers through Lily's hair, still damp from
their bath in a nearby stream. The water had been chilly
but clean, and the smell of moss still hung about them like
a day-old sprinkle of fine men's cologne.

"It's not one of her old drawings," Pasha explained. "She
sketched it last week when she went mushroom-picking,
and I believe it's meant to depict you and me."

Lily turned toward Pasha and pushed herself up, leaning
on her elbow. "Are you kidding me?"

"After all this time," Pasha chided. "You still don't understand Russians."

He took her face in his hands and kissed her nose and

her lips. "Bones don't merely convey the end of life; they are our very foundation. Without them we would be a quivering blob—easily scraped up, leaving only a stain where we once stood."

Lily turned back to the drawing and shook her head. "You're right," she said. "I don't understand Russians."

Pasha's expression sobered. He looked at her for a long time, reading the *story within her eyes,* as he would say. It was the type of penetrating gaze that Lily had worked hard all her life to avoid, yet it didn't make her uneasy when Pasha did it. She wondered if he detected within her the remorseless drive that she had only recently begun to acknowledge. The drive Lily's subconscious mind—and she had always denied there was such a thing—had tried to keep sated with a steady diet of debauched affairs, glamorous languages and expensive trinkets. She'd even endeavored to tame it by dropping out of school and becoming engaged to Richard Putnam. Lily supposed Pasha was the realization of that kind of drive. She stared back at him, trying to imagine if she, too, could have tortured a man like Ivanov or killed one of her lovers like Pasha killed Brenda "Brandy" France, as the newspapers had taken to calling her.

"I'm a wreck, Pasha," she said.

He ran his finger along her jawline and over her chin, resting it in a tiny, barely observable dimple. "You are a work of art," he said.

When he said things like that, she believed him.

"Maybe I'm just a piece of work."

"That, too," he whispered. "But a fine piece of work at that."

Lily nestled her face into the crook between Pasha's chin and shoulder, wrapping her arms around him. Pasha's injuries and their subsequent flight from Moscow had stripped him of his extra girth. No longer did he carry with him the luxuriant fare offered at the homes of public officials, embassies and posh restaurants. This change from diplomat to fugitive was equally present in his face, where his weight loss brought into relief a series of deep lines around his eyes and mouth. Somehow, this new hardness of features made Pasha more appealing. It lured attention away from his heavy brow and to his eyes, which had softened since Lily had first met him at the Hotel Rude. The story within his eyes now conveyed who he once was—the boy, the brother, the son—as well as the long, burning chronicle of the man he'd become. Lily placed her hand on his cheek—warm and freshly shaven.

"Pasha," she asked. "Have you ever been in love?"

"Of course," he said.

"How many times?"

Lily felt his chest rise and fall in a deep, wistful breath.

"Only twice," he said.

"Twice," she repeated. "I've been in love just once."

CHAPTER 33

SERGEI POSAD

Theron Tassos stood in the center of the Church of St. Sergius refectorium, his arms folded across the breast of his navy silk suit. Indigo, blood-red and gold flickered over his travel clothes. They were technicolor shadows reflecting the lavish spread of Byzantium that covered the walls and ceiling of St. Sergius like honeycomb. Apart from their astonishing beauty, they provided a source of meditation for the troubled Greek, the sorrowful, heavy-lidded eyes of Mary hypnotizing him in particular. He could imagine them as his wife's eyes, were she to ever learn of the danger their daughter had stumbled into.

"Lilia," he whispered.

Life was full of tragic coincidences, and he'd seen his share. They were often, when one looked at the string of events leading up to them, seemingly inevitable. But the Greek was truly at a loss when it came to deciphering how his daughter had gone from vacationing on Monemvasia to being the target of a rogue assassin at the seat of the Russian Orthodox Church. It was by God's grace, Theron decided, that his brother, Baru, had enlisted his help in getting revenge for the murder of Etor. Had Etor not been sacrificed, the Greek would have never had any reason to seek out the Hungarian killer. He may have never even heard the Hungarian's name until his own Lily had been found—perhaps hanging from a drainpipe like Etor—and Baru's revenge would be his own. Yes, Etor might have been vain and idle during his life, but his death might redeem him after all, Theron reasoned.

No longer was the Hungarian exclusively a favor for an estranged brother. Until Lily was safe and back in her mother's arms, wiping Beryx Gulyas from the face of the Earth was the Greek's most supreme priority.

But capturing Gulyas and locating Lily were proving more difficult than Theron had expected. By the time he had been able to establish a chain of events and get word to Alyona Artemieva's place, the Russians had gone, taking his sweet Lily with them. Theron didn't like doing business in that part of the world—even if necessity mandated it. Telephones—when there were any—didn't work well and were monitored by all manner of official and unofficial eavesdroppers, including men of his own. And the hand-to-hand network of any proper organization that worked like a well-oiled machine from metropolitan area to village began to break down as one headed into the badlands. These were places dug with the homes of disaffected individuals—like Alyona—and littered with drunken bands of career hobos. They were, when judged by land mass alone, what constituted most of the Soviet Empire. And once you entered their kingdom of despair and squalor, it was easy to lose your way and never return.

"Brother," the slender monk, Albert, beseeched him, presenting a cup of steaming black tea sweetened just to his liking. Albert had news of Lily, though nothing concrete. She and the Russians had passed through Astara some days before. The caravan they had been traveling with had moved up to Yardymli without them, leaving them at the border of Iran—it was assumed. Alyona alleged that Lily and the Russians wanted to go to Tehran. They had business there with the Americans, but about what she didn't know. And Lily, specifically, had insisted they go, Alyona said. There was someone she wanted to see.

"But *who*, in God's name," Theron wondered. Tehran wasn't exactly the kind of place where Lily would cultivate friends.

"He would cut the throat of the orange blossom; reckless act of hatred, enemy of delight." Porphyri Ivanov stood at the entryway, his lips pressed gently into a smile.

"It's not the best translation, of course." Theron bowed to the holy man. "It assumes the cutting of the orange blossom was the act of hatred—and I've never read Nassa that way."

Ivanov opened his arms wide, as if he was going to embrace Theron Tassos, but he never did. "The cutting of any vine is an act of hatred," he said. "I think the translation, though somewhat artless, is all too accurate."

Brother Albert knelt at a fresco of the Crucifixion before backing out of the refectorium. Ivanov bid him a happy day, weaving his fingertips through a beam of sunlight streaming in from a slotted window.

"Why would my daughter want to go to Tehran?" Theron inquired.

Ivanov took a deep breath, scratching his white beard.

"And what do you know of this?" Theron removed a bundle of singed papers from his breast pocket. They were crinkled, missing several pages and smelled of a campfire. Ivanov flipped through them as if they were pages in a coloring book.

"This is of no interest to me," he said.

"You know what they say, don't you?"

Ivanov nodded.

"Assuming these are authentic, your government is building a spaceship."

"Not my government," Ivanov said. "I have no governor."

Theron Tassos folded his hands. "But you can at least

acknowledge the importance of such a plan—if it is, indeed, true."

Ivanov smiled.

"And you can understand that if these plans have anything to do with my daughter—that she's probably being hunted by the Soviet regime as well as this Hungarian psychopath."

Ivanov shrugged and nodded.

"That's all?" Theron persisted. "My daughter comes here unannounced, stays for weeks on end and no one bothers to contact me, to tell me—and this"—Theron mimed Ivanov's shrug--"is all you have to offer?"

Ivanov took the Greek's hand and held it. "Miss Lily is on a path that has already been charted," he said. "It is one she has chosen and one she must finish. And I will help her in any way I can."

The Greek's silk lapel moved up and down like a tortoise shell as he heaved an enormous breath.

"You can help her?" Theron said. "I don't even know if I can help her."

Ivanov leaned in and touched the Greek nose to nose. "You, I'm afraid, have no power to help her."

The Greek backed away from Ivanov and extracted his hand from the holy man's grip.

"You know, Ivanov," he said. "I can't figure out if you're the damned fool or I am. But either way, I'm going to Tehran and you're coming with me."

Ivanov turned on his toe and walked toward the door, kneeling at the same fresco Brother Albert had honored. "I'm not needed in Tehran," he averred. "And neither are you."

FALL, 1956

CHAPTER 34

TEHRAN, IRAN

The poet Mansoor Nassa lived in a brick family house much too large for a single man. The house rested on a quiet, unlit street that was still host to a small procession of outdated horse-drawn carriages called doroshkehs. Though the horses were often emaciated and abused by their impoverished drivers, Nassa preferred the doroshkehs to the taxis and buses that now saturated the streets of Iran's most populated city. It wasn't at all that Nassa disliked modernization—he liked most of the comforts being imported by the Shah's regime. It was in this one instance and one instance only that Nassa—a modernist, a lover of all the virtues of the imagination, a disciple of both HG Wells and Orwell—clung to the past. Mansoor Nassa's grandfather had been a doroshkeh driver, and the poet felt a kinship with the men who made their living by them. He simply couldn't bring himself to take a taxi any other way.

But that didn't mean he ever enjoyed the ride.

Prone to motion sickness, Nassa typically spent the entire distance swallowing his nausea as the weakling horse yanked the carriage to and fro while the driver whipped the creature bloody. Every time Nassa swore he'd never take another. But then, as soon as he left his house, there they were. Like a bad woman, he couldn't resist them.

Mansoor Nassa thanked Jalal, his customary driver, in his native Farsi and stepped down from the wooden cart, pressing a rial into the man's hand. Such was their ritual. The toothless imp, only forty-four years of age, grunted and steered away. Jalal would pretend to go off to fetch other passengers, but Nassa knew he would turn around at the end of the street and be waiting all night, if necessary, to take the poet wherever he needed to go.

"Good evening," Lily Tassos bid him in Arabic. Nassa turned toward her silhouette. The moon, plump and nearly full, cast enough light to expose her beauty, and for a moment Nassa felt unable to move.

"Can I help you?" he inquired.

"Most certainly," she said. "May we come in?"

Nassa put his hands in his pockets and stepped toward his front door. "We?"

Pasha and Fedot stepped into view.

"We were told to come here," she said.

"By whom?" Nassa asked.

"By Porphyri Ivanov," she said.

Nassa scratched his head. "I don't know anyone of that name," he told her.

"He said we should see you," she persisted.

Nassa watched her lips closely as she spoke, cocking his head and breathing through his nostrils. "My God," he said in English, quite suddenly delighted. "Are you American?"

Lily smiled.

The walls of Mansoor Nassa's house were of whitewashed plaster and rose to a high ceiling. Painted silk taffeta and Persian rugs—their *kermans* in crimson and gold and central medallions in emerald and cerulean—were splashed over the floors and walls, while English antiques had been arranged to create separate stations in the mainly open floor plan. A Star of David, imprinted into the ceiling plaster, reigned over the room as surely as the sun did the sky.

The impeccable trappings were at odds with the cobwebs that dotted the ceiling and the undisturbed layer of dust that coated the once highly polished furnishings. Nassa's mother, who had died in her sleep some months before, had made them her obsession. She'd been a servant, after all, until her son had done so well for himself, and the house ached of loneliness without her.

"Please," he said, offering them a seat on a plush rug his mother had woven.

Although it was late—well after ten in the evening when he returned from a production of *Tartuffe*—Nassa insisted on their sharing a meal. He got his servant, Goli, out of bed and asked her to prepare a supper of fish and yogurt, pomegranates, tangerines and sweet lemons. Most Iranians ate on the floor around a *sofreh* cloth, but Nassa insisted that when the time came, they would be sitting at a table using utensils.

"Boris Karloff is the greatest actor of all time," Nassa asserted, twice over the blaring music. He played Persian *setar* and *kamancheh* records so loud that they had to repeat everything they said at least once.

"*Frankenstein*, yes," Lily agreed. "Great movie."

Pasha and Fedot nodded.

"And *Dracula*," Nassa chimed, drawing his hand in as if he were Bela Legosi. "Sublime. But nothing can defeat *Nosferatu*." He closed his eyes and sucked in, pursing his lips. "Chilling."

Pasha glanced at Lily. She had sat through dozens of such negotiations with her father. And while her father was a Greek and Mansoor Nassa a Persian, the tell-tale social cues were there. This was a culture that never got right down to business. As eager as Mansoor Nassa was to know what an American girl and two Russians were doing lurking outside his house this late, and as much as they wanted to tell him, it would've been unthinkable not to share some food first and talk. So, horror movies it was.

"My personal favorite," Pasha intoned. "Is *Dr. Jekyll and Mr. Hyde*. But not the Spenser Tracy version."

Mansoor Nassa smiled wide and embarked on a lengthy monologue about the sins and virtues of the 1931 and 1941 films.

Finally, well after midnight, they adjourned to the poet's garden. It was a walled-in, with an oval pool surrounded by red—and only red—roses. And there were hundreds of them, making the lush garden a direct counterpart to the horrid summer heat that had left the city parched and peppered with a thin coat of powder the color of ashes. Lily, by this time, was starving—as Goli had returned to bed after fetching them some watermelon juice and the promised meal had never materialized. As far as servants were concerned, Goli was next to useless, Nassa explained. But she had been a dear friend of his mother's and was like family to him.

"You know, when I first saw you—for a moment I feared for my life," the poet said, appraising Lily from head to foot. "I wondered if I had done or said anything to draw the attention of the Shah's police." He bit his bottom lip and narrowed his eyes as if reading tiny print. "I could think of nothing. Then, I said to myself, 'Why would the police send a woman? And one speaking Arabic, no less? No one of any character or national pride speaks Arabic in Iran. Especially not an agent of the Shah.'"

Pasha began to laugh, and Nassa joined in. Lily knew they understood the nature of a police state in a way she never would.

"I didn't mean to frighten you," Lily explained.

Nassa shrugged.

"So, Ivanhoe, you said." The poet raised his finger in the air. "Like the novel."

Lily started at the beginning, more or less, telling him about meeting Ivanov and later escaping from the Lavra. She then explained his suggestion that they come to Tehran and pay a visit to the poet Mansoor Nassa.

Nassa, for his part, listened intently. His eyes were wide, engaged—almost excited. When Lily finished, the poet sat, thinking, his chin balanced on his knuckles.

"Mr. Nassa," Lily said softly. "We're not quite sure why we're here, but we do need to get to the American Embassy somehow, and that may be a little bit difficult. Because, you see, we've been followed."

"To my house?" the poet inquired.

"No," Lily assured him. "But to Iran, and here, to this city."

"And we're quite sure our stalker knows we intend to contact the American government," Pasha added. "The Embassy, I fear, will be surrounded by all sorts of surreptitious characters by now."

Nassa paced for a few moments around his oval pool, staring at its surface until his reflection came into relief. He squatted down and pricked the water with his finger, watching his image ripple into an abstraction.

"It's very simple," he said. "Assuming they truly don't know where you are."

Nassa explained that the weekend was to usher in the crippling heat again, as the weather teetered between summer and fall. Anyone with any means would be fleeing to their mountain retreats—including, for instance, the British ambassador.

"So you know Ambassador Pearce?" Pasha inquired.

"Know him?" Nassa said. "I'm his weekend landlord. And I can tell you this—he and that American fellow— you know, the ambassador; they call him Sandy."

"Ambassador Chandler?" Pasha said, smiling.

"That's right! The three of us have had quite a game of cards going."

CHAPTER 35

KANDOVAN, IRAN

"They're like modern cave-men!" Rodki Semyonov marveled as General Pushkin's single-engine plane glided low over Kandovan, giving him a close look at the hundreds of medieval dwellings—carved out of rock and looking like beehives—that swarmed the rough, volcanic terrain of the East Azerbaijan Province of Iran. Rodki even forgot the discomfort he felt inside the General's favorite toy as he eyed the remote village. He was charmed by its otherness, its ancient beauty and the comic indifference to it all of Kandovan's inhabitants—men wrapped in colorful cloth resembling the desert sunset and women in plain, head-to-toe Muslim garb.

Rodki, who had never flown until early that morning, found it ironic that he detested flying. Especially since his main objection had nothing to do with fear of crashing, but of the intense claustrophobia he experienced sitting for so long in such a confined space. He knew the Great Leader, Josef Stalin, would have found that funny, too, were he still alive, since it was he who had so ruthlessly enforced Rodki's Moscow strictures in the first place. And contrary to what many people thought of the Great Leader—particularly those he had sentenced to death without more cause than seeing their name written on a page—Stalin had a demonstrative sense of humor complete with a boisterous laugh and quick wit.

Rodki missed his company sometimes. General Pushkin, though far more reasonable in his countenance, seemed to find very little to amuse him in the world. Except for his airplane, of course, and the on-command pilot that came with it. *Tedious man,* Rodki thought. Though it was true that without him The Great Detective would never have had the opportunity to see the Lavra, except from a photograph; or Moscow from above; or the cottony threads of cirrus clouds at close range; least of all the jagged stone dwellings of a centuries-old village in Persia. Take-off and landing were a thrill, he had to admit, as the plane skipped and skidded to a halt on a little-known Soviet-operated runway just over the border in Iran.

"How long to Tehran?" Rodki asked the pilot. An empty, idling bus—presumably for him—waited on a dirt road that intersected with the runway.

"I don't know," the pilot replied. "Hours, probably."

The distances were what most amazed Rodki. He had known the world was vast, but seeing an estimation of miles on an atlas and actually traveling those miles was entirely different. Where once he'd been but a single flower in a greenhouse, he was now a microbe in a forest.

"Your map," the pilot said, handing Rodki a folded square of thin paper, frayed at the edges.

"You're joking," Rodki told him. "The General must have told you I don't drive."

The pilot sniffed and cursed. He stormed out of the cockpit and jumped out of the plane, motioning for Rodki to follow him to the bus. Once there, he showed The Great Detective how to start and turn off the ignition, shift the gears and work the pedals.

"Not so hard for a man like you, eh?" The pilot said, unraveling a cigarette and stuffing the tobacco in his mouth. "General's waiting back in Moscow. General doesn't like to wait."

Rodki watched—incredulous—as the pilot strode off the bus and back to General Pushkin's plane. He taxied briefly on the runway before picking up speed and taking off to the north, the way they'd come.

It was nearly midnight when Rodki Semyonov arrived at the gates of the Shah's palace in Tehran. The bus jerked and heaved as Rodki shifted gears inelegantly. The open roads of the countryside had been relatively easy to handle—even for a first-time driver like himself. But once Rodki hit the city, with its starts and stops and indecipherable traffic rules—even for a man with his deductive and inductive skills—it all went to hell. He'd run over a man on a bicycle, gnarled the front end of the bus with two significant collisions, and scraped deep gashes into the sides of the vehicle on a turn he made going, perhaps, a bit too fast. *Doesn't matter,* Rodki thought. He parked the bus in the middle of the street a few yards away from the palace and abandoned it. He much preferred public transportation, and it seemed to be aplenty in Tehran.

"Good evening." A manservant bowed to Rodki before showing him the way into the palace. "Your bag is being delivered to the Faberge suite, where General Pushkin stayed the last time he visited."

"I'm sure he felt right at home," the Great Detective remarked. He was drenched in sweat and embarrassed by his own pungency. In Moscow, his body odor would have blended in, more or less, but here, in this cool, marble corridor smelling of Persian buttercups, he stunk like an animal.

"Is that lamb cooking?" Rodki asked.

"Yes, of course, sir," the servant replied. "Dinner is waiting for you."

The Great Detective explained there was no need for a full dinner. Some meat would be good, as he was hungry after his journey, but nothing fancy for him, please. It was late, after all.

"But you're not the only guest who arrived late, you see," the servant explained. "It's common for guests to come late to the palace. And the Shah insists that a guest must eat."

The servant and the Great Detective entered the glittering dining room, its walls studded with thousands of gold and platinum mosaic tiles. A gold and crystal chandelier the size of a small bedroom dangled from the ceiling, hovering above an antique French dining table that seated twenty. Seven of the chairs were occupied: one by the Shah, another by his wife—as bejeweled herself as the chandelier—another by the American ambassador—a man named Chandler—and two more by his aides. The Shah's secretary sat next to the ambassador, and next to him was another man—one the Great Detective had definitely met before. He was dressed in a bespoke featherweight suit of pearl gray raw silk and looked up at Rodki, continuing to stare as the servant guided the Great Detective to the empty chair next to him.

Rodki nodded.

The Shah stood, guiding his wife up from her chair, as the rest of the visitors followed suit. The Great Detective bowed deeply to the Iranian monarch, thanking him for his hospitality, and was subtly ignored. The Shah's wife smiled warmly at Rodki, however, and continued to smile as the Shah welcomed his guests, reciting "The Road Not Taken" by Robert Frost. His Highness then illuminated the midnight diners about the seventeen-course meal they were about to share—its origins, the names of the dishes in both Farsi and English (though not Russian), and the studies and travels of his personal chef. As this was a casual occasion, there was little pomp and circumstance, he explained. *Apart from the usual standing, sitting and compulsory obsequiousness,* Rodki thought to himself. In this way, how little difference there was between a Shah's palace and the Politburo.

"Brother," Rodki said to the man in silk. "I've only come from a long drive, but I feel like I've gone six rounds with a brute double my size." The Great Detective took a deep gulp of water from the delicate crystal glass set in front of him. "Having never traveled before," he continued, "I'm afraid I had no imagination for the way this kind of heat would feel under a wool suit. Of course, it's my only suit apart from my bathing suit, and I hardly could've come here in that." The Great Detective laughed, but the man in the silk suit did not. "And I had no idea the Shah himself would be here. I thought he was on a diplomatic mission! Tell me, you seem to be quite comfortable around these good people, does His Excellency talk much?"

"You like to talk, Mr. Semyonov, but you never really say anything, do you?" the man in silk said. "I suppose that's the tactic of a great detective. At least that's what they say about you. That you are great."

Rodki Semyonov shrugged and smiled. "By *they* do you mean the other monks at the Lavra?" He patted the man's padded shoulders and leaned in to examine the delicate stitching on his lapel.

"I must say," Rodki said. "Your current ensemble suits you much better than the monk's robe you wore when we first met. Your suit, if I may say—*suits* you as if it were a second skin."

The man in silk ran his fingers through his thick, salt-and-pepper hair. A quail's egg, floating in its half shell, was placed before them on gold-trimmed china. The server dipped a miniature mother-of-pearl spoon into an iced, silver bowl and applied a coif of caviar to the tiny yolk.

"By *they*, Mr. Semyonov, I mean Ambassador Chandler, and our distinguished host and hostess, *Shahanshah,* the King of Kings, Mohammed Reza Shah Pahlavi and his wife, the *Shahbanu.*"

Ambassador Chandler nodded his greeting—affable, business-like, while the Shah appraised the Great Detective disdainfully. It could have been Rodki's disheveled appearance that offended him, or simply his being Russian. The Shah was now good friends with the Americans and may have wanted to make a show of disapproval over his Soviet visitor. Or perhaps it was the man in silk he wished to impress—a man whom Rodki was willing to bet was selling the Persian ruler his weaponry.

Rodki slurped down his quail's egg, licking a tiny cluster of caviar from his upper lip. "And what would these distinguished gentlemen say of you, brother?"

The man in silk leaned forward. His breath was nearly odorless and his movements as strong as they were measured.

"They say I'm a ruthless bastard, Mr. Great Detective. And one who wants his fucking daughter back."

The Shah put his cutlery down, and Ambassador Chandler folded his arms.

"Great Caesar's ghost," Rodki heard the American ambassador grumble. "Is that really *the* Great Detective?"

"Ah, your daughter," the Great Detective said, pulling

Lily's passport out of his breast pocket. "I'd like to talk to her myself, but I have a feeling someone will have beaten us to it."

CHAPTER 36

TEHRAN, IRAN

"This is the largest market of its kind in the world," Mansoor Nassa boasted as he and Lily bumped and pressed their way through the Southern foyer of the Grand Bazaar. It was sweltering—even at nine in the morning—and made worse by the crowds that packed each corridor of the market's ten-kilometer spread. The heavy linen tunic Lily wore, disguising her as a maidservant, was already soggy with perspiration, as was her head scarf. She felt like a wet kitchen rag.

It was hard to believe—as Nassa insisted—that this was the least congested time in the day to do their shopping. By noon, the poet contended, the market would be swarming with five times as many shoppers, and it would be difficult to move from one corridor to the next.

The poet assured them it was indeed the least conspicuous time for them to attend to household business as well. Not a soul in Tehran would expect a man of Nassa's stature to be attending to his own needs, especially at this time in the morning—a time for sipping tea and reading the newspaper. Perhaps enjoying a neighborhood stroll before the sun became burdensome. Only servants were hustled out of their bedrooms this early, charged with not disappointing their masters with later-day goods that had been picked through.

"Pomegranate syrup, quince, rice, saffron, dried limes, cinnamon, a new copper serving tray." Nassa read his list aloud, as if inviting commentary—*No, no—not cinnamon.*

I'm sure the ambassador would prefer cloves! Lily had told him she couldn't boil water. Still, he was insisting on her input as he and Goli, his servant, burrowed their way through the dense throngs of buyers, sellers, and seekers. Lily scampered behind them, pointing out various spice vendors and coppersmiths who called out to her in any number of languages. She went largely ignored, as Nassa and Goli knew exactly which vendors offered the finest fare for the best prices—as far as they were concerned. They plotted their course through the maze of dripping gold, foodstuffs and dazzling textiles that covered every square inch of the market—except for the high, arched ceiling and its crumbling mosaic tiles.

"*Kann ich ihnen helfen?*" a stout man with vivid green eyes inquired in stilted German. He beheld a gleaming copper bowl filled with an iridescent yellow powder he had labeled as turmeric.

"*Nein danke,*" Lily replied. But the man wouldn't leave her alone—offering her a cup of tea and maintaining that he had the most premium spices in the market.

"*Deluxe,*" he said. "*Die meisten ausgezeichnet.*"

"I'm sure you have," Lily told him. "But I have to go." Lily had never enjoyed haggling. She was an American shopper tried and true, who loved the comforts of a nice grocery store, a pretty boutique, a cosmetics counter—and not all crammed into essentially the same space and smelling of incense and animal blood.

"*Bitte, bitte,*" the spice vendor entreated, stirring the golden seasoning with the tip of his index finger. Goli and Nassa were a few steps ahead of Lily now and would soon disappear from her vision, swallowed by the horde and the stratigraphic layers of merchandise.

Lily wished Pasha had come with them, but everyone

agreed it was best he keep as low a profile as possible, especially now that they were in a city. He hadn't wanted her to go at all, calling her silly and reckless, but she was desperate to walk, to be among people and do her best thinking. Pasha's protestations, however noble in their intention and perhaps sensible in their reasoning, would not move her.

"Quickly, okay? *Schnell*," she said.

The vendor nodded and made an attempt at a smile, but the gesture seemed forced, a misanthrope's attempt at levity in a dreaded social milieu. He dug his fingers—plump like breakfast sausages—into the bowl of shimmering powder and cradled a tablespoon of the substance in his hand. Lily bent down to smell its aroma, as the vendor insisted, but could detect no scent at all. She shook her head and bent down farther as the vendor pressed his thin lips together—this time into what was probably the closest thing to a smile that he could manage. He flattened his palm, blowing the weightless powder into Lily's face. Lily drew a sharp breath—but before she could cough or try to expel the tiny, yellow granules from her nose, the market went black, like a movie screen. Lily closed and opened her eyes in a useless effort. Inside her eardrums came a high-pitched scream—*mimi-mimi-mimi-mimi*—compelling Lily to drop to her knees and lie down on the filthy market floor. She would remember nothing else of that day, or the day after, or the day after that—even if Beryx Gulyas would insist to her that she was quite conscious the whole time.

CHAPTER 37

Theron Tassos welcomed Fedot into the hotel lobby and locked the door behind him. It was his hotel, one of many, and perfectly nondescript. Theron preferred using hotels, where an influx of various people—or not at all— went largely unnoticed. Today, his hotel stood empty, except for his manager who smoked languorously at the front desk as he peeled through a weeks-old *Tehran Daily*.

"I came as soon as I could," Fedot explained.

"No, Fedot," Theron countered. "As soon as you could would have been the moment you met my daughter in Moscow. I'm the one who had to find you—here, in Persia."

Fedot appeared unfazed by his castigation. "I've been hunting the Hungarian, as you instructed," he said.

"Unsuccessfully."

"Yes."

It was a delicate business with men like Fedot, and Theron Tassos knew it. Unlike the other men in his employ, Fedot worked for no money—only for the belief that he was doing the work Divine Providence had apportioned for him. This made what should have been a normal boss-underling relationship somewhat complicated. Especially since Theron Tassos was not used to being a middle manager whose commands could be overridden—even if by a deity, or a deity's direct report.

"I met a very interesting man, recently," the Greek baron said. He took a photograph out of his breast pocket, displaying it on his palm. It was of a police officer—bulky man, ugly face—staring forward, unsmiling, as was the custom for any official photograph in the Soviet Union. "Do you know him?"

Fedot shook his head. But he'd seen him once—at the Hotel Rude.

"He has a unique job description, unlike any I've ever known," Theron said.

Fedot took the photo and tucked it into his trousers. "You would like me to kill him or follow him?" Fedot asked.

"Follow him—though he in all likelihood has been following you already. Doesn't matter. He'll lead you to wherever that Hungarian took Lily."

"Assuming it was the Hungarian, of course," Fedot said.

"You have any doubts?"

"No."

Theron Tassos smirked. He was a hard man, but behind his eyes—past their animal curiosity and pitilessness—there was a swell of fear that he was using every bit of strength in his being to suppress. Children—especially daughters—were a weakness for a man like him.

"When he leads you to Lily, then kill him," the Greek commanded. "And the other Russian, too—Tarkhan."

Fedot looked away from Theron Tassos's eyes and slipped his hand into his canvas bag. He stroked the crucifix Ivanov had fashioned from birch branches, scratching some of the charred pieces of bark with his thumbnail.

"And what about the film?" he said.

"The what?"

"The microfilm," he said.

Theron narrowed his eyes and sat down on a white lambskin chair.

"Tarkhan stole it—images of it, anyway," Fedot illuminated. "They're plans of a spaceship. He thinks it will be done in a year or two and that the Americans are far behind on their own plans."

The Greek folded his arms across his chest. "Geiger knew, didn't he? About this spaceship."

Fedot nodded. He gripped the crucifix in his palm, removing it from the bag and holding it flat against his belly.

"Do you have the film?" the Greek asked.

Fedot shook his head. "I could get it."

"Yes, get it," he said. "And get that damned Russian, too."

Theron Tassos lowered his voice into a hiss. One seething with hatred—of the Hungarian, of the men in Lily's life, of the unfamiliar helplessness he was feeling.

"Rip him to shreds for getting Lily caught up in this mess."

CHAPTER 38

"Wine?" It was terrible, of course, not that Beryx Gulyas knew anything about wine. But he did know this wine was terrible. It would take a rube not to know that, and Gulyas had worked hard to shed his peasant tastes.

He held the goblet up to Lily's swollen lips and poured the wine into her mouth, massaging her throat as if he were force-feeding a goose. She winced. Even with her eyes ringed in purple bruises, she looked beautiful, and her torso, sadly, was still too sore to allow her to get up for a short dance. He'd longed to dance with her since the end of their first day together, but by then he already knew she wouldn't be getting up for some time. It was a good thing he hadn't marred her body very much. Gulyas knew how to inflict pain without the resulting unsightliness, but until Lily Tassos had come into his life, there had never been any point in keeping a would-be corpse in tip-top shape. A disfigured body, Gulyas believed, made a good statement in most cases. It let people know who they were dealing with.

"Careful," he said. The wine had gone down the wrong pipe, and Lily began to cough. She moaned as he turned her onto her side and patted her back.

Normally, Gulyas wasn't the soft velvet and scented oils type of man. He liked an earthier woman. It was why he had dismissed Lily at first—spoiled little rich girl who got in over her head, he thought.

But what a surprise!

Though the effects from the Muralti powder were temporary—lasting no more than a few hours—the nature of being suddenly blinded, then tortured was enough to make even the most hard-boiled crumble. Not so Lily Tassos. She screamed and cried at first like any woman, like most men for that matter. But only a short time into their encounter something changed. Her breathing slowed, and she began to nod, as if she were in a dream. She did this for some time, and Gulyas watched her out of curiosity. Then all of a sudden she smiled a light, guileless smile—like a child—and said, "Thank you, Holy One."

"You're welcome," Gulyas said. And he meant it.

From that point on, things were different between them. He tortured her carefully, bringing her to points of unbearable pain—yet he knew she would endure, saying nothing about the *Sputnik* or her Russian friends no matter how many times he asked her, no matter how many ways. Lily was in a different place now, a place where pain and uncertainty meant little. Gulyas touched her lips, and she started to sing again, this time a Greek hymn, then she talked about the trees in the Lavra.

"They were very nice trees," he said. It was true. He couldn't help but notice them even if he'd had other things on his mind at the time.

Gulyas removed a midnight blue scarf from his back pocket. It had belonged to his Aunt Zuzanna, and he'd taken it some time ago after losing the monogrammed handkerchief his wife had given him as a wedding present. Gently, he lifted Lily's head and tied the scarf around her eyes, making the knot good and tense.

"Porcia Catonis was Marcus Brutus's second wife," Gulyas said. "The one who killed herself by swallowing hot coals." He took Lily's jaw in his hands and pried it wide open, placing a wooden block between her teeth. "I always admired her fortitude."

Lily resisted, of course, but he'd tied her wrists behind her back and secured them to her ankles, binding them with a kind of slipknot that pulled her hands and feet closer together as she struggled. The more she moved, the more unnatural the position became, and the more agonizing. He enjoyed her struggle—although not because it gave her pain. He enjoyed it precisely because she was able suffer the pain. It was yet another attribute they shared.

Gulyas reached over to the dying Bunsen burner at his side and removed a dish from its frame. It was filled with a pharmacological capsaicin mixture and bubbled the way he imagined lava might bubble inside a volcano on the brink of erupting. An active component of the chili pepper, the capsaicin would certainly feel like hot coals.

"This shouldn't take too long," he said.

Slowly, Gulyas poured the mixture down Lily's throat. She gasped and coughed as the capsaicin foamed in her mouth, but finally, she was forced to swallow. It was either that or drown.

"There we go," he murmured.

In most cases, Gulyas found mock executions to be an extremely effective method of psychological torture. The capsaicin provided the added benefit of physical anguish as well.

But Lily, as he'd come to expect, was not most cases. She rolled onto her side, her wrists and ankles pulling closer together. Her eyes were tearing heavily and she was wheezing, but she'd suffered her fear and discomfort very well. There was almost a sense of serenity to her countenance.

The Hungarian took a sip of his wine and blotted Lily's forehead with a cool, damp cloth he dipped frequently in a tin of rosewater. He heaved a breath, admiring the strong slope of her nose and the elegant line of her jawbone. She whispered something, but Beryx Gulyas couldn't hear it. He bent down, putting his ear to her lips. "Love, did you say? Yes, love."

Lily Tassos had been changed by love, he mused to himself. *His love.* And Beryx Gulyas had waited all his life for someone like her. The funny thing was . . . she wasn't even Hungarian.

"What was that?" he asked her. She endeavored to speak again, this time meeting his eyes with an intensity that surprised him, given her general condition. With the burns from the capsaisin, she was difficult to understand, but he was pretty sure she'd said *love you.*

But this time Gulyas was wrong.

Lily had, in fact, said, "Fuck you."

CHAPTER 39

Pasha felt as if he was going to crawl out of his own skin. Lily had been gone for more than two days, and he feared the worst for her. A marked man, absent his usual channels and back-ups, he felt powerless to help her and frantic to remedy the situation.

"*Bolván!*" Pasha smacked his palm to his forehead. He hated himself for having caved in to her demand to go with Nassa to the market. It had seemed at the time that she would simply not take no for an answer, but why, he wondered, hadn't he forced her to stay? She was certainly no match for him physically. And since when did he take his orders from a woman? *Since you met Lily Tassos, it would appear,* an inner voice told him. *Since, for the first time in nearly twenty years, you put a woman's interests ahead of your own.* He had long forgotten how such a simple action—so natural to a young groom, or a new mother—began to forge a bond that is increasingly difficult to break. And how easy it was to make a habit of such a dangerous endeavor.

In addition to this disturbing storm of emotions, he was beginning to chafe at his increasing dependence on Fedot, especially since his friend had seemed the slightest bit unreliable since they'd reached Tehran. *But no,* he thought. *Unreliable was too strong a word . . . unfocused, perhaps.*

"Where have you been?" Pasha demanded as Fedot slid in through the doors of the servant's entrance. "You were gone an awfully long time." He held up the note Fedot had written and placed next to his pillow. It stated quite simply that he had gone out and would return soon.

Fedot smiled, removing a box of Persian pastries from his sack and placing them on the engraved silver coffee table that stood as the centerpiece of Mansoor Nassa's living room.

"Breakfast," he said. "And where is the poet?"

"Out," Pasha told him. "On one of his doroshkeh rides. He wants us to depart for his mountain retreat this afternoon as we planned."

Pasha had lost affinity for Nassa since he'd returned from the market without Lily. How he could have allowed her to fall behind and be abducted was beyond Pasha, but then poets did tend to dwell in the sanctuary of their thoughts far more than most beings. At least they knew it was the Hungarian who had taken Lily. Nassa and his servant had described him definitively, from his doughy form to his striking eyes.

And the fact that the Hunagian had taken her and not killed her meant that she held some value for him—although how much was difficult to say. Pasha knew their only chance to help Lily now was to reach the Americans. He hoped that Chandler fellow knew something or could at least contact Lily's father. If anyone could extract a hostage from a hired assassin, it was Theron Tassos—especially if that hostage was his daughter.

"Ambassador Pearce should already be at Nassa's house," Pasha continued. "An invitation has also been extended to the American ambassador, as I understand it. He certainly won't want to stay in the city with this kind of heat."

Fedot sat down.

"Fedot?"

The Russian shook his head. He picked up a nut-filled

kooloocheh pastry and took a small bite, chewing slowly. "You should go to the Americans," he said.

Pasha Tarkhan squatted down at the coffee table. "Alone?"

"Someone should be here in case we hear word of Miss Lilia," Fedot said, weaving his hands together in his lap. "There's no need for both of us to go, is there?"

Pasha Tarkhan dipped his fingers into one of many small bowls of anise seed that Mansoor Nassa kept around as breath freshener. He pinched some of the seed between his thumb and index fingers and placed them on his tongue, crunching the tiny pods between his molars.

"I suppose not," Pasha said.

"You don't like this idea?" Fedot asked. "I thought you would."

"It's just a change, that's all," Pasha said. His eyes met Fedot's, and he studied the little man. Calm, still as a puddle. "I've never been afraid of change, Fedot, and I sense that neither have you."

Pasha turned away from Fedot and ran his hand over his breast pocket, feeling nothing but the smooth bed of muscle and bone that Lily liked to lay her head upon. Gone were the brown bottle of Myer aspirin and the scroll of microfilm that had left Brandy France lying in a considerable pool of her own blood. Pasha Tarkhan blinked heavily and chuckled. He bent down and slid the metal card, with its symbols and Cyrillic lettering, out of his shoe and ran his finger over the Russian word for tree—дерево.

"When did we meet, Fedot, was it five years ago or six?"

The Russian spiritualist shrugged. He cared little for time.

"You were involved in smuggling then," Pasha recounted. "Religious artifacts for The Patriarch." Pasha rubbed the card between his fingers the way he used to rub his daughters' hair when they were little. "You gave me this card, do you remember? You said it guided you during times of moral dilemma."

Fedot smiled his prim, monastic smile and touched Pasha's forearm. He took another bite of his pastry, washing it down with the sulfurous-tasting mineral water Nassa kept around the house.

"Perhaps we should pray for an answer to our troubles," Fedot offered.

Pasha returned the card to his sole and looked up at his friend. "I'm afraid that's your domain."

Fedot put his pastry down. He stood up from the coffee table and knelt directly under the Star of David embossed onto the ceiling plaster. As he closed his eyes and held his palms up, Pasha Tarkhan walked behind him, placing his giant hands on Fedot's shoulders. The young Russian inhaled deeply, making them rise and fall like a wave. Outside, he could hear the clippety-clap of the poet's doroshkeh cart as it pulled up to the front doors. The horse was antsy, and it brayed. Fedot relaxed, as Pasha dug his fingers deeply into the base of his neck. He anticipated the crack of the doroshkeh driver's whip, and it came as Pasha's mighty hands squeezed tighter, compressing his esophagus and fully impeding Fedot's ability to breathe. The young Russian remained impassive and unmoving, except for gently unfolding his hands.

CHAPTER 40

It was only the light that Lily remembered from those first few hours—or maybe they were days, it was hard to tell. Light that seemed foggy and yellow—blurred shapes, indecipherable. It must have been how an infant viewed the world shortly after birth. Lily wondered, at first, whether she had died and been reborn. Ivanov believed in reincarnation. It was his contention that when a child was born, he remembered everything from his former life, but would slowly forget as he might a vivid dream after being jerked awake.

As her pain swelled and the man she assumed was the Lavra assassin called her Lily—*my Lily, it's breakfast time, Lily—get your strength up, Lily, we have a long day ahead of us*—she knew that she was still inhabiting the same life, the same body. And that revelation made her wish she was dead, even if she had never had a suicidal thought in her life.

Then Ivanov came to sit with her.

He knew a thing or two about torture—Pasha's torture specifically—and held her hand, talking to her about the whispers of God heard only in times of unbearable agony. *A gift. Candy stuffed into your shoe on St. Nicholas Day,* Ivanov sang. *A gift of love.* And God didn't speak to just anyone—but wait—*yes, he did,* Ivanov insisted. Most people just didn't hear him. Lily wasn't sure she heard him, either. But she did hear Ivanov.

"Are you hungry?" The Hungarian had broth for her. All she could stomach was broth. Beryx Gulyas smiled often at her now, but it didn't soften his appearance. *How dare you smile at me?* she wanted to say. But Lily had neither the strength nor the inclination to speak to anyone but Ivanov, or Pasha if he had been there.

Lily missed Pasha—desperately. It was Ivanov's chronicling of the Russian's every move and emotion that kept Lily from going insane. That, and the holy man's assurance that Pasha was looking for her. Spaceship or no spaceship, he would never leave her behind, the Holy One insisted. Any more than she would leave him. She believed Ivanov, even if she couldn't quite figure out what a man like Pasha Tarkhan saw in her—apart from what men usually saw in her.

"I could've been killed on Monemvasia and would've left behind a few ex-friends, an ex-fiancé, and a great wardrobe. Hardly Nobel Prize material," she'd told Pasha one night, as their caravan neared Astara. He'd smiled at her in that way she loved. A smile that told a thousand stories about women he'd cherished and men he'd buried—with his own hands if necessary. It was a smile, she realized, that was not unlike her father's.

"Courage is a muscle you didn't have to develop," Pasha had said, stirring the liver stew the circus Mongols had shared with them. "It's not one I had to develop, either. I knew more gifted men than myself who stayed in Georgia, pretending to be mediocre so that they never had to leave home and never had to make a hard decision."

Lily looked up and away from her reverie. Beryx Gulyas was smiling at her again. He had untied her wrists and ankles for the time being, knowing she hadn't the strength to fight him off. The Hungarian seemed to welcome the prospect of Lily struggling a bit, anyway. It meant he could subdue her. And he seemed to enjoy doing just that—twisting her arms and panting onto her face.

Gulyas was uncouth, and that was what Lily hated most about him. It wasn't lost on her that Richard Putnam's mother—and eventually Richard—had hated her for that same reason. It was why she wasn't good enough for the Putnams of Philadelphia, even if her father could've bought and sold them with the wave of a hand. She wondered if Richard Putnam would even recognize her now if they passed each other on the street. Or Tony Geiger? She decided Tony would. There was a lot about her that made him roll his eyes, but there was one thing Lily was sure of now. Tony had known she was capable of making hard decisions. It was something in her blood, and she couldn't shake it no matter how much jewelry and how many bad parties lay between her and men like Tony. Pasha knew that, too.

"Now look at us," Lily had told Pasha. "Hard decisions are leading us to Persia, being chased by some goon."

"Beryx Gulyas is no goon, and we'll do best to remember that," Pasha cautioned her. "He's a hard-driven sadist and a Hungarian nationalist who lacks polish. It wouldn't serve us to dismiss him as an ignorant psychopath. Beryx, after all, has had some hard decisions to make, too."

Fedot had filled them in on Beryx Gulyas at Alyona's underground apartment: Born in Transylvania to Hungarian parents; a talented assassin with psychological flaws; the personal lapdog for Nicolai Ceausescu—rumored successor of the current Secretary General of Romania. Pasha, of course, had heard of him. He was surprised that General Pushkin would send a man like that to take him out, but Fedot explained that he hadn't. Whoever the Hungarian was working for had hired him out of Romania, not brought him into the Moscow fold.

"Romania," Pasha repeated, shrugging. He seemed

incurious as to why someone other than the Soviets would want him dead—as if it was an expected development in his life's story and the particulars were hardly important.

"Never underestimate your enemy," Lily had said. "Sun Tzu says as much in *The Art of War*. My dad told me that."

"I've never read it," Pasha told her. "My knowledge of war is through experience."

Lily felt the gentle press of a warm palm against her head and for a moment thought it might be Pasha. But no, this hand wasn't big enough. The Hungarian petted her hair, raking his fingers across her scalp. She heard him burrow into the front pocket of his trousers, grunting as he yanked his hand out from under the snug woolen material. He placed several small stones and crystals on the floor tiles next to her: dioptase, moonstone, opal, rhodochrosite and green amber—all for love, he told her. He added garnet this time, for physical love.

Beryx Gulyas then forced her mouth open with a spoon and dropped the various stones—one by one—into the back of her throat, forcing her to swallow them. He lit a match, tossing the box, labeled *Hotel Salonika*, on the floor near Lily's shoulder. As he heated the cradle of the metal spoon, boiling the pharmacological capsaicin again, Beryx Gulyas's breath became audible. Lily listened to the way he exhaled—like a bull, in short and forceful puffs—and walked her fingers over to the matchbox. Slowly, she slid the box toward her shoulder, tucking it into her armpit.

Pasha was right. Lily nodded. It was of no use thinking of Beryx Gulyas as a goon—a coarse and simple caricature of a man. He'd gotten this far. Both of them had. Lily rolled onto her back and looked fully at him. The Hungarian's face was contorted in a mask of concentration. If he messed up, like he had once before, the capsaicin would become too acidic, too volatile. It could even explode, he had told her. The substance needed to be just right so that, when he poured it down her throat again, it would merely burn and savage—like shards of scorching glass—leaving her with a raw and excruciating sore throat for a number of hours and swelling her lips and tongue until she thought she would suffocate.

Lily touched the Hungarian's knee, and he glanced down at her, careful not to take his eyes—the color of English peas, and his only desirable feature—off the spoon for too long. In its purest form, the capsaicin was odorless—and needed to stay that way. As soon as the substance began to overheat, a sour smell would tinge the air—scarcely detectable at first. The white curl of smoke emanating from the tiny pool inside the spoon would become highly combustible from that instant. It would ignite if ever the tip of a flame crossed its ribbon and would spread toxic acidity to every available molecule in the air around it.

Lily rolled over slowly, pulling the top of the Hungarian's sock down with the tip of her finger and pressing her lips to his exposed ankle, biting gently and playfully along the bone. She let the matchbox drop from her armpit into her hand, pushing it open with her thumb.

In a distant corner of the room, Lily could swear she heard Ivanov giggling.

CHAPTER 41

Pasha opened one eye. There was light—morning light—in the top tier of his field of vision and clear, bold cerulean in the bottom. He rubbed his hand over the short, silken rug that he was lying on facedown and lifted his head, moving his neck to and fro. Nothing hurt—not really—but he felt dull and groggy, like the victim of one too many glasses of young wine. Standing up was dizzying, but not painful—another good sign.

A few feet in front of him, on a table next to the settee, was a small tray left for him by Fedot, he assumed. *Fedot.* Yes, now he remembered. Something had changed with Fedot, something that had given Pasha enough cause to kill him—his friend. Who are friends, after all? Most of his own friends had tried to kill him at some point or another, for this or that reason. Not Fedot, however. He hadn't expected it of Fedot—and he turned out to be right. It was a good thing the little Russian was so strong and resourceful. It made Pasha laugh. Nobody ever saw it coming with Fedot.

The last Pasha remembered, he had been strangling Fedot, his own considerable might halting any flow of oxygen to his friend's lungs or brain, and then he, Pasha, was on the floor. Was it minutes later now? An hour? Couldn't have been more than an hour, judging by the light in Mansoor Nassa's living room.

Pasha walked over to the tray that had been assembled for him. There was a cup of Turkish coffee, a colorless shot of something severely alcoholic, a fresh apricot pastry with poppy seed and nuts, and a small, mint green envelope. Pasha touched the coffee—it was still hot—and drank the liquor (quite a good vodka—*thank you, Fedot,* he said aloud), before forcing the pastry into his mouth. He didn't want it, not exactly, but he knew that he needed it and so had his Russian friend. Inside the envelope lay an official type photo of a policeman. It was some years old.

"Hello, Great Detective," Pasha said, scrutinizing Rodki Semyonov's jagged features. They'd met before, at Stalin's Kuntsevo residence, not long before the Great Leader headed off to the Great Beyond or the Great Below, as many of faith would believe.

"Now here's one that makes sense," Pasha said. Beryx Gulyas and why he would have it in for Pasha was a mystery, but the Great Detective? Who else would General Pushkin send after him? Pushkin was no fool, after all.

Next to the tray lay the thin, paper box that had contained the pastries Fedot had bought for their breakfast. It was white and stained with large, greasy ovals, but at the bottom right was a small stamp of partially smeared Hebrew words and numbers. *Sabourjian,* it read—the name of the bakery—and listed the address.

"My *favorite* bakery!" Mansoor Nassa had exclaimed as he fed them *Sabourjian's* flatbread the morning after they arrived. Fedot had been dispatched to the Jewish quarter at the crack of dawn while he and Lily slept.

Pasha didn't know quite what Fedot and Nassa were up to, but it was clear they were keen to take him along. Maybe not to Mansoor Nassa's mountain retreat—at least not today—but to wherever Fedot believed God was leading them. And wherever that was, Pasha needed to find Lily there.

He wondered if it was Lily's uncommon beauty and smarts that had put a spell on him. Of course, Pasha had known plenty of fine-looking and intelligent women, some of whom had loved him with a passion that he found as touching as he did curious. No, beauty was a commodity for a man like him. Intelligence was nice, but even that wasn't necessary for his emotional fulfillment. His ex-wife hadn't been particularly bright, and he'd loved her. Even if he did begin to tire of her early on in their marriage.

More likely, it was as simple as the fact that Lily had cared for him when he was unable to care for himself. Selflessly, or at the very least, not in her self-interest. Such a cliché of love. Yet as he'd fought for his life after Beryx Gulyas had tried to kill him, as he struggled to regain consciousness, it was primarily because he wanted to see Lily's face. Her skeptical gaze and prickly demeanor. Her smile that both understood the joke and told it. In fact, now he found himself in the same fix. To both his thrill and dismay, he'd never needed something so much right then as to glimpse the face of the woman he loved.

"Lily," he said aloud. "I fear you'll be the death of me."

The Mahalleh, the Jewish Quarter of Tehran, looked nothing like the Jewish Quarters Pasha had known in cities like Krakow or Prague—at least before the war. Those were clean, dignified and showed evidence of prosperity even during dark times.

The porous, graffiti-engraved walls of the Mahalleh, the rusted iron bars on the windows, and the broken metal doors indicated not only decay, but impending abandonment. Mansoor Nassa himself lived outside these parameters, and Pasha wondered what it must have looked like here when Nassa was but a boy, running wild through the narrow alleyways and central courtyards studded with fuzzy-leafed trees. Perhaps it had been bustling then, or maybe its very paucity had been what led Nassa to poetry and out of the Mahalleh for good.

A young boy—no older than eight—peeked his head out from behind a sky blue door with a large diamond shape on it. It was a door left unmolested by rust and apathy, clearly leading to a family home.

"Young one," Pasha called in Hebrew, and the boy craned his neck to get a better look at him. "I'm but a visitor," Pasha explained. "Could you tell me how to find this address?" None of the street signs were written in Hebrew, and Pasha couldn't read the Persian language.

The boy pointed down the alleyway and spoke rapidly of several twists and turns the Russian would have to make in order to reach his destination. He then took off into a courtyard and hid behind a wooden drum, watching the giant stranger as he made his way.

In truth, Pasha didn't know if the address meant anything—or at least anything concrete. He was sure, however, that Fedot and Nassa had left it for him deliberately. And given that he had nowhere else to go and really nothing else to do since they had—presumably—already left for the mountains, he might as well have a look.

As he rounded onto a wider street, he finally saw evidence of vitality—the kind of commerce, game-playing and conviviality that Pasha would have expected in any living, breathing city neighborhood. Next to a cobbler stood two gentlemen, deep in conversation while their sons played jacks in the street. A fruit merchant sang a complex melody in a sonorous voice barely tamed by years of heavy smoking. And from a tiny door—a door straight out of a children's book—came two women carrying a bounty of bread. Above that door was a scratched wooden sign no bigger than a license plate. It read: *Sabourjian.*

Pasha took out his handkerchief, wiped his neck with it—already hot at this time in the morning—and took a step toward the bakery. It had long ago ceased to amaze him how ordinary a place could look—a place that was perhaps an important link in a dramatic chain of events. But then again, maybe it was only a bakery.

He ducked through the door and found himself in a space even smaller than the one he had anticipated. There was little room for more than a handful of customers at the counter, which was brimming with stacks of flatbread, soft loaves, and the pastries Fedot had brought to the poet's house. Behind the counter stood a man and his wife, their three children huddled around their mother's ankles.

Pasha greeted them in Hebrew and pointed to a pairing of honey-glazed buns. The baker nodded, his eyes darting toward his wife, who looked to the floor. The children were unmoving, except for the littlest one, a child of about three, who stroked her mother's calf with her tiny fingers. It was quiet in the bakery—unnaturally quiet, it seemed, for this time of day. There should have been a line out the door, the bounty picked through.

The baker held out the thin, white box containing the honeyed buns, and Pasha took it, handing him a few rials he'd collected from the poet's house and telling him to keep the change. He had the distinct feeling the baker did not want him to leave. Pasha looked over at his wife. Her eyes were still held to the floor, petting the head of her youngest child, when he noticed what looked like a deep cut around her wrist—the kind of cut that came from a pair of tight handcuffs.

"Your wife doesn't look well," Pasha said. "Would you like me to fetch a doctor?"

The baker shook his head. In the silence that followed, Pasha heard a baby crying upstairs. The child's cry turned to a wail when it was clear no one was going to tend to his needs. Now Pasha understood.

"Good day," he said. "And God bless you."

Pasha exited the bakery, staying close to the wall, and looked up at the small, dark window on the second floor—the one that looked out onto the street and, from the proper angle, into the baker's flat.

"Mr. Gulyas," Pasha said under his breath, "I'll bet you're a terrible houseguest."

CHAPTER 42

Rodki Semyonov had been following Fedot Titov all morning, and it could have been a tedious ordeal. Going to this place and that, looking for meaning in mostly banal transactions. Rodki, by fate, had been forced to accomplish most of his detecting work within his imagination and had few fond memories of tracking suspects gum-shoe style. In this and only this regard, Stalin had done him a favor by plucking him from the police force.

But Fedot Titov was never what he seemed and did little that was straightforward. That, in and of itself, captured Rodki's interest. They had been playing what was to the Great Detective an amusing game of cat and mouse. Amusing not because Rodki enjoyed such activities. Being good at something didn't necessarily translate into pleasure for him. He'd never liked bare-knuckle fighting, after all, even if he did gain a certain sense of achievement from it.

What had amused him was the walking tour of Tehran it had provided—especially the affluent northern neighborhoods with their wide boulevards and sumptuous gardens. He almost felt as if he were back in Moscow—pounding the pavement, riding the buses—and it gave him a sense of well-being that had eluded him since he'd left home to find General Pushkin's old friend and once-trusted ally.

"Mister, how bouta cigarette?" a young man pleaded in English.

Rodki flipped him a butt and motioned for him to move along. He realized how much he must look like an

American to someone young and relatively untraveled outside of Iran. Even a rich kid like the boy who'd wanted a cigarette. The Great Detective had bought a beige linen suit at an American luxury hotel, wanting to look like a tourist. He could never credibly fit in as a Persian and didn't bother trying to don their style—even if most of them wore Western dress. Much like the young man, in his loafers and banana-hued linen trousers, there was something *other* about the way the Persians wore their Western attire. The fabrics were overly crisp, as if pressed twice a day, and the colors tended to be brighter, complimenting their darker skin tones. The Persians looked, overall, quite beautiful. In this way, they appeared in stark contrast to the dreary uniform of factory dress and quasi-military style that had been imposed upon the Moscow citizenry. The forced ugliness of Soviet Russia had made even his Polina look haggard and sullen on the days she visited Rodki's imagination. Her plump cheeks and full lips, however, would always defy the look of collective doom and unspeakable boredom that Rodki had grown so accustomed to in his native land.

"More cigarette, for later day? Yes, please?" The young man—*Banana Pants*, as Rodki had begun to call him in his mind's voice—had returned, wanting to make a friend. The Great Detective shushed him.

Out of a shuttered house—one that looked as if it were still closed for the summer months—came Fedot Titov. The Great Detective had lost him once he'd entered the Elahiyeh neighborhood—an elegant and cosmopolitan-looking district. The homes were stately but tasteful there, housing senators, scientists, artists, writers and a good population of Persian Jews. It was a mystery as to how a man like Fedot Titov could have gained entry to a manor house, but then, perhaps the little man had befriended a hotel guest at some point or another. It wasn't unheard of. Also likely, Fedot Titov's accommodations were the result of having friends in high places—friends like Theron Tassos—even if Fedot seemed too capricious a character to reap such favors. And Theron Tassos, as far as Rodki could tell, was hardly the type of man who provided anything for anyone in his employ—apart from loyalty and a very nice paycheck. Anything else could give the impression of favoritism, or worse, could lay the groundwork for a personal relationship.

Still, the Great Detective had first spotted the former assistant manager of the Hotel Rude that morning entering a decent but cut-rate hotel run by one of Tassos's minions. Fedot Titov wasn't there long—barely long enough to finish a cup of coffee –before he slipped out onto the street and travelled back to the manor house where he was staying.

"You wanna supper?" Banana Pants inquired, although it was still morning. "My mother inspires so good food in our servants."

Rodki gave him the kind of look that had always stirred fear in his adversaries. A look of ruthless indifference that he'd cultivated for intimidation purposes. A look that told the young man, "You will suffer if you persist in wanting to satisfy your curiosity."

But Banana Pants was too enthralled with the idea of having garnered the attention of such a curious foreigner to care. He practiced his English, deluging the Great Detective with questions and invitations, imitating Bogart as he smoked his cigarette and centered his hat, tossing a gemstone in the air and catching it in his breast pocket.

"You like, Louie?" he said. "Is this start of our beautiful friendship?"

Near the front entrance of the splendid house out of which Fedot Titov had come, a doroshkeh appeared, its withered horse releasing an anguished bray. Fedot Titov got in. He whistled twice, and the doroshkeh began to move, pulling onto the boulevard and immediately rounding a bend.

The young man looked up from his gem-tossing. "In the shadows of the rose garden," he said, quoting the first line of what the Great Detective believed to be a poem. One by a Persian poet, if memory served him. Something about the blood of spirits infusing the white roses in a garden—making them red.

"What was the next line, Bogie? I can't remember." The Great Detective called him Bogie, as Banana Pants seemed too condescending.

But Bogie wouldn't say. In the flash of a moment, he was gone—running down the boulevard, his crisp banana pants fluttering around his slender legs.

Funny people, these Persians, Rodki thought.

He flagged a taxi and motioned for the driver to round the same bend as the horse and cart carrying Fedot Titov. There, the boulevard curled onto another tree-lined street, where the tops of the trees curved together like interlocked fingers, and the road was quiet—determined not to disturb its illustrious residents. The doroshkeh had vanished, and for the life of him Rodki could not see where it had gone. He asked the driver to creep along the street, looking for an alley or drive-way where the weary horse could have wandered in.

The taxi driver gestured, shrugging to ask his customer where he wanted to go. They couldn't inch along a prosper-ous street indefinitely, after all. It attracted all the wrong kinds of attention.

The Great Detective sat back and sniffed, scratching his crooked nose.

"The Mahalleh," he said, though he didn't know why. It was just a hunch.

"Okay, Mahalleh," the driver said. He turned around and headed back to the boulevard.

As they drove by the shuttered house where Fedot Titov had emerged, the Great Detective peered out the taxi window, admiring the brick manor home. It was handsome, yes, but a bit lonely. As if it had once been loved deeply and was mourning the loss of that affection. It was a feeling familiar to Rodki. One he ate for breakfast nearly every morning at his apartment in Moscow, his wife's spirit seated quietly next to him—her soft-boiled egg untouched, her tea too hot to sip—asking him, as she had the morning she was taken from him, "Do you think we could acquire an extra satchel of milk this week? Your mother would like me to make her a Charlotte russe for her birthday." That morning he had replied, as he had every time since, "Charlotte russe? Rich tastes for a woman who grew up eating kissel." Polina's laughter still echoed at their table.

Out of the corner of his vision, Rodki spotted something—a color—sticking out of a barberry bush. As the taxi moved closer, he recognized Banana Pants, kneeling amidst its plum wine leaves, his Bogie hat crushed to his chest. He was talking to someone—Rodki could see the outline of a man's figure behind the bush. Banana Pants seemed to have lost his look of wide-eyed curiosity, replacing it with a rather cool demeanor.

"Ah," Rodki said. "I should have known. The boy was an agent of the Shah."

CHAPTER 43

Pasha was flicking his cigarette butt into the gutter when the ground shivered beneath him and the sound of a minor explosion, like a collective sneeze, shot out from a second-floor window above the *Sabourjian* bakery. A plume of smoke looped up into the air and a wild scream—*kurva anyádat!* Something about a whore, from Pasha's understanding—was hurled in Hungarian from the broken window.

"Lily," Pasha said.

He rushed to the bakery entrance, but it was locked, bolted shut by the slide of a wooden plank. "Let me help you!" he shouted in Hebrew, pounding the door with his fist. He heard scuttling inside the bakery—the family was gathering their few things and moving toward the back of the building through the bakery kitchen, where a back door must have lain in wait.

The Russian looked up and down the street, searching for a shortcut to the back of the shop—one that didn't require his circling the block—but there was none. The street itself was emptying rapidly, as if its population had been waiting for something like this to happen. The children were gone, and the remaining handful of adults was fast disappearing into windows and behind the metal gates that guarded every home and commercial structure.

"You, there," Pasha called to a middle-aged man as he jiggled his keys just a few doors down from the bakery. The man let go a torrent of blasphemies, then slipped in and quickly slammed the door before Pasha could intercept him.

"Lily!" Pasha cried, kicking at the middle-aged man's door. The hinges were strong and the metal unforgiving.

Pasha stopped and looked up. All was silent now from the second story window. Black smoke belched from its empty frame, and his eyes began to sting as if they had been sprayed with onion and lemon. It may not have been the type of explosion that would tear limb from limb, but it was diabolical—clearly chemical in nature. He had an uncanny suspicion that it was Lily's doing and not the Hungarian's. "Hold on, Lily," he said as he began to sprint down the now-deserted street. It would take him as long as two minutes to race around to the back of the Jewish bakery, and he had to believe that his Lily could take care of herself in the misery of that chemical haze for such an interminable length of time.

The blast had blown away from Lily as she'd hoped it would, though refuse still clung to her body—some of it embedded in her skin, as tiny rivulets of blood steamed down her bare arms and legs. She was in a pair of panties and nothing else, but she didn't care. Despite being battered and half-conscious, she knew enough to grab a sheet wet with spills from rosewater and wrap it around her body. A naked woman wouldn't do well on the streets of a Muslim country, even one as forward-looking as Iran.

"Goodbye, lover," she rasped. Her throat was still raw. "See you in hell, I'm sure."

Beryx Gulyas lay curled in a fetal position beneath the window. His palms were pressed into his eyes, and he was cursing bitterly in his native Hungarian. She couldn't understand what exactly he was saying, but she was sure his profanities were directed at her. His face, neck and shoulders had been burned badly, but the capsaicin was the source of his real discomfort. At this close range, it was thick in the atmosphere, and Lily knew from experience the agony it caused—especially when it came in contact with any mucous membrane. She, herself, had grown used to it, or perhaps it was Ivanov's voice in her head that helped her stand on her weakened legs and stomach the burning in her throat, lungs and eyes. "Come, come, Miss Lily," she imagined him saying. Without another word to her Hungarian captor, she tied a knot in the sheet at her shoulder and stumbled toward the stairs. "Yes, good, Miss Lily, good."

In the back bedroom she heard a cry and remembered the baby. She'd heard it on and off over the course of the last few days as she drifted in and out of consciousness. Bracing herself against the wall, she made her way to the child's small, wooden cradle and picked him up, cuddling him into the sheet and shielding his face from the capsaicin that lingered in the hallway.

Downstairs, it was empty. Lily was sure there had been others there—a woman, a man, more children perhaps. Or maybe they were merely visitors. The child had to belong to someone.

Lily moved slowly through the bakery kitchen, her legs gaining strength with each step and her arms tightening around the yowling white bundle she was carrying. Finally, at the back: a door. *Thank God,* she thought. Lily stepped outside into a gloriously muggy, overcast day and appraised her surroundings. She was in a poor and narrow alleyway of some kind, one too thin to support the usual tangle of clotheslines that were strung from window to window in other parts of the city. The alley was too slim for even a taxi and seemed to go on forever—or perhaps that was only an optical illusion? Lily had, after all, been in nothing but dim light for some time—Beryx Gulyas waving a lone candle in her face, or a match and a spoon. And despite the gradual return of her strength, Lily was nowhere near up for a run through the streets of Tehran clad only in loosely tied bed linens.

A woman cried out in Hebrew, waving her arms in the air as she lurched toward Lily. There was a toddler hanging on her skirt. She pushed Lily and grabbed the child out of her arms, kissing the baby's face and holding it to her breast. She shouted something else in Hebrew before turning and running down the alley, disappearing into a slit of a doorway. Lily wasn't sure if the woman had thanked her or cursed her, but she was glad the child was back in his mother's arms. Lily endeavored to run, but in a sudden shift, her legs collapsed beneath her, and she fell to the ground.

Behind her, Lily heard Beryx Gulyas heave and slip down the stairs. He swore again, louder and angrier, but got up onto his strong legs and stomped through the kitchen toward her. Lily's heart began to pound. The gravity of her situation was all too evident now; her clever escape from Gulyas had bought her a few minutes, had gotten her out the door leading into the bakery's alleyway, but it wouldn't get her to safety. She would die in this place.

"You duplicitous piece of ass!" Gulyas bellowed. He took a long knife—sharp and serrated—from a block on a chopping table and held it out in front of him.

Lily didn't look over her shoulder. She didn't have to. In her weakened condition, there wasn't a chance in a thousand she could outrun or overpower the Hungarian assassin, regardless of his injuries. Instead she did what she hadn't done since she was a child of eight—and even then her efforts had been half-hearted. Lily bowed her head, folded her hands close to her chest—where the squirming baby had been moments before—and prayed.

CHAPTER 44

Pasha ran down the lane, banging on windows and calling Lily's name. As he came to the end of the tiny street, he cursed viciously in Russian, kicking a cinderblock that sat under a window as a perch for peeping Toms. He'd reached another dead end. The interior maze of lanes, alleyways and courtyards in the Mahalleh made no journey a linear one—even one that appeared as straightforward as a shotgun corridor that went from the front of one building to the rear. It was maddening.

The Russian ran back the way he came, this time leaving the passages of the commercial lanes and entering a full-fledged street—albeit a deserted one.

"I'm here for the very bad man," he called out in his rusty Hebrew. "I will chase him from here and leave you in peace." But no windows opened or doors cracked to reveal a tentative eyeball. The sound of a baby crying could be heard in the distance.

"Gulyas! I'm here!" Pasha bellowed, grabbing a broomstick that had been leaning against a doorjamb and banging it over and over on an adjacent water pipe. He felt like a lunatic.

He heard the clip-clop of horse's hooves behind him and turned.

"Hello," he shouted as he caught a glimpse of Fedot rounding a corner from a lane leading out of the Mahalleh. Fedot stopped at the curb and smiled.

"The Hungarian—he's here," Pasha told him, although

Fedot was unquestionably aware of the fact. "And Lily. I'm sure of it."

"Yes, she's here," Fedot said. His face was impassive—even in light of his smile—and his eyes were penetrating. Pasha had seen this look on the young man's face before. It was the way he had beheld the crucifix Ivanov had fashioned from a birch branch; the way, years ago, Fedot had revered a seventeenth-century Russian icon of Saint Mary of Egypt that he had stolen from a member of the Politburo.

"Please, my friend," Pasha entreated. "We have to find Lily. The Hungarian can wait. I'll help you get him, I will. It's me he's looking for anyway."

Fedot nodded, allowing the smile to melt from his face.

"It's so good you're alive," Fedot said, putting his hand on Pasha's shoulder. "I wasn't sure I wouldn't kill you until I didn't."

Lily's prayer echoed inside her head as if it were a bat trapped in an attic room. *I want to live* was all she said, but she meant a great deal more than that. Gone was the Lily of Fifth Avenue shopping, of Monemvasian debauchery, the girl with her nose pressed up against the glass of the Chilton Club—waiting—hand outstretched for a Boston Brahmin to guide her in and give her a seat. The new Lily was, perhaps, a question mark. A girl who had fallen in love for the first time. Love, finally, love, and with Pasha Tarkhan. *This* was love—invasive and total. She would do anything for Pasha. And this new Lily—this woman in love—was also one who could make hard decisions but had no idea where that skill was going to take her. Still, it seemed like a waste to let her die in a Tehran alleyway.

"*Kurva!*" Gulyas howled at her back. She heard the baby—the one that had been taken from her arms by his mother—bawling in the distance. Still, her legs betrayed her, and she couldn't get up.

A clamor of pots and pans from the baker's kitchen alerted her to Gulyas's approach. His eyes were still painful and tearing, causing him to trip over a bucket of cake flour. The powdery grain puffed up into his face, settling into his burns and causing him to shriek.

Lily started to crawl, but before she could advance farther into the alleyway, at least putting some distance between herself and the Hungarian, a crack of a whip caught her attention. There, roosted on his doroshkeh, was Jalal—his tooth-poor mouth open wide as he chided his miserable horse. He was a beautiful sight.

With every scrap of strength she could muster, Lily pulled herself to her feet, quivering, yet holding steady. The doroshkeh didn't fully stop at the door to the baker's kitchen, but Lily was able to mount it, heaving her body into the cab. The baby stopped crying as soon as she settled into the seat, as if he knew now that Lily was safe and was glad.

Lily dared look behind her now. Beryx Gulyas was running after the doroshkeh, but Jalal was keeping ahead of him. She could hear Jalal laughing as he snapped the reins. Still, the Hungarian would concede no defeat. He threw knives he'd gathered from the baker's kitchen—one landing at Lily's feet and another, a short paring knife, grazing the horse's behind. The wretched thing whinnied and redoubled his efforts, galloping faster than he had in years until finally leaving Beryx Gulyas in the dust.

"You and I, Lily," Gulyas shouted from the cloud of earth and city grime that obscured Lily's vision of him. He didn't finish whatever it was he wanted to say. Instead he turned his back on the speeding doroshkeh and walked back to the bakery, looking once more over his shoulder before disappearing inside.

CHAPTER 45

Rodki Semyonov's taxi pulled up to a curb on an unmarked, vaguely commercial street in the Mahalleh. His driver sucked hard on his teeth and popped a chew candy onto his tongue, letting it melt slowly as he awaited further instruction. The foreigner paid well, and he was in no hurry.

"I want to stretch my legs," the Great Detective told him, miming a stretch and little walk around the car. He pulled out a few rials and handed them to the driver, assuring him he had no intention of giving him the slip.

The moment he closed the taxi door behind him, he heard it. It was the unmistakable sound of the doroshkeh cart that had pulled up at the manor house in the Elahiyeh, taking Fedot Titov with it. It felt close, as if it was coming up on his back, but when Rodki spun around, nothing was there. Only a hot breeze as thick and tacky as pine sap.

Rodki slid down the side of the taxi, peeking up into the side-view mirror. The oval glass displayed nearly the entire street, and the Great Detective instantly spied Fedot Titov—his graceful stride more kitten than cat-like—as he ran tip-toed down the pavement and rounded a bend. Rodki stood and sprinted toward the end of the street, not wanting to lose the nimble Russian around another corner. He knew the streets leading into the bowels of the Mahalleh were intricate, having walked it once already. And the Great Detective wasn't keen to test his memory in a chase with such an unpredictable character. He stood at the top of the street where Fedot Titov had turned, his back pressed up against a spattering of worn graffiti. Slowly he twisted his neck, letting his left eye get a look onto the lane.

"Great Caesar's ghost," he said, imitating the American ambassador's favorite phrase from the Shah's midnight supper. It was at times like this Rodki's instincts genuinely amazed him. In the middle of the lane stood Fedot Titov—as Rodki had hoped, but not necessarily expected—while next to him was a bear of a man close to his own size and, he suspected, as skillful a puzzle solver.

"Pasha Tarkhan," he said under his breath. The Great Detective reached into his coat pocket and pulled out the pistol General Pushkin had supplied for him. It felt oddly comfortable in his hand, although it had been years since he'd actually held one with the intent of using it. When orders were issued to bring someone in dead or alive, as they had been in the case of Pasha Tarkhan, the real message was that this man knew too much to be allowed to get away. Sure, it would be nice to question him before his execution, but ultimately, stopping him was the principal goal. *Do what you need to do* was the unspoken instruction. And Rodki had a clear shot to Pasha Tarkhan's head that any assassin would have considered a gift from fate.

> *Not even a whisper is heard in the great, great night,*
> *Just a faint wind, like the breath of a woman.*
> *If you only knew how I crave them when I go,*
> *The lights of Moscow nights!*

The song, "The Lights of Moscow Nights," was familiar to just about any urban Russian. It was a song that held particular significance for Rodki and one that Pasha Tarkhan—his voice low and lugubrious—had sung some years ago when they'd met briefly at one of Stalin's residences. He'd

performed it at Stalin's request—eyes closed, as if waiting
for his death. Rodki would never forget it. And now, as he
prepared to put Pasha Tarkhan to death, he couldn't get it
out of his mind.

The wind is blowing, so cool and original
Dressing the moon in the jeweled sky.
The whispers that ride the wind are but fleeting words
from a part-time lover,
Behold the lights of Moscow nights.

Rodki Semyonov shook his head, then readied his pistol
once more.

Why, oh why, my darling do you doubt me?
Watching my face like a gypsy thief.

Porphyri Ivanov flashed into Rodki's mind, naked and
singing the very same tune. He'd tried to keeps thoughts
of the Russian mystic at bay. The Great Detective knew
Ivanov from his time in the psychiatric prison where he was
being held after the war. Deprived of food, except for a potato on some days, and stripped of clothing, he had ignored
the indignities hoisted upon him and spent most of his
time—when he wasn't in the interrogation facilities—in
prayer and song. Every day, when the guards came for him,
he smiled, as if they were meeting in a tavern. *Disassociated
personality*, the Great Detective had deduced at the time, a
disorder most commonly observed during wartime. In fact,
everyone indulged in it to some extent—how else could
a human being function in times of tremendous stress?
But in the extreme cases, a soldier, or someone like Ivanov,
might actually convince himself that he was, say, among
friends, when he was in fact being tormented day and night
by people who meant him deadly harm.

No matter how far I go, I can never leave behind
These lights of Moscow nights.

With the Russian mystic's voice still in his head—high, mellow, almost feminine in its countenance, a fine compliment to Tarkhan's tone—the Great Detective stepped out into the lane, aimed his gun at Pasha Tarkhan and fired.

CHAPTER 46

The force of the bullet propelled Pasha Tarkhan headlong, causing him to stumble. He gripped his shoulder, the blood pouring over his fingers, then stood upright, running toward the rusted, iron gate into which Fedot Titov had disappeared. The Great Detective wasn't about to give him another reprieve. The first one—when he had shot the former Russian diplomat in the shoulder rather than the head—had surprised Rodki as much as it must have surprised Pasha Tarkhan. It was a decision made with no deliberation, a last-minute change of plans. It was so unlike Rodki—opposite anything the Great Detective was prone to do. The Great Detective was a deliberative man, pragmatic in his thoughts, unsentimental about outcomes. He'd lost too much to indulge himself in either curiosity or empathy for other people's miseries.

The Great Detective aimed the gun again, easily tracking the hulking Russian as he wobbled his way out of the street. As curious as Rodki was about Pasha Tarkhan's self-directed mission in Tehran, he wasn't about to let that curiosity get the better of him again.

Yet he did.

The twinkling lights, little fires lit by our souls,
More beautiful than the eyes of a woman,
Ah, the lights of Moscow nights.

The gate creaked and slammed shut. Tarkhan was inside. And the Great Detective remained unmoving at the top of the street, his legs apart, his gun still pointed to where he could have effortlessly taken his target down. As the song gradually faded from his mind, Rodki put the gun down. He wondered if his own imagination, the one that had kept his Polina so close to him all these years, had followed him from his apartment in Moscow all the way to Persia. Or if Pasha Tarkhan had a friend in the netherworld. It didn't matter, he supposed. All he knew was that he now had to undertake a chase.

With the gun at his side, Rodki walked toward the decrepit gate and let himself in. It smelled musty and damp, full of urine and perhaps a dead animal or two. It was dark. He could scarcely see his hand in front of him.

"Tarkhan?" he whispered. No one answered, but the Great Detective could feel Tarkhan's ragged breath on the back of his neck. In a sharp movement few would attribute to a man his size, Rodki Semyonov, The Iron Knuckle, The Great Detective, spun and shot, hoping, despite himself, that he had aimed low enough not to kill his target.

Pasha Tarkhan fell to the ground in a slide. Fedot turned around at the sound of the shot and saw his friend go down. The Great Detective stood at the entranceway, the gun wrapped so fully in his muscular hand that it almost seemed to disappear. There was no point in running to Pasha's aid—all, in that case, would be lost. Instead, Fedot said a silent prayer for his friend as he disappeared behind another rotted metal gate and into a damp, fungal corridor.

Pasha, for his part, was glad to see Fedot continue on without him. Time was of the essence, and he was only a liability now. His shoulder burned; the second bullet had ripped straight through his side, just under his rib cage, and he found it difficult to breathe. He looked up at the man who had shot him—the one Stalin had loved like a prized thoroughbred—and wondered why General Pushkin hadn't ordered an immediate termination. Even an under-skilled marksman could have killed him with such an easy shot, and Pasha Tarkhan knew the bullet that had breezed so artfully in and out of his shoulder had not been meant for his skull. Nor had the one that had penetrated his torso been meant for his heart or any other vital organ.

He ran his hand over the new bleeding hole. The Great Detective continued to aim his gun at him as a warning not to move. *Get a hold of yourself,* he was saying. *But don't think of trying anything funny.* Of course, there was nothing funny Pasha wanted to try. He had been present at dozens of interrogations that preceded an unceremonious execution, and he had no intention of allowing himself to become a victim of one of those. As merely a principal interrogator, it would take him days to recover—not just mentally, but physically. And he had told himself every time that he would die rather than succumb to that unlucky destiny.

Pasha couldn't for the life of him think of why Pushkin would want him alive, but he did know that the general would never want him to escape. Since that comprehension was the closest thing to comfort that he was going to get, Pasha took an anguished breath, rose and faced his executioner. He nodded to the Great Detective, acknowledging that he remembered him and that he understood what he needed to do, and wished him no ill will. Looking ahead at the gate Fedot had vanished into, Pasha made a break for it, knowing full well that as a vassal of Moscow, The Great Detective could never allow him to reach its rusted bars.

CHAPTER 47

The doroshkeh cart stopped at the corner of a street lined with stores offering basic services: laundry, transportation, and film development—even if the latter was a bit fancy for this neighborhood. The district certainly didn't seem poor, like the Mahalleh, but Lily could detect nothing particularly handsome about it either. Its only aspiring feature was a hotel—clean, but clearly for second-class tourists—and Jalal had stopped his cart directly in front of its doors. Lily slouched farther into the belly of the doroshkeh as two men walked by arm-in-arm. Chuckling, they ducked into a tiny, galley coffee house without having noticed her.

"Jalal," Lily whispered in Arabic—she hoped he understood. "What are you doing?"

Jalal smiled and pointed to the front doors of the hotel.

"Jalal," she grunted between clenched teeth. "I'm wearing nothing but a sheet. Can't you please take me back to Mr. Nassa's house?"

This time, Jalal laughed. He gestured again at the hotel, saying "Go, go, go. Go, go, go."

It occurred to her that perhaps Mansoor Nassa was waiting for her inside the hotel. He had, after all, sent Jalal for her—although she couldn't for the life of her understand how he'd known where she was. *Pasha! Of course,* she realized. It had to be Pasha. He was undoubtedly in the hotel with the poet and Fedot. Lily smiled for the first time in what felt like years. Even that small adjustment of her facial muscles made her hurt all over, as if each tiny movement was joined to an infinite assortment of raw nerves.

"Thank you, Jalal," she said.

Slowly, Lily lowered herself from the doroshkeh and limped toward the front doors of the hotel. She'd been more agile when Beryx Gulyas was chasing her, but now that her adrenaline was no longer pumping with a fury, every step was an effort. It seemed to take a long time to get to the lobby.

"Hello," she said in Arabic, as the doors swung closed behind her.

Inside, no one was at the front desk, although a freshly lit cigarette lay gently against the rim of a full ashtray.

"Pasha," she called. But the lobby was silent.

Lily picked up the cigarette and held it to her swollen lips. Given the state of her throat, she could hardly believe that she desired a cigarette, but she did. It even felt good as she inhaled the smoke—an Oriental blend with both depth and sweetness—holding it in her lungs and enjoying its taste again as she exhaled. Lily couldn't remember the last time something had felt so pleasing to her senses.

She finished the cigarette and still, no one had come.

In the corner of the foyer was a boxy but comfortable-looking divan—roomy and upholstered in bright orange leather. Lily shuffled over to it and sat down. Beryx Gulyas had taken a lot out of her.

Outside, various people—servants mostly—walked by the hotel's tall, slender windows. No one looked in. The service class of Tehran was too busy carrying their packages and rushing to make sure things were just right in the homes where they worked: water needed to be boiled, bed linens to be refreshed, lentils to be soaked. They weren't curious about who could be lurking in a hotel lobby.

Before she knew it, Lily had lain down on the divan, tucking her feet up behind her and nestling into the now-dry sheet that still smelled of rosewater. She fell asleep a moment short of her head touching the scrolled and padded armrest that would serve as her pillow.

"Lilia," the gravelly voice murmured. It was familiar to Lily—very—but seemed far away. A voice from another lifetime. She felt much as she had when she first awakened to find Beryx Gulyas looming over her. Unsure of whether she was dead or alive. Uncertain about the time, or even the day. All she knew was that the voice had awakened her from a dream. In her dream, she was standing on the cliffs of Monemvasia in her billowing, white dress again. It was daylight this time, and she wasn't afraid of being spotted by Tony Geiger's assassin. Instead, she felt powerful—as if the sky, the cliff she was standing on, the chamomile and wild thyme that dripped from the crumbling sixth-century convent walls behind her, the wind, all belonged to her. And she felt alone.

"Lilia," the voice said again.

Lily opened one eye and lifted herself up onto her elbow. The sun had broken through the overcast sky and shined in a beam into the lobby of the hotel, backlighting the man who stood before her and making him appear more like a shadow than a human being. But even as little more than a silhouette, Lily knew him. She would have known him if he were nothing more than a breeze coupled with a faint voice that rode the airstream like a wave.

"Daddy?" she said.

CHAPTER 48

Theron Tassos walked over to Lily and sat next to her on the divan. When she lifted her head and placed it on his lap, he cradled it in his arms. Bending over her, he kissed her hair, her brow, her bruised eyes, her cheeks, her dry, distended lips, her chin and finally, her nose. It was a nose Lily had never liked, but her father's favorite of her features. When she was little, he had assured her it was a fixture on all truly great Greek beauties. He despised the small, upturned noses that had become so fashionable in America and Europe. They made a woman look eager for approval. Helen of Troy would've never had such a nose.

"You smell of roses," he said, rocking her for a tender moment—as if she were a baby again. Lily's mother had been ill for a time after Lily was born, and Theron had stayed up with his youngest child night after night, feeding her, singing her to sleep. Lily was the only one of his children whom he'd cared for in this way, and as a result, she had always been his most beloved.

"How did you get here, *paidi mou*?"

Lily sat up and unraveled herself from her father's embrace. She looked into his soil-brown eyes—the kind of deep, fertile soil that looked like Turkish coffee. Pasha's eyes were just as rich, but his were brighter, more like the Belgian chocolate her mother was so fond of. Right then, she fell into the shelter of her father's eyes as she had into Pasha's. They were eyes that sheltered grave, untold memories, that loved deeply and hated without sentiment. The only eyes she had seen in recent memory had been the Hungarian's, and his, though improbably beautiful, had been shallow. Whatever pain Beryx Gulyas had encountered in his life had been channeled into anger and fantasy. Never had it been pondered, scrutinized and absorbed.

"The poet brought me here—his driver. Or maybe Pasha. Is Pasha here? He might have sent for me."

Theron shook his head.

"I will get you some clothes," he said. "And we'll go directly to the airport, so you can be home with your mother by morning." Theron sighed deeply and rubbed his hand over his twice-shaven face. He knew he should wait to confront his daughter, but some things he couldn't let pass.

"Getting the American ambassador to help me wasn't as easy as I'd anticipated, Lily," he said. "It appears you've taken a membership in the Communist Party."

Meeting a man and becoming entangled in deadly intrigues because of him was one thing, but a deliberate act of subterfuge—like joining an enemy political organization—showed that his daughter had strayed a lot farther than her heart.

Lily pulled the sheet up to her collarbone and put her hand on top of her father's.

"I'm not a Communist," she said, smiling a little. It didn't hurt so much to smile this time. She was feeling better. Maybe it was just being in her father's company. "I don't really know what I am. But I know I'm not going to the airport with you."

The Greek baron rolled back his shoulders, sat up tall and loomed over his daughter. Lily, however, was unmoved.

"Daddy," she said. "I'm not here by accident. A twist of fate, maybe, but not by accident."

Her father had a way of sitting like a dormant volcano:

tall, inert, but with an occasional tremor capable of re-
minding every surrounding animal what kind of fate he
could unleash upon them. If Lily hadn't been looking into
the eyes of a hardened predator for several days now, imag-
ining each morning to be her last, she might have complied
with her father's wishes.

"Pasha Tarkhan has stolen the plans for a spaceship from
the Russians," she said. "We have to find him. And we have
to get those plans to the Americans."

It sounded mad, but Lily knew that nothing could
surprise her father, and little was out of the realm of his
imagination. He'd seen too much in his fifty-two years not
to believe in spaceships. And for all she knew—given her
father's network and the fact that he'd been able to track
her to Tehran—he was aware of the *Sputnik* plans already.

Lily's father, of course, had always been able to secure
the best table at the best restaurant, the best suite in the
best hotel. But until recently Lily had never thought of
her father's name as one that could gain her entry into the
homes of monarchs or manipulate world events. In Boston,
men like her father were able to live very well, but the doors
to the finest families and establishments—unless they were
peopled by politicians with an open palm and a certain casual attitude towards ethics—had been hermetically sealed
to keep people like them away. While that fact had nearly
driven Lily mad with resentment, it had never seemed to
bother her father. It was no wonder to her now. What interest could he have in a Putnam or a Peabody, when they
never held the keys to the kingdoms he was interested in to
begin with? And today, Lily could hardly believe she'd ever
been interested in them, either.

"Daddy," she told him. "You can help me or you can get
out of my way."

A contained collage of emotions crossed her father's face—ones only detectable by those who loved him and had a long, intimate knowledge of his expressions. Lily saw raw anger shaded with a trace of pride. Her father, after all, had been the only person in her life—her life before Tony's murder—who'd never rolled his eyes at her, had never expected less of her. In fact, he had told her on more than one occasion that there would come a day when she would stop wasting her time and become the woman her blood had predetermined her to be.

There was something else on her father's face, too, but it was an emotion that was unfamiliar to Lily. One she had never encountered in her father and wouldn't decipher until later. By then, it would be too late.

CHAPTER 49

OREKHOVKA VERKHNY KONDRYUCHY, RUSSIA

Porphyri Ivanov's home was a typical Russian country cottage: French-blue painted wood, one story with the exception of a tiny attic room, and roof tiles like overlapping gingerbread cookies. Its window frames were a golden brown and carved into a lace pattern every bit as intricate as the hand-sewn lace curtains that hung in every window, excepting the kitchen. There, the light spilled in without a filter, and Valentina, a woman with once-black hair now streaked with ribbons of iron, tended to a fire, boiling a pot of tea over its dying embers. She sighed, staring out at her husband, who stood nearly naked in the chilly, early autumn air, wearing only a thin, bone-colored scarf tied around his groin. The axe she had thrust into his hands when she shooed him outside was lying in a bed of wildflowers, and the man she had loved for some two and a half decades now was dancing around a Norway Maple, its leaves just beginning to redden.

Valentina smoothed her eyebrows and removed her apron, hanging it loosely over the back of a wooden chair. She stepped outside, squinting up into the cloudless sky before looking back at her husband. He stroked one of the maple's branches and inhaled the smell of her leaves. He tapped his bare foot onto the dry soil that housed the roots of the tree and sang "The Lights of Moscow Nights" in a sweet timbered soprano.

The woman smiled, sighing deeply. She marched into the wildflowers, shaking off a bee sting between the knuckle of her index and middle finger. The offending creature had been flung to the ground, and she stomped it into a black and yellow smear. Picking up the axe her husband had discarded and tucking her long hair into the collar of her blouse, the woman made her way toward the cellar doors of her cottage. There, she rolled a slice from a tree trunk away from a rusted iron crucifix nailed into the side of her house. It faced southwest, toward Jerusalem.

Raising the axe high above her head, she struck the tree slice, splitting it in two. She stepped back to brace herself and repeated the motion over and over again, until the slice had become several jagged logs that she then piled onto a wheelbarrow and rolled into her kitchen. Peering out the window, she saw that her husband was no longer singing. He was standing, his arms outstretched and looking directly into the sun.

TEHRAN, IRAN

Fedot was facing east, peering openly at the hot, mid-morning sun when Lily spotted him. She called his name, and he turned in her direction, blinking hard to readjust his vision and letting tears stream unhindered down his face. Lily ran to greet him, while her father remained standing outside the hotel lobby where they had emerged. Lily took Fedot's hands and kissed both of his cheeks.

"Where's Pasha?" she asked. Fedot had come alone from the decrepit lanes of the Mahalleh, and its smells of cement dust, citrus and raw sewage still clung to his clothes.

"I thought you'd be gone by now," Lily said. "To Mr. Nassa's mountain retreat."

Fedot had few answers for her and even fewer questions, despite how long Lily had been gone and how peculiar she must have looked to him in a pale blue Givenchy dress her father had supplied and a thick coat of waxy red lipstick that clashed with the fading bruises under her eyes.

The fancy dress and the bright lipstick were a sufficient enough distraction from the way Lily's facial muscles tightened whenever she swallowed. And from the look of world-weary knowledge she'd acquired in just three days with Beryx Gulyas. A girl her age, in her clothes, could look discontented, perhaps, without drawing a more skillful observer to her eyes and what lay behind them. But Lily had not yet learned how to mask her hardening emotions and needed tricks and distractions to do the work for her.

Fedot would notice that change in her, of course. Fedot noticed everything. She liked that about him. Lily had never liked answering questions about herself anyway, and would grow to like it even less in the coming years. It was why she almost married a man like Richard Putnam, why she had always found herself in bed with any attractive man who crossed her path. They would never know her, and it had suited her that way. But, of course, Pasha Tarkhan was different, and that was why she'd fallen in love with him. Pasha never had to ask—he knew. At least about what really mattered.

"Fedot, we have to find Pasha," she said, and the Russian nodded. He focused his stare across the street, his sun-stung eyes taking in the image of Theron Tassos, who stood watching their exchange. It occurred to Fedot that perhaps the Greek was wishing him dead now as well—for not stopping Lily from coming to Tehran, for not contacting him when she first arrived at the Hotel Rude. It didn't matter.

Fedot was no more afraid of Theron than he was of any earthly being. And like Tony Geiger, he'd never particularly liked Lily's father—if you could qualify his feelings in terms of likes and dislikes. He did like Lily, though, and he was glad to see her alive.

"Find Pasha, yes," he agreed. "But first, perhaps, we should deliver this." Fedot reached into his pocket and pulled out the brown bottle of Myer aspirin, holding it up for Lily, but out of her father's sightline.

"Pasha gave that to you!" Lily gasped. "Where is he, Fedot?"

Fedot shook his head. "He's been captured by Moscow."

Lily took the bottle of Myer aspirin and held it to her chest. Her face felt hot, and she bit down on her lip.

"We can't go to the Americans now, Fedot, not until we find Pasha."

"Miss Lily," Fedot said, lowering his voice. "I fear the Americans are the only ones who can help us find Pasha. And they'll feel much more inclined to give their assistance if we have something for them."

Fedot took the Myer aspirin from Lily's fingers and tucked it into his palm. Theron Tassos was crossing the street and walking toward them, one hand in his pocket and the other hanging loosely at his side. Fedot felt sure the Greek wouldn't acknowledge their acquaintanceship, and he was right. Theron waited for Lily to introduce them and then extended his hand.

"Have you spoken to Mr. Nassa?" Lily asked Fedot after the necessary pleasantries had been exchanged. The Russian shook his head.

"I suppose he's gone to the mountains, then," she said.

"The Americans will want to help us find Pasha Tarkhan," Fedot said, asserting himself. "Especially once we tell them about the *Sputnik* plans Mr. Tarkhan still has on his person."

Lily looked curiously at Fedot but decided against contradicting him. She glanced down at the *Sputnik* microfilm and watched as Fedot tucked the bottle of Myer aspirin into his trousers with a slight of hand so deft Harry Houdini would have been impressed.

"Shall we go, then?" Lily's father ventured. "My car is just around the corner."

CHAPTER 50

"Reza Shah Boulevard," Fedot instructed the driver, guiding them out of the city and toward the Alborz Mountains. Fedot sat in the front seat with his eyes closed while Lily and her father were in back—he, sipping the cup of coffee he'd missed that morning and smoking a cigarette. She thought of taking her father's fingers in her hand, but a coffee and cigarette signaled his time for reflection and mental preparation. She didn't wish to disturb him.

Lily's father, like many constant business travelers, became a man of rigid habit when he was on the road. The Chrysler Imperial that was shielding them from the Persian sun and whisking them off to the mountains was the only car he would drive or be driven in. Theron Tassos owned at least a dozen of them around the world—maybe more.

It felt like a long time since Lily had had any creature comforts in her life, and while she certainly was at home in her father's black Imperial, its leather seats and air-conditioning didn't feel like the necessities they once were, even in the cruel heat of Tehran. Perhaps they wouldn't until Pasha was safe and next to her again, his muscular arm enveloping her shoulders and one of his giant hands holding both of her own. Or perhaps a full surrender to the enjoyment of luxuries was a thing of the past for Lily.

She considered her father for a moment and realized that she couldn't remember a time when he'd actually enjoyed any of the expensive architecture around him. Luxury and routine were interchangeable to him. While his cars, hotel rooms, clothing and the like were essential, just as compulsory was his black coffee in the morning—Illy brand only, please—with a cigarette. Nothing more until eleven, then yogurt and honey—regardless of where he was. No lunch until two, that being his only meal unless he was obligated to have another. Necessity often forced him to eat the local fare out of courtesy as well, but Theron preferred Greek food no matter how good the cuisine happened to be in his host country.

Lily had always assumed that her father's particular tastes were a form of snobbery, but recent events had caused her to rethink a great many things. Certainly, Theron Tassos surrounded himself with fine effects—very specific, fine effects—but a man of his position needed something besides his own wit that he could rely on. And fine things tended to be reliable—whether they were automobiles or delicate threads of saffron in a honey pudding.

It occurred to Lily quite suddenly that she hadn't had a proper meal since the morning of her abduction by Beryx Gulyas. On that day, Goli, Mr. Nassa's servant, had laid out a delicious assortment of fares that Fedot had purchased in the markets: flatbreads, feta cheese and exotic fruits ranging from sweet dates to the pomegranates that Pasha loved so much—placing fingers-full of the tiny, juice-bubble seeds on Lily's tongue. The large, tough-skinned fruits hung heavily from trees all around the city and lined the increasingly open road before her father's Imperial. The mountains seemed so close, and her ears began to pop.

It won't be long now, Lily told herself. The Americans could surely give her some idea of where the Russians had taken Pasha.

"You would like Pasha, Daddy," Lily said, so softly that her father didn't seem to hear. Unlike Richard Putnam, Pasha was no *Malaka.*

Lily leaned toward the front seat. She wanted to ask Fedot once again about the last thing Pasha had said to him, and about the final moments before the two of them were separated. Fedot had told her so very little—only that Pasha had been searching for her and that a man he called the Great Detective had found them in the street. Lily touched Fedot lightly on the cheek. His eyes were closed, and his breathing exhibited the steady rhythm of sleep—or perhaps merely deep meditation.

"Fedot," she said, but as soon as the words left her lips, Lily heard the shrieking crush of metal upon metal. A split second later, she was thrown against the right-hand window in the back seat. The window cracked, cutting Lily's head as she fell unconscious into her father's lap.

From the outside, the crash site was lonesome and quiet except for a hiss coming out of the Imperial's engine. The truck that had rammed the left side of the Imperial was mangled in the front but still running. Had there been a driver in its cab, he no doubt would have suffered the same fate that Theron Tassos's driver had suffered.

Staggering toward the crash—about twenty meters behind the truck—was a grimy and tousled Beryx Gulyas. The Hungarian had jumped out of the truck only seconds before the crash and rolled like tumbleweed across the arid terrain before landing in a silver-leafed shrub.

Gulyas circled around to the unmarred portion of the Imperial and opened the back door. Gripping Lily under the arms, he dragged her out of the car and sat down, panting heavily. Although he'd lost two kilos in the excitement of the past few days, he felt no lighter in his bearing, and this realization made him kick the Imperial's tire from his seated position. It would take at least five kilos until he would start feeling more agile, and a few more after that to notice the difference in a mirror.

The Hungarian wanted to take a longer rest, but the sun—nearing noonday—was intolerable and causing him to sweat. And the salty beads of perspiration that were rolling from his scalp to his face stung terribly as they settled into his burns.

He got to his feet, stretched and shook off his aches and pains. Finally, with his back muscles feeling less taut, he crouched down, hoisted Lily up over his shoulder and, with a grunt, tottered over to the truck, depositing her in the passenger's seat of the cab. The hood of the truck was crumpled like tin, but the engine was purring softly, with only an occasional sputter from the generator. It sounded like a cymbal's ching after a low drumroll.

Down the long, straight road leading out of Tehran, Gulyas could see a small, blue dot that with every ticking second was growing bigger. Traffic. Quickening his step, the Hungarian climbed into the driver's seat of the truck, reversed away from the mangled Imperial and drove back in the direction of the city well ahead of the approaching car.

His father's ring glinted in the dazzling sunlight, and Gulyas admired it as he drove. Although he'd never liked his father, Gulyas did respect him, as he did anyone who had served in the Royal Hungarian Army. Lily had noticed his ring when he was holding her in the baker's apartment. She even recognized what it was, so Gulyas knew she respected him, too. That was why he couldn't understand how she could have betrayed him so. He would find out soon enough, however, and when he finished punishing Lily for her transgression, perhaps they could finally have that dance he'd been longing for.

CHAPTER 51

Theron Tassos could feel pearls of sweat behind his ears and under the collar of his shirt. At first, the Greek baron thought it might be blood, but the wetness he felt all over—on his back, his legs, under his arms, soaked into his underclothes—was too thin and pervasive.

"Lily?" he whispered, and opened his eyes. A swooshing sound—sudden, fast—came and went, and Theron looked out the window. A blue sedan had driven by and continued on toward the mountains, uninterested in the steaming, mangled Chrysler Imperial on the side of the road.

"Lily," he said—louder this time—as he looked around the automobile. The muscles in his neck tensed, making him wince.

The back seat showed no sign of her, except for a stripe of blood on the leather seat that continued over his pant leg as if she'd dragged herself—or been dragged—out of the car.

Theron opened the door and spilled out onto the parched ground. He crawled to the front of the car, steadied himself on the bumper and stood up. The truck that had rammed into them was gone. The grooved imprints of its tires showed a forward-crash-reverse-and-turn pattern, then led back in the direction of Tehran.

The Greek went to the driver's side of his Imperial and leaned in through the shattered window. There, the driver sat nearly decapitated by a shard of glass that came from the other vehicle. The man's hands were still gripping the steering wheel, and his right foot was on the gas pedal. His one intact eye was open, but not wide—there was no look of surprise frozen on his face. The eye was fixed on the road, as if the driver had been deep in thought when they were struck.

Fedot, on the other hand, looked as if he were sleeping. A gash in his skull had matted his honey-brown hair with blood, but otherwise he appeared unharmed. He was certainly breathing—although in the restrained way that a deeply unconscious man takes his breath, as if he were sucking his air cautiously through a straw.

Between Fedot and the dead driver was a perfectly undisturbed bottle of Limonata, and when Theron spied it, he became consumed by a rabid thirst. The Greek uncorked the bottle and put it to his lips, drinking down the warm soda in nearly a single gulp. He tossed the empty bottle at Fedot's feet, whereupon it hit another glass object. Theron ducked out of the driver's side window and walked around to the passenger's side, where Fedot was seated. He opened the door and squatted down, lifting the empty Limonata and hoping another drink had survived the crash.

But it had not.

Underneath the empty bottle of Limonata was a small, brown bottle, cracked in half. It was a bottle of Myer aspirin—easily recognizable—and when the Greek looked closer, he could see a coil of equally brown film amidst its broken glass.

Theron plucked the film from the floor of the Imperial, blowing the dusty glass particles off its thin, shiny surface. He slipped it into his front trouser pocket, where he would have kept his car keys had he not had other people drive him where he needed to go.

The Greek was not in the least surprised that Fedot had

kept this precious information from him. But with Lily gone again, the microfilm was secondary at the moment.

In the warped air of the heat, a smoky gray mass caught Theron's eye in the distance. He mounted the hood of the Imperial and shielded his gaze from the sun. It was, indeed, an automobile. Theron Tassos climbed down, careful of his back, and stepped into the middle of the road. His right shoulder was growing sore, but he shook off his discomfort and began waving his arms until the gray car—a Ford—began to slow. It pulled up, stopping just where the truck and the Imperial had collided.

"You need a hospital?" the driver asked Theron in Farsi.

The Greek shook his head. "Tehran. Just Tehran," he said, and the driver of the Ford motioned for him to get in.

"Terrible accident," the driver said. "The others are dead?"

Theron Tassos nodded.

The driver pulled a jug of water out of his back seat and offered it to the Greek, who took several massive swigs.

"Please, let's go quickly," Theron said.

"Yes, yes—hospital."

"The city."

"Yes, the city."

As they pulled around the Imperial, Theron looked into the passenger's seat where Fedot had been lying unconscious. The bench was empty—the imprint of Fedot's body in the leather being the only evidence that the spiritualist had ever been there at all.

Theron spun around, taking in the arid landscape—but there was no Fedot. A pair of footprints—new and small—was visible near the passenger-side door but disappeared as they rounded the hood of the Imperial. Otherwise there was nothing.

Fedot Titov was gone.

CHAPTER 52

"It is said love can tame the most ferocious monster," Beryx Gulyas whispered, not wanting to wake her. Not yet. "Perhaps even the most stuck-up slut."

The Hungarian patted Lily's bottom lip with the tip of his index finger. Her lips—they were his favorite of her many splendid attributes—pouted unwittingly as she lay unconscious. He was disappointed, however, that she had painted them with lipstick, even if it had, for the most part, faded, leaving only a dessert-cherry stain. The Hungarian was still furious with her, of course, and she would pay for his injuries. But for these last few moments as she lay wound into a feline curl in the truck's cab, he wanted to admire her.

Re-buttoning his pants—they were too tight for his comfort when he was sitting down—the Hungarian stepped out of the truck and went to the passenger's side door. The road was quiet—not a visible soul in this verdant and empty part of Tehran, an oasis away from the bustling shops and dusty streets that characterized much of the city. He looked once more to the right and left, then wrenched open the cab door.

Lily screamed—a little too quickly—when he grabbed her by the hair and dragged her out of the truck. She hadn't been unconscious after all, and Beryx Gulyas wondered how long she'd been pretending. She writhed and dug her nails into his wrists as he pulled her inside the small, brick building hidden by the side of the road. He'd spied it when he was tailing the American car belonging to Lily's father, and it had seemed ideal for his purposes. Modest, off the beaten path, and leading into what looked like a garden. That was the feature he liked most of all. Lily looked most beautiful when she was surrounded by flora. He had laid lilies, her namesake, and palm fronds around her when she was his captive.

A man in a black robe appeared from behind a gated door, yelling in Farsi and waving his arms. Gulyas let go of Lily's hair and shot him in the face, the sound of gunfire echoing unpleasantly around them. He then darted around the foyer and behind the gated door, poking his gun around corners and into structural crannies until he was satisfied they were alone.

"What is this place?" Gulyas wondered aloud, tapping his fingers on a thick plate of colored glass that separated the entrance from the main body of the interior.

Like many places in Tehran, the structure's outward appearance did not match its inner character. While the exterior was that of a simple brick bungalow, its only flourish being a light green metal roof resembling a beret, the interior was magnificent. Silver and gold—pressed into thin, decorative motifs—ran along the border of an arched ceiling, while gemstone mosaic tiles, so tiny, embellished the walls, breaking only for a line or two of Arabic script. The floors were a cool, blue marble.

"It's a cemetery," Lily told him.

"How do you know?" The Hungarian loved her less when she spoke.

"Because it says so." Lily pointed to the wall.

"You can read this?"

Lily shrugged.

"It's not just any cemetery," she explained. "It's for the

Imam-born. For any immediate descendant of a Shi'a Imam."

Beryx Gulyas ran the barrel of his gun along the ocean-like waves of the engraved script that Lily claimed to be able to decipher. He'd never understood the need for elaborate death rituals. Upon his own death, he couldn't care less if he was picked apart by vultures, although Nicolai Ceausescu had promised him a fine stone somewhere in a cemetery designated for men who served him.

"Idiotic," he sniffed.

He led Lily out into the back garden, where several dozen tombstones lay like single beds in a dormitory. Most were covered by a smooth, black cloth—blacker than night and undamaged by the Persian sun.

"You know, you could've just shot me on the road back there," Lily said. "That's what I would've done."

Beryx Gulyas actually chuckled. Low and grunting, but it was a chuckle. Lily smiled, gazing over the shrouded tombstones.

"Of course, a cemetery is sort of like one-stop shopping for you. I mean in terms of having to dispose of a body—you couldn't ask for a better place." Lily unpinned her hair, running her hands through it. "Much better," she said, shaking it out.

Gulyas adjusted his pants. "I don't dispose of bodies," he informed her. "Not my job."

"Mmm." Lily rolled her neck from side to side. "Well, I would think in this case you'd make an exception." Lily leaned on her hip and dropped her hand, running her knuckles along one of the black cloths. She took in a deep, slow breath. Her hand was shaking, and she made a tight fist. Lily bit down, and when she released her fingers, they were still. "I love black," she said. "It seems like such a shame that people only wear it to funerals." Plucking a burial cloth off one of the tombs, Lily held it to her cheek. "I think this would flatter me, don't you? I mean if I took my dress off right now and laid down on one of these tombs, draping only this cloth over me?" She traced her neckline with the cloth and swept her eyes over his body. "You'd like that, wouldn't you?"

Gulyas was breathing heavier now.

"I bet you'd take me dead or alive," she said, reaching back and unzipping her dress.

He took a step forward. Lily took two.

"But if I'm alive, I can run my hands all over your body." Lily blew on her fingers, then trailed them under the black shroud. "And if I'm not, you have all the power. That's a very difficult decision on your part."

Both options certainly were appealing to him, but one more so. He imagined her bathing him, the way his Aunt Zuzanna had done, guiding the slippery bar of soap over his body, lathering his most sensitive places. Lily had delicate hands—unlike Zuzanna. With long, slender fingers. And she was trembling—the way he used to tremble with Zuzanna in the beginning. When he still loved her. When her very presence made him quiver with anticipation.

"I want you to touch me," he said. "Everywhere."

"I thought you would." Lily took another step toward him. "I bet you'd like me to do a lot of things."

Gulyas swallowed and blinked hard. The many, many things that he wanted Lily to do to him flashed through his mind. They involved her teeth and fingernails, her hair, of course, and her lips most of all. He wanted her to look on him fully naked and with desire. And to eat a pistachio out of his navel. Just one.

Sadly, for him, his erotic musings were cut short when

Lily flung the cloth over his head. He clawed and pulled at the thing, shooting randomly until he could yank it off and aim his gun. But Lily was no longer standing before him. Gulyas spun this way and that, peering around the tombstones. He pointed his barrel into the shrubbery and was about to shoot again when he heard a scratch coming from behind a narrow marble wall near the back entrance to the brick edifice. It was the heel of a woman's shoe scraping over a groove in a tile.

"You didn't get very far, did you?" he said.

Lily had not. She'd hoped to make it into the building and, with any luck, out onto the street, where Gulyas had parked the truck, but she'd only gotten as far as a small cubicle meant for ceremonial bathing. "Maybe I was just wanting to play a little hide-and-seek," she said.

The Hungarian pulled a handkerchief from his pocket and dipped it into a bowl of water that floated several blossoms of Persian Lilac. Sweat rolled from his hairline down his temples. Gulyas blotted the handkerchief over the burns on his face and neck, all at once wincing and sighing with relief. "Do you believe in destiny, Lily?"

It was a rhetorical question.

"Some of us create our own destinies, Mr. Gulyas," said a man's voice.

The Hungarian twisted around and trained his pistol on Theron Tassos. It was the first time he'd gotten a good look at Lily's father, and he was impressed by the man's presence. Although his suit had been sullied and his hair was out of place, the Greek baron stood with the confidence of a brigadier general. It was because he was fit; Gulyas knew it. A man with a good physique was always poised, regardless of what shape his clothes might be in. The Hungarian envied him his metabolism and self-discipline. Gulyas sucked in his belly as he cocked his gun. "You don't seem like a man who wants to lose his balls," he said.

"And you don't seem like a man who wants to die in agonizing pain." Theron smiled. "But then, who does?"

The Hungarian angled his pistol, directing it at the Greek's genitals.

"Daddy?" Lily's voice came from behind the cubicle.

"Your daddy's unarmed, and I'm going to shoot his balls off if you don't step out here right away," Gulyas said. He saw the pointed toe of her shoe first before Lily slinked fully away from the relative safety of the marble wall.

"You don't have to get all cross," she said. "We were just playing, weren't we?" She allowed her dress to slip lightly off her shoulder, letting Gulyas know it was still unzipped.

"I like it when you're reasonable," he told her. "Now be a good pet and come sit at my feet."

"But can't we go inside?" she asked. "It's so hot out here. And we could all get to know each other." Inside wasn't much better than outside, but it had some possibilities. Doors that led places, and the fact that it was one step closer to the street.

"I told you to come sit at my feet, you mouthy whore!"

Theron Tassos ignored both his daughter and the Hungarian's outburst. "I came alone here, Mr. Gulyas, but I'm not one man—do you understand?"

Beryx Gulyas did not. His index finger beckoned Lily, and she obeyed this time, taking short, careful steps until she reached his side.

"I cover more ground than a certain member of the Romanian Politburo, for instance," Theron explained. "In fact, I could have someone in Mr. Ceausescu's house within the hour if I wanted to. Leaving a stubborn stain on that enormous Ottoman rug in his Great Room. Do you understand now?"

The Hungarian pulled the gun close to his chest. He didn't put it down, but he tipped the barrel toward the ground, slightly.

"You're a good listener, Mr. Gulyas," Theron said. He glanced briefly at his daughter, who had seated herself at the Hungarian's feet. "And I'm a good negotiator."

Lily's heart sank as her father removed a curlicue of microfilm—Pasha's microfilm, the *Sputnik* plans that Fedot had so deftly slipped into his pocket earlier in the day—and dangled it before Beryx Gulyas.

"No, Daddy," she said, but her father ignored her.

"I know what the Americans would want for this," Theron continued. "And the Soviets. But what, I wonder, would an ambitious Romanian like your boss be willing to pay for a trip to the moon?"

Beryx Gulyas scratched his neck and looked Theron Tassos up and down.

"Why wouldn't I shoot you and take it and whatever else here belongs to me?" He caressed Lily's hair with the barrel of his pistol. "You don't even have a weapon."

Theron held the microfilm steadily between his thumb and middle finger.

"I don't need a weapon," he said.

Gulyas watched the man. He had become an expert at detecting a bluff over the years, and it was clear to him that in Lily he hadn't stumbled upon just any rich, American girl. There was no doubt in his mind that if he didn't relinquish Lily to her father and call Ceausescu with the opportunity to bid on the *Sputnik* plans, Theron Tassos would have him hunted to the far corners of the earth and killed in a way that would make Etor's end peaceful in comparison.

"Good, Mr. Gulyas," Tassos said. "Fear of the Lord is the beginning of wisdom."

The Hungarian looked down at Lily and then once more at her father. As he looked into the Greek's eyes—their bottomlessness and certainty—he understood. He had taken things too far with Lily and managed to conjure hatred in a normally cold-blooded adversary. Tassos wanted Lily, he wanted a lucrative deal for the *Sputnik* plans, and he wanted Beryx Gulyas to suffer a protracted and pitiless end.

Breathing in deeply through his nose and letting his belly protrude, Gulyas lifted his gun and shot Theron Tassos through the throat.

CHAPTER 53

"*Kurva!*" the Hungarian howled as Lily sunk her teeth into his calf. Lily would remember the distinctive metallic flavor of Beryx Gulyas's blood for the rest of her life. As an old woman, telling this story to her only living grandchild, she would swear that she could distinguish the flavor of his blood from any of her other enemies.

Gulyas snarled, losing his grip on the gun. It fell with a muted clank on the cloth-covered marble tomb of a significant Imam descendent.

Wheezing deeply, the Hungarian doubled over and gripped Lily's ears. She clamped down harder, wrenching her head from side to side. Lily knew her only advantage was the Hungarian's shock at being attacked so decisively during his cold execution of her father. Already he was adjusting to the pain of her bite, thinking clearer, and a mere second or two away from reclaiming his upper hand and breaking her neck.

Ivanov. He came into Lily's thoughts like an idea—suddenly and accompanied by a rush of adrenaline. She remembered what he'd whispered to her in her torture-induced daze at the baker's apartment, when she was fully under the Hungarian's control. It was of her ability to endure what he called the agony in merely one possible world among an infinite number of universes. It almost made her laugh. All at once, she felt someone else's presence as well—a real presence, not a memory or a dream. Physically—right there. As she no longer believed in figments of her imagination, she knew what she felt in the cemetery was as real as the dense chunk of calf muscle that pulsed inside her mouth. As absolute as her father's inert body—his flesh cooling and pale from the emptying of his jugular vein.

In that same split second of realization, the Hungarian let go of her. Lily could feel his pointed stare, and slowly she released his leg from her jaws. Wiping his blood from her chin, Lily looked up into Beryx Gulyas's face. His eyes were distended, and he was biting his bottom lip as if he had something unpleasant to tell her—something that pained him.

"What do you want from me?" Lily grunted, barely recognizing her own voice.

But the Hungarian remained silent. His gaze was broken only by Fedot, who emerged from behind him and clasped his elbow around his neck. Lily watched as Fedot pressed the knuckles of his right hand deep into Gulyas's kidney, triggering shockwaves of agony. The Hungarian was strong, but the Russian was exceptional in his purpose and calm. As if he were merely opening a difficult jar of pickles.

"Fedot!" Lily shouted. Her eyes had darted to the Imam descendant's grave, where the killer had managed to hook his gun under his fingertips and drag it back into the grip of his palm.

The Hungarian's movements were jerky and erratic as he raised his arm; he was still gasping for breath. Gulyas pointed the barrel back at Fedot's head, but Lily shot to her feet and grabbed his wrist as he fired. The bullet scraped Fedot, taking part of his ear and causing him to stumble backward. Lily thrust her knee into the Hungarian's groin, and once again, he dropped his gun. This time Lily dove on top of it, but Beryx Gulyas made no attempt to retrieve the weapon. Instead, he leapt over her and ran to the cemetery wall. It wasn't a very tall boundary, and he was able to scale it, although not without some difficulty. His sausage-shaped body rolled over the top just as Lily dug her hand under her belly and pulled his gun out. She shot at him, although it was a futile gesture. He had already fallen to the ground, and she could hear him get up and run.

CHAPTER 54

"The Hungarian has written an end for his life, Miss Lily."

"Yes, Fedot," she said, but her heart wasn't in it.

They were riding in the truck Gulyas had stolen with Fedot at the wheel, bleeding from his halved ear. Lily had torn the lining out of her dress and bandaged Fedot's head with it. She stared out the window, first watching the Tehran neighborhoods flip by like pages, then following the hypnotic turns of the road winding up into the Alborz Mountain range.

Lily could not fathom the death of her fathere. And she couldn't allow herself to mourn him, either—not yet. Not with Pasha still out there and everything at stake.

For now she would pretend that her father was merely gone—unavailable to her, but not dead. Not lying under a black shroud on an Imam's grave and waiting for Lily to return and give him a proper burial. She wished it was Gulyas lying dead—his body bloating in the hot Persian sun. That image was her only pleasure.

"Where do you suppose he'll turn up?" she asked Fedot. He shook his head.

Lily believed the Hungarian was very close. Beryx Gulyas couldn't, after all, return to his master without the microfilm she had pulled from between her father's fingers. The dangerous "piece of candy" that Pasha had risked his life for and that her father had been willing to sell to the highest bidder. Nor would the Hungarian go back to

Romania without Lily. Or at least without her blood under his fingernails.

"I wish Pasha was here," she sighed as Fedot rolled in behind Mansoor Nassa's mountain retreat, pulling up the emergency brake and hoping it still worked.

"So do I, Miss Lily," Fedot said. Lily adjusted the side mirror so that she could look at her face. She spit-cleaned her cheeks and applied a thick coat of lipstick before pulling her hair into a neat braid.

They left the banged-up vehicle on the side of the road between Nassa's house and another, giving the appearance that a service truck had broken down. Despite looking ruffled and fatigued, they walked the steep slope of Mansoor Nassa's driveway without hurry—as if they were invited guests just in time for tea.

The door to the house was hidden behind a vine-covered panel, and Lily stepped forward, banging a triangular knocker against its metal base. For several seconds, the house was still—as if no one was or ever would be there—but slowly it came to life, and the sound of footsteps echoed up from the first and second floors.

"Good evening," Lily said.

The woman who opened the door was Iranian. She wore her hair in a tight bun, and her lips were even tighter.

"Lilia Tassos is here for Ambassador Pearce," Lily affirmed. Fedot stood at her side, his head turned away so the servant woman couldn't see his crude, blood-soaked bandage.

The woman, in perfect English with a distinctly British accent, asked them to remain where they were while she summoned the ambassador.

"I'm Lilia Tassos, Theron Tassos's daughter," Lily said as Barnaby Pearce came up from the stairs and entered the foyer.

"Yes, I know who you are," the ambassador said. "May I help you?"

"I'm terribly late, I know, but Mr. Nassa was sure you would see me."

"Mr. Nassa?"

"Ambassador Pearce, may we please come in and talk to you?" Lily said. "It is of the utmost importance."

The ambassador blinked twice and nodded, showing them in. He seemed less than delighted to have them there but resigned to their presence nonetheless.

"This is Fedot Titov." Lily made the introduction as Fedot extended his hand. "Mr. Titov, as you may have already heard, is traveling with us. He came to Tehran with me and Pasha Tarkhan."

Ambassador Pearce dispatched his maid to fetch proper bandages for Fedot—casually, as if his wounded ear was little more than a stubbed toe. He extended the usual pleasantries, offering to lead them downstairs into the main cavity of the residence. There, he said, they could have a proper drink and discuss things in a civilized fashion.

"Will your father be joining us later?" he asked.

"No," Lily said. "My father has nothing to do with this."

Pearce raised an eyebrow.

"Whatever *this* may be," he said.

Mansoor Nassa's mountain retreat was a deliberate antidote to his house in the city, eschewing antiques and unconcealed anglophilia for the modern chic of steel and glass. Built into the mountain and three stories high, it offered unparalleled views of Tehran, which would glimmer like a starlit sky once the sun fell. A plateau supported a descending garden at its side. Nassa couldn't live without a garden.

"You do have a poison, don't you?" Ambassador Pearce asked. Theron Tassos never touched alcohol, but he and Lily differed in that way and always would. She asked for bourbon.

"Never trust a teetotaler," Pearce snickered as he led them down to the second floor and motioned for Lily and Fedot to take a seat.

The Great Room on the second floor was a study in minimalism and furnished only with a lime-green, semi-circular couch and a table of petrified wood. There was no art on the white walls and no rug on the polished, marble floor. Anything else would have been a distraction from the glass wall that angled down onto Iran's capital city. Flanking that wall of glass were two enormous mirrors that gave the illusion Tehran went on for eternity.

Standing at one of those mirrors and turning toward Lily and Fedot as they sat down was a jowly man with round, heavily-framed glasses, his graying hair slicked back and parted in the middle.

"Miss Tassos and Mr. Titov, this is Sandmore Chandler, the American ambassador to Iran," Pearce offered.

Lily extended her hand. "Mr. Nassa has told me a great deal about you, Mr. Ambassador. He says you're quite a card player."

Sandmore Chandler nodded, looking from Lily to Pearce.

Chandler—Sandy, as Pearce called him—joined Fedot and Lily on the couch, crossing one leg over the other and leaning back. Despite the effort, he didn't at all look relaxed.

"I'm sure you'll both appreciate it if I get to the point," Lily said.

"Ah, we're used to roundabout discussions," Sandy Chandler said. He seemed like a genial enough man.

"Then hopefully, I'll be refreshing," Lily told him.

"My dear," Pearce said. "You already are."

Ambassador Pearce opened a hidden door on the back wall and produced an excellent bottle of bourbon. He poured four crystal highball glasses, three fingers full, and brought them to the seating area.

"Pasha Tarkhan has defected," Lily said. Chandler and Pearce remained poker-faced. "Mr. Titov and I travelled from Moscow to Iran with him, but in the course of events, Mr. Tarkhan has been recaptured by the Soviets."

Chandler and Pearce exchanged looks again but remained patient—a study in the diplomatic arts.

"Perhaps I should start from the beginning," Lily said, receiving neither encouragement nor contradiction.

She began her story where she felt her life had begun—or was reborn—with Tony Geiger's death on Monemvasia. Lily continued with the Hungarian's attack on Pasha in Moscow, the massacre at the Lavra and their escape to Tehran, omitting any mention of *Sputnik*, her kidnapping by Gulyas, and her father's murder.

"Miss Tassos," Sandy Chandler began. "As far as we know, Mr. Tarkhan is still in Moscow."

"A high-level defection is hardly something the Soviets would want to advertise," Lily said. "Especially to their enemies." She hoped a big fish like Pasha would be enough to bring in the cavalry, so to speak. And instinct told her not to bring *Sputnik* into this—not yet.

"Mr. Chandler, I—we—Mr. Titov and I, came to Iran with Pasha Tarkhan. I helped nurse him to health after he was injected with acid by an assassin and brought him to Mr. Nassa's house in Tehran. From there, we intended to come here to see you, but as I explained, we ran into some difficulties."

With the Hungarian around, Lily was starting to feel worried for Mansoor Nassa. It didn't appear he'd made it to the mountains yet, and judging by the reactions of Pearce and Chandler, he'd never been in touch to brief them about her arrival either. Her heart feared Beryx Gulyas could have somehow intercepted the poet, though she couldn't imagine when he would have had time.

"Miss Tassos," Sandy Chandler said. He put his drink to his lips, then set it down on the petrified wood. "I'm not sure why you've come here, of all places, and not to the American Embassy where your rights as an American citizen are unequivocal."

Lily knew her explanation had to be careful and plausible. The truth about Ivanov and his spiritual directives was lunacy—at least to anyone who'd never met the "Russian saint."

"Ambassador Chandler, Ambassador Pearce, we thought a private residence might be a less conspicuous place to meet than an embassy—especially one that is in all likelihood being watched by people looking for me and especially for Mr. Tarkhan. And we were so fortunate to have this house offered to us by its owner."

Pearce shook his head. "The British Embassy?"

Lily smiled. "I'm sorry?"

"This house is now owned by Her Majesty's Foreign Service."

Lily sat back and took a long, deep swallow of her drink. "But Mr. Nassa . . ."

"Yes, of course, Manny," Pearce said, clasping his hands. "It did used to belong to him, poor chap."

Lily bit her lip.

"Good man, he was," Pearce said.

Chandler nodded in agreement. They both took another swig of their bourbons.

"He left this house to the British Embassy. Always said he would, but, uh, didn't expect it so soon," Pearce clarified. "I don't quite know what'll come of his city place. Or his money. Don't think he had any heirs."

Lily's hand began to tremble. She balled it into a fist and placed it in her lap. She looked to Fedot, who continued to stare at the ambassadors.

"Yes, poor man," she said. "I never did get the details."

Pearce sighed heavily. Lily could see his affection for the poet.

"A doroshkeh accident," he said.

"He and his doroshkehs," Chandler lamented. "Crushed between two city buses. He and his servant girl killed instantly. Only the driver survived. Not a scratch. Imagine that."

"Not a good way to go," Pearce remarked. "But fast. The corpses were unrecognizable, of course. Good thing the driver could identify them."

Lily wanted to speak, to say something in protest, but instead composed herself. She couldn't afford to look like a fool—or worse.

"A doroshkeh accident," Lily said.

"And he went owing me money, too," Chandler said.

The ambassadors chuckled.

"Never could play a decent hand of cards."

CHAPTER 55

KANDOVAN, IRAN

"An ancient legend—Sardinian, I think—alleges that the bodies of those born on Christmas Eve will never become dust like the rest of ours, but will be preserved until the end of time."

The Great Detective opened the wooden shutter above the tiny propane stove, but just barely. Outside the sun was completely obscured, and the swirling air was the color of sepia. His hair and skin felt coated in a film of sediment that was somewhere between the consistency of cake flour and ash. Even Pasha Tarkhan's bandages—fresh only a couple of hours before—had already taken on the look of ancient parchment.

"It's a shame you can't get a good look around here," Rodki continued. "It's an interesting place. Of course, you're much more travelled than I am, so perhaps this is all passé for you."

The weather had held up General Pushkin's plane, and judging by the sound of the wind battering the tiny beehive of a place they were staying in, the plane wouldn't be arriving any time soon. Dust storms in this part of the world were legendary. Hazardous, and with the potential to last for days. The one that had begun that morning had started typically enough, but by afternoon, as the storm picked up strength—first obscuring the mountains, then the town, then even their last few feet of vision—locals were already speculating that this might become the worst storm in memory.

"Just the same," Rodki mumbled.

He was not looking forward to handing Pasha Tarkhan over to General Pushkin anyway. It spelled the end of a brilliant man, and Russia was fast running out of people with any real brains—what with his former master's purges. The Great Detective thought it was a marvel the Soviet Union continued to function at all and wondered how many decades it could survive on merely the fumes of its revolution.

"Quite a predicament," he said, though mostly to himself this time.

"I thought I was the only one of us in a predicament," Pasha said.

Rodki Semyonov smiled; he couldn't help himself. Pasha Tarkhan hadn't uttered a word in their time together. Not as Rodki removed a bullet from his upper chest, and not during their endless ride back to Kandovan. The Great Detective, having met Tarkhan before, knew what good company he was. And if there was one thing for which he had a weakness, it was for good company. So much of his life was solitary.

"Your predicament is certainly grimmer than mine, but we are both in a predicament," the Great Detective alleged. He hummed a few lines of "The Lights of Moscow Nights."

This time Pasha Tarkhan smiled. "You don't belong here," he said.

"Here," Rodki asked. "In Kandovan?"

Tarkhan shook his head. "Moscow."

Tarkhan adjusted his position and tried unsuccessfully to sit up. The morphine was starting to wear off. Rodki Semyonov removed a blanket—a rich tapestry of henna, mustard seed and eggplant—from the top shelf of the pantry and stuffed it carefully behind Pasha Tarkhan's shoulders. The morphine was running low, and he only wanted to use it when absolutely necessary.

"Why would you say such a thing?" he asked.

"Why would you be interested in my comfort?" Pasha countered.

Rodki shrugged and smiled again. "I'm interested in you, of course. What can I say? I'm a detective."

"Precisely."

The Great Detective had nothing further to add. To his disappointment, this spelled an end to their brief exchange, and Rodki wondered if there was anything he could have said to save the conversation. That he couldn't leave his wife, perhaps, whose memory sat with him every morning at his breakfast table? Or worse, that he simply loved the taste of Russian coffee, though he knew it was terrible by any rational, objective standard?

"Mr. Tarkhan," he said. "You are Georgian by extraction. But I am a Russian tried and true."

"Then perhaps you're right," Tarkhan said, his voice trailing off as a wave of pain overtook him. "I'm not the only one in a predicament."

Rodki Semyonov watched Pasha Tarkhan slip further into an exhausted sleep. He liked the man—very much—and held his general character and abilities in high esteem. He knew little about him, of course, at least specifically. But nobody in Moscow talked about Tarkhan much, and that in and of itself told him a great deal.

It occurred to him he should kill Pasha Tarkhan now, rather than let Pushkin get ahold of him. Such thoughts were rash, and the Great Detective knew it. How could he explain shooting a sleeping man *before* his interrogation? If he'd shot him like he should have—when Tarkhan had attempted to flee in the Mahallah—this wouldn't be an issue. Damn "The Lights of Moscow Nights."

No, the Great Detective would have to let him go under some sort of plausible circumstance and then kill him as he made his escape. It would be best for everyone that way. Even General Pushkin, who despite his cruel nature, would surely have felt a brief pang of regret as he sent his one-time friend to die in a gulag.

CHAPTER 56

"*Sputnik*, you said?" Pearce repeated. "Sounds like a board game."

"Or a game of dice," Sandy Chandler offered. They'd both agreed it was a funny-sounding name for spaceship. "Not at all dignified," Pearce concluded while Chandler poured himself another bourbon.

Lily's mention of *Sputnik* at this point in the game was undoubtedly reckless, but she could think of no other alternative. The horrible news about Mansoor Nassa had been a considerable blow to her position of strength.

"How about *Dostoyevsky 1?*" Pearce chortled.

"Or *The Brothers Karamazov*, if there were three of them?" Chandler chimed in.

"Dostoyevsky intended the work to be the first part of an epic titled, *The Life of a Great Sinner*. He died, of course, before he could complete it."

Pearce *hmmm'*d.

Lily put her drink down, uncrossed her legs and cupped her hands over her knees.

"The satellite is a five-hundred-eighty-five-millimeter diameter sphere, assembled from two hemispheres which are hermetically sealed using O-rings—whatever those are—and connected using thirty-six bolts," she recited. "It has a mass of eighty-three point six kilograms. The hemispheres, covered with a highly polished one-millimeter-thick heat shield, are made of an aluminum-magnesium-titanium alloy, and are two millimeters thick. Shall I continue?"

Pearce blinked hard and looked at Chandler, who put his drink down and folded his arms across his chest. Behind them, leaning with his back against the gigantic picture window, Fedot stood smiling.

"Please," the American ambassador said.

"The satellite carries two antennas. Each is made up of two parts, two point four and two point nine meters long. Each of these antennas resembles whiskers pointing to one side, at equal thirty-five-degree angles with the longitudinal axis of the satellite. The power supply, with a mass of fifty-one kilograms, is in the shape of an octagonal nut with the radio transmitter in its hole. It consists of three silver-zinc batteries. A temperature regulation system contains a fan, a dual thermal switch and a control thermal switch. *Sputnik* is filled with dry nitrogen, pressurized to one point three atm—or atn, I'm not sure. The typeface was smeared. While attached to the rocket, *Sputnik* will be protected by a cone-shaped, payload fairing, with a height of eighty centimeters and an aperture of forty-eight degrees. The fairing will separate from both *Sputnik* and the rocket simultaneously when the satellite is ejected."

Pearce and Chandler stood together at the bar, unmoving. Finally, Chandler cleared his throat.

"You, uh, remember all that?" he asked.

"Yes, sir."

"I see. Well, that was quite a recitation, I must say." He sauntered over to Lily and hovered above her. "And one any pretty little actress could have memorized on the long journey from Russia to Iran."

Lily held the American ambassador's gaze and then glanced over to Pearce. Judging by the look on Barnaby Pearce's face, Lily had struck a nerve. The British ambassador was a trained engineer, after all, and Mansoor Nassa had made a point of his passionate interest in astronomy. Pearce would know her level of detail and explicit knowledge could be neither lie nor fantasy. Lily stood up and placed her hands on her hips.

"I'm not an actress, Ambassador Chandler," she said. "I'm the daughter of a very powerful man. And it took me thirty seconds to memorize the information I just gave you. I've heard it's called a photographic memory, but I've never paid such monikers much thought. To me, it was always just a great tool for getting good grades without having to try too hard—you know?"

Chandler scratched his neck and sniffed. It was a gesture meant to buy him time, not satisfy an itch.

"Well, then, Miss Tassos," he said. "Why don't you write down these *Sputnik* plans for us so that we can actually share them with someone who might know what a—what is it you said, 'O-ring,' is?"

Lily sighed. It had been imperative that she describe the *Sputnik* plans perfectly and convincingly for credibility's sake, but she also needed to sound just naïve and frightened enough that the ambassadors would never suspect she had any more than what she'd given them.

"I can," she explained. "But I'm not sure they'd do you much good. I only looked at a couple of pages worth of the written designs. The complete plans are copied onto a tiny roll of microfilm—one that only Pasha Tarkhan can provide, I'm afraid."

It occurred to her that she had been too direct for Ambassador Chandler's liking. Most men liked their tough-talking women on a movie screen, played by women like Lauren Bacall. Lily sat back down and buried her face in her palms.

"Oh, please," she begged. "I must help Pasha. I love him."

It was true, of course, but she laid it on thick the way she did back home when she was stopped for a traffic violation. There was always a crisis, a vindictive boyfriend, a broken engagement (although that one had been true) she could pull out of her back pocket. That and a tear or two would soften the stern look on any policeman's face. The few times she'd told the truth, remained stalwart and taken responsibility—*Yes, Officer, I certainly have been drinking, but I'm not drunk per se*—she got the ticket. She couldn't afford to get the ticket with Pearce and Chandler. Pasha's life was at stake.

"There, there," Chandler said, patting her shoulder.

"I guess I should call Daddy—maybe he could help after all. Do you suppose I could use your telephone?"

Pearce and Chandler looked to one another in unison.

"I can't imagine that will be necessary," Pearce countered. Chandler nodded. "I'm sure I could make a couple of calls and get some idea of where a Soviet agent might take a high-level diplomatic defector around here."

"How much longer?" Lily yelled over the wind. Her goggles were pressed on too tightly, giving her a dreadful headache. Lily despised motorcycles. "Fedot!"

Fedot didn't answer –perhaps he didn't hear her. He was pushing the cycle's engine to its limits and it—along with the sidecar Lily was crouched in—practically hovered above the road. Actually, Lily wished it was a road—by her standards, anyway. The divots, pea gravel, dust and potholes that characterized the main artery leading to Iran's rugged northwest could hardly be called a road. She held on tightly, nearly getting bounced out and into a ditch, where the leather cap, jacket and thick canvas pants she was wearing might protect her from the worst kinds of road burns and scrapes but couldn't keep her from bashing her head on some of the larger rocks at the road's edge.

"Watch it, will you?" she chided.

Lily was still angry, and unfairly taking it out on Fedot. She had expected more help from the Ambassadors Chandler and Pearce. Especially after coming clean not only about *Sputnik*, but the Soviet directive to put a nuclear arsenal into space in sight of a decade. For all that, she'd gotten the name of a province where Pasha had likely been taken, a village with a rudimentary airstrip frequented by the Soviet Union, and a BMW R69 motorcycle with sidecar.

Pearce had also given her some of his younger son's biking clothes, making Lily look something like Amelia Earhart, though not, she hoped, on her way down and into oblivion. He would have liked to do more, she thought. As she and Fedot prepared to leave, Pearce had come out to the cycle to "bid them farewell." In reality he'd come to slip her a gun. It was a .44 Magnum—bigger and better than the one she'd taken from Gulyas—and likely an indication of the kind of trouble Barnaby Pearce thought she was getting herself into. Ambassador Pearce, for all his back-slapping and bourbon-swilling, was a serious man who held his cards very close.

Lily wondered what Mansoor Nassa thought of Pearce. She imagined he'd liked him very much—perhaps they'd talked of horror movies together. Nassa's death weighed heavily on her heart in an unexpected way. Perhaps it was his lovely and peculiar way with words, or the quotes he could summon so effortlessly. What was it he had said to her on that morning as they left for the market? *Is not pacifism cowardice dressed in the frock of ideology?* Pasha had laughed heartily at that.

"We're close!" Fedot shouted. "But I'm afraid not close enough, Miss Lily."

He pointed toward the horizon—or at least to what would have been the horizon. Up ahead, billowing, coming straight for them, was an enormous russet-colored cloud that stretched from the sky to the soil.

"What the hell is that?" Lily cried.

"Looks like a dust storm."

"How on earth are we going to get around it?"

Fedot glanced toward her and revved the engine. "We're not."

Lily watched as the distance between them and the dust cloud closed.

"Fedot, we can't do this!"

"Have faith, Miss Lily," he shouted. "If there were another way, surely God would have shown us by now."

CHAPTER 57

In a moment, day turned to night. The wind churned the air around them as the storm enveloped Lily and Fedot completely, obscuring everything but a few feet of vision. The air was dense and chalky, difficult to breathe. Lily pulled a handkerchief from her pocket, holding it over her mouth and nose. Up ahead, there came into view what looked like a large shadow shaped in the form of a termite's nest and studded with hazy, twinkling lights.

"Kandovan," Fedot said as the motorcycle slowed.

The village of crude dwellings began to take shape as they entered its perimeters. With its streets deserted, Kandovan had the feel of an abandoned archeological site, except for the scattering of lanterns in the windows of various caves and hives. The only sounds were those of the storm—the wind, the tiny bits of refuse being blown about, the bray of an animal in pain.

A little pension sat at the foot of the village, accessible only by a stone staircase leading down to a rounded doorway. The entrance resembled a tomb, Lily thought. She and Fedot parked the R69 and made their way to the pension step by step, enduring the assault of pebbles, dust particles, chips of wood and assortment of granules that whipped at them like a gauntlet of cat o' nine tails.

"Good evening," Lily bid the pension owner in Arabic as they entered the lobby. The room had curved ceilings the color of bone and was furnished with Persian rugs, pillows and the occasional wooden end table that held worn and charred kerosene lamps.

The owner—sporting a quilted tarboush and a midnight blue tunic—introduced himself as Ismayil. He stared blankly at Lily, a study in incomprehension as he tried to grasp what kind of woman would dress the way she was dressed. It was odd even by the modern, Western standards the Shah had imposed upon Persia.

"A room, please, Mr. Ismayil," Lily said. "For my husband and myself." She took off her goggles, revealing two white rings around her eyes, and smiled. The pension owner laughed.

"What a weather," Ismayil said in his native Azeri-Turkic. "Allah is angry with someone." With its Arabic influences, Lily was able to discern roughly what he was saying. His intent was another thing altogether. She wasn't quite sure whether he was implying it was she who had angered Allah or if Allah was simply taking his wrath out on some other unnamed offender.

"I'm sure Allah will be just in his dealings," she said in Arabic. Ismayil seemed to understand, or at least get the gist of her comment. From behind a thick, embroidered pillow, he procured a wooden block the size of a deck of cards. It hung on the end of a loop of rope, and the owner swung it around his index finger as he led them through a honeycomb of guest rooms. Theirs was tucked around a corner, and he opened the door for them, hanging the block on an irregular, handmade nail that protruded from the wooden door at eye level. Ismayil stepped into the darkness of the guest room, lit a lantern and scurried away, giggling after bidding them a good night.

"I guess they don't believe in locks around here," Lily

said. She swiped at the hanging block—the only apparent marker that their room was now occupied.

Lily stood outside their door for a moment and listened—familiarizing herself with the various noises specific to the pension. There weren't many of them, as the pension couldn't have had more than one other occupant: she could hear the habitual snorting of a man—probably middle-aged—with a sinus problem, and the clinking of water glasses being washed in a small tub. Having no windows, the pension was ventilated by a series of narrow tunnels leading to its plateau rooftop, and these were the only conduits to the sounds of the storm outside. Its incessant howling—nearly deafening in the streets—was barely audible over Isamyil's alto soprano hum.

"Have a nap, Miss Lily," Fedot prescribed. "It's been a long day. I'll wake you when Kandovan is asleep."

Lily wanted to protest, insisting they begin their search for Pasha at once, but she was too dog-tired. Besides, if Pasha was in Kandovan, as Chandler and Pearce believed, then he certainly wasn't going anywhere during a violent dust storm. She went over to the simple washbasin on their night table and splashed her face with tepid water that instantly turned a brownish-gray. Lily then lay down on one of the cots flanking each side of the guest room and slept until Fedot's cool fingertips touched her shoulder some hours later.

"Your *sucuk* looks like a turd," Ismayil complained, pointing to the spicy Turkish sausages.

Rasul was a nothing and always had been. The only

reason Ismayil did business with him at all was because of how fine a person he believed Rasul's father had been.

"They are fresh—just brought up from Elmira's cellar," Rasul said. It was a lie.

"They are months old and have been improperly stored." Ismayil shook his head and crossed his arms.

"It's the air," Rasul persisted. "The weather makes them look too dry, but they are as new as the dawn, I tell you—and firm, not hard."

Ismayil rolled his eyes.

"How could it be the air when your mother's house is connected to mine?" he demanded. "They've never seen the air!"

Their arrangement worked well most of the time: Rasul brought a breakfast platter for the pension guests the night before, and Ismayil stored the *peynir*, butter, eggs, tomatoes and *sucuk* in the root cellar until morning. A sunrise delivery system would have been nice, but Ismayil felt an obligation to Rasul's family, and Rasul was no good in the morning. He stayed up late drinking *raki* with his friends and was rarely seen around the village until noon. And with the exception of tonight, he'd never pulled anything like this.

"I won't pay for them," Ismayil said, stomping his heel.

Rasul shrugged. "Take them. Take them for nothing."

"And what will I feed my guests? I have an American couple here, and they'll think I'm cheating them."

Rasul laid the platter of food at Ismayil's feet. "I'll tell Mami to bring you a *simit* first thing in the morning."

Ismayil waited for Rasul to skulk away before he picked up the platter. Rasul's mother would have never allowed him to bring such sausages if she had seen what he'd prepared. Especially not for foreigners. Ismayil picked up one of the sausages and examined it under the light of a lantern. Dry as a bone. He could never serve them to a guest, of course, but it would be a shame for them to go to waste entirely—and on such a terrible night when all he'd had was a bowl of lentil soup for supper.

CHAPTER 58

"I'm here, Barney," Sandmore Chandler said, nearly shouting. He'd placed the telephone receiver on his desktop while he unpacked his overnight case. "The site isn't far from ancient Praaspa, you know. It's practically the same place Marc Antony failed to capture in 36 BC. Antony's expedition there, in fact, ended in utter failure with heavy losses to the Romans."

Chandler fancied himself an expert on world history, and Barnaby Pearce supposed he was, but that didn't make his dry, pompous lectures any easier to bear. But having gone to Cambridge, Pearce had a lot of experience in suffering pompous lectures.

"Mmm, yes," he said, as Chandler expounded on Marc Antony's various deficiencies. As a general, he found the man overrated.

Overall, Pearce liked Chandler okay. He was a good card player and drinking companion most of the time. Where they differed—and often—was in their approach, and on occasion, their conclusions. Pearce had to admit, when Chandler was right, he was spectacularly right. But his wrongheaded notions had been devastating as well—letting betrayal escape unpunished and leaving true friends to hang. In fact, Pearce believed it was Chandler's paranoia and arrogant misreading of a similar situation that had resulted in the death of Mansoor Nassa. He had come to believe, wrongly, that the poet had anti-Pahlavi sympathies because of a comment

Nassa had once made about the speed with which the Shah was modernizing Iran.

"Sandy, he's Jewish," Pearce had reminded him. "Pahlavi's the only leader in the region who not only doesn't want to kill the Jews, but lets them thrive."

"All the same," Chandler had said. "Plenty of pink Jews in America, and look how the Russians treat them."

Pearce hadn't bothered to try and explain the difference, culturally and politically, between Jews in the Middle East, in America, and in Russia. It never did any good to contradict an enumerator of facts. And Chandler, while unrivaled in his ability to conjure particular facts, was less skilled when it came to understanding themes. Still, Pearce wondered if he should have tried. He would never know for sure if the poet's death was truly an accident or the result of an irresponsible exchange between Chandler and the Shah about Nassa's political leanings. Nassa himself had mentioned to him some weeks ago that he thought he was being followed. He'd noticed a well-dressed fellow, terribly young-looking and affecting the look of Humphrey Bogart—part *Key Largo*, part *Casablanca*. The poet was sure he was an agent of the Shah.

"I hear the local youths still dig up a Roman coin here and there," Pearce said.

Pearce's stomach sank in a feeling he knew well. He regretted telling Chandler that he believed Lily Tassos and everything she'd alleged about the Russian—Pasha Tarkhan.

"I don't know why you would ever trust a word that comes out of that woman's mouth," Chandler said. Pearce could hear him rustling through papers. "She is a member of the American Communist Party."

"Sandy, she says Tony Geiger arranged for that membership. It seems to me entirely possible that--"

"It's right here in black and white, Barnaby," Chandler insisted, thumping his index finger along each word of his type-written fact—MEMBER-OF-THE-AMERICAN-COMMUNIST-PARTY.

"So it does," Pearce conceded. "What do you propose we should do?"

Chandler sighed, exasperated. "You'll leave it to me is what you'll do."

Chandler placed the receiver into its cradle. He shuffled the papers on his lap before tucking them back into their folder and took a drink from his tea. The beverage was already coated with a thin layer of dust, as was everything else in the room. Chandler got up and walked over to the wooden shutters shielding his lone window. He pulled out the felt he'd pushed between crooks of the shutters and peeked outside into the dust storm. It seemed worse than before, and Chandler figured there was no way Pushkin's plane would be landing in this anytime soon.

"Mister-mister," a voice called above the circling wind. A knuckle rapped on the window glass, and Chandler motioned to the door. He opened it just enough to let in a significant puff of dust and debris that was followed by Rasul—covered head to toe in dust as if he were a floured cutlet.

"All done," Rasul said. "Money, money." The mister had promised he would give Rasul three times what Ismayil paid him.

"Here," said Chandler, stuffing a bag of coins into Rasul's hand. "And don't come back."

Rasul didn't understand him, but it didn't matter. He had no intention of coming back there. He had enough money now to buy plenty of *raki* for himself and his friends.

CHAPTER 59

Fedot stood over the pension's owner, Ismayil, studying the anguished look on his face and the way his arms were wrapped tightly around his belly. There remained a nub of dry sausage in the palm of his hand. Stepping over the man's corpse, Fedot walked behind the desk in the pension lobby and rifled through its drawers, procuring for himself and Lily about one hundred rials and a simple iron dagger with a sheath that hung easily from Fedot's belt-loop. The Russian spiritualist crept over to the front door, opening it just a crack and assessing the state of the dust storm outside. If anything, the storm had gotten worse. The wind, though not much stronger than it was upon their arrival, had kicked up a significant amount of dust and debris that now floated freely through the air. The sun had set completely, turning the already dark cloud that enveloped Kandovan black.

"Mr. Ismayil has eaten some bad sausage," Fedot said, as he stepped back into their room.

Lily had been crouching by one of the vents, listening to the storm. She stood up, checked the barrel of Pearce's .44 and tucked it into her waist. It was a sheriff's gun, or an outlaw's, and seemed an odd choice of gun for a British diplomat. Then again, Barnaby Pearce seemed an odd sort of man. It was no wonder he ended up in the Foreign

Service—a professional ex-patriot—instead of a university or London business. She tossed Gulyas's gun to Fedot, who caught it one-handed and slipped it into the inside pocket of his leather jacket—the one he'd borrowed from Sandy Chandler.

"We better work quickly," Lily said. She tied her hair into a knot, securing it at the base of her skull with a pen that still smelled of Pasha's fingers. Lily then spit-cleaned her goggles and pulled them over her head.

In the empty hallway outside their room, the muffled noises of the storm seemed to crescendo. Lily felt as if she were inside a conch shell. She tiptoed past the other rooms to a narrow staircase that she hoped would lead to the roof. Fedot followed, carrying two of the glass lanterns from the lobby. They'd left the lanterns burning in their room, hoping to give the illusion it was still occupied.

As Fedot passed a hanging tapestry halfway up the staircase, he watched the lanterns suddenly flicker.

"Miss Lily," he said, lifting the tapestry. It revealed a passageway that appeared to lead to the dwelling next door.

"You think the whole village could be connected in this way?" Taking one of the lanterns from Fedot, Lily stepped into the passageway, stooping under its low, rounded ceiling. When they reached the end, Lily peeked under the flap of another tapestry—this one frayed and smelling of stale incense—and stepped carefully into the adjoining house. It wasn't as clean as Ismayil's pension, and disappointment seemed to hang in the air as surely as the dust that seeped in from the outside. Lily and Fedot crept past the kitchen, where an older woman sat sleeping in a hard, wooden chair. Her chin rested on her upper chest, and a wet snore came with her every inhale.

"I wonder if this is such a good idea," Lily whispered. The

woman mumbled in her sleep, drooling over her wrinkled bottom lip.

Behind the kitchen was another narrow staircase—this one less than a dozen steps long. A flowered cotton sheet hung halfway up the staircase just as a tapestry had in the pension, and a perfectly square wooden door beckoned at the top.

They would cover more ground in a shorter time if they split up, so Lily slipped through the cotton sheet, while Fedot continued up to the wooden door. He pulled the glass slide over the flame of his lantern, turned the knob and stepped out onto the flat rooftop, holding his lantern high and hoping to see beyond the two feet of visibility he'd encountered earlier. Up on the roof, the wind was less fierce and the debris was considerably lighter—consisting mostly of dust as the harder particles tended to stay low to the ground. He could even see a couple of meters ahead of him and was able to make out the edge of the roof. Fedot walked over to the roof's brink, stepped backward, and jumped to the next rooftop, landing squarely. Getting to the other side of the village wouldn't be nearly as troublesome as he'd thought it might be.

Lily snuck through several archaic dwellings—past toddlers sleeping on hand woven cots, a liaison between a young widow and her sister's husband, an old man who'd fallen asleep during his evening prayers and lay on a prayer rug with his behind high in the air and his cheek nestled into his folded hands—before reaching a dead end where the bridges from home to home seemed to stop. She was on the second story of a domicile smelling of allspice, fragrant tea and something distinctly sulfurous. Downstairs, a radio was tuned to a Turkish music station, and Lily could hear the rhythmic steps of a young man dancing.

Holding her breath, Lily put her lantern behind her back, letting it dangle from her fingers. She stole down the stairs, lurching in one large step past the doorway where the late night dancer was undulating to the opening notes of a Kanto melody. Lily opened the door to a huge gust of wind and grime that knocked over a water pitcher. The music stopped abruptly, and the young man called out for his father. Leaving the door wide open, Lily thrust the lantern in front of her and entered the storm—ducking out of sight just as the dancer arrived at the doorway. He sheltered his eyes, peering into the swirling dust, before deciding that it had been a bluster that had blown his front door open. With a cuss he closed it again, and Lily was finally able to exhale. She looked down at her hands and saw they were gripping the .44 Magnum Barnaby Pearce had given her. She didn't remember taking it out of the waist of her trousers or clicking off the safety. Her finger rested lightly on the trigger.

CHAPTER 60

Pasha Tarkhan softened visibly as the morphine flooded his veins. It wasn't too much; he could still think clearly and scrutinize the details around him—mainly Rodki Semyonov bent over a small metal serving tray, stirring his tea with his index finger and pretending not to pay his captive any mind. The syringe sat empty on the serving tray, the point of its needle still holding a single drop of morphine, like a tear ready to drop from the lower lid of a child's eye.

Rodki straightened up, unhooked the shutter and looked out the window again. The tiny handle of his tea glass broke suddenly, sending the drink to the floor and splattering Rodki's shoes with hot liquid. The Great Detective grunted, plucked a handkerchief from his pocket and crouched down to clean his only pair of shoes. Outside the window, Pasha noticed a glow. It was scant, like a lit match in a large cellar, but noticeable. As Pasha edged up and focused his eyes, he could see it was from a burning lantern. Slowly, a form began to take shape behind the light—the form of a young man, perhaps. Pasha could see the form's profile now. His eyes followed the slender slope of a neck, a pair of full lips, a strong, aquiline nose.

"Lily," he whispered.

Even with her eyes covered by a pair of goggles and her hair tucked into a jacket, Pasha knew it was her. He repeated her name entirely to himself this time. Just saying it was a comfort to him. And seeing her was finer than the rush of morphine he'd so relished. Lily was alive, and she was well. *My lovely Lily,* he thought. Pasha wanted to take something—the three coins Rodki Semyonov had placed on the bedside table—and throw them at the window. The clink of the coins against the warped window glass would be lost in the clamor of the storm, however. In little more than a moment, Lily's profile disappeared from view, and all that was left was the darkness again. He lay down again as the Great Detective rose from his crouch.

"It's a good thing my shoes are black," the Great Detective said. He stood up and tossed his tea-stained handkerchief onto the tray. "My last pair was brown and looked dreadful by the time the soles wore out. And I polished them twice a week."

Pasha sat up, taking a deep breath as the blood rushed to his head. Too much up and down.

"I see you're feeling better," the Great Detective said.

Pasha shrugged. "Just tired of lying down. My back was beginning to cramp."

"Still, a good sign, I think."

Pasha Tarkhan nodded. "Yes, a good sign." He sniffed the air and smiled. "Apple tea?"

Rodki Semyonov leaned against the table and folded his arms.

"You are well traveled. It's Turkish, like a lot of the tea around here. And it's good. Very strong—like coffee. Would you like some?"

Pasha tried to lift his arm over his shoulder. It was painful, but not impossible.

"Oh, yes. I most certainly would," he said.

"Good," Rodki said. "The water is still hot." The Great Detective rubbed his hands together and went to work on the tea. He might just get a good conversation out of this after all.

Lily was standing between two beehive structures, shielded somewhat from the storm. Her lungs ached, and though she'd kept her mouth closed tight, the grotesque sediment lodged between her cheeks and gums was now collecting beneath her tongue as well. She spat it to the ground, wiping her lips against the back of her hand.

Up ahead, a Persian man wrapped head to toe in white muslin was unloading a donkey. The animal hawed in misery even as its burden was eased and it was tied to a drain pipe, a linen sheet thrown over the donkey's head and body for protection.

The Persian stepped away from the animal and stretched his neck and back. He had obviously been riding for several hours. In his hands, he held a corked jug of clean water, a satchel and the pelt of a golden jackal. He looked to Lily like he could be a merchant, and she wondered why he hadn't weathered the storm in Tabriz or another more hospitable place. He threw the pelt and the satchel over his shoulder and put the jug in the crook of his arm. Hunched over and battered by the wind, the Persian made his way toward the narrow gangway where Lily had taken her brief refuge.

"You there—boy," she thought she heard him say in Azeri-Turkic. Although he was shouting, the wind and flying debris made it difficult to hear. Lily covered her mouth with an already filthy handkerchief and shook her head.

The Persian grumbled, pointing to Lily's lantern, but she felt no inclination to be a good neighbor right then. Time was precious, and she could feel that Pasha was close. The Persian, however, was belligerent and continued gesturing toward her lantern. His journey and general discomfort had plainly made him irritable, and he was blocking her path out of the alley in an obstinate manner that made it clear she would not pass. Not without a fight. It would, Lily realized, be easier to light his way for a few steps rather than waste even more time getting into an argument with the man. Begrudgingly, she nodded.

Waving her hand, Lily motioned for the Persian to hurry. He ambled toward her with a slight limp, ignoring her sense of urgency either out of mulishness or genuine pain. As he came close, she lifted the lantern, casting a glow over his muslin-wrapped face. Only a small slit was left open for his eyes, and Lily glanced over them. Even through her soot-covered goggles their color was unmistakable. A brilliant green—gem-like in their luster—the eyes narrowed instantly as recognition set in.

CHAPTER 61

L ily threw down her lantern and pulled Barnaby Pearce's
gun out from the waist of her trousers. A strong gust
of wind, carrying soot and pebbles from the street, blew
a plume of kerosene fumes and fire between Lily and the
Hungarian. Her vision of Gulyas was obscured, but she
shot—three times—until the surge of flames died down,
confined once again to a ring around the broken lantern.
Beryx Gulyas, by then, was gone. The air was too gritty and
dark to allow Lily a quick search for some sign that she'd
wounded him—a smear of blood, perhaps, giving her an
idea of which way he could have gone.

Lily stomped out the fire at her feet, crunching over the
broken glass from her lantern. There were two doorways—
one on either side of her—that led to two different dwellings. Gulyas could have entered either one of them, but
the one to her left was closer. Slowly, Lily stepped forward,
pushed open the door, and stepped inside.

"Did you hear that?" the Great Detective queried. "Sounded
like gunfire."

"Could've been anything," Pasha said. "These storms
make all sorts of trouble." Lily was capable of making all
sorts of trouble, too.

"Bom, bom, bom! Just like that. Rapid fire." The Great
Detective opened the shutters again and strained to look

out the window. He watched a slender young man put out a small fire with his boot. Otherwise, there was nothing.

The Great Detective started to turn away from the window but then looked back again. Something about the young man wasn't right. The way he used his toe instead of his heel to put out the fire; the way his hips moved under his bulky clothing.

"A girl," the Great Detective said.

"I'm sure you can get one of those here, too," Pasha offered. "It's a small village, but they seem accommodating to tourists."

The Great Detective ignored his comment, watching the girl in man's clothing move toward their system of dwellings. Although it was dark and he could barely make out her silhouette, one thing was clear: this girl had a gun. A very big gun.

"Trouble never comes alone," the Great Detective whispered. He stooped down, pulled a coil of rope from a curtained cabinet and tied Pasha's wrists to the bedpost.

"You're being a great sport, as the English would say."

Pasha Tarkhan made no acknowledgement of the compliment, and the Great Detective could feel his prisoner's eyes on him as he slipped out the door and into the unlit hallway. The walls were rough—carved and sanded down from a grainy rock—and the Great Detective listened for movement as he felt his way deeper into the dwelling. The dust storm outside provided a constant melody of ambient noise that played with a certain degree of tone-deaf belligerence, like a marching band. It was a strangely comforting sound, unlike silence. Yet even through the din of the storm outside—the pitter of gravel, sticks and broken glass—the Great Detective could hear—no, perhaps sense—the creeping step of a man in thickly soled shoes on the floor above him.

CHAPTER 62

L ily's father had once told her that in youth, instincts are one's only reliable beacons.

"Good judgment comes much later," he'd said. "After years of experience."

He'd told her this around the time she'd accepted Richard Putnam's proposal of marriage—an offer her untrained judgment told her to accept and her instincts rejected violently—punishing her with a relentless case of insomnia coupled with a nightly craving for three-quarters of a bottle of red wine.

Unlike the case of her *malaka* ex-fiancé, Lily couldn't tell right then if it had been her instincts or her judgment that had goaded her into going after Beryx Gulyas. She might have continued her search for Pasha, hoping to keep hidden from the Hungarian assassin—at least until she had some back-up. But she instead found herself tiptoeing through a dwelling with a floor plan like a labyrinth and gripping Barnaby Pearce's gun so tightly that her right hand felt as if it were in a state of rigor mortis.

And this old structure was not at all as settled as the other ones she'd crept through. There were no lights in the passageways; in the place of stairs, Lily encountered a rickety wooden ladder that led from the first floor to the second. Lily ascended that ladder—her judgment telling her not to—and arrived at an unfinished foyer with pitted walls and a single beeswax candle dangling from a string. It was as if seven hundred years had not been enough time to make basic home improvements.

A hushed, almost imperceptible waft of stale air made the hair on the back of Lily's neck stand up. She could detect no sounds apart from the muffled clatter of the storm, yet she felt distinctly not alone. Instinct—and it was instinct this time—told her that while she could not see anything or anyone from her vantage point, she was without question being seen. She cocked Pearce's gun, readied her finger on the trigger, and slowly turned around.

"Miss Tassos," the voice whispered.

Lily froze.

"Miss Tassos, a shot from a gun like that in an ancient place on its last legs could be a catastrophe."

Lily looked in the direction of the voice—thickly Russian accented, but correct in its English grammar; even in its choice of idiom. "Is Pasha Tarkhan with you?" she asked.

But the Russian was done talking. She heard his footstep—light as a dancer despite the heavy frame she'd sensed from the caliber of his voice. "Don't come any closer," she said, holding Pearce's gun out in front of her.

"I'm afraid I haven't much choice in the matter," he said.

A face emerged into the dim light of the lone candle— fully healed, but once badly broken. It was the man she'd seen at the Hotel Rude. The one who'd followed her, staring blatantly at her as she left for the Lavra with Fedot and a near-dead Pasha. It was that stare she remembered most—even more than his damaged facial bones. A gaze that betrayed nothing—neither intention, nor emotion, nor aptitude. The face of a card player—no, a detective. Behind him, Beryx Gulyas came forward. He was holding something at the detective's back. Perhaps a gun, but Lily couldn't be sure.

Unlike the Russian detective, Gulyas made no effort to

disguise his objectives. His raw, singed face was a contortion of hostile emotions.

"You fickle bitch," he rasped, pushing his weapon into the detective's back. He inhaled deeply, flaring his nostrils.

"Do you expect me to drop my gun?" Lily said. "I don't even know this man." Lily did know, of course, that the broken-faced detective was less the Hungarian's hostage than his human shield. Still, making small talk in this instance was calming somehow.

"We're going to leave here together," Gulyas asserted.

"For another capsaicin cocktail party?"

"Now, now," Gulyas coaxed, curling his fingers.

Despite Lily's second betrayal at the Imam's cemetery, Gulyas, in his heart, felt he could forgive her over time. She was, after all, responding to the death of her father—and what kind of woman wouldn't feel loyalty to the master of her household? Certainly a Hungarian woman would have done the same. Gulyas clung to the belief that one day Lily could see him as her master again. That she would bite a chunk out of a man's calf in order to avenge him. It was an enormously pleasant thought, and Beryx Gulyas did not have pleasant thoughts very often. Unconsciously, he bared his teeth, his lips turning upward into a smile.

Lily inched backward, side-stepping the gaping hole that led to the preceding floor. She wondered if she could jump down and roll out of view before the Hungarian had a chance to pull the trigger, but Gulyas seemed to know what she was thinking. He pushed the Russian detective forward, putting Lily off balance and forcing her to lurch farther away from the hole.

As Lily caught her footing, her eyes darted quickly at the detective. His lopsided face wore an expression of cool surveillance—as if he was not a part of whatever was going on between Lily Tassos and the Hungarian assassin, and he knew exactly how things were going to turn out anyway. Lily took another step backward and felt the heat of the beeswax candle at the back of her head.

"Lily," Beryx Gulyas whispered. He was looking at her, his gun aimed at the detective. Spinning quickly around, Lily blew out the single candle, sheathing them all in the pitch-dark. She crouched low to the ground, anticipating a shot, but none came. Although Lily could still feel the presence of the detective and the Hungarian, neither of them had shifted. It was as if each of them was waiting for someone else to make the first move.

"Gruh!"

The low grunt ended their standoff, and Lily could hear hobbling, then a hard step. It was Gulyas; she was sure of it. Days of being his captive had illuminated her to his mannerisms—to the distinct sound of his every movement—if not so much to the sound of his voice. He'd rarely spoken.

Somehow the Russian detective had wounded Gulyas, or at least stunned him, causing him to stumble. Lily rose up and took a crouched step in what she thought was Beryx Gulyas's direction. The detective's hand—a wide and muscular paw—grabbed her wrist and dug his fingers between her tendons. Lily's grip on Barnaby Pearce's gun began to slacken, and she clutched the barrel of the .44 with her left hand, reinforcing her hold. She didn't mean to pull the trigger, but she did, sending a powerful shot into the wall just below the ceiling. The primitive structure trembled audibly—like a minor earthquake—and then settled.

In that instant, Lily's legs flew out from under her, sending her to the sandy floor. Pearce's gun was plucked from her grip like a twig from a child.

"Stay where you are," the detective said. His presence

faded away into the dark, leaving Lily alone and vulnerable. She pressed her cheek, then her palms to the floor, feeling for the vibration of footsteps—the Hungarian's—but the cold, grainy clay felt as inert as a tombstone.

Slowly, Lily began to slide along on her belly. She timed her movements with the swells from the storm, making her way in what she hoped was the direction of the hole and ladder that would lead her back to the ground level. Lily's fingers explored all around her, coming upon granules, a candy wrapper, a few small shards of glass, but nothing that would indicate the passage out. Finally, her left hand felt a current of air. The hole had to be close. Lily lifted her head, breathing in and trying to catch a whiff of the dank air she'd noticed on the preceding floor of the old dwelling. At first, she could only smell the foyer—earthen minerals and old urine. Straining, she arched her neck toward the cool current until she did at last detect the faintest trace from the odor of the ground floor. Much cleaner, with a bitter tinge.

Lily had just exhaled and slackened her tense shoulder muscles when Beryx Gulyas's boot came down on her. The Hungarian stepped hard onto her neck, making it damned near impossible for Lily to breathe. At her ear, Lily heard the cocking of a gun, and the low, heavy breathing of a man up a few pounds who had clearly exerted himself. She could picture the look of gratification on his face as the Hungarian pressed his heel harder and listened to Lily's desperate, intermittent gasps for air. It would have been the same look she'd witnessed on his face just before she blew out the beeswax candle and dropped in the dark to the floor.

Beryx Gulyas, for his part, had no such look on his face. He puffed his breath and strained to keep the heel of his boot squarely on her shoulder. Although he was cutting off most of her air supply, it wasn't enough to kill her. He didn't want to do that. He wanted her to come with him. If he could get her home, or somewhere they could be alone, he was sure he could once again watch her beam up at him as if he were an angel.

"Love," Gulyas grumbled, just as two shots from Barnaby Pearce's .44 Magnum thundered through the foyer, aimed in his general direction.

A scant moment after the echo subsided, an ominous crackling sound permeated the structure. Beryx Gulyas took his boot off Lily's neck and stepped back. He raised his gun from her ear and fired toward the shots, dealing a death blow to the weakened domicile. The clay floor quivered as half of the edifice collapsed—peeling off, then plunging down to the street like a large tablet from an iceberg. The storm rushed into what remained of the structure, and Gulyas stumbled close to the edge of its gaping side.

Lily rose to her knees and moved to push the Hungarian off the edge when a hand gripped her ankle and began to pull her into the hole she'd been seeking. Lily clawed at the ground, but the hand was too strong—pulling her down until she fell like a ragdoll. Her head hit hard against part of the ladder, breaking a rung. The last thing Lily remembered before losing consciousness was landing onto something soft and unbreakable at the same time—curling into a ball and becoming aware of the fading scent of anise and cigarettes.

CHAPTER 63

From a neighboring rooftop, Fedot watched as the entire façade of one of the ancient Kandovan dwellings disintegrated into a powder that was instantly consumed by the blowing storm. He set his lantern down and ran to the roof's edge. It was too long a distance for his legs to withstand a jump to the street level, so Fedot slid down a drainpipe and struggled to make his way across the narrow road that served as one of Kandovan's main channels. The storm had grown in its ferocity, made worse by the refuse from the collapsed dwelling. Fedot felt his way to the entrance and pushed open the door, only to find himself face-to-face with the Great Detective.

"I ran from the wolf and encountered a bear," Fedot said, but the Great Detective ignored him. He simply covered his mouth with a handkerchief, pushing past him and making his way into the street from where Fedot had come.

"It's no use out there," Fedot told him. But it was no use in there either. The partially destroyed structure—apart from being unsound—was a whirl of rubble and chalky air. But Fedot continued inside, climbing over chunks of debris and using dead Ismayil's dagger to chip through sections of the passageway that hadn't completely buckled. He was sure Pasha Tarkhan couldn't be far away—perhaps stuck in the rubble, or hiding from the Great Detective. It could have been Pasha who had orchestrated the collapse in order to escape. It seemed like something he would do.

"Miss Lily?" Fedot called. He had caught a hint of her

perfume. It clung stubbornly to her hair, eclipsing even the odor of the thick air around them.

A sound resembling a clap of thunder reverberated through the structure. It creaked and groaned like a dying man before beginning to collapse from the middle, caving in on itself like a sinkhole. The ceiling, the walls and the floor crumpled in succession, and Fedot found himself falling—not deeper into the structure, but beyond it, to a place that looked like nothing Kandovan had to offer. A double-headed horse greeted a winged King on his descent; he saw gargoyles with bulging eyes and ferocious smiles—all glimpsed like wind-swept pages in a book.

His fall was broken by water—deep, clean and frigid—then followed by chunks of debris from the crumbled dwelling. Fedot swam toward the bottom, trying to avoid the deluge of falling refuse, but he never reached it. When he could no longer hold his breath, he surfaced—treading water until his eyes adjusted to the dim cavern.

Fedot had plunged into an early cistern—perhaps as old as two thousand years. Faded paintings were inked onto the walls, and partially preserved mosaic patterns studded a pair of great columns that reinforced the grotto. Stone carvings sprung from the bulwarks; gargoyles ogled Fedot from every corner. There was graffiti carved into some of the wall paintings. The most recent, as far as he could see, were from the medieval era—an etching of a castle structure with three lines floating above it, perhaps representing the heavens, or a coming plague.

Fedot swam to the ledge of one of the columns and pulled himself up. He searched his jacket for the gun Lily had given him, but it was gone—probably at the bottom of the cistern. Gone, too, was the pension owner's dagger, only its sheath still strapped to Fedot's waist. Looking up into the hole from where he'd come, the Russian could see nothing other than darkness. He could no longer hear the storm outside.

The cavern itself could have gone on for miles—perhaps linking up with another ancient cistern in Tabriz through a system of underground rivers. Near a vanishing mural that depicted a lion hunt, Fedot could detect a current in the otherwise still waters. He lowered himself back into the drink and swam closer to the mural until he could see the mouth of a tunnel. It swallowed the cold water in frantic gulps.

Behind him, Fedot heard a gentle splash. He looked back to the column that had been his perch moments before. It sat innocently enough in the water—as it had a thousand years ago, as it might tomorrow. Still, Fedot was disturbed. A crescent shadow, slim as a nail clipping, blunted a glimmer of reflected light, and Fedot plunged his head underwater. He could feel something both slim and weighty dive only centimeters away from his skull. He reached out and caught it with his hand, his fingers closing around the rippled edge of a blade. It was the pension owner's dagger.

"You cur," Beryx Gulyas growled. "This time you'll be the one running." Gulyas had fallen into the depths of Kandovan just as he was about to leap from the second floor of the structure onto the street. He was sucked in suddenly, violently, only a moment after he had seen Lily below him, being carried away by someone. Although the little man had nothing to do with how Gulyas had gotten into the ancient cistern and away from Lily Tassos, it seemed he was always, somehow, getting between the Hungarian and his objectives.

"Do you hear me?" Gulyas shouted.

Fedot did not hear him. He was swimming underwater

toward the cavern wall, trying to stay just ahead of the current.

The Hungarian removed his gun from beneath his soaked Persian dress. The white muslin had kept his weapon firm in its place as he fell into the cistern, even as he struggled. He raised the barrel and shot methodically into the water, following a path he suspected Fedot Titov was pursuing. Gulyas had been unsuccessful with the knife, but the little Russian wouldn't escape so easily now that a firearm was back in his hand.

"Russian . . . Russian . . . Russian . . . dead Russian," he droned, shooting with grace and precision as he monitored any undue wrinkle in the water's facade.

At the cavern wall, Fedot's mouth broke the surface and he took in a deep breath before submerging again. The Hungarian didn't see him take his air, and Fedot floated freely underwater as he contemplated his options. A bullet had pierced his thigh muscle, making it difficult to swim, and his only defense against the Hungarian's superior marksmanship was the pension owner's dagger. Fedot felt along the wall of the cavern in search of a divot, but it was smooth and water-worn. He dug the tip of the dagger into the cavern wall, working with a fury until he was able to chip away a large enough piece and could fit his boot heel into the cranny.

From there, he fortified his position and dove out of the water, throwing the dagger in Gulyas's direction. It landed firmly in the Hungarian's right buttock, and while not the mortal wound Fedot had hoped to inflict, it was enough to destabilize him, making Gulyas drop the gun and sending him falling directly into the strongest part of the current. He sailed across the water as if he were sliding downhill and headed straight for the hole.

Fedot gripped the side of one of the enormous columns for a moment, gathering strength and managing his pain. That moment would cost him. The Hungarian seized hold of his hair as he glided by, slamming Fedot's head into the column. Slippery as an eel and able to get out from under his grip and plunge underwater, Fedot grasped Beryx around the waist and began to squeeze. The Hungarian swore and flailed his arms. He worked his knee up to his belly, pushing and kicking Fedot until the little Russian finally released him from his clutches. Gulyas looked around quickly, but Fedot was nowhere in sight.

Behind him, Gulyas heard a loud slurp, and he pivoted. The gaping hole looked as if it had just consumed a meal. Water rushed into it, and it occurred to Gulyas that the hole was the only place Fedot Titov could have possibly gone. Gulyas must have kicked him straight into the current, and, as the Hungarian had experienced for himself only moments before, it was nearly impossible to extract oneself from that powerful stream of water.

Clinging to the slick base of the column, Beryx Gulyas rested. He squinted up into the darkness in hopes of spotting a way out, but there was nothing. His eyes followed the shadowy gargoyles to the damp walls of the cistern, but they, too, were a dead end, as smooth as polished stone, with no ledges for gripping and climbing back up to where the ceiling had once been.

"*Kurva,*" he said under his breath.

But in a deep corner of the cistern, he noticed something. There, in the near dark, seeming to glitter up the far wall, was what looked like a staircase. He couldn't see the actual steps, but it appeared as if a light refractor of a sort—a jewel perhaps—was mounted onto each slab to make them visible to whoever's job it had been to care for these ancient wells. Slowly, Gulyas started moving toward those jewels. He was tired and he hurt all over, but his most recent wound—the one from the dagger in his buttocks—was feeling better.

"The dagger!" he snarled as his hand darted down to where it had plunged into him. It was gone. It couldn't have fallen out—even in his scuffle with the little Russian. The dagger had sunk far too deep into his gluteus muscle. Gulyas swam faster from one column to the next, avoiding the current, until he reached the jeweled stairs at last. *The dagger couldn't have fallen out,* he said again to himself. *That damned little Russian must have pulled . . .*

Before the Hungarian could finish thinking through this revelation, Fedot jumped from one of the stair ledges onto Gulyas. Whirling together through the chilly water, the two struggled, inching ever closer to the ferocious current. The Hungarian was a dirty fighter—biting wherever he could, pinching Fedot's scrotum, scratching at any vulnerable part like an irate woman. For once, Gulyas's weight was on his side; his extra fat made him buoyant in the water. He pushed and pressed into Fedot, trying to shove him into the current, and for a moment it appeared he was having some success. But like in the Lavra, the little Russian always had a surprise for him. Just as it seemed that exhaustion might get the better of him, Fedot Titov's arm broke free from the water, and he plunged the pension owner's dagger hard into the muscle behind the Hungarian's shoulder blade. It was a horrifically painful injury to inflict—purposeful. Beryx Gulyas froze immediately, a look of shock distorting his features. He couldn't move, he couldn't swim—he could only submit to drifting into the waiting current.

Fedot watched him disappear into the underground

river stream. His leg aching and his lungs fatigued, Fedot swam to the column for a brief respite. He knew there was little time for self-indulgence and allowed himself only the reprieve he would need for what he would have to do. Slowly he moved along the wall, parallel to the rushing stream. Finding his divot once again, he used it to steady himself and then push off, pitching his body fully into the current in pursuit of the Hungarian. He doubted he could catch him—and there was no telling where or if he would find a pathway to the surface. But if he did, Fedot knew there was only one place the Hungarian would go after failing in his mission. And Fedot intended to see him there.

CHAPTER 64

Curiosity was both the powerful engine of Rodki Semyonov's greatest skill and the reason he was alone and those he had loved were long dead. Rodki was, at times, powerless against the murmur of its seductive voice—the one that asked, "What is going on here apart from your task?"

It was a dangerous question. As dangerous to Rodki as leaving Moscow had been. That question alone admitted that there was a voice he listened to other than his master's; there was a story other than the one Moscow told.

He had known all of this before, of course, but there had never been any reason to pursue this knowledge. What would he have gained, except an unmarked grave somewhere in the earth where his wife lay, her remains forever frozen in a desperate attempt to take a breath? Even his love didn't extend that far.

Rodki's first taste of freedom had led to his second, and as intriguing as those tastes had been, he didn't wish to be led. Not by Moscow; not by his own impulses. After all, a detective's powers of deduction lay primarily in his ability to impose logic over chaos. And the Great Detective would have been dead long ago if he had been listening all these years to the incessant chatter in his brain that narrated every set of circumstances in which he found himself. The one he had to manipulate at times in order to stay alive.

So, as the Great Detective surveyed the remains of the

dwelling—the approximate section that had housed the very room where he had tied Pasha Tarkhan to the bedpost before going in search of Lilia Tassos—it occurred to him that fate, in this instance, had done his work for him. It had imposed logic over chaos and left Rodki Semyonov to close yet another case as The Great Detective.

"General Pushkin," he would say. "I'm afraid it appears your former comrade has met his destiny." However the General might choose to interpret that, it was true. Also true was the fact that General Pushkin would be relieved to have this ugly chapter closed.

Lily lay comfortably, dreamlessly on a small cot. The room was plain and little, with space enough only for the cot and a weaving nook with a few pillows. A poster depicting Mowlana, in the *Poet of Life's Dance*, was pasted to the ceiling, its edges curling and parts of its golden hue blackened from candle smoke.

She awakened slowly—it must have taken her a quarter of an hour—confused as to her surroundings and nursing a headache that rivaled her worst hangover. It took her a moment to remember everything that had happened—the broken-faced detective, Beryx Gulyas, the strong hand that had pulled her down and out of the ruined second floor foyer. Lily reached up to the back of her head and touched her injured skull. The lesion itself was less than an inch long and mended by several stitches. Someone had taken very good care of her. Exhaustion overwhelmed her. The pain in her head throbbed. Lily closed her eyes again and fell into dreamless sleep. But not before she saw his face—it must have been a hallucination. Mansoor Nassa. He'd tiptoed into the room and leaned over her. Smiling, he put a cool cloth on Lily's head before pulling the light blanket up to her chin.

"There's no hurry, Miss Lily," he said. "None at all."

Lily did not sleep for long this time. Perhaps a couple of hours. The blanket was still pulled to her chin—she must've hardly moved during her nap, a sure sign of total fatigue. Mental. Physical. Lily hadn't noticed until then that she was naked. Her clothes—or rather, Barnaby Pearce's son's attire—had been neatly folded and sat on the cushion of the weaving nook just to her left.

"Nassa," Lily said. Had he been part of a dream, the way Ivanov had entered her dreams when she was being torured by Gulyas in the baker's apartment?

"Would you like some apple tea?"

The voice came from the doorway, and Lily turned her head.

"Yes, I know," the poet said. "I'm supposed to be in heaven."

"Not according to your beliefs," Lily said. She still wasn't sure he was real.

"Oh, I believe in heaven," Nassa said.

Lily breathed in deeply. The smell of fresh-baked dough—in preparation for the approaching dawn—hung in the air as thick as the sand and sediment outside. Lily knew it was of Goli's making. He'd brought her with him. Loyal Goli who had devoted her life to her master. Only Jalal would be left behind in Tehran. He had grandchildren to attend to.

"Smells heavenly, doesn't it?" Nassa said. "There's that

word again. But it is apt, and I like to use the correct word."
Nassa sat down at the edge of Lily's cot and replaced the
cloth at her forehead with a fresh one.

"Pearce and Chandler," Lily said. "They told me you
were dead."

Mansoor Nassa smiled. "I am dead. At least to them.
Crushed beyond recognition. You know I would have been
dead had I not died first."

Lily shook her head.

"It doesn't matter," the poet said. "It was time for me to
leave Tehran. My mother's gone, and I have another calling. Just like you, I think."

Lily blinked and endeavored to stretch. She felt creaky
and rusted. "Ivanov?" she said.

Mansoor Nassa smiled and nodded.

"I thought you said you didn't know him."

"I don't. Not personally. But I've known of him for a
long time. And now I'll join him."

Somehow Mansoor Nassa and *Derevo* did not seem like
such an odd combination to Lily.

"I'd written him many times—poems and letters," Nassa
told her. "And I knew that when you came to my door,
Ivanov had finally sent for me." Nassa put his finger to his
throat and touched a Star of David necklace he was wearing. Lily had never noticed it before and wondered if it was
new. Perhaps a reminder of the star that presided over his
living room in his beautiful house.

"So, from Persia to Russia," Lily said.

"I'll go wherever I'm needed."

Lily understood what Nassa meant. His life in Tehran
could have only ended in his death, and there was magnifi-
cence in starting over and leaving every old thing behind.
It was the sort of predicament a true poet would welcome,

she reckoned. Imaginers were restless, and deep thinkers didn't attach so easily to positions and possessions.

"Will you miss your rose garden?" she asked. Lily didn't know why his roses mattered to her, but they did.

"No," he said. "I can plant roses anywhere, or summon my memory of them." He said it, wanted to believe it, but it wasn't entirely true. He would most certainly miss his roses. "Sleep more," he said. "You look tired. And I won't be leaving for hours."

With that, Nassa left her bedside and walked to the door.

"Thank you," Lily said.

"For what?"

Lily rubbed the back of her head, where her stitches protruded.

"Oh, I didn't do that. He did. I only made you tea."

"He?" Lily said.

"You know who," Nassa said. "He took such excellent care of you."

He let himself out of the room, allowing the tapestry to fall back over the doorway. Another foot soldier for Porphyri Ivanov's motley band of subversives—a poet, a diplomat, a monk, the daughter of a murdered arms dealer.

Lily did not want to sleep anymore, even if her body was demanding it. She sat up, slipping her bum off the cot and crawling warily to her pile of clothes. Her head still throbbing, she dressed piece by piece, until all that was left was the jacket. In a sudden panic, Lily yanked the jacket off the cushion and dug her hand into the interior pocket. The *Sputnik* microfilm was there no more, and in its place was a folded piece of white paper smudged with large tawny fingerprints. Lily opened the paper, her eyes sweeping over the tight, neat cursive. It was the first stanza of a poem called "Tristia" by the Russian Osip Mandelstam, who was Pasha's second favorite poet next to some revolutionary who had shot himself:

I have studied the Science of departures,
in night's sorrows, when a woman's hair falls down.
The oxen chew, there's the waiting, pure,
in the last hours of vigil in the town,
and I reverence night's ritual cock-crowing,
when reddened eyes lift sorrow's load and choose
to stare at distance, and a woman's crying
is mingled with the singing of the Muse.

It was written in Pasha's handwriting.

Lily pinched the paper between her fingers and stumbled to the porthole window above her cot. She tore open the shutters, not knowing quite what to expect. She had no idea how long she'd been in and out of consciousness or what she would see in the predawn haze. Outside, a preternatural stillness was descending over Kandovan. Lily watched the final churn of the dust storm as it blew down the street, leaving behind a thick layer of residue and opening the sky to a sunrise ready to burst with an array of desert oranges. She bowed her head, a ribbon of her black hair tumbling over her face, and let her eyes fill with tears.

CHAPTER 65

"What is it you Russians say?" Sandmore Chandler said. "Without torture, no science. A hell of way to look at things if you ask me—even if there's some truth to it."

Pasha Tarkhan wondered if perhaps what Chandler meant was that he preferred to acquire his science from those with the stomach for torture, rather than have to get his hands dirty.

"Looks like they did quite a number on you," Chandler remarked.

They hadn't, but Pasha was in no mood for explaining. Even the two bullets Rodki Semyonov had pumped into him were meant to impede rather than kill him. The knot the Great Detective had tied around his wrists had been decidedly loose, as well. Not too loose—your average detainee wouldn't be able to unravel his overhand knot at all, but Pasha could, given a little time and morphine.

"Takes forever to get a long-distance line out of here," Chandler grumbled. He picked up his phone and dialed the operator in Tabriz again. Pasha was surprised there was a phone line in Kandovan at all, but then, in his dealings with him Chandler had always been a resourceful fellow.

"Yes, yes, of course I'll wait," Chandler said. "As if I have a bloody choice." Chandler had picked up the word "bloody" during a stint in London and it had stuck. It sounded strange to Pasha when said in an American accent—like a turn of phrase badly translated.

The operator rang.

"Mmm hmm," Chandler said. "Yes, the seasonal vegetables are excellent here. I'll be sure to bring some back." Chandler picked up a bronze statuette of Kali that he used as a paperweight. He rubbed a smudge off her cheek, then tossed her from hand to hand as he spoke, cradling the receiver between his chin and shoulder. "The figs are especially good this time of year."

Pasha Tarkhan knew what Chandler had really been telling whoever was on the other end of the line—Tony Geiger's replacement, he supposed. Roughly translated, Chandler was confirming Pasha's defection and underscoring its secrecy. Pasha had made it clear he had no intention of becoming a high-profile traitor and mere instrument of anti-Soviet propaganda. His knowledge and experience were far more valuable if he remained in the cold— his name changed, his identity manipulated. Besides, the Americans were well aware of how easily Pasha Tarkhan could make himself disappear—along with all of his priceless insights and information.

"Okay, then. Ciao," Chandler said, using another phrase he'd assumed—this time from a stint in Rome. He hung up and put Kali back onto his desk.

"We'll certainly have a lot to talk about with you, Mr. Tarkhan," Chandler said. "Here, of course, and back in Washington."

"I'm quite eager to talk about anything," Pasha told him. "Especially the microfilm of the *Sputnik*."

"Right, yes. Especially that." Chandler patted the breast pocket of his jacket. "Quite a revelation, that."

"Quite," Pasha said.

"And the American girl—we'll have to find her, too."

Not too soon, Pasha hoped. And not here. He needed

some time and distance, and then one day it might be all right to see Lily again. He'd never left a woman too soon before. By the time his relationships were nearing their end, he was relieved to be extricating himself—often from a very complex set of circumstances. But he didn't feel that way about Lily. In fact, he felt as if he could have gone on a long time with her—much longer than with his wife or even his most beloved mistresses. He and Lily were two of a kind, and Pasha hoped—at least from afar—that he would be able to watch her grow further into the woman he knew she would become.

In that moment Pasha felt a pang of regret—much stronger than the general malaise he'd felt since he'd left Lily with Mansoor Nassa. He wondered if, perhaps, the two of them could have made a go of it together. It was a selfish thought, even if born out of a basic human need. Pasha was no good for anyone. Especially now, as a fugitive and traitor. The ruse of his death would work for a while, of course, but not forever. Somewhere, someone would see him, hear about him, feel the touch of his unseen hand. Lily Tassos would have enough to worry about in the coming years without finding herself trapped in the schemes of a high-level Russian defector. Pasha hoped that at some point—some point soon—he would be able to put his emotions behind him.

"You know, General Pushkin's plane will be arriving today," Chandler said, looking out the window at the dissipating storm. "We'd better get out of here."

Pasha nodded. His mind was still elsewhere—with Lily in a bathtub at the Lavra, her wet fingers touching his lips.

"I'll have my boy help you bathe and change your bandages. We'll scare up some pain relief for you between here and Tabriz, too." Chandler rang a small bell on his desk.

Chandler's boy entered the room promptly. A small man of about thirty, although he looked much younger. Wearing a fedora tipped to the side, the boy leaned on Chandler's desk and tossed a stone in the air, catching it in his breast pocket. He looked like trouble. Chandler mumbled something in Farsi, and the man nodded, setting the stone on his desk.

"Mr. Tarkhan," he said, offering Pasha his shoulder to lean on. But the Russian refused his help—at least until they entered the bathing quarters.

Chandler closed the door after they left. He went to his desk and picked up the bronze Kali once again, turning it over and using a letter opener to pry off part of the base. He pulled the curl of microfilm from his breast pocket, rolled it around his index finger and went to stuff it up Kali's back before thinking better of it.

"Not for you, dear Kali," he said, ramming her base back on with a blunt blow from his palm. Instead, he plucked a small bottle of Coca-Cola from the right-hand drawer of his desk and opened it. He poured the cola into a whiskey tumbler and watched it bubble and form a collar at the rim, then dropped the microfilm inside. If Coca-Cola could eat the varnish off his wife's dining table, it could certainly dissolve a little film.

It's nonsense, anyway, he thought. A fanciful tale of clandestine propaganda if he'd ever heard one. Chandler had no intention of sticking his neck out for that. Not when there were so many more important things—real *wars of the world* that he needed to stick his neck out for. And Tarkhan—if his defection was even real, and Chandler had seen no facts to support that at all—was either an unwitting pawn in Soviet misinformation or even the author of this particular ruse. He'd always thought Tony Geiger's recruitment of a "spiritual underground"—whatever that meant—was a load of hooey. He'd seen absolutely no facts to support their existence, other than a few metal cards that anyone could have had made. One of Geiger's *Derevo* spiritualists had probably done him in, too.

"And *Sputnik*," he said aloud. "What a stupid name."

CHAPTER 66

Politically, not to mention from a fundamental human standpoint, the news from Hungary was devastating— even if not surprising.

Lily sank plaintively into her leather club chair and placed the newspaper onto her desk. The chair was nearly identical to one belonging to Richard Putnam's father, and she'd always admired it. Although she'd made sure to decorate her townhouse in as contemporary a style as possible given the limitations of Boston architecture, she'd made an exception for the chair. It was her strategizing chair, her pondering chair, her dreaming chair. The chair she sat in when she allowed herself to think about Pasha Tarkhan.

She picked up the newspaper again. *Fighting in Budapest has died down*, it read. *Up to five thousand civilians are reported to have been killed or wounded. Many buildings in central Budapest have been damaged or destroyed, and thousands of refugees have begun fleeing across the border to Austria. Tens of thousands have been jailed. Some 700 Soviet soldiers are said to have died in the uprising, including some executed for refusing to fight. There are even reports of freedom fighters being hunted down where they live and tortured to death.* The article went on to describe one such death—Lily suspected it was the only such death. An ethnic Hungarian with Romanian citizenship had been found in his hotel room on the 11th of November. He had been dead for at least two days and was discovered wearing a "mask of infamy"—a grotesque and farcical mask made of copper and other metals. Such masks were designed for the individual wearer, and in this case, the mask was one of a comical devil—with three horns, rounded cheeks, and a strange, constipated smile. Masks of infamy were commonly used in medieval Russia as a means of public humiliation, as the masks tended to be permanently fused onto the wearer's face. The ethnic Hungarian was described as having died of extreme "blowt," after having been forced to swallow several hundred rocks and crystals one at a time.

"Fedot, is that you?" Lily called.

Fedot slipped into her study carrying a small bag of groceries. The bounty of America was overwhelming for him, and he preferred to shop for his needs a day at a time. He removed an apple and a sack of pistachios from his bag and sat across from Lily on an ottoman.

"Good work," Lily said, passing him the article.

Fedot scanned it and handed it back to her. He'd spent a day at a library in Budapest when he'd first arrived, researching medieval Russian torture methods—ones he thought Lily and her uncle, Baru, might appreciate.

"Miss Lily," Fedot said.

Lily Tassos was prone to reverie—tapping her pen along her desk, stroking her chin. Right then, she was running her finger along the newspaper's edge, her face a menagerie of recent sorrows.

"I'm sorry about your uncle."

At his insistence, Baru had been present at the Hungarian's death. He had especially enjoyed lining up the various stones—charoite, jade and rhodinite for understanding destinies, green amber for atonement—and watching his son's and brother's murderer swallow them with his customary level of contempt and defiance. Even toward the end, Gulyas was loath to admit his agony. But

Baru knew, and it satisfied him. The Greek died in his herb garden only three days later, falling into a rosemary bush after his heart had simply stopped beating.

Lily was glad her uncle's revenge had been fulfilled, even if Fedot had been concerned that in his physical anguish, Beryx Gulyas might repent and at last go to the arms of God. A rapturous death was a gift Gulyas didn't deserve, and Fedot resented even giving him the opportunity for such an end. An end he, himself, would welcome.

Lily doubted the Hungarian was capable of any sort of penitence, but had shared Fedot's misgivings with Ivanov nonetheless. Ivanov told her that however unworthy the Hungarian might seem, he was, after all, a creature of God, and Lily had relayed this wisdom to Fedot word for word.

"He spoke of you, you know," Fedot said.

"My uncle?"

"No, the Hungarian."

Lily didn't care to know what he'd said. She had gone with her uncle to Hungary when Fedot had sent word that he'd found Gulyas. She stayed for most of the death ritual Fedot had chosen for him and admired the Russian's steadfast implementation of each effect. The way he pushed the individual stones into the Hungarian's throat with a pair of pincers and massaged his esophagus, forcing him to swallow. It was a long, arduous day, but Fedot had hardly broken a sweat.

"Watch me," Gulyas had whispered. "Stay." He wanted desperately for Lily to gaze upon him at his death and had the nerve to request that he be fully naked for the occasion. The request was denied, but Lily did assist Fedot in applying a toxic adhesive to the Hungarian's skin and affixing the mask of infamy to his face before she left. Beryx Gulyas's death was to be her uncle's satisfaction alone.

"We should go, Miss Lily," Fedot said.

He removed an itinerary from his coat pocket and placed it in front of Lily, laying it over her newspaper. She glanced at it absently before meeting his eyes, and it was then her expression changed. Whatever troubles she had been nursing were vanquished from her expression, and her gaze centered on him in a way that reminded Fedot of her father.

"Have you spoken to the general?" she asked.

"General Pushkin doesn't like to be contacted directly, for the obvious reasons. I'm communicating with him through our back channels."

Lily folded their itinerary and slipped it into the pages of the book she was reading—a dog-eared copy of Faulkner's *A Fable* that Tony Geiger had given her the first time they'd met.

"Money impresses General Pushkin," Lily said. "And my father has paid him handsomely over the years. You can tell him that if he's a good boy, my father's daughter will continue to pad his Swiss bank account and allow him the very luxuries he deems capitalist and bourgeoisie. But only if he's a very good boy."

Lily Tassos gave Fedot a look he was coming to know well. It said both *I'm not my father* and *his blood runs deep in my veins*. It was a look, Fedot believed, Lily had been practicing, and wisely so. She would have to give it to a great many of her father's associates in the coming years as she solidified her charge of his affairs.

Lily's new assertiveness had surprised her mother and siblings upon her return with her father's remains from the Middle East. But the shock of grief demanded someone take charge. Whatever her father had been to men like Tony Geiger and Sandmore Chandler, to the Tassos family, he was daddy. His loss was unfathomable, shattering—especially to Lily's mother, who had loved her husband without reservation and had known no other man. In the end, Lily's assumption of leadership had been silently acknowledged as the most sensible course of action for the family. Theron Tassos's death had been violent and mysterious, after all, and deep down no one really wanted to know why he'd been taken from them.

Oddly, it had been easier for Lily to begin doing business in her father's less legitimate endeavors than his straight-up shipping business. In the above-the-board world of industry, skepticism about a woman running things ran high, whereas in the underworld, people were used to going against the grain and cared only about results. Lily had decided to let her brothers front her father's strictly lawful enterprises while she began to navigate the others. And as Lily contemplated General Pushkin, part of her wished she could send one of her brothers in her place. Pushkin, of course, straddled both worlds but, as a military man, felt most comfortable on the more appropriate side of things.

"On second thought," she said. "Tell General Pushkin only you will be coming. I want him to be knocked off guard when I walk through the door. His first acquaintance with his new chief should be a surprise, I think. Don't you, Fedot?"

"Surprises are good, Miss Lily," Fedot concurred.

Lily picked up the newspaper from her desk and dropped it into a tall, cylindrical trash bin. She slid her arms into her raincoat and held her purse in her hands, waiting for Fedot to take her suitcase.

"And after Moscow, Fedot, I'd like to take a trip to the Russian countryside." Lily smiled. "You don't think we'll have to contact His Holiness, Mr. Ivanov, through back channels, do you?"

Fedot shook his head, his smile almost imperceptible. "Perhaps he will be able to tell us something of Pasha."

Lily studied him for a moment. "Perhaps," she said. She didn't wish to appear too eager—not even to Fedot.

Lily opened the top drawer to her desk and removed a pair of gloves, draping them over her purse. Under her gloves was an oval of amber that she'd taken from Beryx Gulyas in Hungary. Trapped in the warm, golden gem was a spider—old as time—and a dance fly that had been less than a moment away from becoming prey but was instead interred within the amber for all of time: one of life's little dramas captured in the prehistoric equivalent of a still photograph. It would always remind her of her father.

"A man holds power in his hands," he'd once told her. It was a long time ago now. She was barely into puberty, and she'd had no idea what he was talking about, really, except that he was perhaps making a vague reference to sex. "But a woman," Theron Tassos had continued. "She weaves power into a web with strong, silken thread and diabolical strategy."

It was true, Lily supposed. And that smooth piece of amber, with its ancient drama and timeless wisdom, would always serve as a connection to her father—between this world and the beyond, if there was such a thing—even if it had come from his killer's trouser pocket, the only gemstone Fedot and her uncle did not force the Hungarian to consume.

Outside, the weather was strangely glorious for so late in the fall. The sun made every remaining speck of color on the mostly-bare trees appear crisp and dazzling. Lily hardly needed a jacket.

"Where on earth is the car, Fedot?" Only minutes earlier, her Chrysler Imperial—hunter green, not the black or navy her father favored—had been parked just outside of her townhouse with her driver waiting inside. She was beginning to hate when such simple expectations weren't met and barely stopped herself from stomping her foot.

Fedot didn't answer her little tantrum and didn't need to. The Chrysler turned the corner at the bottom of the street and coasted to a purring stop at the curb where Lily tapped the toe of her toasted-brown pump. It occurred to Lily how alike in temperament her new car was to Fedot Titov—solicitous, always, but never subservient.

Case in point, her driver opened the back door for her while Fedot turned his back and began to walk away.

"Now where are you going?" she demanded.

"I have business, Miss Lily," he said. "I'll see you at the airport."

Lily rolled her eyes and threw her purse and coat into the back seat. "Of course you have business," she told him. "With me!"

"You, I think, have business, too." He didn't bother turning to face her when he imparted this last bit of information; he simply glided along the sidewalk like he had a date with eternity. No need to rush—the universe would wait.

But it would not wait for Lily Tassos, as they came to a near standstill only a few minutes from the airport.

"Oh, Linc, isn't there another way?" she asked her driver. She habitually cut it too close whenever she had to get to the airport, an unfortunate character trait.

"I'm afraid not, Miss Tassos."

She hadn't thought so. At least it was a nice day. Lily rolled her window down and leaned out, laying her head gently on the crook of her elbow. Despite the filthy stink of car exhaust, she could still make out the scents of fall in Boston, mostly burning leaves and yeast. Comforting aromas. A taxi edged up next to them, however, blowing black smoke out of its muffler. Lily coughed and sat up, waving away the wretched odor. She started to roll up her window but then spotted the passenger in the back of the cab.

Turning to her, the passenger put his palm to the window. His face was defined, almost sculpted—he had never gained back the weight he'd lost at the Lavra.

"Pasha!"

The taxi inched up, then pulled onto the curb and began rolling past the other cars.

"Damn it, Linc—go after that cab!" But they were stuck, sandwiched between the other cars and unable to cross the next lane and pull onto the curb the way Pasha's cab had done.

Lily kicked the seat in front of her, threw open the door and began to run. She could hear Linc calling after her. The cab was a good distance ahead, but it, too, had been forced to stop. Lily ran up the lane between the cars, incurring the irate honks of already wound-up drivers. She pounded on the hood of an aging Ford—at least ten years old—and its driver spit out a string of curses that would make a pickpocket blush.

Finally coming up on the back of the taxi, Lily skirted its bumper and slapped her hands flat onto the rear passenger window from where Pasha had greeted her. It was empty.

"What the hell are you doing?" the cabbie said.

"That man—the man who was in your cab—where is he?"

The cabbie shook his head.

"I don't know what you're talkin' about lady, I didn't have nobody in my cab. I'm going to pick someone up—at the airport, see?" He held up a sign he took from the shot-gun seat. It read: Mr. Donald Frazier.

"Don't you bullshit me, you son of a bitch, where is he?" Lily grabbed his woolen cap and threw it to the ground. She started slapping him, then grabbed the man's shirt, but that was going too far. The cabbie tore her hands away and jumped out of his taxi, coming nose to nose with her.

"You crazy bitch," he hollered. "You touch me again and I'll break your neck!"

"Hey, hey, hey!" Another man, well-dressed, jumped out of his Bel Air. "That's no way to talk to a lady!"

"Miss Tassos!" This time, it was Linc. "Please, traffic is starting to break up." He was out of breath, running to-ward her.

Lily could hardly breathe. She put her hand to her cheek and looked around. Pasha was nowhere. She was afraid she was going to cry or scream.

"Bastard," she hissed to the cabbie. She took Linc's prof-fered elbow and walked with him back to her car. Linc was shaking like a leaf, and so, Lily realized, was she.

Once inside, she reached into her purse and took out a soft, cotton handkerchief. "It was Pasha, goddamnit," she whispered. Lily lifted the handkerchief to her nose and blew. Softly, she began to hum a song she'd once heard Pasha sing at Alyona Artemieva's subterranean apartment. He'd sung it in Russian but had translated its lyrics for her. "It is not a dream, not a dream," he'd sung. "It's all my truth. It's my love, it is my love." It had been one of his mother's favor-ites, he'd explained, although when she'd sung it, she was referring to Stalin and the Russian revolution. It comforted Lily to feel the melody in her throat. She started to sing louder, and another voice joined hers—deep, baritone. Lily covered her ears and shook her head.

"Why is it that when Ivanov sings to you, you believe him, even when he's an ocean away? But when I sing, you shake your head."

Lily looked up, coming face-to-face with Pasha Tarkhan. He was seated in the front passenger's seat, as if he'd always been there.

"Could it be that you've developed some faith after all?" he said.

Lily opened her mouth to speak, but nothing came out. Pasha's bear claw of a hand reached into the back seat. He touched his index finger to her nose with a motion at once so sweet and reverential that he may as well have been touching a breast for the first time.

"Pasha," she whispered.

"Yes, it's really me."

Lily took his hand, kissing the palm he'd pressed against his window. She brushed her lips over the pillow of flesh beneath his thumb and kissed each and every one of his fingers, then his wrist, his knuckles and the thick veins that snaked so close under his skin. His hands smelled like cigarettes, newspaper pages and smoked salmon from his breakfast. It was a heavenly perfume.

"Where have you been?" she asked him.

Pasha pulled a lock of hair from her coif and weaved it around his fingers. "Where I should still be, I suppose."

It occurred to Lily quite suddenly that he might not have come to stay, and it was an utterly unacceptable thought.

"This is where you belong," she said.

Pasha smiled. "If I were a better man, Lily, I wouldn't be here at all. And I certainly wouldn't stay."

"Don't be ridiculous," Lily told him. "I'm a terrible human being. I deserve whatever you bring into my life."

Pasha's chuckle felt as close to a home as anything.

"Because we're horrible people?" Pasha shook his head. "That is, I suppose, why I've returned. Because you and I are on a similar path, in equal danger, as it were. Especially now that you've chosen to assume your father's dealings."

Lily snuggled his hand close to her chest. "Would you not have come back if I'd gone back to shopping and traveling?"

He pressed his thumb over her heartbeat and raised an eyebrow. "I would not."

"Hmmf. Then I'm not sure I want you back," Lily said. "You're clearly far too good a person for me."

Pasha cocked his head, frowning.

"I'm joking!" Lily said. "And speaking of horrible people, I was just on my way to meet an old friend of yours. I think he's even worse than we are."

The traffic stopped again, and Pasha jumped out of the car, pulling his coat over his head as if it were raining. He slid into the back next to Lily and kissed her like he'd been waiting all his life to do it. Like he hadn't kissed her a hundred times, everywhere. When he came up for air, he put his lips to her forehead, then traced a little cross with his thumb right over her brow.

"Fedot can take care of Pushkin," he said. "You needn't concern yourself with the general or his approval."

Lily swallowed. She was embarrassed to admit just how much she wanted Pushkin's good opinion. "Pasha, I need to see him."

Pasha gulped and kissed her again, trailing his lips to her ear. "The general is nothing to you," he whispered. "He'll beg like a dog if you tell him to, and you won't have to ask twice."

Lily broke from his embrace and met the rich soil of his eyes. She couldn't read them. She knew what Pasha was saying. That Pushkin was useful, perhaps, but utterly replaceable. And she hated herself for wanting to prove something to that two-bit Russian general.

"Yeah, I know," she said. "I'm just trying to get familiar with everyone. Make myself known." Despite how much she loved him, she couldn't even let Pasha in on how hard it was for her to come face-to-face with some of the men in her father's network and how badly she wanted them to respect her.

Pasha cupped her hand and brought it to his lips. "There's only one person you need to know—besides Mr. Ivanov, of course."

Lily leaned in to Pasha and bit down on her lip, the waxy film of her Brandywine lipstick clinging to her teeth. "You?"

This time Pasha full-out laughed.

"No, not me," he said. "I'm just your lover. And an in- convenient defector. I was referring to yourself."

Myself, Lily mouthed. "Always the philosopher, aren't you?" Lily nuzzled his chest, stroking her cheek against the crisp thread of his cotton shirt. Her father, the Hungarian, Pasha . . . It was all nearly too much to comprehend at once.

"I think Bombay awaits us," he said.

"Bombay?"

"We'll be flying there tonight after a brief sojourn in my hotel room. Perhaps after Bombay, we can make our way to Hong Kong or Rio de Janeiro. People like us, my dear, don't thrive in places like Boston."

Lily couldn't deny that.

"Rio," she said. Lily looked up at Pasha, trying not to succumb to a smile so easily. "What can I say? I love beach- es." That was one thing that would probably never change.

Pasha took her very suddenly into his arms, squeezing her tight as if he'd just awakened from a nightmare. "Say your prayers, Lily, and commune with our Ivanov. If you and I are to be together, we're going to need every bit of Divine Grace we can marshal."

Lily nestled herself deeper into Pasha's embrace, kissing the hollow in his throat. Bombay, yes, Bombay would be fine on this first leg of their journey. Anywhere would be fine, at least for now. Because in spite of the horrors of the past few months—the fear, the torture, the deaths—there had been a few tiny cells of magic. Lily had completed Tony Geiger's mission, after all—the one he'd died for. The one he would've never guessed she'd take up on her own. That thought alone could make her smile for a week. She'd traveled through Russia, Persia and Eastern Europe with a purpose that didn't even vaguely concern wine, a closet of new dresses or a parade of worthless men, none of whom would have cared about her.

And there had been happiness.

Right there in her Chrysler Imperial, with her Russian and her father's dubious enterprises, her own changing heart and Ivanov's voice in her head—always Ivanov's voice—Lily felt happy.

THE END

If you can spare a moment, the author would be grateful for an honest review of this novel—even if it's just a sentence or two—on Amazon, Goodreads, or the platform of your choice.

ACKNOWLEDGEMENTS

First and foremost, I want to thank my readers. So many of you reach out and share your lives with me. You follow me to some outlandish places, too – exotic times and locals filled with ghosts, assassins and lovers. Your faith and loyalty keep me sane.

A big, big thanks to my street team, aka Coldsters. Your enthusiasm makes launching a new book like a party. I wish I could take each and every one of you out for a coffee. Or a good whiskey.

My husband, Jack, without whom I'd spend all of my time merely wishing I was a writer. And our kids, too, deserve a hug, an ice cream and a trip to Disneyworld for being so tolerant of their mother's imaginary world.

Writing can be a lonely business, and I'm ever so grateful for my fellow writers who have spent so much time with me around the virtual watercooler in our various online writers groups. You are, quite simply, great people and I feel privileged to have gotten to know you. Christoph and Catalina, this means you, among many others who are too numerous to name, but live in my heart regardless.

Josh Getzler of Hannigan Salky Getzler – thank you for your support and terrific editorial feedback. Thanks also to Danielle Burby, who was always there to lend a hand along the way.

Andy Straka, co-founder of *Crimewave*, at the Virginia Festival of the Book, thanks for an ear, a word, and for having such a lovely wife.

Supportive friends are worth their weight in gold. Thank

you Nancy Bishop for championing my work and spreading the word. Michele Kayal and Dale Eastman — I think you've read this book nearly as many times as I have. Thank you. And to all of you kind souls who have read or recommended my work to your friends, shown up at my book readings, and lobbied to have my books featured in your book clubs, you can't know how much that means.

Kate Brauning — thanks for being a great editor. Chris Bell, your design sense makes my words look so great on the page that they actually read better. Brianna Harden — your cover design is gorgeous. Thank you.

VICTORIA DOUGHERTY

Victoria Dougherty is the author of *THE BONE CHURCH*, *WELCOME TO THE HOTEL YALTA*, and *COLD*. She writes fiction, drama and essays that revolve around lovers, killers, curses, and destinies.

Her work has been published or profiled in the *New York Times*, *USA Today*, *The International Herald Tribune* and elsewhere.

Earlier in her career, while living in Prague, she co-founded Black Box Theater, translating, producing, and acting in to sold-out audiences in several Czech plays—from Vaclav Havel's "Protest" to the unintentionally hilarious communist propaganda play "Karhan's Men." Black Box Theater was profiled in feature articles in *USA Today* and numerous European publications.

Her blog—COLD—features her short essays on faith, family, love and writing.

WordPress, the blogging platform that hosts over 70 million blogs worldwide, has singled out COLD as one of their top Recommended Blogs by writers or about writing.

Follow COLD at www.victoriadougherty.wordpress.com

Please visit me on Patreon

WWW.PATREON.COM/VICTORIADOUGHERTY

Patreon is an amazing and empowering platform that makes it possible for artists and their enthusiasts to engage, and even work together towards a common goal.

I want to partner with readers like you not only to create the most singular, comprehensive and knock-your-socks-off story experience a writer has to offer, but to give back.

As little as a $1 pledge will give you access to original essays, works-in-progress, new book excerpts, photographs, art work, videos and more. One third of the proceeds from each goal achieved will go towards supporting worthy organizations committed to improving the lives of children with special needs.

Thank you!

Made in the USA
Lexington, KY
27 September 2018